Joss Wood loves books and travelling—especially to the wild places of Southern Africa and, well... anywhere! She's a wife, mum to two teenagers, and slave to two cats. After a career in local economic development she now writes full-time. Joss is a member of Romance Writers of America and Romance Writers of South Africa.

USA TODAY bestselling author **Natalie Anderson** writes emotional contemporary romance full of sparkling banter, sizzling heat and uplifting endings—perfect for readers who love to escape with empowered heroines and arrogant alphas who are too sexy for their own good. When not writing, you'll find her wrangling her four children, three cats, two goldfish and one dog...and snuggled in a heap on the sofa with her husband at the end of the day. Follow her at natalie-anderson.com.

HOW TO WIN THE WILD BILLIONAIRE

JOSS WOOD

STRANDED FOR ONE SCANDALOUS WEEK

NATALIE ANDERSON

MILLS & BOON

First Published in Great Britain 2021
by Mills & Boon, an imprint of HarperCollins*Publishers*
1 London Bridge Street, London, SE1 9GF

How to Win the Wild Billionaire © 2021 Joss Wood

Stranded for One Scandalous Week © 2021 Natalie Anderson

ISBN: 978-0-263-28244-3

MIX
Paper from
responsible sources
FSC® C007454

This book is produced from independently certified FSC™ paper
to ensure responsible forest management.
For more information visit www.harpercollins.co.uk/green.

Printed and bound in Spain
by CPI, Barcelona

HOW TO WIN THE WILD BILLIONAIRE

JOSS WOOD

CHAPTER ONE

IF YOU GIVE me custody of Olivia, I will forgive your past behavior.

If you don't fight me on this, we can be a family again. You'll be welcomed back into my house, into my life.

Bay Adair pulled up alongside the lavender house in Bo Kaap, two blocks over from Layla and Ali's house—her house now—and lifted her hands off the steering wheel, irritated to see the fine tremor in her fingers. She was shaking. Still. A full day after her ugly confrontation with her father.

He could still, damn him, shake the foundations of her world. And she was furious that, for just a minute, she'd considered his offer, her need to be a part of a family again temporarily overriding logic. But then common sense had kicked in and she'd realized that nothing had changed, that he was just playing her and, worst of all, using Olivia as a tool to bend her to his will.

Her father was an expert in emotional manipulation, Bay reminded herself, and his love was fully conditional.

I will only love you if you do as I say.

I will only love you if you believe what I do.

Well, damn him and damn that!

He'd been playing these games for more than half of her life and Bay was done. He didn't, not really, want custody of Olivia—the fact that neither he nor her mother had tried to see their grandchild in the six months since Layla's death led to that conclusion.

So no, she would not let him use her orphaned niece as a pawn in his twisted game. He wanted control over her, like he had complete control over her mother, and his promise of love and forgiveness was a lure, bait to get her to fall into line. She wasn't stupid enough, weak enough, to believe otherwise.

It was a timely and tough reminder that love always, *always*, came with strings attached.

Bay glanced in the rearview mirror. She frowned when she saw the telltale flush of fever on little Olivia's face. Her big, black eyes normally sparkled with fun and mischief but today, thanks to a vicious cold, they were red-rimmed and flat.

Bay rubbed her fingers across her forehead, hoping to rub away the headache settling behind her eyes. Turning her head, she saw the navy door to the house opening and smiled when she saw Mama B step onto the small landing above the whitewashed steps dressed, as she always was, in a loose, long-sleeved caftan. Today's hijab, her head covering, was a deep, dark purple.

Bay jumped out of the car and jogged up the short flight of stairs to take Mama B's hands in hers. She kissed one wrinkled cheek, then another. "Thanks for taking Olivia. I really appreciate it."

Mama B waved her gratitude away. "She's my great-grandchild—of course I'd help." She frowned. "You said that you think she's coming down with something?"

"I think it's just a cold."

Bay had only been Liv's "mom" for six months and,

after years of world traveling and only being responsible for herself, she was still overwhelmed by her new responsibility. What the hell had her younger sister Layla and her husband Ali been thinking when they made her guardian of Olivia? Sure, she could understand why they didn't name her parents—her father's recent behavior hammered that nail home—but Ali had wonderful cousins, any of whom would've been happy to welcome Liv into their ever-expanding broods.

But no, for some crazy reason Layla and Ali decided that Bay, with no child-rearing experience, was the person they wanted to raise their beautiful daughter. And she was beautiful, with her black curls, her creamy, light brown skin reflecting her dad's Cape Malay heritage, pink rosebud mouth and those deep, super-dark eyes. She was also demanding and willful, energetic and mischievous and, yeah, extremely tiring. Being a single mother was tiring.

Being a single mother trying to earn enough to support her and Liv was freaking exhausting.

"Why are you heading to The Vane today?" Mama B asked.

Bay crossed her arms and rocked on her heels. "I'm going to see Digby Tempest-Vane…"

Mama B's drawn-on eyebrows, thin and arched, lifted in surprise. "The Wild Billionaire? Wasn't he the one who had an affair with that opera singer?"

Mama B was confusing Digby with his father, the notorious, rich-as-a-king philanderer who, together with his equally scandalous wife, kept the city, the country—and pretty much the world—entertained when tales of their parties, fights and licentious affairs made front-page news.

"His father, Gil, had the affair with the opera singer,

Mama B." But the press did call Digby the Wild Billionaire because of his love of speed, adrenaline and adventure.

He also turned over girlfriends—socialites, models and aristocracy—with the speed of a spinning top. His aversion to commitment, marriage and family was well documented. With parents like his, she couldn't blame him. Neither could she judge him, as Bay had, as soon as she could, left the country and put as many miles between her and her parents as was humanly possible.

Bay saw that Mama B was still waiting for an explanation. "Do you remember Brin? And Abigail, they lived in the house on the corner of my street?"

Mama B nodded.

"Brin is engaged to Radd Tempest-Vane and Abigail works for him. A few weeks ago, Brin told me Digby has been looking for an interior designer for months. He wants to renovate certain rooms of The Vane hotel. Brin is away on holiday with Radd but Abby got me an appointment to meet with Digby."

Bay twisted her lips, not feeling confident about the upcoming meeting. Honestly, she thought it was a waste of her time. And his.

According to Brin, Digby had interviewed various interior designers, the best in the business locally and internationally, but he had yet to find anyone who understood his vision.

Bay didn't think that she, an amateur—she'd received her diploma but never worked as an interior designer—would be the answer to Digby Tempest-Vane's prayers.

But she desperately needed a job and this was her only opportunity to earn money doing something she loved. Her savings were rapidly dwindling and while she'd inherited Layla and Ali's house on their death, they hadn't left much in the way of hard cash.

She was fast running out of funds and if she couldn't find work as an interior designer, she'd have to look for work as an engineer. She'd be miserable but she'd be miserable while earning a lucrative salary.

Ugh. She'd rather stab herself repeatedly in the eye with a rusty fork.

Working for Digby Tempest-Vane would give her wheezing bank account a hit of oxygen. It would also, she presumed, open doors to future interior-design business. But, her voice of reason reminded her, if Morris and Campagno, two famous designers, one based in New York and one in London, couldn't nail the brief, Bay didn't hold out much hope that she could.

But she had to try.

"Trust in yourself, Bay darling, and trust your talent. And if you don't believe in yourself, how can you expect that Tempest-Vane creature to?" Mama B asked, her head tipping to the side.

Bay looked down at their still interlinked hands, one light, one dark, and felt grateful she had this wise woman in her life. Bay was the product of a privileged, superconservative family who lived their lives behind the huge walls of their Rondebosch mansion, carefully choosing the people they interacted with. Rich people, privileged people, white people. Their daughter and granddaughter living in the mostly Muslim, vibrant neighborhood of the Bo Kaap suburb was not acceptable.

Luckily Bay had a lifetime of practice in bucking, fighting against or flat-out ignoring her parents' dictates, opinions and demands. Mama B, sweet, tough and proud, had become, in just half a year, her family, and hers was the only opinion she listened to.

After carrying a now sleeping Olivia into Mama B's house, Bay thanked Mama B again, kissed her cheek and hopped back into her car.

Fifteen minutes later, Bay swung her small car into the oak-lined driveway to The Vane, the ancient branches forming a canopy over the road. Table Mountain, dramatic and ever changing, loomed over the rambling pale green-and-white hotel. The hotel had been, for more than a century, an oasis of calm and elegance in the heart of the city. It was where captains of industry did deals in meeting rooms and bars, where royalty and celebrities chose to lay their heads.

Bay parked her car and looked around. She'd never visited the iconic institution before and she allowed her eyes to drift from the impressive buildings to Table Mountain and back again. *Wow.* The grounds, from the little she could see, were also magnificent, with carefully manicured bright green lawns separating beds of brightly colored flowers and interesting shrubs. If memory served, there was an award-winning rose garden behind the hotel, and she'd read that lovely, whimsical fountains and wrought iron gazebos dotted the extensive grounds.

As with all six-star resorts, there were numerous heated pools, tennis courts, a state-of-the-art gym with private trainers, spas, boutiques and a hair salon.

Luxurious, romantic, iconic...

Again... What was she doing here?

Money, honey.

Bay flipped down her visor to check her appearance. She'd twisted her long, wavy hair into a loose knot at the back of her neck and it looked reasonably okay. She'd slapped some foundation on her face but it, as per normal, hadn't managed to cover the heavy spray of freckles on her nose and high cheekbones. Her whiskey-colored eyes—her best feature in her opinion—reflected her anxiety and general exhaustion.

Bay looked down at her pale pink T-shirt and tailored black pants, which were a little baggy around the butt and thighs. Since returning to Cape Town, she'd lost weight and, as she was naturally slender, they were pounds she couldn't afford to lose.

Right. She was here, best get on with it.

Bay tucked her T-shirt back into her pants and pushed her fist into her sternum. Life had taught her to be a realist and she really didn't think she had an ice cube's chance in hell of being employed by Digby Tempest-Vane as his interior designer.

But, if she didn't try, she'd always have regrets and second-guess herself.

She was allowed to fail. And she probably would. But failure was only acceptable when she'd given it her best shot.

Digby Tempest-Vane was experiencing a bad-dream hangover. Having had the same recurring nightmare since he was fourteen, he was familiar with its aftereffects of feeling antsy, unsettled and irritated. Sometimes he wouldn't have the dream for months but, whenever he was dealing with change—like now—it was a nightly visitor.

The image of Radd's coffin, plain black like Jack's, being lowered into a deep, black hole jumped onto the big screen of his mind, and he slammed his eyes shut, hoping to force it away. Because he needed to check on his brother, he wouldn't be able to function if he didn't, he pulled his phone out of his pocket and punched in Radd's number.

This is Radd Tempest-Vane. I'm not available at the moment. Leave a message.

Digby disconnected the call, frustrated and irritated at his inability to reach his brother. They were business partners and best friends but for the past few weeks, their relationship ran a very distant second to Radd's romance with Brin.

He was happy for Radd, he *was*, but he couldn't help feeling relegated to the sidelines of his life, pushed aside and well, yeah, forgotten.

Digby, standing at the window of his sprawling office with its amazing view of Table Mountain, placed the palm of his hand on the glass and told himself to stop behaving like a teenage girl. Radd was in love, he was happy and that was all that mattered.

And yeah, if Digby didn't have the same access to him as before, if he was feeling a little lonely and a lot left out—he'd regressed to sounding like a ten-year-old—then that was his problem, not Radd's.

Radd had only fallen in love; he hadn't, like their parents, disappeared from his life. He hadn't, like their elder brother, Jack, *died*. But Digby couldn't help feeling, just a little, abandoned. It was, thanks to being the youngest son of the world's most neglectful parents, an emotion he was very familiar with.

Intellectually he knew he was being stupid, but his heart refused to listen to reason. It was stubborn that way.

But, seriously, if one more person—friend, foe or reporter—asked him whether he'd changed his mind about love and marriage and whether he was going to follow Radd's example and settle down, he'd punch someone or something.

Radd was the only family Digby had, all he needed.

It was his most closely held secret that he lived in constant fear of losing his brother, so why on earth would he want to increase his stress load by having more people in his life to worry about? No, he preferred to fly solo, thank you very much.

Digby sighed and turned away, eyeing his very messy desk. After wrapping up the purchase of the Botswana diamond mine from Vincent Radebe, Radd and Brin decided to take a month-long vacation in the Maldives. That meant Digby taking on Radd's responsibilities to the Tempest-Vane group of companies as well as his own and he was slammed. And stressed.

He should've canceled his meeting with Brin's interior-designer friend; he really didn't have the time to meet her and he doubted a no-name interior designer would be able to grasp what he wanted when it came to redecorating The Vane. And until he found a kindred spirit, someone who got his vision for the most favorite of all the Tempest-Vane properties, he'd wait to redecorate and renovate.

It wasn't like the wallpaper was falling from the walls or the paint was cracking. The last renovation was completed ten years ago, shortly before he and Radd purchased the hotel, the first business in their quest to restore the Tempest-Vane businesses and assets their father sold in order to line his personal pockets.

The hotel still looked good. Great, even.

But he didn't want good or great, he wanted fabulous, unique, a combination of breathtaking elegance and comfort, sophistication and warmth. Their safari operation, Kagiso Ranch, was known to be one of the best safari lodges in the world; he wanted The Vane to be one of the best hotels in the world. They were close but close wasn't quite good enough…

He intended the hotel to become a favorite amongst the world's elite, and his and Radd's fame as two of the world's youngest billionaires didn't hurt. Over the past few years, he'd made numerous changes and now the only outstanding issue was the decor…

Why couldn't he properly convey his vision for the hotel? He was erudite, many called him charming and most called him charismatic. But, despite his ability to converse with paupers and princes, not one of the designers managed to strike the right balance between sophisticated and luxurious but also warm and welcoming. Some of the designs were too cold and too austere, others were too country house.

He didn't think Brin's friend would succeed where the best in the world had failed. He should've just canceled…

Too late now, Digby thought, glancing at his watch. He was due to meet her—God, what was her name again?—in the lobby in five minutes.

Digby buttoned his loose collar as he walked out of his office and pushed up the knot of his tie and straightened his tiepin. Tucking his phone into the inside pocket of his jacket, he ran a hand over his jaw, thanking God stubble was still in fashion.

"Muzi Miya-Mathews wants to know if you have five minutes for him," Monica, his personal assistant, said, looking at him while she continued to type. How the hell did she do that?

Digby nodded and looked around, not seeing his best friend. "He said he'd wait for you on the south veranda but if you don't have time to spare, he'd call you later."

Digby thanked Monica and hurried to the lobby, rapidly moving across the harlequin-tiled floor to the south veranda. He and Muzi had met at Duncan House, one of the best private boys' schools in the country, nearly twenty-five years ago and had been best friends ever since. Except for Radd, nobody knew him better than Muzi Miya-Mathews.

Spotting the dark-skinned Muzi—he was an exceptionally tall, well-built guy so he was hard to miss—Digby hurried over to him and slapped his shoulder. "Three M," he said, using Muzi's nickname from school.

Muzi shook his hand and pulled him into a brief, one-armed hug. "Dig, how's it going?"

"Good. Crazy." Digby shoved his suit jacket back to push his hands into the pockets of his pants. "I've got a meeting in five so I can't hang around. What are you doing here?"

"I'm conducting interviews for a new winemaker for Tangle Vines." Muzi leaned his shoulder into a pillar. Muzi, he remembered, needed a winemaker for his ever-expanding group of wineries.

"If I think the candidate has potential, I'll take them out to the vineyard." Muzi sent Digby a sour look. "Seven interviews and I've yet to make that drive."

Digby sympathized. He knew what it was like not finding the person who gelled, clicked, the person you were looking for.

"Look, I know you are in a hurry but I wanted to tell you that we've made a formal decision to try to purchase Saint Urban. I was wondering if you could put me in contact with the owner."

The Saint Urban vineyard had been his mom's property, and when his parents died two years ago, the vineyard became part of their trust. Neither he nor Radd were beneficiaries of that trust and had no idea who was.

"Sorry, we still don't know who that is," Digby replied. His parents' heir would not only inherit Saint Urban but also Gil and Zia's art and car collection, a couple of huge insurance policies, their extensive property portfolio and a few healthy bank accounts.

He was bitter and he had a right to be. The trust was funded by the sale of Tempest-Vane assets, and the fact that someone unconnected to them was going to reap the rewards of the hard work of generations was a bitter pill to swallow. But Gil and Zia had no sense of family loyalty. If they had, they would've taken a great deal more interest in their three sons.

Digby always knew he was unwanted. His parents paid little to no attention to him, and his achievements, sports and scholastic, went unnoticed. His oldest brother, Jack, had been more of a parent to him than both his parents combined, and his death, shortly before Digby's fifteenth birthday, rocked his already shaky world. Six months, maybe a year later Digby concluded it was better, safer to push people away before they could leave him.

His greatest fear was loving someone again and having them leave, and his recurring dream of Radd dying had him experiencing cold sweats and sleepless nights. He couldn't lose someone else he loved, he wouldn't be able to survive it. So, despite his charm, his wide circle of friends and his popularity, there were only a handful of people he allowed underneath his tungsten-hard suit of armor.

His anxiety was his biggest secret and no one in the world had any idea that the charming, sometimes reckless, wild Digby Tempest-Vane lived with a constant, low-grade fear of being alone, of being abandoned.

Yeah, the press would love that story…

"Anyway, I wanted to give you a heads-up about the

offer to purchase Saint Urban," Muzi told him. "Let's grab a beer and catch up sometime."

Digby glanced down at his watch. God, he was late; he needed to hustle. He told Muzi he'd be in touch and, as he walked away from his friend, at the entrance to the still-closed bar, he noticed a flash of cream-and-brown fabric next to an ornate pot holding a miniature palm tree. Digby bent down and picked up a slightly battered, two-toned stuffed animal wearing a T-shirt sporting the slogan I'll Always Hang with You.

Digby looked into its funny, weird little face and saw that the stuffed toy was actually a sloth. Cute. Strange but cute. Someone, presumably its owner, had pulled its short hair on the top of its head into a tiny tail and tied it up with a candy-pink ribbon. So this was a girl sloth then.

"Got yourself a new girlfriend?" Muzi teased, shoulder bumping him as he passed him. "I must say, your taste is improving."

"Bastard," Digby muttered, holding the sloth by one arm. Huh, it actually looked like it had Velcro on its feet and hands, allowing the thing to hang from any tree limb or surface. Clever.

He'd hand this in at the front desk and his concierge would send a text message out to all the child minders asking if any of their charges had lost a stuffed toy. It looked well loved and would be claimed within, he bet, the hour…

Digby looked around, hoping to catch the eye of the concierge but his attention was caught by a woman rushing into the lobby. Her hair was a deep golden brown, pulled back to highlight her pixie face. High, sharp cheekbones, more than a few freckles and a wide, sensuous, luscious mouth made for French kissing. She was tall, slim but busty too, all long legs and arms and frantic energy.

She looked around, obviously harassed. But her eyes were on the floor, looking for all the world like she'd dropped something. Digby looked at the toy in his hand and felt a surge of disappointment. If she was looking for the toy then that meant she was a mom…

Probably married or in a relationship.

But even if she was single, she wasn't someone he'd pursue. He didn't date married women or women with children—too much baggage and drama. But damn, she was gut-wrenchingly beautiful in an understated, quiet way. A confusing combination of sexy and sweet.

As if she sensed his eyes on her, her gaze tracked to him and when she saw the stuffed toy in his hand, her shoulders slumped with relief. He saw her chest rise and fall and the tension in her face ease.

Right, so the creature in his hand was important…

Digby watched as she ducked around a group of French tourists, flashing a smile at an elderly man who stood back to let her pass. She adjusted her tote bag over her shoulder and clasped a leather satchel in her other hand as she approached him, a hesitant look on her face.

"I think you have my sloth." Her voice was deeper than he expected, holding a touch of sexy sandpaper.

"He was trying to sneak into the bar," Digby replied on an easy grin. "I think he has a drinking problem."

Her wide mouth tipped up in a smile and Digby caught a glimpse of neat, even white teeth. "Being the poster child for a deadly sin makes him want to drown his sorrows."

He laughed at her quick comeback. Handing the fluffy toy over, his fingers drifted over hers and electricity raced up his arm. *Wow.* It had been a long, long time since he'd experienced such instant, immediate attraction. Working hard to keep his expression bland,

Digby pushed back his jacket and shoved his hands into his pockets.

"Do you normally carry alcoholic animals around with you?" he asked.

She looked at the creature and pulled its Velcro legs apart before slapping them together again. "Ah, no. I was a little early and took a walk outside—he must've fallen out of my bag along the way. Thank God you found him or else I would never be forgiven. Mr. Fluffy is an important member of our household."

"Boy or girl?" Digby asked, thinking that he should walk away, that there was no point in drawing out this conversation. Even if she wasn't in a relationship— and of course she would be—he never had affairs with women with kids.

He liked women who could be spontaneous, who could meet him at ten at night for a late drink or at six in the morning for an early run on the beach, who could leave for a weekend away at a moment's notice or answer the door dressed naked.

Digby worked hard and played harder and liked being the sole focus of a woman's attention. That never happened with someone who had kids.

"Ah, a girl. Olivia… Livvie. She's three and she's besotted with this sloth. She's probably throwing a hissy fit of epic proportions because he's missing."

He saw the worry in her eyes, the flash of panic. He instantly, and strangely, wanted to reassure her. Not that he knew what to say. And that was weird too. He could always think of a quick comment. He could bullshit with the best of them.

But not today. And not, he realized, with her.

Digby saw his most senior concierge rapidly crossing the floor to them and sighed. They were about to be interrupted and he wanted more time with this woman, whoever she was. But time was something he didn't have, he was running so late as it was.

"May I be of assistance, sir?" Benoit said, raising his nose as he looked at the woman and the toy in her hand. Benoit could size up the guests in a flash by their clothing, accessories and attitude, and he was never wrong.

Her plain black trousers and equally plain, light pink T-shirt were clearly off-the-rack and her shoes were scuffed at the toe. Her hair was completely natural and it was obvious she hadn't spent more than five minutes on her makeup.

But she was more lovely than most of the models, actresses and socialites he'd met.

"If you'll accompany me, miss, I'll see if I can be of assistance," Benoit said, looking down his long, aristocratic nose at her.

Digby saw annoyance flash in the woman's eyes and couldn't blame her; Benoit was a hell of a snob. But his stupendously wealthy guests loved the snooty, almost rude concierge, and receiving his deference and approval was something they all aspired to. If you passed muster with Benoit, then you were worthy of your status, your wealth, your place in the world.

It was a ridiculous notion, but Benoit's name was dropped with alarming frequency in the rarefied world he operated in.

Benoit, no last name needed, *arranged a hot-air balloon ride over the wine lands.*

Benoit found me a bottle of Petrus 1990...

Benoit arranged for me to have my portrait painted by Kendall...

Digby didn't particularly like Benoit, but his guests did and that was all that mattered. It would be easy for him to hand her over to Benoit to deal with but, for some strange reason, he wanted to protect her from Benoit's always polite but silently scathing attitude.

"I'll handle it, thank you, Benoit," Digby told him, his tone suggesting that he not argue. Benoit hesitated then nodded, bowing slightly before retreating.

When Benoit was out of earshot, he connected with those cognac-colored eyes again—did his heart really skip a beat or was that his imagination?—and the question he'd been about to ask flew out of his head. He felt the insane urge to find out whether her skin was as soft as it looked.

"I'm Digby Tempest-Vane, by the way."

"My name is Bay Adair."

Bay Adair. The unusual name suited her. What didn't suit him was his fiery, instant, almost out-of-control need to make her his. Again, super strange.

"Are you here to meet someone?"

Irritation flickered in her eyes. "I'm here to meet you, to talk to you about redesigning this hotel."

Hell. Brin's friend. She was here on business, to try to nail a design concept that had eluded ten of the world's best designers.

"Right."

On the plus side, he'd be wasting an hour, maybe two of his time because there was no way Bay would be able to give him what he needed, not in a business sense. Physically, sexually, he had no doubt that she could rock his world.

Life was messing with him by sending him stupid dreams and placing women in his path he couldn't have.

Good thing he had practice at looking it in the eye and telling it to go to hell.

CHAPTER TWO

BAY STRUGGLED TO keep up with Digby Tempest-Vane's long stride as she followed him across the lobby—funny how a space so beautiful and luxurious could still be so cold—toward a set of doors discreetly marked as Staff Only.

Liv's sloth was back in her tote bag and Bay clutched her art satchel to her chest and found herself almost jogging to keep up with him. He was tall, six-two or -three, and his stride was long and brisk. His shoulders were wide, and his short-at-the-sides and raked-back-on-top hair, a deep, rich brown. His eyes, as she'd noticed earlier, were the deep, intense shade commonly used in mosques from Marrakech to Medina, all across the Middle East and North Africa.

Persian blue and brilliant.

She liked his strong jawline under three-day stubble, his straight nose and his sensual mouth. He was panty-dropping attractive, successful and rich. Alpha to the core.

Bay watched as he keyed in a code to open the door leading to the back rooms of the hotel. She'd seen the flicker of annoyance in his eyes and heard his sigh when she told him she was there to see him, and it was obvious he thought meeting her was a waste of his time.

And she couldn't blame him for being skeptical; if the best in the business hadn't been able to nail his vision, then there was little chance she would succeed where they failed. She was, after all, a realist.

When she heard his *Thanks, but no thanks* she could put aside this silly dream of supporting herself and Liv through interior design, and she'd resign herself to living in the real world, the *mundane* world.

After Digby turned her down, she would call Busi Sithebe, of Kane, Sithebe and Pritchard, Consulting Engineers; Busi was her best friend from school and, a year or so ago, she'd told her that when she was ready to return to engineering, she'd try to find a position for her in her company. Bay felt her stomach lurch at the thought of joining the corporate world and working in a field that bored her to tears.

But she was out of options. A girl, and her niece, needed to eat.

It was unbelievable how much could change in a scant six months. Her life—and Liv's obviously—had been flipped upside down and inside out. She lost her sister, and her niece lost her mom and dad…

A picture of their little family—Ali, black eyes flashing, his arm around his pale, blonde wife, and Liv between them, her daddy's child through and through—flashed in front of her eyes and Bay swallowed, blinking to clear her suddenly burning eyes.

She'd been in Goa when she heard the news of their deaths and it had taken her two days to get home. Bay mourned her sister, she *did*, but she'd had to put aside her grief to look after a confused three-year-old who'd had her life ripped apart. She'd initially been in a state of shock on hearing that she'd been appointed as Olivia's legal guardian but that shock soon receded as the enormity of her responsibilities dawned on her.

She was twenty-eight years old and for the past five years, she'd been responsible only for feeding, clothing and looking after herself. Now she had a three-year-old and thoughts of how she was going to pay for Olivia's education, any medical bills, food and clothing kept her awake at night.

Today was D-Day, her very last, almost impossible chance to earn money doing something she loved. If she failed, Bay would have to look for a *proper* job. She sighed at the thought of discussing working hours, remuneration, health insurance and responsibilities.

Honestly, it didn't matter where she found work, whether it was here or somewhere else. Life would change for them and would bring a new set of challenges. She'd have to find daycare for Olivia, dropping her off early and picking her up late. Liv, thanks to losing both her parents, had separation anxiety, and Mama B was the only person, apart from Bay, with whom she felt comfortable. If she went back to work—and she had no choice about that—would Olivia feel abandoned, unloved and rejected? All over again?

But a salary would mean food on the table, money in the bank, a cushion in case of disaster—

"Ms. Adair, I don't have all day."

Digby's cool voice had her jumping back into the present and she noticed that he held a door open for her, waiting for her to step into his office. Bay walked into the expansive and luxurious space and, once inside, turned to watch him shut the door behind him. He immediately shrugged off his tailored suit jacket and loosened his tie. He tossed his jacket over the back of a couch and gestured her to one of the visitor's chairs next to his desk.

"Take a seat," he told her, walking around his huge desk, and dropping into his leather office chair. Almost immediately, he raised his left arm and pushed his hand down the back of his neck in what looked to be an oft-repeated stretch.

Bay watched as the fine cotton of his shirt tightened across that football-field-wide chest and big biceps. He switched hands, elongated his spine, and all the moisture in her mouth dried up.

Digby Tempest-Vane had one of the best bodies she'd ever seen. No contest.

Digby lowered his arms and shrugged. "Sorry, I slept in a weird position last night and my shoulders are tight."

Bay nodded, not wanting to think about Digby in bed. Had he been alone? Did he sleep naked? How big, exactly, was his bed?

Adair! Really?

Digby linked his hands on his flat stomach and Bay couldn't help wondering whether that fine material covered a six-pack. She was damn sure it did…

Digby's eyes—that intense blue—rested on her face and Bay wondered if he'd bring that same intensity to the way he kissed.

Or made love.

She wasn't someone who spent a lot of time wondering about men and their kisses. She'd had a couple of relationships at the university but, for the past few years, she'd lived her life on her own terms, without reference to anyone else. There had been that guy in Berlin, another in Tasmania, but neither tempted her to stay in one place, to stop traveling. To take a risk with her heart, already decimated by her dad.

She was cautious…extremely cautious.

But she couldn't stop imagining what Digby would look like…well, naked.

Aargh! Resisting the urge to bury her face in her hands, Bay hoped she wasn't blushing, so she looked away and forced herself to change the subject.

"Why don't you just tell me your vision of The Vane and I'll take notes?" Bay suggested, proud of her strong, clear voice. Yeah, a lifetime of hiding her emotions from her parents came in handy sometimes.

Digby reached for a folder on his desk and handed it over. "Here are all the dimensions and a set of photos of all the rooms. You can look at it later."

Bay nodded and tucked the folder into the back of her sketch pad. Digby pushed his chair back and placed his ankle on his knee. "I want restful but sophisticated, comfortable but elegant. Do not give me country house, minimalism or avant-garde…"

Bay's hand dashed across the page, making notes as he spoke, idly noticing that he was doing a great job of telling her what he didn't want but not what he did.

"In the first stage on the revamp, because we can't do everything at once, I want the ballroom, a second honeymoon suite and the coffee shop refreshed. The next-steps phase of the project will be the conference rooms, the lobby and all the other public rooms. The third stage will be the bedrooms. I want the same designer working on all three phases, to keep the vision consistent. I'm imagining that this will be a multiyear project and the designer would need to commit to all three phases. After I sign off on the design, the designer would then take over, using their capital to run the project. I'd be happy to consider paying a deposit but I'd expect my designer to purchase all the supplies, furniture, art and accessories and pay the work crews. I'd then issue payment once the work is completed to my satisfaction."

Digby tossed out his sentences in a flat monotone and it was obvious that he'd repeated these words many times before. Bay felt all hope of securing this project fade away on hearing how Digby planned to structure the deal.

The project was massive, much bigger than she thought, and she couldn't take it on. Oh, there was scope to make a lot of money but she'd have to spend money to make money.

She didn't have that sort of cash available. And, without any security or bank credit—the downfall of traveling the world and not having a credit history—she wouldn't qualify for a small loan, never mind the millions she'd need to see the first stage of this project through.

She didn't have the funds to decorate a doll's house, never mind the city's most exclusive hotel.

Bay closed her sketch pad and leaned back in her chair. "Let's not beat around the bush, Mr. Tempest-Vane—"

"Call me Digby," he suggested.

"It's an exciting project but I'm not the person you are looking for. I don't have the experience for a project this big and even if I did, I don't have the finances to take on something of this magnitude." Bay stood up and shrugged. "So, I'm going to stop wasting your time and let you get back to work."

Digby stared at her for a long minute before climbing to his feet. "I respect your honesty—thank you."

"And now you can tell Brin that you did as she asked and met with me." Brin had sent her a couple of messages asking for an update and she was convinced her friend was harassing Digby, as well.

Digby handed her a wry grin. "She keeps texting me, asking if we've met. I can now tell her we have."

Thanks for trying, Brin.

Bay expected him to bid her a brisk goodbye but, instead of showing her the door, he walked around the desk to pick up his jacket. "Would you like to see the rooms, anyway? I've got some time before my next meeting and I'd like to stretch my legs."

Bay bit her lip, knowing that she should leave, that Liv was probably screaming blue murder because she couldn't find Fluffy the sloth.

But Bay hadn't had a minute off in six months and she hadn't had a proper conversation with an adult, never mind a sexy man, for as long. And, yes please, she really wanted to see more of this iconic hotel.

And, more worrying, she really, really, *really* wanted to spend a little more time with Cape Town's sexiest playboy. He was, after all, eye candy.

After today, she'd never see him again, but for an hour, maybe a little more, she could pretend that she wasn't a struggling single mom dealing with her manipulative father, as well as being almost broke and pretty much at the end of her tether. For a tiny sliver of time, she could go back to being Bay, to being the carefree person she was before the world changed.

He should've just ushered her out of his office and carried on with his day. Showing her the ballroom was a complete waste of time, Digby thought, ushering Bay into an elevator that would take them to the third floor and the grand ballroom.

But he was reluctant to bring their meeting to an end, to see her walk out of his life.

Why? He didn't have a clue.

Maybe it was because she was unlike anyone he'd ever met before. Quiet but not a pushover, polite but direct.

She also seemed very unimpressed by him, which was, frankly, a novelty. Most women he met instantly turned on the charm, played with their hair, batted their eyelashes. With Radd off the market, Digby knew that he was the most eligible bachelor in the country. Not because he was anyone special but because he was a Tempest-Vane, had a fat bank account, an okay-ish face and a fit body.

Women craved his attention because of his name and his wealth and his status, because he had a wild streak and a reputation for being a bit of a bad boy.

They wanted to be the one to tame him, to make him settle down. They were all on a fool's errand. He'd never give a woman that much power over his heart and his life. Losing Jack had nearly destroyed him; he was terrified of losing Radd, and he'd never, ever love someone enough to be constantly worried about whether they lived or died.

Bay Adair was just another in a long line of women he was attracted to, somewhat different, a little mysterious. Her fantastic eyes were unreadable and her expression remained cool and impassive. She was the most self-contained woman he'd ever met and, yeah, he was intrigued. And attracted.

And the longer he stayed in her company, the more he noticed. Her eyebrows were arched and S-shaped, a couple of shades deeper than her shot-with-auburn brown hair. Her mouth was uneven, with a thin top lip and full bottom lip, turning the lopsided feature indescribably sexy. She had a long neck and while she was on the skinny side of slim, she had a round, high butt and amazing breasts.

Her fringe covered her forehead and he wondered how long her hair was, unable to tell because it was wound into a messy bun at the back of her head. Freckles covered her nose and her high cheekbones and, he imagined, her shoulders and back, anywhere the sun touched.

She was ethereal and quirky, nothing like the sharp, sexy, successful women he normally dated. Although dating implied that feelings were involved. His had never been engaged and never would be. And the women he dated, slept with, knew not to expect more from him than a few dates and a good time…it was all he could give.

Relationships required taking a risk and while he'd risk his body—and had many, many times—he'd never risk his heart. That was a step, or hundred, too far.

Uncomfortable with where his thoughts were headed, Digby watched as the elevator doors opened onto the small lobby outside the ballroom and gestured for Bay to walk ahead of him. His eyes flickered to her ass again—gorgeous!—and he sighed when he felt the action in his pants. Time to switch gears, Tempest-Vane.

Bay hurried across the lobby to the closed doors of the ballroom. After grabbing the brass handles, she flung the doors open and stepped into the huge, light-filled space. Walking across the parquet flooring, she then stood in the middle of the room, where so many brides had danced in the arms of their new husbands, slowly turning around, her arms akimbo.

Digby sucked in a breath as an image started to form

behind his eyes… Bay wearing a simple, classic wedding dress, fresh flowers in her hair and a broad smile on her face. Her eyes, light and filled with love, were on a man across the room and Digby, unable to help himself, looked in that direction…

But all he saw was an empty room, chairs stacked up against its cream-colored walls.

He rubbed his jaw, thinking that was incredibly weird. And unsettling. He was the type of guy who imagined what women looked like naked, not how they'd look in a bridal gown. This had been a superbly strange day…

"Mmm. The room is very neutral and a little bland," Bay stated, her voice a little raspy. "Neutral, but…"

"Boring?"

"Yeah, boring." Bay nibbled her full luscious bottom lip, and he wanted, very badly, to know whether it tasted as good as it looked. But she hadn't given him a hint that his attraction was reciprocated so no moves, dammit, would be made.

So sad, too bad.

"The light is incredible and the proportions fantastic," Bay said, her light, bright eyes darting everywhere.

Digby tried to see the space through her eyes and admitted it was. It was a double-volume room with crowned ceilings and floor-to-ceiling windows and a highly polished wooden floor. His parents had been married in this room and he'd watched the video of their expensive wedding. His mother looking sensational wearing a Chanel gown, his father in a black topcoat and tails, his face alight with laughter.

Three months after their wedding, his father took over as CEO of Tempest-Vane Holdings and started looting the company. By the time Digby was a teenager, twenty or so years after that society wedding, there was nothing of the family fortune left and the Tempest-Vane holding company was declared insolvent.

There had been no remorse about transferring the company's wealth to their individual bank accounts and, ultimately, to a trust, and their desire to live harder, faster, crazier lives in the pursuit of pleasure simply increased. Man, they'd been useless parents in every possible way.

No wonder he was emotionally stunted.

Bay cleared her throat and tipped her head to the side. "You don't like this room," she commented.

He liked the room just fine, it was the memories he hated.

Needing air, Digby walked over to the floor-to-ceiling French doors and quickly unlocked them, sliding them against the wall. He walked onto the expansive balcony and gripped the balustrade, looking down onto the rose garden first established by his great-great-grandmother. He smelled Bay's perfume, subtle but sexy, as she joined him and he noticed that her head just reached the top of his shoulder.

He wondered how well she'd fit into his arms…

Bay looked down and gasped. In the garden below them, white roses slid into pink roses, then red, then scarlet. It was, he admitted, a hell of a sight and best seen from up above.

"Mama B would love this," Bay said, resting her forearms on the railing, her eyes dancing over the rose garden.

"Who is that?" Digby asked, turning to lean his hip against the railing.

Bay's smile was soft and gentle. "Mama B is Bella Samsodien, my late sister's grandmother-in-law. The

owner of the sloth, Livvie, is her great-granddaughter."
Bay darted him a quick look, as if deciding how much
to tell him. Then she shrugged quickly and continued.

"My sister and her husband died in a car crash six
months ago and they named me as Olivia's guardian."

It took Digby a minute to make sense of her words,
to understand that she was raising her sister's child. Intellectually he knew that her actions weren't that out of
the ordinary, but since he was a product of parents who
hadn't shown any interest in raising their *own* sons, her
unselfish action amazed him.

Digby looked at her profile and saw the tension in
her mouth, in the cords of her neck. He knew what it
felt like to lose a sibling. "I'm sorry. I lost my brother
too and I know how hard it is."

Bay nodded. "I miss her, but I'm lucky to have Liv.
She's the most amazing little girl."

Digby, who had no experience of children, and didn't
want any, didn't know how to respond to that statement.

"Having Olivia in our lives is such a blessing, and
Mama B adores her. Ali, my brother-in-law, was Mama
B's grandson—she raised him from a baby because her
daughter died in childbirth." Sadness flitted across her
face. "She's endured so much loss—I don't know how
she goes on."

You plow on because you have no damn choice. As
he damn well knew. "And you are fond of her." That
much was obvious; he saw her face soften every time
she mentioned the older lady.

"She's amazing," Bay told him, turning to look at
him, her expression earnest. "I was overseas when I
heard about the accident. I returned to Cape Town immediately, only to find out that I'd inherited their house
and was named Liv's guardian. I was reeling, trying

to deal with Layla's death and trying to wrap my head around the fact that I had a child to care for. I knew nothing about children, wasn't even remotely interested in them."

Bay dug into her bag and pulled out her phone, swiping her thumb across the screen. She held it up. "This is Olivia."

Cute, Digby thought. Olivia sported a head of wild dark curls. With her massive round black eyes, rosebud mouth and lovely brown skin, she was the definition of gorgeous.

"We stayed with Mama B for three months, and Liv and I moved out three months ago."

Digby wanted to ask her about her parents, wondering why she hadn't mentioned them, but he could visibly see her retreating. It was obvious that she thought that she'd been too open, shared too much. But he wanted to know more and that was dangerous. He wouldn't be seeing her again...

Pity.

Digby watched as her spine straightened. She pushed her shoulders back and lifted her chin, and their very brief moment of connection wafted away on the slight breeze blowing off Table Mountain.

He shouldn't feel so disappointed; she was just another woman passing through his life.

Yeah, he was attracted to her, found her unusual and unsettling, but he was attracted to women all the time. The days when he chased down everyone who caught his eye were long gone...

"I should get going," Bay said, tucking her hair behind her ears. "I'm sure Olivia is awake, and you have work of your own to do."

She had no idea of the length of his to-do list but

meeting Bay was worth having to work late to catch up on lost time today. She was a breath of fresh air. "I do. But before you go, I have something else I want to show you."

Bay frowned. "Another room?"

"No, this can never be redecorated or improved on," Digby said, walking down the balcony. At the corner of the building, where the balcony made a right-angle turn, he stood back and gestured Bay to walk around the corner. She sent him a puzzled look but did as he asked and her sharp intake of breath was what he'd been waiting for.

Joining her at the railing, he smiled at the incredible view of Table Mountain looming over the hotel. His forefathers had purchased this plot of land purely for the view of the mountain, and it was said to be the best view of the world-famous landmark in the city. Rising above them to an impressive height, it was frequently covered when a rolling cloud, also known as the table-cloth, formed when the southeaster blew. But today the mountain was bare and utterly impressive.

"It's so beautiful. You're so lucky to live here, to have this view," Bay told him, her voice soft with awe and appreciation.

"Standing here on this balcony and looking at the mountain is my very first memory," Digby told her, unsure why he was revealing something so personal. "When my brother and I decided to rebuild the Tempest-Vane group of companies, I insisted that this hotel should be the first business we wrestled back."

A smile touched Bay's lovely mouth. "And was it a wrestle?"

He shrugged. "We made the owner an offer he couldn't refuse. He didn't so it was reasonably easy.

"Unlike the bloody mine," he added, wondering why he was running his mouth. "Now that was a nightmare."

"There's a story there," Bay said, sounding curious.

"Complete with a slightly crazy, utterly demanding bride, my brother meeting Brin, him falling in love and tough negotiations with a greedy mine owner."

Bay smiled, a proper, wide, open smile and Digby placed his hand on the balustrade to anchor himself. Holy hell, that smile was definitely her superpower.

He stared at her, she stared back and he couldn't help his eyes going to her lips, wondering whether her mouth would taste like sunshine. Would her eyes lighten or darken with passion? Would her long fingers slide up his neck, into his hair?

He couldn't let her leave without finding out.

He lowered his mouth, bridging the gap between them. Her lips formed a small "oh"—excitement or surprise?—and because she didn't pull or push him away, he covered her lips with his, lifting his hand to trace his thumb across her cheekbone. Yeah, soft. So soft.

Her mouth was land he wanted to explore, tempting and luscious, but Digby knew he couldn't push; if he did, she'd bolt. He carefully placed his hands on her tiny waist and gently pulled her into him, surprised at how well their bodies fit. Feeling her tension, he ran a reassuring hand down her back and increased the pressure on her mouth, teasing her lips to open, and when she allowed him in, his world—normally so steady—tilted off its axis. Digby felt like he'd taken a hit of something illicit. He felt shaky and disorientated, hot and cold…weird.

He wanted to shake his head to clear it, but that meant dislodging his mouth from Bay's and that was impossible. He'd find the willpower to stop ravaging her mouth, but he'd need a minute more. Or ten.

Bay softened, released a small noise of approval and then those hands were in his hair, running down his neck, across his shoulder blades. She felt like warmth and home and comfort, emotions he didn't normally associate with foreplay.

And this *was* foreplay.

Digby lifted his hand to her shirt, sighing when his hand covered her breast, pleased when her responsive nipple pushed into the palm of his hand. He rubbed his knuckle over the tight point and that action broke the connection between them. Bay jerked back, looking up at him with wide, startled eyes.

"What are we doing?" she whipped the question out, looking as unsettled as he felt.

Digby hoped she wouldn't notice his bobbing Adam's apple and the slight tremor in his hands. "Kissing in the sunlight," he answered, resorting to flippancy.

Bay pushed her hands into her hair, loosening the knot on the back of her head, and Digby watched, fascinated when tendrils fell down her back. He'd love to pull those pins from her hair, to see the contrast between her dark hair, shot with red, and her pale skin, to see where else he could find freckles on her.

"I need to go," Bay said, bending down to pick up her bag and art satchel. He'd been so entranced by her, having her in his arms, he hadn't noticed that she'd dropped either.

He had so much work to do, a meeting to attend, but all Digby wanted to do was to keep kissing her in the summer sun. He knew this property inside out and, following a series of seldom-used corridors, he could walk them through the hotel unseen. They could be in his house at the back of the property in ten minutes; he could have her naked in eleven.

Why this woman and why now? Sex, finding it and enjoying it, was easy. He had at least a dozen women whom he could text and set up dinner, followed by some bed-based fun. Or he could go to a club and pick up a woman, or even, if he was feeling lazy, a guest sitting in his world-famous bar downstairs.

But Bay Adair, Digby realized, was most definitely not easy, in any sense of the word. She wouldn't, he knew, indulge in sex for sex's sake.

Bay sent him a quick, embarrassed smile. "I really hope you find a designer who'll do this place justice. Please don't let them take their inspiration from the decor in the lobby."

"What's wrong with the lobby?" Digby asked. He rather liked the look of the lobby.

Bay wrinkled her nose. "It's cold. It reminds me of a snooty museum or art gallery."

Well, he'd asked. Digby felt Bay's hand on his forearm as she stood on her tiptoes to kiss his cheek. "Thanks for your time. Don't bother seeing me out— I'll find my way."

She moved her lips to his mouth, tasting him quickly before pulling back. "Have a good life, Digby Tempest-Vane."

Digby, still trying to catch up, stared at her slim back as she walked away, wondering how one kiss—admittedly a stunning, earthshaking, volcanic kiss—could make him feel so shaken, so utterly off balance.

But it had and he was. He didn't, he silently admitted as he gripped the railing with both hands, like either sensation.

CHAPTER THREE

BAY WALKED OUT of the ballroom, caught the elevator to the lobby and ducked into the first ladies' bathroom she came across, grateful to find it empty.

Gripping the basin with both hands, she stared at her reflection, wincing at her flushed cheeks and bright eyes. Her lips looked swollen and red, and anyone with any observational powers would immediately know she'd been thoroughly kissed.

It had been a lot of fun, Bay thought, touching her lips with her fingertips. In the space of a few minutes, Digby turned her to liquid wax and she'd lost track of where she was...

And *who* she was.

Bay hadn't had many lovers—okay, a grand total of two—but she'd kissed enough guys to know that Digby Tempest-Vane had a master's degree in the art of smooching. It had been, by an African mile, the best kiss of her life.

And, probably, her last. For a long, long while.

Pity.

Pulling her thoughts off his expert lips and exceptional body, Bay splashed some water on her hot face and told herself to pull it together. Staring at her reflection in the mirror, she touched her lips, her thoughts returning to how wonderful it felt standing in his arms. She'd felt secure and protected, emotions she hadn't experienced in a long, long time.

Was that why his kiss rocked her off her feet? She'd been completely on her own for five years but, since she was a young teen, she'd been on the outside of her family looking in, on unstable emotional ground. Had she responded like a wild woman to Digby because he was tall and strong, the ultimate alpha male, somebody bigger and stronger than her? Because she'd needed to feel safe?

Was she doing that age-old, biological thing, looking for a strong protector, someone to slay her dragons for her? And if she was, then she was being a complete moron.

She was a strong, independent woman who could, and would, wield her own sword, thank you very much. Relationships—and love—were a quid pro quo, a trade-off, the price always too high to pay.

As she'd suspected, working for Tempest-Vane was an impossibility. She'd taken her shot, missed the basket and it was time to move on. She had a little girl relying on her and she wouldn't let her down.

Pulling her phone from her bag, and ignoring her hollow heart and dread, Bay called Busi's cell. When it went straight to voice mail, Bay called Busi's office. The receptionist told her that Busi was away from her desk and would be unavailable for the next few days. Would she care to leave a message?

Bay left her details and heard the beep of an incoming call. Switching calls, and frowning at the strange number, she stated her name.

"Ms. Adair, my name is Bradbury, and I'm a lawyer representing your parents."

Okay. So why was he calling her?

"This is a courtesy call to inform you that your parents intend to sue for custody of one Olivia Jane Samsodien…"

For the second time in the space of an hour, Bay felt her head swim. Bay caught a glance of herself—her face deathly pale and her lips now bloodless—as she dropped into the wingback chair, thankful it was there because her knees no longer seemed to be working.

This couldn't be happening…

When the first wave of denial and shock passed, Bay rested her forearms on her thighs, staring down at the plush carpet beneath her shoes, and did some deep-breathing exercises. When she felt her panic receding, she pushed her emotions back and forced herself to think. Almost immediately, two thoughts became crystal clear.

First, she needed a lawyer who specialized in family law.

And, second, there was no way she'd allow her rigid, demanding, emotionally crippled parents to raise Layla and Ali's wonderful child.

Unbidden, the memories rolled in, tipped with acid. For the first thirteen years of her life, she'd been her father's model child, happily echoing his macho beliefs about patriarchy and protection. Charismatic and charming, his were the viewpoints she embraced, whether it was on religion, on feminism or on politics.

Then she went away to boarding school and met Busi, her sister of the soul. She'd asked her parents whether Busi could spend the weekend at her house and her parents refused, not giving her a reason for saying no. After badgering them, her father finally snapped, telling her that Busi wasn't like them and that they didn't want her kind in their house.

Her *kind*? Someone sweet and thoughtful and seriously smart? It finally dawned on her that her father's sole objection was to the color of Busi's skin.

Furious, she'd started questioning their racist and misogynistic beliefs and challenging the status quo. She and her father argued about race and religion, feminism and misogyny, and when she refused to back down from a point—or change her mind—he started to withdraw his approval and his demeanor grew cooler.

Then he started to blatantly ignore her and then, to punish her further, turned all his attention, affection and love onto her older sister, Jane, and younger sister, Layla, leaving her to waft in the wind, feeling unsure and abandoned. She lived in their house but her presence was simply tolerated. The only thing that she and her parents agreed on was that they all couldn't wait for her to leave home.

Bay had fought for her freedom, for the right to live her life on her own terms, and she'd never allow Liv to be raised in what she now realized was a toxic environment.

And she'd never allow herself to love someone because it was better to not taste, touch and feel love than to have it and then lose it.

Bay shook her head, conscious of her tight throat and the concrete block resting on her chest.

Her father had tried to bully her into giving him custody of Liv yesterday but when she refused, he'd approached a lawyer and instructed him to sue. He didn't want Liv...he just didn't like hearing the word no.

But, because he and her mother were wealthy, established, charming and personable, and had raised three girls of their own, there was a good chance of them winning.

It didn't help that Bay had no child-rearing experience, was currently unemployed and was, mostly, living off her savings.

Bay found a tube of lipstick in her bag. She removed the lid and carefully…oh, so carefully, since her hand was shaking…slicked on the pale, taupe color.

She needed work, something to show the courts that she could look after Olivia, that she was the best person for the job. She would not allow her niece to grow up in an environment that stifled creativity, individual thought, that promoted intolerance and didn't celebrate individualism. She wanted Olivia to grow up in a home where she was free to be herself, to explore ideas and faiths and to make up her own mind about what she did and didn't believe in.

She wanted Olivia to know that she was strong, that she was capable and that she would always, always be loved.

Bay would make very sure Olivia knew that her love wasn't conditional.

Digby far preferred Cape Town in summer; he wasn't a fan of short days, wind and rain. In summer, the long, hot days stretched on endlessly. Not that he'd seen a lot of sun lately since he spent most of his time in either of his two offices, the one at The Vane or at the headquarters of Tempest-Vane Holdings.

Digby loosely held the wheel of his Maserati Levante Trofeo, the luxury SUV he bought himself a few months back to celebrate his thirty-fifth birthday, enjoying its growly engine, its great handling and luxury finishes. He glanced down at the fluffy toy on his passenger seat and reached across to rub the nubby fabric between his finger and thumb.

He was on the way to the Bo Kaap neighborhood of Cape Town to deliver Fluffy, the sloth and ultimate escape artist, back to Bay Adair.

After Bay left, he'd walked into another meeting and when that was done, he told Monica he wasn't to be disturbed and immersed himself in work, ignoring his cell and emails as he attempted to whittle down his insane to-do list. When he finally surfaced, it was after seven and he heard a frantic message from Bay Adair on his company voice mail. Bay asked him to please retrace their steps because she'd lost the damn sloth again. Hearing the exhaustion in her voice, and a trace of panic, he did as she asked and found the stuffed toy lying on the balcony where they exchanged their hot-as-fire kiss.

Digby twisted his lips, feeling like a total ass for not sending one of his many drivers, interns or underlings to deliver the toy. He didn't need to play the role of the courier but he did want to see Bay Adair again.

Why her? Why now? Why did she affect him in a way no other woman had managed to? She made him feel like he did when he jumped out of a plane or skimmed down the face of a massive wave. He loved adrenaline, adored the thrill, the kick of his heartbeat, the dry taste of fear in his mouth, feeling alive, powerful, like the world made sense.

He had experienced all that when he kissed Bay Adair earlier today.

Madness. But it was a madness he couldn't resist.

Digby pushed his hand through his hair. He never pretended to be a monk; he was a virile, healthy single guy in the prime of his life and he enjoyed women, liked sex and refused to apologize for that. He never gave anyone false hope or empty promises, treated his partners with respect and hopefully, kindness, and managed to remain friends with most of his previous lovers. Because of his parents' hedonistic lifestyle played out in the world's tabloid press, he only dated women who were single, childless and unencumbered. He never dated women who had any type of baggage.

And Bay had baggage. And lots of it.

But, when he kissed Bay earlier, he felt like he was rushing down a black-diamond ski run or increasing the lean on his superbike to negotiate a tight hairpin curve. Up until this point, women and chasing adrenaline were two of his favorite pastimes, but when he held Bay in his arms, both gelled, morphed and became one.

And that, folks, was why he was traveling to Bo Kaap at half past eight at night, to return a stuffed toy. It was also why he had to keep a firm rein on his emotions, to control what he was thinking and how he was reacting. It was easy to confuse attraction and lust with affection, desire with connection. He was looking for a lover, not the love of his life.

Love, after all, was easily imitated and just as easily destroyed. Through neglect, death or disappearance. Love, if it existed at all, was intensely fragile and something to be avoided at all costs.

Digby knew he'd entered the Bo Kaap neighborhood when he started to notice the brightly colored houses dotting this exceptionally pretty area. Digby remembered his history, that back in the eighteenth and early nineteenth centuries, the houses in this neighborhood were leased to the slaves the British brought in from Southeast Asia and beyond. The leased houses had to be painted white back then but when the Malays were granted their freedom and were allowed to buy their houses, some of the new owners embraced color. After apartheid ended, bright, bold and stunning color swept through the neighborhood as a way for the owners to express their joy at true freedom.

He turned right, passed a tangerine-orange house, then a lime-green house, looking for number twenty.

The house Bay lived in was bright pink; the color reminded him of cartoon flamingos. Searching for a parking space, he spied an empty spot three houses down and whipped the Maserati into it, grateful for power steering. After exiting the car, he locked the door with the keyless lock and shoved the remote into his pants pocket and strolled up the street to Bay's glossy navy blue door, lifting his hand to acknowledge the kids across the street who were already making their way over to look at his car.

His Maserati tended to attract attention…

But then again attracting attention was something the Tempest-Vane family knew how to do. Digby banged his fist on her front door, waited a minute and finally heard footsteps on the wooden floor. The door cracked open and his heart settled as his eyes connected with hers.

What was it about her that made him relax, that pushed the tension from his body? No one had ever had this effect on him before and he had to get this craziness under control.

"It's about bloody time," Bay muttered, flinging the door open. She snatched the toy from his hand. "Do you have any idea of the hell I've gone through today?"

He was right about her looking exhausted; her eyes were red rimmed—had she been crying?—and her face looked a shade paler. He smiled at her outfit: a pair of loose cotton pants and a tank top showing off her slim but still sexy body.

Before he could respond to her fiery greeting, Digby felt a small bump against his legs and looked down, astounded to see a mop of ebony curls and two tiny arms encircling his leg. He found his balance and heard deep, snotty sobs coming from the little girl.

Aw, crap. The little girl tipped her head back and his breath caught at huge round wet eyes the color of obsidian. She lifted her arms up and Digby, who tended to avoid children as much and as often as possible, immediately scooped her up and placed her on his hip. She took the sloth Bay held out to her and her sobs immediately stopped. She tucked the toy into her tiny chest and rested her head on his shoulder, her thumb in her mouth.

"I finded Fluffy."

Bay nodded and held out her hands, obviously expecting the little girl to fall into her arms. Olivia surprised them all by shaking her head and laying it back on his shoulder. "Tired, Mommy Bay, and my head hurts."

"I'm sure you are, baby girl," Bay crooned, her hands still outstretched, "so let's get you into bed."

"Nuh-uh. Stay here with Fluffy's friend."

Now, there was a name he'd never been called before.

Digby patted Olivia on her tiny back. "Sweetheart, I need you to go back to your mama," he told the sweet-smelling handful in his arms.

Olivia immediately let out a screech and wrapped her arms around his neck, squeezing with everything she had. "No! Stay here."

Bay pulled a face. "Sorry. She's just feeling sick and has a bad cold," she explained.

Digby winced, thinking of his designer suit. Yay,

snot and tears, just what he needed. Thank God he was as healthy as a horse and never got sick. Not knowing what else to do, he kept patting her back, keeping his touch light. A minute or so later, he heard her sigh, felt a tiny puff of breath against his neck and her tiny body sag. He lifted his eyebrows at Bay, who had a satisfied look on her face.

"She's asleep," she mouthed, gesturing for him to follow her.

Digby walked into a tiny second bedroom, white and pink, and laid the little girl into a single bed. She tried to open her eyes but when he tucked the sloth into the crook of her arm, she rolled over, yanked her legs up and fell deeper into sleep.

Bay pulled up a light blanket, kissed her head and then they both left the room. In the passage, Bay closed her eyes and her lips moved in what Digby thought might be a heartfelt prayer.

"I need a drink." Bay softly muttered, leading him into the small living room.

The room was a pale, creamy pink and the fronds of a huge fern tumbled off a side table. Seascapes adorned the wall, along with a huge photograph of a dark-skinned man holding a gorgeous strawberry blonde in his arms. Digby immediately saw the resemblance between the woman and Bay; she had to be her sister. And Olivia had inherited her father's black hair and wide, smiling mouth. They'd been a good-looking couple, Digby thought, and looked so vibrant and happy.

Like Jack, they'd died young, before they could even start to tap into their potential. Digby squared his shoulders, trying to push that familiar pain away.

Then Digby looked at Bay and he felt lighter and

brighter. The pain was still there but it felt toothless and weak. How did she manage to do that?

"Let's go onto the veranda—that way we won't disturb Liv. She normally sleeps like the dead but let's not take the chance."

He'd kill for a solid eight hours. He hadn't slept for more than a few hours a night, four at the most, since Jack died. And lately, when he did sleep, he dreamed of burying Radd.

Not exactly restful.

Hoping that Bay didn't notice his shudder, Digby walked through the small sitting room and open French doors onto a tiny patio with a garden the size of a postage stamp. Herbs—he recognized lavender and parsley and mint—spilled from pots and tinged the air with their fragrant scents.

Bay gestured to a small wrought iron table, covered with colored pencils and a sketchbook. A half-full glass of white wine glistened with condensation and Digby wondered whether she'd offer him a glass.

Bay sent him a small smile and told him to take a seat. "I've had an exceptionally crappy day—I'm sorry if I was rude or snappy. Thank you for delivering Liv's favorite toy." The next words out of her mouth were the ones he really needed to hear. "Can I offer you a drink?"

He nodded and sat down, stretching out his legs and crossing his feet at the ankles.

"Whiskey or wine?"

"Whiskey would be great, thank you."

Bay nodded and turned to walk back into the house, narrow hips swinging. She had a truly exceptional ass; Digby couldn't help noticing.

Needing something to distract him from the party

in his pants, Digby looked down at the table, his eyes taking in the upside-down sketch. Recognition flared and he sat up slowly, before twisting the pad. It was a rough sketch of the ballroom at The Vane, *his* ballroom.

Instead of plain white paint, the walls were covered in a subtle pattern—wallpaper?—and huge, luscious plants sat on simple, stylish pedestals. The curtain treatment was luxurious and sophisticated but not ostentatious…

Digby hauled in a quick breath.

This, *this* was what he wanted. Somehow, with barely any input from him at all, she'd nailed the brief.

Forgetting that it was her sketchbook, that he had no right to invade her privacy, he grabbed the pad and started flipping pages. She'd started a sketch for the honeymoon suite, another room he wanted redecorated, but it was only a preliminary sketch and didn't give him an idea of what she was thinking. Her next sketch was of Olivia, easily capturing the mischief in her eyes and the perfect curve of her chubby cheek. Bay was a talented artist, he thought, flipping back to the sketch of the ballroom.

Man, she'd completely captured the look he was going for.

Digby heard her approach and didn't try to hide the fact that he'd been snooping. "Your sketches are amazing."

Bay's eyes jumped from the pad to his face and back again. She handed him his whiskey before sitting down opposite him and crossing one long leg over the other. "It's how I relax," Bay replied, before taking a hefty sip of her wine. "I needed a distraction this afternoon so I started to sketch."

He was scared to say it, in case he was making a

mistake—she was an inexperienced designer without a track record—but what other option did he have? He wanted the hotel revamped and Bay was the first person who'd come even close to giving him what he wanted.

"I love it—it's bloody fantastic." He pointed to the sketch and tapped the paper with his index finger. "That is exactly what I want."

Almost as much as he wanted her.

Bay's eyes widened, obviously surprised by his emphatic statement. "It is?"

Digby nodded. "Yeah." Very much so. On *both* accounts.

Excitement flashed across her face and her eyes turned a lighter shade of gold. Then the excitement faded, she bit her lip and looked away. "Thank you, I guess."

Digby frowned, wondering why she looked like he'd popped her favorite balloon. "I'm trying to offer you a job, Bay."

"I realize that."

She'd succeeded where many of the best designers in the world had failed. Why was she acting like he'd offered her a lump of coal on Christmas morning?

Digby watched as Bay played with the fabric of her cotton pants, carefully folding it into pleats on her thigh. Her hair fell down the sides of her face and he saw that she was biting the inside of her lip, her thoughts a hundred miles away.

"You do want this job, don't you? I mean, that's why you met with me today."

Bay stood up and stepped onto the tiny-sized lawn, digging her bare toes into the rich verdant grass. She held her wineglass against her chest, her eyes troubled. "Of course I would like the job but—"

Digby folded his arms and waited for her to verbalize her thoughts.

She pushed the fingertips of her hand into her forehead and wrinkled her nose. "I have to be honest, Mr. Tempest-Vane."

"We kissed so I'm pretty sure you can call me Digby."

Bay blushed and he worked hard to hide his smile. He couldn't remember when last he'd seen a woman blush, and he rather liked the fact that she did.

Bay ignored his comment and drew patterns on the grass with her big toe. "I pretty much knew, before I even arrived at The Vane, that I wasn't experienced, or established, enough to handle the project. I shouldn't have wasted your time…"

But she had. And he was curious to know why. And, because they'd shared that intense kiss, pretty damn grateful she had.

Instead of explaining why she felt it okay to carry on with their meeting instead of canceling it, Bay veered off. "Look, I can do the design—I think I know what you are looking for, but I'm not set up to take on a big project, financially or otherwise. To be honest, while I have a diploma in interior design, I've only done a couple of small projects—"

"How small?" Digby asked, interrupting her.

She pulled a face. "A couple of kids' bedrooms and a sitting room or two."

Crap. That wasn't inexperienced, that was home decor.

"And when I say that I decorated the rooms, I accompanied my friends to the shops and advised them what to buy. Then I painted their walls and rearranged their furniture," Bay admitted.

Wonderful.

"I've applied for jobs in the sector but nobody is hiring, and you were my last, and only, chance at working in a field I love. But I knew I was very out of my depth."

Bay walked back over to the table, sat down and started to put her pencils back in their cardboard box, and in the correct order. Greens, then blues, then the red shades…who did that?

Digby reluctantly added curiosity about her to his unwanted fascination.

She was different, unusual and captivating.

Strange because those weren't emotions he was familiar with. Digby seldom delved beneath the surface with people. He liked them well enough—and the world saw him as an extrovert, someone always up for a good time—but he didn't open up, or let people in. The term *extroverted introvert* fitted him perfectly.

He could be the life of the party one night, and he could also be the guy slinking away as soon as he could the next night. And he never, ever allowed anyone to look beneath his charming exterior. Who wanted to see chaos, anyway?

Bay placed her forearms on the table and tapped her fingers against the smooth skin of her bare arm. "The long and short of it is that I'm simply not in the position to work for you."

She was right. Digby lifted his glass to his lips, allowing the whiskey to slide down his throat. He couldn't afford to have someone inexperienced running the project; the renovations had to happen quickly, causing minimal disruption to the guests. That meant teams of laborers working in shifts, coordination of deliveries, sourcing furniture and supplies.

He needed someone with experience in these types

of projects, someone who knew how to crack the whip, who could negotiate with suppliers and who had excellent time-management skills.

Bay wasn't that person. She could be, in the future, but she wasn't experienced enough to handle a project of this magnitude. But she was completely suited to be his designer because she was the only one who'd managed to capture what he wanted, design-wise. That, up until now, had proved impossible.

Digby, a million thoughts flying around his head, stood up and, echoing Bay's actions, paced the small area behind the table, his hands in his pockets, picking his problem apart.

"If I gave you the job, what would be your first step?"

Bay rolled her eyes in exasperation but eventually answered him. "I'd set up mood boards for each room, do detailed sketches, source pictures of the furniture I think would work. I'd give you a detailed drawing of my vision which we can discuss." She wrinkled her pretty nose. "I'm pretty anal when it comes to decor—everything has to be perfect. Lines have to be straight, upholstery has to be perfect, patterns have to match perfectly."

Exactly what he needed for The Vane.

Bay was what he needed, and what *she* needed was a project manager. Something he could do in his sleep…

Digby shook his head, lost in his thoughts. He couldn't possibly be thinking he'd project manage the renovation of The Vane? He had the holding company to run, the hotel to oversee. There were a dozen other projects that should take precedence until he found someone to take over the renovation of the hotel in its entirety. And it had been weeks since he'd had any spare time; if he wanted to compete in the grueling Roof of Africa motorcycle rally next year, he should do some training. And it had been an age since he surfed or skydived or even took a weekend off.

If he took on the role of project manager, working with Bay, he might be able to find some spare time in, maybe, five years or so.

But renovating The Vane was close to his heart, it always had been. Many of the good memories he had of his childhood took place within its high stone walls. He recalled playing tennis with his brothers, Jack teaching him to swim in the smaller of the three pools. His grandfather's sixtieth birthday party, Jack's twenty-first. Trying to keep up with his brothers as they scoffed down the delicious treats on offer during high tea.

So many memories…

Because he had an emotional connection to the place, there was no way he would leave any interior designer to his or her own devices. He was a control freak and he knew he'd spend a lot of time looking over shoulders, checking on the progress, making sure they were on track and keeping the standards high. If he took on the project management and Bay provided the design ideas, he'd be in control of the renovation.

And that was a situation he was fully comfortable with. And let's be honest, it would probably be a hell of a lot cheaper than hiring the best designers in the world. Not that money was an issue but Digby didn't believe in wasting cash when he didn't need to.

"Together, we could do this together," Digby murmured, feeling the flicker of excitement in his belly growing into a fire.

"What are you talking about?" Bay demanded, placing her heels on the edge of her chair and wrapping her arms around her knees.

Digby pushed his hand through his hair and gripped the back of a wrought iron chair. "Work for me. Be my designer. I'll be the project manager, will provide the cash and funding and source the crew."

He watched her eyes widen, excitement flashing then fading. "I'd love to but, jeez, Digby, I don't think I can."

"Why on earth not?" Digby demanded, unable to believe she was passing up this opportunity. "If you work with me, you will not only be earning an excellent salary. You can say that you were the designer on a hell of a project. Provided you do a good job, and I don't see why you wouldn't, I would be happy to write a letter of recommendation for you. Working for me would open up a lot of doors for you."

"I understand that and I'm grateful for the offer but it's not that simple!" Bay cried, standing up abruptly. "Can I be honest?"

"Please do."

"I didn't really think this through. I was so caught up in the design work and forgot about the practicalities of working for you, working for anyone, actually. I'm guessing that there would be very tight time constraints, wouldn't there?"

"Yeah, obviously. Shutting anything down means losing money so, yes, you'd have to work long hours and plenty of overtime. You'd be recompensed accordingly."

Bay twisted her lips. "But that's my problem, Digby. I can't work long hours and loads of overtime. I'm responsible for a little girl who lost both her parents six months ago and who is, I'm quite sure, suffering from separation anxiety. While I desperately need an income, and a steady job, I can't leave her for extended periods. I especially can't leave her alone at night and Mama B is too old to look after a three-year-old every day."

Digby stared at her and scratched his head. Damn, he'd forgotten about Olivia. And he remembered how he felt, as a young teenager losing Jack—he'd suffered terribly and had clung to Radd—so he understood Olivia's fear of losing Bay.

Hell, he was *still* terrified that he was going to lose Radd. As his dreams kept reminding him.

But he couldn't lose Bay's talents either. If he did, he didn't know how long it would take before he found someone else who got him.

Got his vision, got what he wanted for The Vane, he clarified.

He thought for a minute, then a minute more. "What if you brought Olivia to work with you?" he asked.

"Then I would get no work done," Bay crisply replied. "She's sweet and lovely but she's demanding. And willful.

"And she doesn't trust strangers," Bay added.

"She seemed to trust me," Digby said.

"I know and that was super strange. But you did bring Fluffy back so... Are you offering to look after her while I work?" Bay asked him. She smiled. "I give you a half a day and you'll be begging me for mercy."

"She can't be that bad," Digby protested.

"She's worse," Bay cheerfully replied. She hesitated, started to speak and shook her head.

Digby encouraged her to voice her thoughts and after a moment she spoke again. "Maybe I can do the drawings for you, set up the mood boards for you, and you can take it from there. You can pay me for doing that."

Digby thought about her suggestion and pretty much instantly dismissed it. "I worked on the design of Kagiso Lodge with Radd, and things we thought would work on paper sometimes didn't. I'd need you to be there to give immediate input, to make changes on the fly."

"That's fair." Bay's expression closed down and she lifted her shoulders in a weary shrug. "I appreciate your offer, Digby, and your faith in my work, but I just don't see how it would work. And I don't want to start something, be excited about it and have it come crashing down around my ears. I desperately need a stable, secure job."

He heard the tension in her voice, saw the way her fists clenched and opened and thought that there was a lot Bay wasn't telling him. And that was okay…

For now.

"I'm prepared to offer you a decent contract," Digby informed her. "And I have an idea about what to do with Olivia…"

Bay lifted her sexy eyebrows—he'd never thought a pair of brows could be sexy until today—and waited for him to continue.

"Today I signed off on some new hires from Human Resources, including a three-month contract for an American looking for temporary work as a waitress…"

He hesitated, wondering if Bay would go for his proposal. There was only one way to find out…

CHAPTER FOUR

As DIGBY BEGAN outlining his proposal, Bay felt like she was on a Tilt-A-Whirl, or that she was a dandelion trying to survive a hurricane. What was *happening*?

Earlier this evening, she'd bathed Olivia and read her endless stories trying—and failing—to distract her from the loss of Mr. Fluffy. Finally, at the end of her rope, she'd allowed Liv to watch her favorite TV show. Leaving her to it, Bay, staying in hearing distance, had gone outside to think, knowing that she needed to make some tough decisions. Bringing her sketch pad—because thinking was so much easier when her hands were busy—she'd contemplated her options, idly drawing the ballroom at The Vane as she considered her next move.

But her thoughts had kept veering to Digby's lips on hers, remembering the feel of his strong biceps under her hands and the silky texture of his wavy hair. Remembering how sexy it had been feeling his stubble on her skin as he kissed her jaw was far more fun than contemplating her return to the world of engineering.

She'd spent five years at the university studying a subject she hated just because her father told her she shouldn't, that she'd never succeed, that it was a man's job...

Stupid.

Pulling her thoughts back to what was important, she'd tried to reach Busi again, relieved to hear her old friend's voice. But Busi hadn't any good news for her—the partners had recently resolved to place a freeze on new hires. There weren't many openings in the sector either, Busi had told her and, because she had little experience, she might find it difficult to find a position.

Awesome.

Having had enough of reality and unable to deal with any more bad news, Bay had allowed her thoughts to drift back to Digby again, recalling how good he smelled, of expensive products containing spice and lemon and something that made her brain shut down and her ovaries sit up.

Nobody had ever made her feel as out of control as Digby Tempest-Vane did.

And he should be the last guy in the world she should be attracted to. He was a player, flitting from model to actress to celebrity to princess with astounding regularity. He had a reputation, deserved or not, of being a playboy, irresponsible or, as her grandmother used to say, a flibbertigibbet. Flighty, flirty and yeah, charming.

She didn't trust charming.

But that hadn't stopped her traitorous body from wanting to plaster itself against his broad chest, to bury her nose in his strong neck, to explore the ridges of his ribbed stomach or the strength of his thighs.

Oh, Lord, she was in so much trouble.

And she knew this because, right now, although she should be thinking of his outrageous and frankly amazing proposal, she was also thinking of how he would look naked. Pretty wonderful, she imagined.

Argh! Really?

Right, time to act like an adult, Adair. Think!

He was offering her a hell of an opportunity, a way to establish a career doing what she loved, but how could she take that up without neglecting Liv? The little girl was wary of strangers and she hadn't been lying earlier—she hated being separated from Bay.

Working long hours for Digby, or anyone else, would be impossible. She needed to spend time with Liv—that was nonnegotiable. Her mental well-being was all that was important.

Along with feeding and clothing her and educating her and...

Rock, let me introduce you to Hard Place.

Bay pushed her hand through her hair, feeling like a hundred years old. Sometimes the responsibility seemed overwhelming.

Today I signed off on new hires from Human Resources, including a three-month contract for an American looking for temporary work as a waitress...

Digby's mind was, obviously, operating at warp speed. He rarely, she supposed, heard no, and she guessed that finding solutions to problems had to be something billionaires excelled at. If they didn't, they wouldn't be so rich, right?

She tightened her grip on her knees and waited for him to continue, interested in what he had to say but knowing that, eventually, he'd walk out of her house and her life.

That was just the way life worked. He was a rich, free-as-a-bird playboy; she was a broke, single mom trying to survive.

"The waitress I hired has a degree in early childhood education and has experience working in her mom's playschool in San Francisco. What if I hired her to look after Olivia?"

Bay blinked, not sure if she'd heard him correctly. "What?"

"We have specialized programs at The Vane to entertain children so that their parents can eat in our Michelin-starred restaurant, drink cocktails on the veranda with other adults or take quality time on their own. We do have family-friendly areas, obviously, but we aim to keep the kids entertained and I employ specialized staff to do that.

"I have a team of au pairs at the hotel but let me employ the American to look after Olivia, exclusively. She can join the playgroup if she wishes to. I don't know anything about three-year-olds, but don't they need the company of their own kind?"

Bay's lips twitched at his choice of words. But he wasn't wrong, it would be good for Liv to play with kids her own age.

"If you need to see her or spend time with her, it's a ten-minute walk across the grounds to the buildings, ditto if she needs to see you. You could work, knowing she's safe and cared for and in easy reach."

Oh, my, he'd cut away her biggest objection to working with him. He was making it exceedingly difficult to say no. And why should she? This job was the answer to her many, many prayers.

"You design, you source paint and materials and stuff you need and you request quotes. I'll organize the work crews, haggle with the suppliers for better prices and arrange for delivery."

He mentioned a monthly salary that had her eyes bugging out. Her tongue, she was sure, was an inch from the floor. She wasn't certain what the going rate for interior designers was but, man, that figure sounded like four or five times what she'd hoped to earn.

"Are you being serious?"

His deep blue eyes connected and held hers. "Deathly."

Well, then.

Bay ran her hands over her face, her mind racing with possibilities. Needing to see it on paper, she pulled her sketch pad toward her, grabbed a bright purple pencil and did a quick calculation, working out her salary for the next six months. Another quick sum gave her the figure of her expenses over the same period and there was a healthy profit. And she wouldn't have to pay for Olivia's childcare so that would increase her disposable income.

She could pay off some debts, buy Olivia a new summer wardrobe and service her car. She could also stash some money away every month for emergencies and best of all, she could afford a good lawyer to help her in her quest to keep custody of Liv.

She couldn't say no; this opportunity was heaven-sent.

Except for one thing…

"What about…" Bay hesitated, her eyes going to his sexy mouth. She bit her lip, knowing she was blushing. "…what happened earlier?"

"Do you want me to tell you that it won't happen again?" Digby asked her and she noticed that his hands were gripping the back of the chair, his knuckles white.

No. Yes. She didn't know.

"I am attracted to you, you know that," Digby said, his voice harsh but his eyes not leaving her face. "All I can promise you is that, no matter what, your job will never be in jeopardy because of anything that happens between us."

She should demand more, to make him promise that nothing would happen between them at all. *Ever.* But she couldn't make herself voice that thought.

Digby's deep blue eyes slammed into hers. "I never play where I work, Bay, and if something happened between us it would be the exception rather than the rule. What if I put the power into your hands?"

Sorry? What was he talking about? Bay frowned at him. "I don't understand."

"If you want something to happen between us, *you* make the move." His sexy mouth quirked in a half smile. "I'm not saying that I won't try to tempt you into bed, but if we get there, it'll be your choice, your timing. Your terms."

Bay's mouth fell open; she was not sure how to react. No man, not her father, either of her two previous lovers or any of her boyfriends, allowed her to be in the driving seat, to take control. Bay turned over his offer, looking for the catch. Because there had to be one. Nobody made that sort of proposal without getting something out of the arrangement.

What was Digby's angle?

She didn't trust him; she didn't trust anybody, so she shook her head. "Nothing will happen between us, Digby."

He frowned at that. "Are you involved with someone?"

She shook her head.

"No. But I can't, for a lot of reasons, get involved with you." Bay said, dropping her feet to the floor.

"It would be an affair, Bay, not an involvement," Digby told her, his voice soft, but she heard the determination in his words. So, like her, Digby wasn't looking for love or commitment. She wondered if his reasons were as complicated as hers.

It didn't matter; they weren't going to go there. Her life was convoluted enough without adding an affair with her employer to the list of things guaranteed to stress her out.

She saw his flash of disappointment when she didn't offer a reason, but she couldn't, wouldn't explain. She was a private person, used to keeping her own counsel. She'd spent too many years fighting with her father for her voice to be heard, her opinions respected, only to be dismissed and rejected, so she'd decided, a long time ago, to keep her thoughts to herself. If she didn't share them, they couldn't be stomped on.

Bay thrust the purple pencil in his direction. Digby raised his thick eyebrows and took the pencil. "And what do you want me to do with this?"

"Scribble a note about providing a nanny for Liv and sign your name next to my calculations and we'll take that as a preliminary contract. You can send me an official one later."

Digby nodded and bent over her sketch pad, his hand dashing words across her page. His signature, bold and confident, just like the man, followed. He straightened, placed the pencil in the box and sent her a small smile. He held out his hand for her to shake. "Deal?"

Bay had no choice but to place her hand in his, trying to ignore the tingles racing up her arm and the heat settling in her belly. "Deal. When do you want me to start?"

He nodded to her sketch pad. "You already have, Bay. Keep doing that and I'll be in touch in a day or two."

Digby released her hand and walked around the table, dropping his head so that his lips were close to hers, sending anticipation and heat swirling through her. "I thought you said that I was in the driving seat."

Digby had the temerity to grin at her. "And you are. But I told you I'd try and tempt you, remember?" He stood so close to her that all she'd have to do was tilt her head upwards and… "Are you tempted, Bay?" Digby whispered the words against her lips.

Desperately so. But Bay didn't think that the super-confident Digby needed to hear that. He was far too cocky as it was…

"Good. Night, Bay."

Bay watched, openmouthed as he walked into her house and out of sight. Then she heard the front door closing behind him and dropped her forehead to the table, feeling both exhilarated and unbalanced, thanks to Digby's professional offer and the heat in his eyes.

And Bay knew that the contradictory feelings wouldn't disappear anytime soon.

Digby sat on the edge of his desk and watched Bay introduce Olivia to her new nanny, Roisin. Row-sheen, he remembered, was the way her name was pronounced. It was Irish, the tall, dark-haired American had explained. And, yes, she was happy to look after Olivia…

Excellent news.

When Roisin tipped her head to the side to explain something to Olivia, she looked a little familiar but Digby immediately dismissed the thought. Roisin had a strong American accent and she'd only been in the country for a month, having flown out from San Francisco six weeks ago, so he couldn't have met her before.

His thoughts moved on from Roisin to Bay, looking fresh and lovely in a pale pink sleeveless shirt and tan capri pants, funky sneakers on her small feet. She wasn't conventionally pretty but something about her kept her constantly on his mind.

In between imagining what she looked like naked, he also had random questions about her, like was she a coffee-first-thing-in-the-morning type of person and did she prefer cats or dogs? Did she prefer chocolate or vanilla and how did she feel about being responsible for raising someone else's child?

In between making mental lists and planning strategies, or finding solutions to a dozen big and small problems, his thoughts often drifted to the kiss they'd shared, remembering how wonderful her mouth felt under his, how her slim body seemed to fit his perfectly, her lovely, subtle scent and the spice of her mouth. And how the world seemed to stop spinning whenever she was in the room, how his heart settled and sighed whenever she was around.

God, he had to stop thinking like this. This wasn't who he was, what he did.

She was taking up far too much of his mental energy. He couldn't offer her anything; he wasn't capable of long-term relationships or even wanted one. Oh, he could play the part of the charming rogue, the life and soul of any party, but he was, deep down where honesty resided, a loner, someone completely comfortable with living his life solo. He'd had parents who never paid him any attention growing up—hell, he remembered not seeing them once over six months—and when they were around, they ignored him to focus on their pursuit of pleasure.

But he and his parents did share some common traits. Like them, he liked his freedom, liked being able to do what he wanted when he wanted, without having to answer to a wife or significant other. But the difference between him and his parents was that he realized how hurtful neglect and disinterest could be and he'd never ever do that to a partner or a child.

Besides, he'd never risk loving and losing someone again. Radd had been, for the past twenty years, his only anchor, all the family he wanted, needed or could cope with.

So why was he, mentally, linking Bay with thoughts of his family? God only knew. What he was certain of was that seeing her, working with her and knowing she was solidly off-limits was going to make the next few months pure torture.

Fingers snapping in front of his face pulled him back to the present. He blinked and Bay's amused face came back into focus. "There you are. Did you take a nice trip?"

Digby looked around his office to find it empty. "Where did they go?"

"To the nursery. Liv was more than happy to go with her, thank God," Bay told him, her eyes reflecting her relief. Her eyes turned to gold when she was happy, darkened when she was stressed. *Good to know*, Digby thought.

Bay placed her hand on his biceps and squeezed and Digby realized it was the first time she'd initiated physical contact. The heat of her hand burned through his cotton to brand him.

"Thank you for hiring Roisin—she's amazing."

Digby risked placing his hand on her hip and moving her so that she stood between his outstretched legs. "Pleasure," he murmured, his hand skating over her hip bone.

Digby looked down into her face and saw the blue stripes under her eyes. Wondering why he hadn't noticed how tired she was, he pulled back, just a little, to look at her properly. Her shoulders were hunched and the cords in her neck were pulled tight.

She was stressed to the max.

She had a job and a nanny for Olivia, so what else

was worrying her? And why was he so desperate to know, and worse, to fix, all her problems, to protect her from anything that was causing her pain?

Lifting his hand, he clasped the back of her neck and rested his forehead on hers. "Are you okay, Bay? Can I do anything, anything at all, to help you?"

Bay's extraordinary eyes met his and he saw a brief hint of tears. She opened her mouth to speak but then snapped it closed before shaking her head.

Instead of answering his questions, she rested her head on his collarbone and placed her hands on his waist. Her next words weren't something he expected. "Can you, for just a minute, hold me, Dig?"

Dig.

Nobody else but Radd and Muzi shortened his name and he liked hearing it on her lips. And, while hugs weren't something people, specifically women, associated with him, he was more than happy to wrap his arms around her and pull her in close.

And, he acknowledged, this had nothing to do with sex and attraction; she was looking for, needed, something else from him. Comfort, maybe? Support? Did it matter? Maybe not.

"Come here, kid."

Digby didn't give her a chance to object, or rethink her question, he just wrapped her up, holding her tight. He placed his cheek on her hair and smiled when her arms encircled his waist to hug him back. They were in his office and they had a ton of work to do but he'd hold her for as long as she needed.

Anytime. Anywhere.

And strangely enough, at that moment, with her in his arms, the thought didn't scare him as much as it should.

* * *

"Mama B, Roisin is wonderful. Liv has really taken to her," Bay explained, her phone tucked between her neck and shoulder.

"I want to meet her, to decide for myself," Mama B replied, her tone suggesting that Bay not argue.

Bay grinned, knowing that Mama B's concern came from a place of great love. "I'll ask whether she can bring Liv to you for a playdate and you can meet her then. You'll like her. I promise."

"We'll see," Mama B replied, before abruptly ending the call. Bay grinned. Mama B had said what she said and was done talking. Bay envied the freedom that came with being old.

Bay, sitting cross-legged on Digby's sofa, put her pencil down and stretched, raising her arms high above her head and bending from side to side. When she was traveling, she'd carved out time to do daily yoga and Pilates sessions, but since returning to Cape Town, yoga and any form of exercise had fallen by the wayside.

God, she missed it. She also missed quiet cups of coffee in the morning, the excitement of buying a ticket to a new destination and stepping off the plane to soak in the sights and sounds of a different land and culture. The noisiness of Bangkok, the sophistication of Florence, the serenity of Bhutan.

She missed the feeling of only being responsible for herself, being able to act with spontaneity and being as free as one could be in the twenty-first century.

As always, a wave of guilt broke over her and she felt terrible for mourning her free, uncomplicated and easy life. *And let's remember why you aren't in Kathmandu or Kampala right now, Adair, and that's because your sister is* dead.

If she handed over custody of Liv to her parents, like they wanted her to do, then she could return to traveling, to exploring the world. She could go to Iran, or to Alaska, or she could pick up a job working on the yachts in the Med.

But how could she enjoy, well, anything, knowing that Layla's little girl would be at the mercy of her rigid, controlling and austere parents?

Initially, Bay knew, her parents would shower her with love and affection, and Liv would be the happiest little girl alive. She'd blossom and shine but, if she was anything like her mom and aunt, as she hit her teens she'd start to question the rules, the rigidity, the lack of trust and their protectiveness. She'd want to spread her wings and they'd be clipped. There would be lectures and then more lectures, and if those didn't work, attention would be withdrawn and love withheld. Affection would become a thing of the past. And because she was strong-willed and stubborn, Olivia wouldn't back down but would be left swinging in the wind, unsure and alone and feeling like she was dying inside.

Bay knew exactly what that felt like.

She thought back to her meeting the previous day with her new lawyer, a friend of Busi's, and to the million questions she'd answered about her life, her job and her romantic interests. Gillian Crawford had deep dived into her life and Bay had told her about her altercation with her father and admitted to her attraction to Digby.

Gillian, an experienced family lawyer, then took her through the legal process and pointed out possible pitfalls. Her parents were well respected, good people, who could give Olivia every opportunity. Because they had children young, they were only in their early fifties and they were fit and could keep up with a three-year-old.

They were perfect.

Bay, on the other hand, was not. She was single, and while her new job working for Digby was a good start, it wasn't permanent and, thanks to her traveling, it could be argued that her lifestyle was a trifle unstable.

But, Gill continued, Layla and Ali wanted her to have custody of Olivia, not her parents. The judge would, probably, respect their wishes.

Unless she gave the judge cause to question her judgment.

Until this lawsuit went away, her lawyer also advised her to downplay her connection to Digby Tempest-Vane. Working for him was one thing, but if the press linked them together romantically, they could and would make a meal of her supposed relationship with the playboy billionaire. Digby was a guy who played hard and fast, who hadn't had a long-term relationship in his life and who had been raised by the most notorious and dissolute couple on the continent.

Her name linked with his would result in her judgment being questioned and that was something that needed to be, at all costs, avoided.

Damn, it wasn't right. Sure, Digby's parents had indulged in drugs and affairs and wild parties—orgies had been mentioned on numerous occasions—but they'd died two years ago and she didn't think it fair for Digby to be judged by the sins of his parents.

It was so unfair that the only man she'd been attracted to in ages was the one man she had to avoid. But, fair or not, she couldn't risk losing Liv.

Nor would she risk allowing herself to bask in his affection and attention. He'd jerk both away when he was done with her, when she no longer interested him, and she'd be left feeling hollow and empty again.

But, like a child who'd been told not to eat the sweets she'd been left alone with, all she wanted to do was gorge herself on him. To taste his wonderful mouth again, to push his shirt up his chest to reveal his exceptional body, to scrape her teeth along his jaw, tug his earlobe in her mouth, put her hands down his—

Whoa, boy! Getting a bit hot in here. Putting her sketch pad aside, Bay stood up, walked over to the window and stared past the incredible rose garden to Table Mountain, covered with its rolling tablecloth. *You can't think about Digby like that, Bay, it's too dangerous.*

She knew it but it was so damn hard, especially when the man was temptation on two feet.

Bay heard his footsteps behind her and felt his hands on her shoulders. She knew she should step away, but when his hands skated down her arms, to slide across her stomach, she leaned back into him, enjoying the way his arms encircled her waist. It was so nice to have human contact, to have a hard man with big arms holding her tight. To feel like she wasn't quite so alone…

"Tempting me again, Tempest-Vane?"

"Trying to," Digby replied.

Bay felt Digby's lips on her neck, sighed when his teeth scraped over the sensitive cord of her throat, along her jaw. She had to stop this, and she would, in a minute. Bay wanted just one minute to enjoy his scent and his solidity, his masculinity and the way he electrified every inch of her body.

"Is it working?" Digby quietly asked.

Bay turned to face him, resting her hands on his chest. "You know it is and it's so unfair."

"You should know that I don't play fair, sweetheart." Digby pulled her in close, her breasts pushing into his pale blue button-down shirt. Her nipples hardened and

Digby placed his hand on her back, a fraction above her butt, pulled her hips to him, and Bay sighed at the hard ridge in his pants.

Yeah, she really should step away...

But he did tempt her and, damn, she wanted just one quick kiss. One *last* kiss. Bay, silently, cursed herself and her lack of control. She had to pull herself together; she couldn't afford to allow him to wear her down, to put herself in a situation that would have huge consequences for Olivia. She couldn't give in to the madness he pulled to the surface; there was too much at stake. She wasn't the only one who had skin in the game and she had to make the best possible choices to keep her tiny family together.

Transient pleasure, a few hours in Digby's arms, wasn't worth the risk.

Digby was far too good at this temptation game, Bay conceded. She'd step away soon, she *would*, she just needed a minute.

That minute passed, and Bay didn't move away, she simply *couldn't*. She wanted this, she wanted him.

"Time is up, sweetheart."

Digby's lips covered hers but Bay, despite her frustration at being so damn weak, didn't hesitate. She immediately invited him in. His tongue, wet and wild, slid across hers and Bay whimpered, loving his heat and his intensity. He wanted her, of that she had no doubt. She felt his desire in the way his gentle fingers traced the line of her jaw, roamed over her lower back before he was digging his fingertips into her butt and groaning into her mouth.

She could stand here in the morning sun and kiss him endlessly, drinking in his power and earthiness, spice and strength. He was *such* a man, strong and hard and rough and sexy. Everything she'd never known she needed in a lover.

He wouldn't treat her like a fragile flower; he'd demand that she give him everything she could, and then he'd teach her to give up more. Bay had no doubt he could persuade her to give him everything...

But that wasn't possible. She needed to keep their relationship professional and Digby at a distance. Right now, they couldn't slide a piece of paper between them.

Bay wrenched her mouth off his and slapped her hands against his chest, pushing against his strength. Digby resisted, just for a second or two, and then he stepped back, lifting his hands off her to scrub his face.

"Dammit."

Bay didn't know whether he was upset with her or himself, but it didn't matter, this couldn't happen again. She had to resist him; she was playing with fire. If the circumstances were different, there was a chance she'd say to hell with it and sleep with the gorgeous man. It would be highly unusual, but there was a first time for everything.

But, if anyone linked them together, Liv's custody battle could be affected by her actions and that was intolerable. She would not risk her future, or her heart, for a quick, or slow, orgasm.

She was bigger and better than that.

She hoped.

CHAPTER FIVE

BAY HAD BARELY managed to pull Olivia's pajama shorts up her chubby legs before the little girl took off down the short hallway, running as fast as she could to get back to Digby.

Her little girl had a crush, Bay thought. Her new mama did too.

He'd been caught up at Tempest-Vane HQ today and they hadn't had time to discuss her suggested color and decor schemes for the hotel. When Digby suggested that he come to her place, she'd been hesitant. What if the press followed him here? The assumption would be that they were lovers and she couldn't, in light of her custody battle, allow that to happen.

But she hadn't had the willpower to say no. And they did need to catch up on work…

Too late now, he was here.

Bay sighed and followed Liv to where Digby sat on the small patio, a glass of whiskey at his elbow. As she suspected, Olivia, and Fluffy, were in his lap and her sweet head rested on his broad shoulder, her thumb in her mouth and her eyes heavy.

She'd be asleep in minutes, Bay realized. Roisin had taken her swimming in The Vane's family pool this afternoon and Liv had by all accounts loved every second of being in the water and had no fear.

But, after a full day, the little girl was completely exhausted.

A glass of wine, courtesy of Digby, sat on the wrought iron table and Bay took a sip, allowing the icy and tart liquid to slide down her throat. Cape Town was experiencing a heat wave. Her cottage didn't have air-conditioning and she felt like she was about to melt.

In contrast to her, Digby looked cool and comfortable in chino shorts and a loose linen shirt, flip-flops on his sexy feet. He'd asked for some time tonight—they hadn't finished their discussion about her mood boards—and Bay invited him to her cottage any time after six. He arrived, to both her and Liv's delight, at six fifteen.

Bay sighed and rubbed the back of her neck in frustration. She wanted, much to her chagrin, to spend as much time with Digby as possible, even though he was dangerous to her self-control.

And her future…

He was *that* addictive.

But addictive or not, it was very annoying that he'd found the time to have a shower before arriving at her door and Bay frowned. She hadn't had a moment to herself after collecting Olivia from Roisin. Before making her way home, she'd needed to stop and buy some groceries, hit a cash machine and put fuel in her car. When she got home, she had to feed and bathe a fractious Olivia. And if she didn't put laundry in tonight they'd have no clothes because they were out of, well, everything.

Bay felt like she'd run a marathon. The idea of making herself something to eat was a step, or ten too far. No wonder she was dropping weight. And God, she hoped Digby didn't expect dinner.

"I'm not cooking," Bay told him, feeling defiant. Her mother, no matter how long a day she'd had, would've made sure her father had a two-course meal ready the moment he stepped through the door.

She was not her mother; she would *never* be her mother. And Digby was her boss, not her lover or boyfriend or husband.

Digby raised his eyebrows at the rather snippy tone. "I know—that's why I ordered Chinese. You do like Chinese, don't you?"

Who didn't? "Sure, I like Chinese." Feeling embarrassed, she sat down on the chair opposite him and hiked her heels up onto the seat. She rubbed her eyes with the balls of her hands. "Sorry, it's been a long day."

"For me too, and I didn't have to deal with the human dynamo," Digby replied. He looked down at Olivia, his face reflecting his confusion. "I don't understand why she likes me. I've had zero interaction with kids."

Bay smiled at his statement. "I think it's a gut thing. She immediately liked Roisin, as well. I trust those initial impressions."

Digby picked up his whiskey glass with his spare hand. "Did you also trust Roisin immediately?"

Bay heard an uncertain note in his voice and cocked her head. "I did. Didn't you?"

Digby seemed to choose his words carefully. "About her qualifications and her love for children, I did. But there's something…"

"What?" Bay asked. She'd spent enough time with Digby to realize that under that very hot face and exceptional body was a scalpel-sharp brain. If he had concerns about Roisin then she'd listen. "Should we be looking for another nanny for Liv?"

The thought made her heart sink. Liv loved Roisin and was completely comfortable with her. Even Mama B liked her, enough to offer to teach Roisin how to make her famous bobotie, something she rarely did. Finding another nanny would not be easy.

Digby held up his hand, his expression wry. "No, relax. I have absolute faith in her ability to look after this peanut." Digby patted Liv's thigh. "I'm not sure that I believe that she's in Africa just because she's traveling…" Digby stared at his whiskey before shrugging. "But her personal life has nothing to do with me."

Bay glanced at Olivia and saw that the little girl was fast asleep on Digby's chest. She gestured to her. "I can take her and put her to bed if you like."

"You just sat down," Digby pointed out, "and she weighs about as much as a feather."

Bay sipped her wine and rolled her head on her shoulders, trying to work out some of the knots in her neck.

She looked at Digby, who was looking very at ease despite the soft bundle lying on his chest. But he did look tired and his fabulous eyes had dark rings under them. Because she was sharing his office at The Vane, she knew how many balls he had up in the air. His meetings and calls never stopped. "You're looking a bit shattered too, Digby. When are you expecting your brother back?"

Digby shrugged. "God knows. He's been away for a few weeks already and I am hoping that he'll be back in time to help cohost our View of Table Mountain Ball."

Bay had heard of the ball—it was one of the premier social events on Cape Town's social calendar.

The tickets were stunningly expensive, hard to come by and were snapped up months before the event. The ball raised funds for numerous causes throughout the city, including HIV/AIDS clinics, literacy and school feeding programs.

The attendees were the most influential, richest and powerful people in the country, including politicians, kingmakers and captains of industry.

"This year is the centenary anniversary of the ball— my great-great-grandmother hosted the first ball at The Vane in 1921—so Radd, and Brin, had better bloody be there," Digby stated. "I am not dealing with that lot on my own."

Bay raised her eyebrows. "I'm sure you can host the ball on your own with one hand behind your back." He was charming and fully comfortable in every social situation, could work the crowd with ease and make everyone feel welcome and important. Radd, she'd heard, was quieter and far less sociable than his brother.

"I miss him," Digby said, surprising her with his admission. For a hugely popular guy, Digby rarely spoke about his personal life.

"Radd?" she asked, just to be clear.

"Yeah. It's been just the two of us for a long, long time and not having him around feels…strange," Digby quietly replied, his blue eyes a shade darker with an emotion she couldn't identify. Could it be loneliness? No, that didn't make sense; Digby was one of the most popular people in Cape Town and, according to everything she'd read, had a hectic social life.

"You're so lucky to have a lot of friends," Bay said. She'd been around Digby enough to realize that he was one of those rare individuals who pulled people into his orbit, someone people gravitated to.

Women wanted to be with him, men wanted to be him…

"I have a lot of acquaintances," Digby corrected her. "I only have a few people I call my friends. Radd, obviously. Muzi Miya-Matthews—"

She'd heard of Muzi Miya-Matthews; he owned and operated some of the best vineyards in the country and was the CEO of a famous wine brand. "The wine guy?"

Digby laughed. "Actually, he has a double degree in business and oenology."

Impressive. "Anyone else?" Bay asked, wanting to hear more about his private world.

Digby lifted a broad shoulder. "No, not really. I mean, I know a lot of people, but people who know me? Muzi and Radd…that's it, I guess."

Bay lowered her glass, her eyes searching his face. He wasn't being serious, she thought, because there was no way one of the most popular bachelors in the city could only call two people—two!—and one was his brother—a close friend. Hell, she'd been out of the country for years and she still had a few close friends.

Bay moved her legs, tucking her heels under her bottom. Needing to dig deeper, she tossed out another question. "Tell me what you and Radd were like as kids?"

Digby flashed his hot-as-the-sun grin. "Naughty as hell. Jack, because he was so much older than us, tried to keep us in line, and he frequently said it was like trying to herd rabid cats. Basically, we were, to a large extent, feral."

Bay smiled. She could easily imagine the Tempest-Vane brothers causing havoc. Especially Digby. "But you grew up, eventually."

"Radd is more grown-up than me—he's even engaged. I never thought that would happen."

Digby reached for his whiskey glass and took a long swallow. He sent her a wry look and she caught the flash of embarrassment in his eyes. "I'm trying really hard to be an adult about him and Brin."

Bay cocked her head to the side. "You don't like Brin? Why not? She's lovely!"

Brin and Abby were her friends and she wouldn't listen to him, or anybody else, denigrate them.

"Relax, spitfire, I'm not about to insult her," Digby told her, his eyes amused. "I like Brin. I really do, and she's perfect for Radd."

"Then what's the problem?"

Digby stared down into his nearly empty glass, his eyes darkening to a shade off midnight. "I'm the problem, Bay. This will sound completely ridiculous since I am a guy in his midthirties but—*Jesus*."

Bay waited for him to continue, trying not to show her impatience. If she pushed, Digby would retreat and she'd never know what he was about to say.

"It's been Radd and me, against the world, since I was fourteen, fifteen years old. As you and the world know, our parents were bloody useless." Digby's already deep voice dropped an octave and she heard a slight tremor to his words. Speaking of his past wasn't easy, but she thought that it might be necessary. Everybody, even sexy playboys, needed to vent.

"Radd is, has been, the only constant in my life for two decades—" Digby's thick eyebrows pulled together and he drained his glass. "Can we talk about something else? We've both had a long day and this is depressing."

Bay shook her head. "No. Tell me what you were about to say about Radd." Yeah, she was pushing him but sometimes thoughts needed to be expressed before they festered. Though maybe that horse had already bolted…

Either way, it would be good for him to voice his frustration.

Digby glared at her, not happy to be pushed into a corner. "You're not going to let me change the subject, are you?"

Bay handed him a small smile. "Nope. Now, stop stalling and tell me."

Digby rubbed the back of his neck as his words poured out in a rush. "I'm jealous of her, jealous that she has his time and I don't. Jealous that he's not mine anymore."

Oh, Digby. Bay placed her hand on her heart but remained quiet, knowing that the dam wall had, well, not broken but cracked.

Digby's sigh was both heavy and embarrassed. "As I said, we've been on our own since our teens. Radd tended to put himself between me and the world when we were younger but, as we grew up, our relationship evened out. Our school offered a gap year after we graduated and, because there's less than a year between us, he chose to do that gap year so that we could attend the university together. We started our internet business together, developing a new payment system, worked together, planned our future together."

Digby stared at her, his expression telling her that he was ready for her to mock him, or to dismiss his fears. For someone so personable on the surface, he really wasn't good at emotionally deep conversations.

"We were a team," Digby said and Bay heard the pain in his voice.

Bay allowed her eyes to connect with his. "And now you think you're not because he's going to marry Brin?"

"Stupid, right?"

Seeing his confusion, Bay decided to put him out of his misery. "You're allowed to feel that way, Digby. Change is always scary."

"I feel like an idiot. And, worse, like a crap brother!"

"Actually, you sound human," Bay told him. "And normal."

Digby grimaced. "I sound like a moron."

Bay's lips quirked up at his low grumble and grumpy face. Unable to resist, she stood up, placed a hand on his shoulder and brushed her lips across his mouth. Funny how perceptions were often wrong, she thought. She'd genuinely believed Digby had a wide circle of friends, but what he had were acquaintances and he was, actually, emotionally isolated.

Digby lifted his free hand to hold the back of her head, to keep her mouth on his. His tongue slid into her mouth, and want and need replaced sympathy. Knowing that she was on a runaway train, Bay slammed on the brakes and lifted her mouth from his. They were venturing into emotional-connection territory, heading toward some sort of nonphysical intimacy. Such connections—expressing feelings and vulnerabilities—were dangerous, especially for her. She refused to step onto that magic carpet only to crash and burn when the wind powering her flight died or changed direction.

She liked Digby, loved the way he made her body sing, but she refused to be another crash victim. Although he was becoming harder and harder to resist and here she was, giving herself more opportunities to be tempted.

Ignoring the whole custody-battle issue, there was a very real chance she could fall for Digby. And if she did that, she would get hurt. She'd throw herself at him, offer him everything, and he might, for a little time, return her affection. But then, because the man never had long-term relationships, she'd start to bore him and he'd begin looking around for something new, someone different.

Then, as her dad did, he'd pull his affection and attention and she'd be left swinging in a cold wind. God, having and losing love had hurt so damn much.

Not happening, never again.

And if that wasn't enough of a reason, she couldn't afford, according to her lawyer, to be romantically linked with Digby.

She wasn't ready to tell him, or anyone, about her custody battle. That would mean explaining that she was estranged from her parents, that they didn't think her capable of raising Liv, that her parents no longer loved her. Or even liked her.

Bay slid her hands under Liv's thighs and back and easily lifted her into her arms. "I'll put Olivia to bed and then we can get to work."

Digby frowned at her, obviously confused by her sudden change of subject. But before he could respond, the peal of her doorbell drifted through the house.

Saved, she decided, by Chinese takeout.

"Digby, you're a freaking maniac!"

A week or so later Digby laughed as he whipped his Ducati between two minibus taxis and smiled at Bay's voice in his ear via the intercom system between their two helmets. She was tucked up behind him on his superbike, her arms around his waist, working with him as he steered his bike down the still busy Cape Town highway. Lifting one hand, he patted her slim, denim-covered thigh.

"Relax, I'm not going that fast." Okay, maybe he was going a little fast.

Digby returned his hand to the handlebar and smiled as he recalled Bay's confused face when she opened the door of her cottage earlier. She'd obviously been asleep; there were crease marks from the cushion on her cheek and her spectacular eyes were a bit foggy. Taking advantage of her confusion, he quickly established that Olivia was sleeping over at Mama B's and that Bay was, blissfully, alone.

And a plan started to form.

He'd been on his way to Muzi's; they'd made vague plans to hit some bars, maybe a club or two. Needing a hit of adrenaline, he decided to take his bike, even if it meant he couldn't drink for the rest of the night. But instead of heading to Muzi's flat in Camps Bay, his bike found itself—strange, that!—on Bay's street, and then he was knocking on her door…

He'd invited her out for a ride and she'd hemmed and hawed and then hemmed and hawed some more. After promising that he wouldn't stop anywhere where he would be recognized or, worse, photographed—a complete novelty because his dates tended to want to be seen on his arm—she finally agreed to join him.

At that point he hadn't had a destination in mind but, on hearing that Bay preferred casual and very low-key, an idea occurred. While waiting for her to change— he'd told her to wear jeans and flat boots—he'd texted Muzi and told him that he was heading for Kwezi's if he wanted to join them.

Muzi might or might not; either way it was sure to be a fun night out. He was with Bay, how could it not be? And best of all, their destination, he was sure, would surprise Bay. She wouldn't expect him to take her into the heart of Gugulethu, one of Cape Town's oldest townships. Hell, he'd never expected to take a woman there either. He couldn't think of a single woman he'd ever dated who wouldn't wrinkle her pretty nose at the thought of joining working-class folks at a working-class place. His dates expected haute, innovative cuisine and extensive wine lists, not barbecued meat and cheap beer.

Bay had spoken a little about her travels, how she always sought out the places where the locals ate, and he knew she wasn't squeamish or snobby. Bay, he'd come to realize, didn't give a rat's ass about expensive champagne and modern cuisine, about seeing and, more important, being seen.

In fact, she'd told him, quite emphatically, that she did not want to appear in any social column. Ever.

Luckily, he'd never encountered a reporter, photographer or any of Cape Town's A-listers at Kwezi's Tavern. Kwezi's was his, Radd's and Muzi's secret, the place they headed to when they wanted complete anonymity.

He could've, Digby thought as he took the off-ramp and stopped at a traffic light, left Bay at home and met Muzi here on his own but…

But the hell of it was that he enjoyed Bay, liked her company. She was a great designer and had a fantastic work ethic, but she was also quick and witty and thoughtful. And so damn sexy he frequently forgot to breathe.

Digby tightened his grip on the throttle and sighed. What had he been thinking when he suggested that she be in control of their going-to-bed timing? God, he hoped she caved soon because not having her was driving him crap-bat insane. When he wasn't having his Radd dying dreams, he dreamed of her naked and writhing and he frequently woke up at the crucial moment, hard as a rock and groaning. Sleep, never easy, had become something he started to dread.

He really had to start getting his attraction to her under control. Yeah, he liked her, adored her body, couldn't wait to get her into bed but...

But that was it.

He didn't believe in love, didn't want it in his life. He couldn't see himself ever having what Radd did with Brin. He couldn't imagine himself engaged or being in a committed relationship. First, he'd been on his own, doing his thing, for a damn long time and didn't think he could change now, but more than that, he didn't want to...

He wasn't brave enough. He knew what it felt like to have love and then to lose it, to feel like he was being ripped apart. Why would he ever put himself in that position again?

No, the sooner he and Bay slept together, the sooner he could get her out of his system. The sooner he could move on and return to his normal life.

So, genius, let me ask you this...

The light turned green and Digby tried to ignore the sarcastic voice coming from deep in his soul.

If sex is all you want, then why didn't you stay in her empty house and try to seduce her there? Why is she on your bike? Why are you taking her to one of your favorite places in the world? The place that you've never, ever taken a girl before?

Good questions and, annoyingly, not ones he had answers to.

From the minute she climbed on the back of Digby's bike, Bay cursed herself for accepting his invitation out, terrified that, despite his promise, he'd take her somewhere where he'd be recognized, where someone would photograph them together.

If that happened, she might put her custody of Liv in jeopardy, and Bay mentally kicked herself. She'd started to, fifteen times, maybe more, ask Digby to take her home, but on his bike, their faces hidden by the black helmets and visors, they were unrecognizable. And she loved flying down the highway, the warm wind whipping her cotton shirt, confident in Digby's handling of the monstrously powerful bike.

She'd see where they ended up, she decided, and if she felt that there was the slightest chance of recognition, she'd ask Digby to take her home. And he would, she knew that for sure.

But of all the places to eat in the city, she hadn't expected to arrive at a colorful tavern in Gugulethu. There were plastic tables and chairs outside the restaurant, filled with jovial patrons tucking into mounds of barbecued meat.

Inside the tavern, rows of wooden tables left little space to walk, and to one side sat a bank of display fridges. Inside the fridges were plastic tubs of meat, waiting to be cooked on open fire behind the restaurant. Digby, after greeting the owner and the man behind the display case, ordered steak and ribs, a soda for himself and beer for Bay. He asked after Muzi but was told he hadn't arrived yet.

The tables were full to bursting and Bay wondered where they'd sit, but Kwezi, the owner, led them to the middle of the room and booted two teenagers out of their seats. When Bay protested, he waved her words away, telling her that they were young, they would survive. She and Digby sat down in the middle of what was a jolly party and were instantly welcomed by the other customers at the table. Nobody, she was sure, knew who Digby was and if they did, they didn't care.

Bay was completely surprised at how at ease he, a multibillionaire, was in this working-class restaurant. Despite having eaten in the best eateries in the world, owning one himself, he didn't seem to care that the plates were mismatched, that there wasn't a wine menu or servers. He was also perfectly content to wait in line for his meat to be cooked, to eat with his fingers.

Her boss, the lover in her dreams, was anything but a snob. His lack of entitlement and ability to talk to anybody anywhere made him, if it was at all possible, even more attractive in her eyes.

She hadn't thought that was possible but here she was, falling a little deeper...

After eating more meat than she normally did in a month and drinking a few beers and laughing at the quips of the middle-aged couple to her right, Bay leaned her shoulder into Digby's and turned her head to smile at him. "Having fun?" he asked.

"So much fun," Bay replied. "This was not how I expected to spend Friday night. I wanted to be at home, relaxing, but I'm here and I feel like I *am* at home. And I am so relaxed."

"That could also be the three beers you've had," Digby told her on a lazy grin.

Bay wrinkled her nose before shaking her head. "Seriously, thank you for bringing me here. I've eaten street food and local dishes on five continents, but I've never visited a traditional African tavern before. The meat is awesome."

Digby popped another piece of steak into his mouth and grinned. When he finished chewing, he picked up her beer and took a swig. He looked longingly at her bottle and when Bay suggested he order his own, he shook his head. "I'm going to be in control of a super-powerful machine in a couple of hours and I can't afford to have my judgment impaired. Especially since I have a gorgeous passenger I'm responsible for."

Bay showed him her appreciation by dropping a kiss on his lips. Before she was tempted to take their embrace further, she pulled back. "Thank you for that."

Digby turned to face her, his elbow on the table. "Are you still okay to work tomorrow?"

Bay nodded. "Why wouldn't I be?"

Digby pushed a strand of hair off her forehead, his fingertip light on her skin. Yet she still quivered. Bay was starting to think that she could be ninety, having experienced a lifetime of Digby's caresses, and she'd still respond like this. "Tomorrow is Saturday, you've been working like a demon and you deserve a day off, to sleep in."

"My boss is a hard taskmaster—he's been working me to the bone," Bay teased. When Digby didn't respond to her teasing, she allowed her fingers to drift over the back of his broad hand. "I'm fine, Digby. A little tired maybe but we need to press on ahead or else we won't get the ballroom done in time for your foundation's ball in two months."

Digby grimaced, moving his hand to wind his fingers through hers. "Fair point." He thought for a moment before speaking again. "I'm just so sick of the four walls of my office…why don't we work out of my house tomorrow?"

She was also getting cabin fever so she quickly nodded. Okay, truthfully, she also wanted to see where Digby lived. And, because his house was within The

Vane's grounds, she didn't have to worry about being spied on, least of all by nosy reporters. She nodded. "Nine-ish?"

"Perfect," Digby said, squeezing her fingers before pulling away to turn his attention back to his food.

Bay, marveling at how much he could eat, changed the subject. "Now, tell me, how do you know Kwezi? Is he another of your friends from your smart boarding school?"

Digby shook his head. "Kwezi's dad was a foreman on our vineyard and we've known each other since we were kids. He, Radd and I spent a lot of time together between the ages of six and thirteen. Then his father was hurt in a tractor accident and they moved back to the city and we lost touch until ten or so years ago."

Bay placed her elbow on the table and her chin in the palm of her hand. "And how did you reconnect?"

Digby saw Kwezi standing at a nearby table and motioned him over. "Bay wants to know how we reconnected, dude."

Kwezi asked a customer to scoot up so that he could sit down opposite Bay. He took a long sip of water from the bottle in his hand. "Digby was playing rugby for his university. I was playing for a local club. We met again on the field. I gave him a concussion that knocked him out cold."

Kwezi, as Bay had already noticed, was a huge guy, six-four or six-five, all muscle. Being tackled by him would be the equivalent of being run over by a tank. "What? *Really?*"

Kwezi shrugged, not at all remorseful. "Not my fault he's weak."

"It was a high tackle." Digby pointed a rib at him.

"High tackle my ass," Kwezi stated. He looked at

Bay and shook his head. "Your boy couldn't take the heat."

"You did go on to play topflight rugby, dude," Digby grumbled, but Bay saw the amusement in his eyes. He looked so very relaxed, so at ease in this casual restaurant. It was a good look on him.

Looking at Bay, Digby continued his explanation. "Kwezi was on track to play for our national team but his mom fell ill and needed help with his siblings, so he came back here and opened up this tavern."

Kwezi reached across the table and snagged a rib from Digby's plate. Holding it in his enormous fingers, he bit down, chewed and looked thoughtful.

"I'm thinking about expanding—there are premises across town I think would be good for another tavern."

Digby pushed his plate away and wiped his hands on a paper napkin. "You sound hesitant."

Kwezi lifted one enormous shoulder. "Money is tight out there and unemployment is skyrocketing. I'm not sure if there is enough money in the system to sustain another tavern."

"That's what you said when we first discussed you opening up this place—no money, high unemployment, too much competition." Digby made a show of looking around the packed-with-people joint. "It looks like you are doing okay.

"Trust your instincts, bruh," Digby told him. "They were spot-on back then—they are sharper now."

Bay—who'd been watching the intricate moves of a young, gorgeous dark-skinned woman on the makeshift dance floor in the far corner of the room, her hips shimmying and her braids flying—pulled her attention back to Digby when he stood up abruptly. Holding his hand out to Bay, Digby nodded to the full dance floor. "Do you want to dance?"

Bay cocked her head to listen to the music, feeling the deep bass lines reverberating through her body. Like the tavern, the music was rough and raw and wholly authentic.

She nodded, stood up, placed her hand in Digby's and smiled. "Yes, please." She turned to Kwezi and excused herself. "I hope to see you again."

Kwezi left his seat and walked around the table. He gave Bay a brief hug and a wide grin. His dark eyes twinkled with mischief. "Digby dances nearly as well as he plays rugby," he pulled a face and shuddered theatrically, "so if you need someone to show you some moves, I'll be around."

Digby's shoulder bumped Kwezi's in retaliation and Bay couldn't help laughing when Digby failed to move him at all.

Bay led Digby to the crowded dance floor, enjoying the rhythmic beat of Kwaito music pumping at full blast from the massive speakers on either side of the makeshift space. She felt the beat in her feet, in her heart, deep in her soul. Hitting the dance floor, she turned to face Digby, noticing that they'd been separated by a couple getting down and a little dirty. Not waiting for Digby to join her, she lifted her hands and instinctively started to move with the beat, shimmying her hips and rolling her shoulders, turning on the spot, her hair flying.

Dancing made her feel sexy and sensual and hot, and the African rhythm connected her to her country and its people. As she waited for Digby to join her, Bay wondered whether he could really dance. Like all women, she found men with rhythm incredibly sexy.

But even if Digby couldn't dance, his willingness to dance with her without caring what anyone thought was pretty damn cool. She liked guys who were carefree enough, confident enough to look let go, have some fun, not caring whether they appeared silly or not.

And Digby had confidence in spades.

As it turned out, Digby was a very good dancer and came off as anything but silly.

On reaching her spot in the middle of the floor, he placed a hand on her hip, his thigh between hers, and immediately started to move in time to the beat. His eyes slammed into hers and in all that blue she saw desire and need.

Bay, conscious that she held all his attention—such a turn on!—caught his small grin before he was gripping her hand, spinning her out, to pull her back into his chest, then leading her into an empty space with a quick, confident shuffle.

He spun her out again and let her go and Bay instinctively realized that, while he was an excellent dancer, he wanted to spotlight her, that this was her moment, her chance to let loose and fly. Shaking off the last of her inhibitions, Bay fell into the music, allowing instinct to take over. She shimmied and shook, twisted and turned, knowing that whatever she did, wherever she was, Digby was there, urging her on, to let go, to dip and swirl, to allow the music to carry her away. Sometimes he held her, most times he allowed her space to move on her own but he was there…

Always there.

She was the picture; he was the frame. Dance was emotion in motion and she reveled in every note, every beat, understanding the lyrics even though she didn't understand the language. As she moved, she flirted with Digby, with herself, with life in general and God…

She felt so very alive.

After three fast songs, the track switched to a song that was slow and sensual and, without hesitation, Bay moved into Digby's arms, looping one arm around his neck and placing her other hand above his heart, enjoying the steady thump-bump under her fingers. His hands rested low on her back, just above the curve of her ass, keeping her anchored to him, his hard erection pushing into her hip. They swayed in place, still flirting without words, seducing in silence.

Dancing was, as someone far cleverer than she once noted, "the vertical expression of a horizontal urge."

Indeed…

CHAPTER SIX

THE NEXT MORNING, a few minutes after she left Olivia with Roisin—the two were off to the beach today—Bay followed Digby's directions to his house. She ambled to the back of the property, through the impressive flower and vegetable garden, another rose garden and across a swath of lawn, to a double-story structure right at the back of the parcel, as far away from the guests as she could possibly be on the huge acreage. Feeling the sun on her bare shoulders, she stopped at the end of the path and looked up, sighing at the incredible view of Table Mountain. Today the mountain loomed over the tract, so close she felt like she could reach out and touch its crags and slopes.

She had, she admitted, a bit of a hangover, not helped by too little sleep and a few beers. She'd had so much fun with Digby last night.

But, admittedly, she'd been very disappointed when, somewhere around three in the morning, Digby dropped her off at her cottage. He'd kept his distance and when she tried to kiss him, he told her she was a little drunk, tired and that she needed sleep more than she needed sex.

He'd been wrong there and she'd been prepared to argue but Digby told her that, while he wanted her more than he wanted his heart to keep beating, it wasn't the right moment.

He didn't want her to have any regrets, to be able to say that alcohol lowered her inhibitions, that her ability to make good decisions was affected. If she wanted to sleep with him, she could just say the word, but preferably when she was completely sober.

Digby was, despite his reputation, a gentleman. Damn him.

Bay slipped her sunglasses onto her face, passed through a small grove of trees and lifted her eyebrows as she approached a large stone building. Digby had informed her that he'd only recently moved into this converted stone barn; up until a few months back he'd been using one of the larger of the hotel suites as his primary residence.

She couldn't pretend; Bay was eager to see his home.

Bay touched the wall of the barn, admiring the work of the stonemasons. Needing to see more, she hurried around the side and placed her hand on her heart when she noticed the monochromatic glass windows rising from the floor to the pitch of the roof, opening up the entire house to the view.

Fabulous. Good job, architects.

Seeing that one of the sliding doors was open, Bay rapped on the frame and stepped inside, straight into the huge open floor space. A freestanding fireplace stood in the center of the room, with a spacious lounge on one side and a dining area on the other. Beyond the eight-seater table with dining chairs upholstered in rich jewel colors was a sleek, gourmet kitchen.

Entranced, Bay looked up. A set of spiral stairs on each side of the barn provided access to what she presumed to be the master bedroom and a guest bedroom on the mezzanine level, with a thin walkway against the back wall joining the two rooms. The ancient beams of the structure were exposed, and light poured in from skylights above.

"I'm in love," she murmured.

"I presume you are talking about my house and not me."

Bay turned to see Digby lying on the couch behind her, her breath hitching when she saw he was only wearing running shorts and sneakers on his feet. Taking a moment, she admired his gorgeous body, the light sprinkling of hair on his chest, the ridges of his muscular stomach and those gorgeous hip muscles disappearing into his shorts. The bicep muscle of the arm resting over his eyes was hard and impressive. God, he was physically powerful and stupendously sexy.

Down, girl.

Digby pushed himself to his feet and gestured to the kitchen. "I'm going to take a quick shower and then we can get to work. Make yourself comfortable, help yourself to coffee, whatever you want."

Bay nodded. "Do you mind if I explore?"

"Not at all." Digby walked to the closest stairs before jogging up the steep curves to his bedroom. Bay dropped her bag, laptop case and art satchel on the dining room table and wandered into the kitchen, peeking into a pantry and beyond that, a utility room. Backtracking, she saw another door at the end of the room and opened it to reveal a smaller lounge complete with huge couches, a massive flat screen and speakers everywhere. There was an interconnecting door that led to a study, lined with shelves. A huge desk was pushed to the wall and held files and expensive-looking computer equipment.

The office's second door opened back onto the main living area and from there she walked up the spiral staircase and onto the landing outside the spare bedroom. It was the standard double-bed guest room with en suite shower, perfectly decorated but, in her opinion, a little bland.

Bay thought about going back downstairs but she was curious, so she walked across the narrow landing thirty feet above the living room below and ended up outside Digby's room. The stairs were to her right and she should use them, but his bedroom door was open and she wanted a quick look. His bedroom had glass on two sides and Bay could easily imagine him waking up every morning in that enormous bed, covered with plain white linen, and rolling over to look at the city's favorite landmark.

Amazing.

Then her view improved considerably when Digby walked across her line of sight, with only a towel wrapped around his waist, his hair wet and droplets of water running down his tanned shoulders.

His body was even nicer to look at than the view outside and that was saying a hell of a lot...

She should go before he saw her, should walk down those stairs. But Bay's feet were glued to the landing and she knew she wasn't going anywhere...

"You're welcome to come inside but, I have to warn you, if you do, I'm going to do my best to tempt you into getting naked," Digby said, turning around to look at her.

Her eyes slammed into his and a million thoughts bombarded her. He was keeping his word; sleeping with him would still be her decision, her choice.

She should go...

She wanted to stay…

She was playing with fire…

But she wanted to burn…

The past six months had been all about Olivia, about doing what she had to do, what she'd promised to do. She couldn't remember one occasion lately, apart from last night, when she'd done something for herself, spoiled herself in any way. She hadn't bought new clothes, gone out to eat or clubbing. Her entire focus had been on Olivia and nursing her through this catastrophic change in her life and dealing with her own grief.

She loved Olivia, she *did*, but wasn't she allowed, just once, to spoil herself?

And sleeping with Digby would be a hell of a treat. He would be a memory she'd have for the rest of her life.

She liked him, was crazy attracted to him, and she'd love to learn all he had to teach her. They were both single and unattached and best of all—no one would ever know.

Digby must've seen the capitulation on her face because he smiled and gently ordered her to come to him. Bay hesitated, but only for a moment. Then, with a tiny shrug, she stepped into his room, walking around the huge bed to stop in front of him. Digby lifted his hands to hold her face and he gently rubbed his nose against hers, his mouth curved into a smile.

"I'll go slow and if you change your mind at any point, just tell me and I'll stop, okay? And there will be no hard feelings."

Bay bit her lip. "Promise?"

"I promise. You're in control here, sweetheart. We'll go as far as you feel comfortable with."

Yeah, as she'd noted last night, under all that charm, Digby was a gentleman, a man with honor.

Reassured, Bay placed her palms on his bare chest, sighing at his smooth, masculine skin. Needing him, she put her hand behind his neck and pulled his head down to reach his lips with hers. "Will you kiss me, Dig?"

"Abso-freaking-lutely," Digby muttered, covering her mouth with his. Bay instantly opened her lips, allowing his tongue to slide against hers. She couldn't help moving closer and pushed her breasts into his chest, wishing she could step inside him, to know him from the inside out. Digby's hands skated up her back and then burrowed under her sleeveless top to find bare skin. After many minutes of thought-and-reason-stealing kisses—or was it hours, since time no longer had any meaning?—Digby pulled back to rest his temple on hers. "You have far too many clothes on, darling."

She knew that he was asking for permission to carry on so, instead of speaking—she doubted her brain's ability to form words—Bay stepped away from him and reached for the button of her shorts. After pulling down the zip, she allowed the garment to fall down her hips to the floor, leaving her standing in her T-shirt and panties.

"Gorgeous," Digby said, on a low whistle. And at that moment, Bay did feel lovely, appreciated, even a little adored.

It gave her the courage to continue so she criss-crossed her arms, gripped her shirt and slowly pulled it up her chest, revealing her rather prosaic sports bra.

She glanced down and grimaced. "If I knew that we were going to be doing this today, I would've worn something sexier."

Digby shook his head as his eyes traveled up her long legs to her breasts, to her face and down again. "You could be wearing the sexiest, most expensive lingerie known to man and I'd barely notice. All my attention is on the present, not the packaging. I'm taking in your incredibly smooth skin, that incredible shape of your legs—" his hand stroked her hip and slid around to palm her butt "—and you have the most perfect ass I've ever seen."

That had to be a lie—he'd dated models and actresses—but she wasn't about to argue. And she wouldn't spoil this moment by comparing herself to his previous liaisons. That way madness lay.

She wanted Digby to drive her out of her mind but not like that!

"Take off your bra, Bay," Digby commanded, and Bay stepped back to lift it up and over her head, feeling a little self-conscious when Digby stared at her chest. She wasn't a C or D cup, hell, on good days she was barely a B cup. But the admiration in Digby's eyes was hard to miss and he groaned when his thumb skated across her nipple, making it pebble.

"Beautiful," Digby murmured, bending his head to suck her into his mouth. Bay held his head in her hands, moaning with pleasure as he sucked her to the point of pain, before lifting his head to blow on her bud. Then his gentle tongue soothed the tiny sting.

So, so good.

Digby dropped to his knees to place kisses on her flat stomach, dipped his tongue into her belly button and eased her panties down her hips. He nuzzled his nose into her thin strip of hair before going lower, then lower still.

Bay sank into his caresses, utterly comfortable with the intimate act. She trusted him, she thought. Trusted him with every inch of her body, knowing that he'd never hurt her, or push her beyond what she felt comfortable doing. Then, as pleasure began to build and he did something amazing with his tongue, all thoughts faded and she concentrated on the enjoyment only he could give her.

But she didn't want ecstasy to be one-sided, not this first time, so she urged him to his feet and pulled his towel from his body. She licked a bead of moisture off his chest and lifted her eyes to his as her hand encircled his erection.

"I'm not on any birth control so I'm really, really hoping you have condoms," Bay told him, dropping butterfly kisses on his chest.

In her hand Digby hardened again—how was that possible?—and he released a small groan. "I do."

Bay nodded and looked at the bed.

Digby dropped a hard, sexy kiss on her mouth before lifting her in his arms and all but throwing her onto it. She laughed and her breath caught at the sapphire-blue color of his eyes, burning with lust, desire and what she hoped might be affection.

Digby walked up the staircase, carefully carrying a tray, Bay's cell phone tucked under his arm. Nudging open the door to the bedroom, he found Bay sitting on the window seat in his room, hair wet from the shower and wearing one of his T-shirts, her legs tucked up underneath her. Seeing her there, sitting in the muted sunlight, she looked so...

When no other word would do, he eventually acknowledged the only word that did...

She looked and felt...

Right.

And that scared him senseless.

Digby placed the tray on the bench at the end of the bed and, unable to resist, bent down to drop a kiss on

Bay's wet head, still able to pick up traces of her citrus-and-jasmine scent underneath the masculine smell of his shower soap. Casual affection wasn't something he engaged in so he had no idea where this need to touch her came from.

Bay sent him a smile and took the phone he held out to her. "Roisin called," he told her.

Her body immediately tensed, her hand flying up to her chest, and alarm jumped in and out of her eyes. "Oh, God, really? Is everything okay? Is Olivia okay? What did she want?"

"She's fine, Bay, really. She just called because Liv wanted to tell you that she saw the penguins at Boulders Beach. Liv also informed me that she wants to bring one home. She's convinced it would be quite happy living in the biggest of The Vane's pools."

Her panic subsided but her hand remained on her chest. "Olivia spoke to you? On the phone?"

He nodded and pushed the bench seat closer to the window so that they could reach the tray of coffee and pastries he'd ordered from room service. "She asked to speak to you. I told her you were in the bathroom, not a lie, and she was happy to babble away. I heard about sand castles and birds and that Roisin bought her an ice cream."

For someone who didn't want children, and didn't know how to deal with them, some sort of rapport was growing between him and Olivia. He didn't seem to be able to resist her and that was, for him, unusual in the extreme.

Digby comforted himself with the thought that he doubted many people in the world could resist Miss Olivia. She was, at three, a force of nature, and he was thankful he wouldn't have to guide her through the teenage years. He was not that brave.

Give her thirty years, Digby decided, and Olivia would be President of the World.

Digby lifted Bay's legs and sat down, placing her legs across his thighs, as she reached for a Danish and then bit down. Her eyes widened as she chewed and a look of bliss crossed her face.

"So, so good," she mumbled taking another huge bite.

Digby smiled, enjoying the look of pleasure on her face as she finished the pastry. "My pastry chef is world-class."

"I'd say," Bay replied.

He reached for a cup of coffee and handed it to her, smiling as she wrapped her hands around the mug. She'd had the same look of anticipation on her face when she wrapped her hands around his erection earlier. Digby sighed, felt the action in his pants and told himself to stand down. They'd made love twice and fooled around again in the shower; he needed some time to recover and so did Bay.

But damn, it had been the best sex of his life. How had that happened?

Forcing his thoughts from how they'd loved each other and how right—that word again!—it felt, Digby turned his thoughts back to Olivia. "You're an amazing mom, Bay," he quietly told her, reaching for his own mug. "If I had said there was a problem, I imagine you would've been out that door in a flash."

"Of course I would," Bay replied. "That's what moms do. Or even what aunts, trying to be moms, do."

He knew that wasn't true. "Not all mothers, Bay. I should know."

"What do you mean?"

Digby grimaced, wishing he hadn't opened this door. Then again, with Bay, the doors he normally kept locked seemed to spring open without any help from him.

He looked at her curious face and knew he was going to tell her. He couldn't not. Bay was his truth serum. "When I was twelve, I suffered an injury on the rugby field and was rushed to hospital in an ambulance—they were worried about my neck. The coach called my mom, who happened to be in the country at the time. She was at the family farm, our vineyard, not twenty minutes away from where I was playing. She told my coach to let her know if something more serious developed. Jack was the one to rush to my side."

Bay looked at him, aghast. "That is truly shocking."

Digby shrugged and looked out the window, idly noticing that his private lap pool was full of leaves, and made a mental note to remind the maintenance crew to have it cleaned. "It was just the way she was."

"And your dad?"

"He followed my mom's lead." Digby told himself to stop talking but his mouth was on a mission of its own. "You've got to understand—my parents didn't engage with us, me in particular. They were very over having kids by the time I came along."

Bay frowned. "They could've chosen not to have any more kids after Jack was born. I mean, I'm glad they didn't, obviously, but that was a choice they could've made. They had their heir, why have more kids?"

Digby wasn't sure whether to tell her that the reason he was born came down to hard, cold cash. Would she understand? Would she recoil away, and would her disgust taint him? Taint what they'd just shared?

He hesitated and Bay put a hand on his arm. "Digby? What is it?"

Despite his hesitation about sharing something so private, the words came tumbling out. "The Tempest-Vanes weren't good at stocking the family tree and my father was the sole Tempest-Vane heir. My great-grandfather told my father he'd give him two million for every male child he produced. Three boys resulted in a hefty paycheck."

Bay looked, as he expected, shocked. "That's dreadful. And if you'd been a girl?"

Digby shrugged. "No money if that's what you are asking."

"Wow, that's a superb example of misogyny," Bay commented. "Your parents weren't very likable, were they?"

Now, that was the understatement of the century. Sometimes he actively hated them for being so damn selfish, so reckless, so impossibly self-centered. For leaving them to raise themselves. His biggest dream, as a kid, was having two parents who put him and his brothers first, who gave them both roots and wings and were a soft place to fall when things went wrong. But he'd never had that. As a result, he didn't know how a family worked and couldn't see himself giving a family the things he most needed as a kid. And if he couldn't do it properly, he wouldn't do it at all.

So, no family for him.

"Radd and I were definitely surplus to what was required. Zia had no interest in us at all and she frequently told the press that she wasn't cut out for motherhood."

He'd repeated her words to reporters, saying he wasn't cut out for a family, but the difference between them was that he wasn't a father and his kids couldn't read what he said about them online or in the papers.

Bay's soft hand stroked the ball of his shoulder and her touch calmed him. It was so strange that, when he spoke about his parents to her, the subject didn't sting as much as it normally did.

"Did you see much of her growing up?" Bay asked softly, waiting for him to continue.

Digby placed his hand on her thigh and drew patterns in her soft skin with his thumb. "When I was about ten, there was a stretch when I didn't see either Gil or Zia for about six months. They went to the States for an extended holiday and didn't return."

"But your dad was running Tempest-Vane at that time."

"Running? No. Looting the company of all its assets? Hell, yes," Digby stated. He turned, moving his legs so that they were on either side of Bay's legs, lifting her calves to rest on his thighs. He smiled when she rearranged his T-shirt to cover her intimate area. It wasn't like he hadn't explored her from tip to toe but he wasn't going to embarrass her by mentioning that. And he liked her modesty, it was a nice change from models who had no inhibition at all.

"I suppose they are the reason why I was, am, such an attention hound," Digby said. He'd never said that to anyone before and couldn't believe that he'd voiced such an intimate thought to Bay. Next, he'd be telling her about his nightmare and his dread of Radd dying. The dream had visited again last night, harder and deeper and darker than normal. But instead of seeing Radd's face in that coffin, the features and body had been indistinct. And scary as hell.

Bay placed the last bite of Danish on the side plate

and her coffee mug on the tray. After wiping her fingers with a linen napkin, she placed her hands on his knees and squeezed. "Will you explain that remark, Dig?"

He knew that if he changed the subject she would respect his need for privacy and he considered doing exactly that. Then he saw the sympathy in her eyes and shrugged. "They never gave me any attention so I looked for it everywhere I could. At school, I excelled at sports and worked hard at it because those guys were recognized and acknowledged, respected. I became the class clown because making people laugh was attention. After Jack died, I acted out because any attention, good or bad, was better than none at all."

He'd admitted so much this morning already—would he regret his loquaciousness later?—so he might as well tell her the rest. "When I left school, I went to the university and nobody cared who I was or what I did. There were so many kids there and I felt more lost than ever before—every day I felt like I was jumping out of my skin. So, in the few moments I had between studying and setting up our internet security company, I chased adrenaline. And I loved it, it allowed me to get out of my head."

Bay threaded her fingers through his and simply waited for him to continue.

"Somehow the crazy stunts I did started to attract attention, press attention, and I liked that. I liked reading about myself in the papers—it was an acknowledgment, you know?"

Bay nodded.

"I was called the wild Tempest-Vane, the fun brother, more like his parents than the brilliant Jack and introverted Radd."

Bay tipped her head to the side. "I suppose that after

you sold your company, the tech one, and you became instabillionaires, the press attention skyrocketed."

Digby nodded. "Yeah, that was a crazy time. Every date I went on, every function I attended, was covered. According to the tabloid press, I was engaged twice, secretly married once and have a couple of secret babies." Digby heard the bitterness in his voice and closed his eyes, mortified. "The women who dated me enjoyed the exposure—many of them translated their brief moment of fame into careers as reality stars, actresses and models."

"Did it annoy you that they used you?" Bay asked.

"I guess it just got boring. Although, I was pissed when one snuck a photographer onto the hotel's grounds and he hid out in the bushes and snapped a photo of her topless in the sunshine."

"Yeah, I saw that photo," Bay said.

Digby winced. Of course she had. He cursed.

"He got a great snap of your hand on her breast," Bay pointed out. He pulled a face, uncomfortable at the reminder.

"The press taking photos of me at functions and in public places is something I can handle—it's part of the deal of being a Tempest-Vane. But her invading my privacy, bringing someone into my home, was unacceptable."

"Damn right," Bay agreed. After a moment's silence, she asked another question. "Is that a warning? To me?"

Digby took a moment to connect the dots, to work out what she meant. He shook his head, a touch more violently than he normally did. "No! Hell! I never thought that for a moment!"

"Okay."

He could see a trace of skepticism in her eye but then

she turned her gaze off him to look out the window. Since she was keeping her eyes on the view, he felt her retreat and cursed himself for being insensitive. *Way to go, Tempest-Vane, you fool.*

"Tell me about your relationships with your parents," Digby said, wanting to engage her again. "I bet you were showered with affection and attention."

Pain flashed across her fine features and her shoulders tensed. He thought she wouldn't answer but then she released a heavy sigh. "I was showered with attention and affection until I went to high school. Then everything changed."

"What happened?" Digby asked, refilling his coffee mug.

"I left my expensive, small, insulated primary school on a scholarship to Foresters…"

The exclusive girls-only school in Paarl? Yeah, he knew the school and was impressed that she'd won a scholarship to the prestigious institution. "Did you hate it?"

"No, I loved it. But I was exposed to new people, different views, and I embraced the diversity of the school. Within a couple of months, I'd been exposed to new ideas and literature and I had to confront, and deal with the notion, that my parents, especially my father, were narrow-minded, misogynistic, homophobic and ridiculously conservative.

"Worst of all, I realized that they were also full-blown racists," she added.

Digby winced.

Bay ran a hand over her face, her eyes darker with pain. "Yeah. I challenged them and they pushed back. I refused to back down, and my father became irrationally angry. He's old-school, he believes his word is the law and his are the only opinions that matter. I'm not sure what annoyed him more, that I was calling him out or that I had an opinion different to his.

"Before I went to high school, he was affectionate and loving. We were exceptionally close and I idolized him. After I started challenging him, his attitude toward me changed and he became, well, mean. And nothing I said could sway him. Just made it worse. And when he realized that I wouldn't back down and that he couldn't intimidate me into changing my views, he pulled away and started to ignore or ridicule me. I went from being daddy's girl to being a pariah in my own home. By the time I was sixteen, we could barely greet each other."

Digby wished he could hug, or love, all her pain away. "I'm so sorry, sweetheart."

"My mom told me to stop rocking the boat, to just agree with him but I couldn't—I couldn't condone what he was saying," Bay explained, her whiskey-colored eyes murky with unshed tears. "After years of either him screaming at me or flat-out ignoring me, I left home, went to the university, again on a scholarship, and we didn't have much to do or say to each other. Layla followed me to the same uni and those were the happiest years of our lives. She met Ali there and they were so in love. She couldn't tell our parents that she was dating a mixed-race, Muslim man. She still had a relationship with my parents."

Digby waited, knowing there was more.

"My parents surprised us at our flat early one morning. They rang the doorbell. I opened the door to them, half-asleep. Layla came stumbling out of her bedroom, quickly followed by Ali, and you didn't need an interpreter to know what they'd been doing."

"And the crap hit the fan."

Bay nodded. "Big time." Bay closed her eyes and Digby knew that her memories were still fresh. "My dad turned on me and blamed everything on me and my radical education and liberal views. If I had just stayed home, been a good girl, content with the status quo, none of this would've happened."

Digby noticed the sheen of tears in her eyes and gently plucked her from her seat and cuddled her against his chest, kissing her hair as he did. God, parents were supposed to love their kids, not rip them apart.

"After telling us that we were dead to them, they left and Layla was gutted. I was angry and horrified and embarrassed and so, so sad. But Ali was so cool. He just picked up Layla, told her his family was hers and that they would be happy. And they were, they really, really were."

"I'm glad that they found each other," Digby said, lifting his lips off her hair to say the words.

"I am too. Anyway, Ali's family is now mine too." Bay used the balls of her hands to wipe the tears from her face. She sniffed, took a sip of coffee from his mug and scooted off his lap. She walked over to the second wall of windows, folded her arms and stared at the mountain, watching the tablecloth settle over the previously clear top.

Her next words were a bombshell he didn't expect.

"They want Olivia, Dig."

Her words were flat and cold and he couldn't make sense of them. "What? What do you mean they want Olivia? *Who* wants her?"

"My parents are applying for custody of her and are going to tell the court that I'm unfit to raise her. They have money, they are still young, they are only in their

midfifties and they have experience raising children."
Bay tried to smile. "It's a good argument."

Digby struggled to digest this new information. He
stood up and walked over to her, noting her pale face.
"But she's mixed race. And you said that he's a racist."

Bay sent him a wan smile. "Ah, they'll ignore that
inconvenient fact. But I'm terrified they'll raise her as
they raised us, to be a good wife and daughter, to not
have her own opinions, to believe that a man's opinion
is more important than hers will ever be. And if I lose
her, Layla will haunt me forever."

"You're not going to lose her, sweetheart," Digby
told her, his hands reaching for hers. "Layla and her
husband gave you guardianship—the court will take
that into account."

"God, I hope so. But the fact remains that I have
no child-rearing experience and I've spent the last few
years bouncing around the world. I'm also self-em-
ployed and my income stream isn't long-term steady."

"I think you are borrowing trouble, honey. I think
you have an excellent shot of retaining custody."

When her eyes connected with his, Digby knew he
wasn't going to like what she was about to say. "Unlike your previous girlfriends, Digby, you don't have
to worry about me using you to up my visibility. In
fact, my worst nightmare would be us hitting the gossip columns—I cannot tell you how much I'd hate that."

She removed her hands from his and wrapped her
arms around her waist. She briefly closed her eyes and
her chest rose and fell; her agitation was obvious. "I
can't be linked, in any way, to you, Digby. It might hurt
my chances to keep custody of Olivia."

Digby felt like she'd shoved a knife into his chest.
"What? *Why?*"

"My lawyer says my judgment might be called into question if they—my parents or the press—discover that I'm dating or sleeping with you." Bay bit her lip, her shoulders lifting to reach her ears. "You've led a bit of a wild life and…well…"

"Just spit it out, Bay," Digby said, his voice cool. He knew what was coming—he'd been here before, taking on the sins of his parents. But, damn, it had never stung this much before…

Bay sucked in a deep breath and her words rushed out. "Some people think you are like your parents and, obviously, they'd wonder what effect you'd have on Olivia if you were to become a permanent fixture in my life. I told my lawyer that you are anticommitment, that nothing like that would happen, but she says that it doesn't matter, that perception is all that's important."

"I'm not like my parents, Bay, not when it comes to the important stuff," Digby said, his voice stiff with annoyance. God, he hoped she didn't hear the hint of hurt under his irritation.

"I know that, Digby, but the judge and lawyers don't. And I can't take the chance of losing her, Dig." In her eyes, he saw defiance and determination and knew that whatever they had was now lost, that the spark between them had been doused. "This is Olivia's life we are talking about—I cannot take any risks that might backfire."

"So you have to choose between her and me," Digby said, his tone frigid. Would anyone ever put him first? Then the wave of shame broke over his head when he remembered that Olivia was innocent, a child, and he was an adult with a crapload of resources.

Bay looked sad but resolute. "This isn't about choosing, Digby. What I said was that I can't be romantically linked with you. Besides, you haven't been shy about stating your antimarriage, anticommitment stance. Have you changed your mind about that?"

Digby scrubbed his hands over his face. Hell, no. But also, yes. Maybe a little. God, he didn't know…

Bay folded her arms across her chest, looking fiercely determined. "I'm going to court in two weeks to fight for custody. I can't take any chances. I *won't.*"

If Bay were his mother, she'd say to hell with Olivia and take what she needed, what she wanted, putting her needs before her child's. But she wasn't Zia, she was Bay and loved her sister's child as her own. She was prepared to sacrifice anything and everything—including him—to do what was right. Digby felt annoyed, hurt and pissed off but he couldn't fault her for that.

A part of him even admired her commitment to her niece and to fulfilling her sister's wishes.

"I need us to go back to being what we were before today. Friends. Colleagues. Client and service provider."

He couldn't argue with her; he didn't have a leg to stand on. And he wouldn't, he had far more pride than that. And Bay was right, Olivia was all that was important.

Digby stepped back and slapped his hands on his hips. What else could he do but nod? "I get it," he growled.

Bay stroked his arm from elbow to shoulder. "I really don't think you do. You might not believe this, but I don't sleep around. Sleeping with you meant something to me, Digby, and I loved being with you. But the price I might pay if this gets out is too high. And I know that you understand that."

He wanted to argue with her, to persuade her that everything would be fine, that they could carry on, that no one would discover they were sleeping together. He was selfish enough to do that, ruthless and egotistical enough to put his needs before hers. And Liv's. He had, after all, learned from the best.

But he couldn't do that, not to Olivia and not to Bay. Neither of them deserved his selfishness and disrespect, and he wouldn't be able to live with himself. Olivia was not at fault and he wouldn't do anything to jeopardize her chances to stay with Bay.

Damn, putting other people first sucked. This was why he stayed single, why he didn't get involved.

"Once I get custody, we can rethink this," Bay quietly told him. "I just need two weeks, Dig."

But Digby knew that so much could happen in two weeks, in less time than that. Businesses could be lost, brothers could die, life could change in an instant. Nothing stayed the same, neither should it.

"I'm sorry our morning ended this way…"

Yeah, they should've just kept their mouths shut. Talking never did anyone any good. Bay lifted her shoulder up in a slight shrug and continued. "I'm going to get dressed and get going. Thanks for…" she gestured to the bed and her cheeks turned pink "…that."

Bay bit her bottom lip, shook her head and started to gather up her clothes. Quickly dressing, she shoved her feet into flip-flops and, after sending him another regretful look and quietly telling him that she'd see him on Monday, walked out of his bedroom, leaving him standing there and feeling like a fool.

Not something he liked, or was used to feeling.

CHAPTER SEVEN

DIGBY STOOD TO the side of the grave, tears running down his face in a continuous stream. Above him, hard rain pounded on the roof of the white gazebo they'd erected over the grave to keep the matte black casket from floating to the top of the eight-foot pit.

Digby looked around, surprised to see Roisin standing behind him, and behind her Radd and Brin.

If Radd was here, then who was in the coffin?

Digby yelled for them to stop lowering the casket and sprang forward, desperate to see who he was burying.

His fingertips struggled to open the coffin.

His rough voice begged Radd to help him.

But Radd didn't step forward and he knew he was on his own.

Using all his strength, Digby lifted the heavy lid, sensing that the casket was fighting him, that it wasn't happy to be opened.

With a final heave, Digby lifted the lid and allowed it to rest on its hinges. Taking a deep breath, still not wanting to look, he forced himself to open his eyes...

She looked peaceful.

The thought was coming from a place far, far away.

But everything that made her Bay was gone. Her vitality, the passion in those unusual eyes, her humor and her spirit. Her soul was gone and she'd taken his heart with her...

Digby was about to shut the lid of the casket when her eyes flew open and her hand reached out to grab his tie.

He stared down into her sad, sad eyes and waited for her to speak.

But instead of saying something profound, deeply meaningful, her eyes fluttered closed and Bay slipped away. And this time Digby knew she wasn't ever coming back...

His heart pounding, Digby shot up and looked around his bedroom, relieved to see the first rays of light peeking through the edges of the motorized blinds in his bedroom. Picking up the tablet from his bedside table, he tapped the button to open the blinds and as they rolled up he rubbed the sleep out of his eyes with his fingertips.

Damn, that had been a hell of a nightmare. Digby felt moisture on his fingertips and stared down at his hands, slowly registering that he'd been crying in his sleep.

Well, that was a first.

It was an overcast day, the mountain was concealed behind a thick cloud and the weather perfectly matched his mood. Sitting up, Digby rested his forearms on his knees, staring down at the damp print his palm left on his white sheet. He was, he decided, a basket case...

He'd had the same dream for most of his life but it was morphing into something deeper and darker, and every time he had the dream, he felt like he was losing a little bit of his soul. Maybe he should see someone...

And what would he say? *Hey, Doc, I've been having dreams about my brother dying most of my life. But this morning he was replaced by a woman I've only just recently met, whom I crave with every breath I take,*

*with every beat of my heart. I want her; I need her. But
I won't let myself have her. Because if I love her and
she leaves me, that's me done. I'm not brave enough
to take that risk...*

Loving someone and losing them? He refused to do
it again.

Digby scrubbed his face with his hands, uncomfortable with the roiling, churning emotions swirling inside his gut.

A week had passed since Bay walked out of his bedroom and back into the friend zone and he was over
it. Over the stilted conversations, over trying to keep
his hands off her, over boycotting his office because it
hurt too much to be around her and not be kissing her,
laughing with her, goddamn talking to her.

Somehow, Bay Adair had snuck under his carefully
constructed armor.

One week. In seven days, the custody hearing would
be over—though he suspected Bay would want to wait
a few weeks while the judge considered his decision—
and then...what? What did he want from her, from this
thing that was growing between them?

If he couldn't love Bay the way she needed to be
loved, then he should let her go. But how could he? She
was everything good and bright and colorful in his life.

She'd make his life better; the converse wasn't true.

Irritated with himself, Digby pushed the sheet back,
thinking that he was damned if he did and damned if
he didn't. He wanted Bay with an intensity that scared
him but he'd never imagined himself settling down,
making a solid commitment.

But neither could he imagine her not being in his life.

However, along with Bay came Olivia; that meant
sharing Bay with Liv, and he wasn't ready for an instant

family. That was one step too far. But, if they got to the point of dating, he and Olivia would start to develop a relationship, as well...

And if he ran true to form, and he always did, and decided that he wasn't cut out for attachment and permanence, Bay wouldn't be the only one who'd be hurt.

He didn't want to cause either of them any pain. So he wouldn't. But that meant not being with Bay, ever again.

His stomach lurched into his throat.

Digby swung his legs over the edge of the bed and picked up his phone, looking for a distraction. As always, there were a slew of emails but one caught his eye. He read through it quickly, cursed, and immediately called Radd.

Radd, very unusually for him lately, answered his call.

"I take it you got the email then," Radd said, dispensing with their normal "how's business?" and "how's your holiday" small talk.

"Yeah."

"So, the beneficiary of our parents' trust is asking us to meet with them early next week."

Yeah, he got that; he'd read the damn email not five minutes ago. "Thank you, Captain Obvious," Digby muttered.

"Did you get out on the wrong side of the bed?" Radd asked him, sounding a trifle amused.

Digby told him what to do with himself and immediately felt bad. It wasn't Radd's fault that he was horny and tired and frustrated. And confused. So damn confused.

"What's his motive?"

"You're assuming it's a man," Radd pointed out.

"His, her, *whatever*. Why does he want to meet us?"

Digby demanded, standing up to pace his bedroom. He needed to work off some excess energy and when he was done with this call, he'd head for his lap pool and push his body until he banished Bay's lovely face from the big screen in his head.

"I guess we'll find out next week," Radd laconically replied.

"On one hand, I don't care about the money or collections of cars, art and property—we both have enough to carry us through several lifetimes. But I am curious as to who Gil and Zia thought important enough to warrant such generosity."

"Me too," Radd admitted. "Once we know, we can put the parents behind us."

He'd like nothing better than to put his parents, their deaths, his past with them and the mystery surrounding their inheritance to bed, forever. He had more important things to worry about.

Like Bay…

Annoyed with himself for allowing his thoughts to return to her—not that they were ever really off her—Digby told Radd he was looking forward to seeing him, and to him getting back to work, and disconnected.

Digby tapped the face of his phone against his forehead and hoped that the day would be kind to him. Honestly, at this point, he didn't know if he needed a liter of coffee, six shots of tequila or to sleep for a month. Or all three.

Or Bay.

Mostly, he reluctantly admitted, he just needed Bay, any way he could get her.

Later that day and on the other side of the property, Bay sat on the Persian carpet in Digby's office, surrounded by fabric swatches and wallpaper samples. She'd yet to find the exact fabric and wallpaper combination she wanted for the ballroom.

She was not usually this indecisive and it was driving her nuts. Maybe she needed to take the sample books up to the ballroom and look at them in the natural light, but she'd tried that already and the entire exercise just made her feel more confused.

And self-doubt was creeping in…

She'd told Digby she couldn't do this. What made her, or him, think that she could take on a project this size? It was nuts; she had no experience, no track record. This fabric cost thousands of dollars a yard, what if she made a mistake?

Bay leaned forward and banged her forehead on the book in front of her, feeling her back muscles stretching as she did the once-familiar movement. She hadn't done any yoga or Pilates for months; she was risking tearing a muscle thinking she was as flexible as she was earlier in the year.

What she wouldn't do for a hot-stone, full-body massage…

Digby had told her, a while ago, that she could use the hotel's spa at no cost, but it wasn't something she felt comfortable doing, especially since they were…well, not at odds, but their relationship had shifted.

Since sleeping together, they were both behaving like polite strangers, both pretending that they hadn't been intimate, physically as well as mentally. These days their meetings and interactions were both brief and rushed, mostly because Digby was rarely around.

Bay wasn't a fool; she knew that Digby was spending more time at Tempest-Vane headquarters to avoid her.

But she missed him, she missed who they were together.

Bay sat up slowly, picked up her water bottle and took a long sip. Leaning back on her hands, she stared at the art on Digby's walls, seascapes that never failed to soothe her. Except today, today she was fairly certain that not even a strong hit of Valium would do the trick.

She was tired, she hadn't slept well in weeks, her creativity had all but dried up and Olivia, obviously picking up on her stress, was being a monster and fighting her on anything and everything.

Thank God for Roisin.

Thank God, and all his angels, archangels, saints and deities, for Roisin.

Feeling like the walls were closing in on her, Bay stood up and walked out of Digby's office and down the staff corridor. Thinking that she'd take a walk in The Vane's impressive gardens, she slipped into the lobby and ducked around three businessmen waiting for a lift.

The lobby was full of guests and Bay wrinkled her nose as clashing perfumes and the scent of the huge floral bouquets drifted over her. Heading left, she crossed the lovely harlequin floor, aiming for the wide French doors that led to the wraparound veranda.

The back of her neck tingled and Bay recognized that sensation; it meant that Digby was near. Looking around, she saw him standing by the concierge's desk, talking to a small group who'd obviously just arrived.

Italian, Bay decided. Florence or Milan. Big money, judging by the Birkin bags, the Louboutin shoes and the huge diamonds on fingers and earlobes.

One woman had her hand on Digby's forearm, and

he was laughing. The man added something and Digby clapped him on his back, before turning to the waiter standing behind him holding a tray of glasses filled with what she knew to be a superb vintage of Moët & Chandon.

Digby handed out glasses, flashing his broad, sexy grin.

He loved this, Bay realized. He loved interacting with his guests, playing the part of the genial host. Some of it was based in his need for attention but a good portion of it was his genuine love for people, for making them feel welcome, happy and looked after.

All the things he'd never experienced growing up within his own family. Neither, she admitted, had she.

Bay stopped by a column, concealed by a huge bouquet of mixed flowers, and watched as another two men approached Digby, who was standing to the side of the group. Digby caught their eye, held up a discreet finger asking them to wait and, with ease, disengaged himself from the Italians. The men waiting for him shook his hand and Bay saw the genuine pleasure on their faces.

People liked Digby, she realized. They liked him a lot.

He was extraordinarily self-confident and bold and in being so unapologetic about it, he silently encouraged people to follow his lead. People felt more alive around him; she certainly did. Just knowing him promised some sort of adventure, and people were attracted to individuals who could make their lives more interesting.

Bay was.

Ah, hell. Attracted to him? She was more than halfway in love with him. What a stupid thing to have done, Bay thought. She could just, well, kick herself.

Bay held her hand up to her face to hide her yawn

and slowly made her way across the floor, hoping a brisk walk would raise her flagging energy levels and, hopefully, spark her creativity. And clear her head…

Bay felt her phone vibrate and she pulled it out of the pocket of her cotton pants. Swiping her thumb across the screen, her heart—stupid, stupid thing—leaped when she saw Digby's name on the screen.

My office. Now.

Frowning at his unusually autocratic text message, Bay looked around, didn't see Digby and retraced her steps back toward his office. After punching in the code that gave her access to the back rooms of the hotel, she pulled open the door and walked down the passage. Stepping into Monica's office, she started to greet Digby's assistant and realized that she wasn't there. Hearing the door shut behind her, she whirled around and slammed into Digby's hard chest. She clocked the sound of the outer door locking but before she could make sense of what was happening, Digby's mouth was on hers and she spun away on a vortex of pleasure.

She allowed herself a minute to indulge in the wonderful feel and taste of him before pulling back and putting some distance between them, her breathing so labored she felt like she'd run a fast five miles' race.

"I saw you walking across the lobby and realized that I couldn't go one more day, one more goddamn minute, without touching you."

Bay looked into his eyes, midnight blue and a little feral, a lot wild. Needing to connect with him, just a little, she placed her hand on his chest, feeling his thundering heartbeat. Hers was pumping at maximum capacity, as well. God, she'd missed him. Working near him and not being able to touch him had tested her willpower every minute of every day.

She was thrilled that Digby was suffering, as well.

But, as powerful and as feminine as that made her feel—having a man like Digby looking at her like she was everything he wanted and needed was a high she'd never experienced before—she *had* to be sensible and cautious.

"We can't do this, Digby. I told you that."

"One kiss, Bay. I've missed your mouth."

She'd missed him too, dreadfully. And what would one kiss hurt? There were no cameras in Digby's private offices; nobody would know. She needed this quick interlude to slake a little of the desire that raged through her.

Digby's mouth connected with hers and Bay felt that hit of lightning, that spike of need. Yeah, this. This man, this moment…

When Digby moved his hands up to hold her face in his, tilting her head to take their kiss deeper and darker, Bay stroked his waist from hip to rib cage.

"I think about you all the time and not being able to touch you is so damn hard," Digby muttered as he dropped sexy kisses on her jaw, across her cheekbone. "I'm so damn hard. All the time."

As if to prove his point, Digby pushed his erection into her stomach and Bay released a tortured moan. She wanted him, in her hands, in her mouth…everywhere. She'd never felt so out of control and she loved it.

She loved kissing this wild man, charming and complicated.

His mouth came back to hers and his tongue found hers, stroking it. His taste was delicious, his breath sweet. And with every thrust, each parry, she could feel herself losing control. She wanted him, no, worse, she *needed* him.

And because that need was so fierce, so crazy intense, Bay knew she had to back away before he overwhelmed her senses and desire shut down her ability to think rationally. Her body was betraying her; her willpower had gone AWOL. And because she couldn't afford to lose herself in him, she yanked herself out of Digby's arms and moved back until she was out of arm's reach.

In his eyes, she saw lust and regret and frustration. Stepping back, he raked the fingers of both hands through his hair.

"We can't do this," Bay whispered.

"I know," Digby replied, his voice sounding strangled. He pulled in a deep breath, rubbed his hands over his face and tipped his head back to look at the ceiling. After a minute he spoke again. "Monica will be back in five minutes."

Bay nodded and watched as Digby, before her eyes, transformed from her wild, intense lover into the debonair, suave businessman he always was. While she knew her cheeks were still burning, her nipples were throbbing and her intimate area was screaming for him to touch her, he looked like he'd just come from a business meeting.

Even his pants had subsided. He was in control and she wasn't. The realization that she was the one who could lose everything—Olivia and her heart—yet he'd lose nothing, smacked her in the gut.

Bay placed her hands flat on Monica's desk and blinked back unshed tears. She would be, she knew, easily replaceable in his life—sex was easy to find and this was the guy who didn't do commitment or forever, remember?—but Bay doubted he'd ever be replaced in hers.

Sure, he wasn't the only guy in the universe...

But he was the only one who mattered.

Hearing Digby's low curse, she sighed when he placed his hands on her waist and gently turned her around. His eyes drifted across her face and he lifted a thumb to graze its pad over the soft skin under her eyes. "Goddammit, Bay, you're exhausted."

Bay looked into his red-rimmed eyes and raised one eyebrow. "Kettle. Pot. Black."

Digby acknowledged her verbal hit with a quick half smile. Hearing the office door open, he stepped away from her, his eyes not leaving her face. "And that has to change," he said, ignoring Monica as she pushed past them to settle in behind her desk.

Digby took Bay's wrist and pulled her into the passage, away from Monica's flapping ears. He slid his hands into the pockets of his suit pants, his expression intense.

"Do you trust me, Bay?"

What a strange, out-of-the-blue question. Behind her back, Bay placed her palms against the cool wall and considered how to answer him. She did trust him, with her body and her feelings, but not with her heart. Never with her heart.

Digby spoke again before she could answer. "If I solemnly swear to respect your privacy issue and that not a word of us being together will reach the press, will you come away with me, for a few days?"

She'd love nothing more but she had Olivia to think of. "I can't be separated from Liv, Digby, not right now. I need to be with her, especially if the custody hearing doesn't go my way."

"It will go your way, and I understand that," Digby said, darting a look down the still empty hallway. "My invitation includes Liv—I get that you two are a package deal.

"Besides," he added, "Olivia is my favorite three-year-old."

"She's the only three-year-old you know," Bay pointed out, amused and touched at his easy acceptance of Olivia.

"Fair point but I still like her. With regard to going away, I'll see what I can organize," Digby said and winced at Monica bellowing his name.

Bay watched him walk back into his office and shook her head. Going away sounded like a lovely idea but she knew how busy Digby was, how inundated they both were. When he hit his desk and work rolled over him, he'd realize how ambitious the thought was and that leaving for the weekend really wasn't an option.

The thought counted, Bay thought, touched that Digby was worried about her. It was a lovely idea but it wasn't practical so Bay pushed it from her mind.

The next day, Digby had just finished making a series of calls to put his plan into action when he heard a quick rap on his office door, quickly followed by Olivia's high-pitched squeal. He lifted his head and there she was, barreling across the room to him, her smile powerful enough to compete with the sun.

"Dig, I was looks for you."

Digby caught her, swung her up onto his lap and lifted an eyebrow in Roisin's direction. The nanny shrugged and rolled her eyes. "She got this bee in her bonnet and I've heard nothing but your name all morning. I asked around, heard you were in here and thought you could give her a little attention."

"And you a break," Digby dryly replied, and Roisin flashed an unrepentant smile. Roisin was his employee but didn't act like it. "I'm glad you are here—I was about to call you."

Roisin frowned. "Problem?"

Digby quickly shook his head. "You have the weekend off. I'm whipping these two away for a long weekend."

Roisin smiled. "Nice. Where to?"

Digby reached around Olivia's little body to minimize his computer screen. "I wanted to go to our safari operation, Kagiso—I thought someone would get a kick out of seeing an elephant. But it's fully booked and my villa is being used by a friend this long weekend."

"I wants an elephant," Olivia told him, proof that she was definitely listening to their conversation. "He can sleep in my bed and I'll call him Fluffy."

"The penguin she wanted last week was also called Fluffy," Roisin told him, sotto voce.

"I'm taking them to a luxurious beach resort in Mozambique," Digby told Roisin. He'd thought long and hard on where to go, looking for a place that was both isolated and interesting, finally remembering that the Tempest-Vane Holdings leisure division was considering buying a five-star resort in Mozambique on one of the small islands in the Bazaruto Archipelago. He and Radd had been meaning to make a trip up there but hadn't gotten that far...

Five minutes later, he had a number in his hand and ten minutes later, he had the excited owner promising him their best villa. He'd fly the Tempest-Vane helicopter to the airport, hop on their private jet and in a few hours the three of them could be sitting on the beach as the sun went down.

"I'm worried about her. She's tired and stressed," Digby told Roisin, remembering her blue-ringed eyes and gaunt face.

Roisin looked worried. "I know. She came to see Olivia earlier and I could tell she'd been crying." Roisin tucked a long dark curl behind her ear. "If you take her away, you can't let her work—she has to eat decent food and you have to make sure she relaxes and sleeps. She needs to be at her best next week."

"Yes, mom," Digby dryly responded. Roisin was acting like a mother hen. Then again, he was acting like one too.

Wait, she'd mentioned next week...

"So you know about the custody hearing?" Digby asked. If so, she and Roisin were closer than he'd realized.

"I do. And I made a witness statement saying what a great mom she is," Roisin replied. Digby saw the concern in her eyes. "But how are you going to make sure that nobody knows she's with you, Digby? She's terrified of the press linking the two of you together."

He was aware. While he knew it was necessary, it still pissed him off.

"I've snuck in many a high-profile guest for a press-free, low-key weekend at The Vane. I'm sure I can use those same skills to smuggle them off the premises without anyone knowing. Helicopters and private planes ensure privacy."

"And what about clothes and toiletries?" Roisin asked.

"I put in a call to the manager of the boutique on the

premises and if she needs to, she'll employ the services of a personal shopper to get everything they need."

Roisin, finally, looked impressed. "You've thought of everything."

He hoped so. Now he just had to get Bay and Liv to the helipad at the back of the property. Digby, impatient to leave, turned back to the screen. His eyes fell to Olivia's hands and he muttered a quiet curse when he saw she was drawing squiggles on his tie. How the hell had she managed to do that without either of them noticing?

Digby saw that Roisin was about to chastise Olivia but he lifted his hand to wave her off. "It's just a tie."

"It's a damn expensive tie."

Pale green and ever so slightly embossed with a fine gray pattern, it was Hermès and a limited edition. But still, just a tie.

Digby stood up and placed Olivia, who was still holding his ink-covered tie in her hand, on his hip. Roisin held out her arms to Liv and Digby transferred his sweet-smelling bundle to her. "Let's go, princess, we've got stuff to do."

Olivia pursed her rosebud mouth. "'Kay. Are we going to see Mommy Bay? 'Cos I want to ask her if I can have an elephant."

Digby grinned and dropped a kiss on her nose. "You do that, kid. Maybe she'll be more reasonable than Ro-Ro."

"Funny," Roisin said, as she left his office.

Again, no deference. And, again, he really didn't mind.

CHAPTER EIGHT

OLIVIA LOVED THE helicopter ride to the airport, Bay not so much. It wasn't that she didn't like flying and, while she was fully confident of Digby's ability to handle the craft—like everything else he did, he operated the helicopter with complete control and confidence—she just wasn't crazy about the amount of space between her and the ground.

But the combination of a helicopter and private jet flying meant a quick trip to Bazaruto Island. They'd arrived way before sunset and had been able to take Olivia to the beach and to explore the rock pools directly below the house. There were, Bay thought, perks to being megarich.

She'd never been to Mozambique before and she was very happy to have been kidnapped and whisked away to this aqua playground with her two favorite people. The Bazaruto Archipelago was, as Radd had told her, a protected marine reserve and national park, a place where the sand dunes rolled onto the white sand beaches playing kiss-kiss with the clear, azure ocean.

It was all that and more. Stunningly beautiful and indescribably romantic.

The villa was also amazing. It was a modern, super luxurious open-plan building with four bedrooms, as many bathrooms and a huge living area with one-eighty-degree views of the sea and sand. The shaded entertainment area, dotted with comfortable loungers, overlooked the rock pools. It was a minute walk through the dune grass to a private beach. The next house, Digby told her, was a distance away; they were completely and utterly secluded.

Bay pulled a sheet up Olivia's tiny body and pushed her curls off her forehead. She'd run herself ragged on the beach, and bathing and feeding the exhausted toddler had been a nightmare. But Bay managed both and, not two minutes after her head was on the pillow, she was deeply asleep.

Bay straightened and walked to the window of this room she'd chosen for Olivia to sleep in, looking at the dark sea and the rising moon. When she had arrived at the helipad, situated at the back of The Vane's property, and listened to Digby's plan for a weekend away, her first instinct was to refuse. Then he told her that it came with no strings, that they'd both been working like demons and they all deserved a weekend away. They both needed, he insisted, to relax.

She just had to step into the helicopter; everything else had been taken care of. Nobody would know they were together. It was a break from reality and God she needed it.

And now that she was here, and after swimming in the lukewarm ocean and watching a magnificent sunset, she was glad she hadn't refused. Digby was right; she needed this…

Needed peace and quiet. But mostly she simply needed to be with Digby.

Bay dropped a kiss on Olivia's head and left her sleeping, leaving the door ajar in case she woke up and called for her. Heading back into the open-plan living area, she looked around for Digby and saw that he'd jumped into the pool situated in the corner of the deck. Bay watched as he broke through the surface of the water to rest his forearms on the paving, his chin on his wrist as he looked out to sea.

Seeing a bottle of wine and two glasses sitting on the wooden table, she poured the wine, picked up both glasses and walked over to the pool. Sinking to the pavement, she handed Digby a glass and dropped her bare calf and foot into the water.

Digby looked at her and smiled. "I like this place."

Bay sighed, tipping her head back to look at the stars popping through the black velvet sky. "It's fabulous."

"Do you think we should buy it?" Digby casually asked. "It's up for sale."

Bay nearly choked on her wine when he told her the selling price.

Holy cupcakes, that was a hell of a lot of money.

"Ah, maybe you should see the rest of the property before you make a decision," Bay suggested, her tone wry.

Digby picked up her foot, kissed the arch of her instep before dropping her foot back into the water. "Good point."

Bay rested the cool wineglass against her cheek. "Thank you for bringing me here, Digby. For bringing both of us. I…well… I needed this."

Digby's eyes and the darkening sea were both the same intense shade of blue. He stared at her for a long moment before nodding. "I know."

Bay watched as he propelled himself out of the pool, arm muscles bulging as he left the water. He walked over to the lounger, picked up a towel and started dry-ing his body. Wrapping his towel over his wet swimming shorts, he walked back over to her, holding out his hand. Bay placed her hand in his and he hauled her up, keeping hold of her as she found her feet. Because she wanted to, Bay placed her hand on his chest, her thumb brushing water off it.

"I missed you," Bay said, the words slipping out without her permission.

Digby placed his lips on her temple and his big hands on her hips. "I missed you too."

Bay slid her arms around his waist and rested her cheek on his wet chest and listened to his strong heartbeat. His arms encircled her, hauled her closer and it felt like he was putting himself between her and the world. She was a strong, independent woman but sometimes it felt so wonderful to lean, to soak in someone else's strength.

And Digby had a lot of it, mental and physical.

Digby's hands left her body to hold her face, his thumbs on her cheekbones and then her jaw. "This place is utterly secluded, Bay, so we can pretend that there's just the two of us—"

"Three," Bay reminded him.

"Two and a half." Digby's lips twitched into a smile. He rubbed his thumb across her bottom lip. "I have a lot on my mind, so do you, so the aim of this weekend is not to think but just to be. Think we can do that?"

God, that idea sounded like heaven. She needed a break from thinking about the fight for custody of Liv. She couldn't stop the thought that losing Liv would be like losing Layla all over again and, as a result, her stomach was twisted in a perpetual knot.

Bay rubbed the back of her neck. She wanted to stop thinking, to take a break from missing Digby and worrying about the future. She desperately wanted to live in the moment, this moment, and Digby was offering her the opportunity to do just that.

Digby tipped her head up with a finger under her chin. "Is that a deal?"

Bay nodded. "Absolutely. Can I just ask you one thing?"

Apprehension jumped into Digby's eyes and she felt bad for putting it there. "Sure," he replied, sounding a little wary.

Bay hesitated before deciding to take the plunge. If this was the only time she'd have with him then she wasn't going to waste it. "Will you kiss me? Like you did before?"

Passion flared in Digby's eyes. "I have no problem with that request…" He started to lower his mouth to hers but Bay stepped back and held out her hand.

"One more thing?"

Impatience warred with desire as both emotions danced across his face. "Getting impatient here, Adair," Digby muttered.

She loved the fact that she could make him growl. Not being very experienced in dirty talk or in the art of seduction, she looked for words to turn him on. Though, judging by his tented towel, he was already halfway there. "I'd like to spend the weekend in your arms, in your bed."

"Excellent news," Digby muttered.

She could tell him; she was sure he'd understand. He knew that Olivia and her happiness and stability were her driving force. "It's just that, when we are back in Cape Town, I can't—"

Digby placed his broad hand over her mouth and

shook his head. "No, sweetheart. No explanations, not now. I just want to love you."

Oh, thank God. Wonderful.

"Right now, I think it's time the kissing began," Digby murmured, pulling her against his body. He started at the corner of her mouth and Bay felt the tilt of his lips as he smiled. Tension and stress swirled away as his hands ran over her shoulders, down her arms, up her sides. Holding her rib cage with both hands, he spread his fingers and his thumbs brushed her nipples. They immediately flowered under his attention. Her tongue met his in a long, lust-soaked tangle and Bay noticed that he went from hard to concrete in a nanosecond. She was back, in his arms, in his life, for this weekend.

It felt more than right.

It felt like perfection.

Bay ran her hands up Digby's back, over his butt, across his stomach. Her fingers danced over his six-pack and hit the band of his towel. Unhooking the edges, she allowed it to fall to the deck. That was the first barrier; the second was the ties of his board shorts. Undoing the knot, she loosened the ties and pushed the fabric down his hips and past his knees and then dropped the shorts to the deck. Her hand unerringly found him, encircled him, her thumb sweeping across the tip while her mouth supplied him with emotion-soaked kisses.

"Let's get your clothes off, sweet Bay."

While it would be wonderful to make love outside, she still had to consider Olivia waking up and needing her. "Can we take this somewhere a little more private?" Bay asked him. "We have a child in the house."

It took a moment for Digby to remember Olivia and when he did, he nodded. Taking Bay's hand again, he picked up his towel and shorts and, walking naked

across the deck, led her to the end of it. They turned
the corner and stepped onto a semiprivate deck. Two
more loungers lay outside what she knew to be the master bedroom, and Digby sat down on a lounger and
guided her to sit on his bare thighs. She was still dressed
in her T-shirt and shorts and she wanted him to rip the
clothes from her body, feeling like they were slowly
constricting her.

She wanted to be naked. *Now.*

"Digby," she pleaded as he dropped kisses on her
jawline.

"Mmm...?"

"I've got far too many clothes on and I need your
hands on me."

"Do you?" Digby smiled as he toyed with the hem
of her T-shirt. "You sound a bit impatient, darling."

"You have no idea," Bay grumbled, holding his chin
and jaw with one hand before covering his mouth with
hers. She sighed when he allowed her tongue to slide
in, to explore his masculine mouth. She'd missed him;
she'd missed this so much. Making love to Digby made
her feel powerful, like a pagan woman, put on this earth
to pursue pleasure.

Loving Digby made the world stop, problems fade.

But kissing Digby and only having his hands resting on her waist wasn't doing it for her. She needed him
wild and passionate and out of control.

"Digby, if you don't start touching me, I'm going
to lose it," Bay warned him, after pulling her mouth
off his.

"We can't have that now, can we?" He lifted her to
sit closer to his knees and spread her legs wider. Bay
gasped as Digby slid his hands up her inner thighs,
under the loose cotton of her shorts, his knuckles flirt-

ing with her feminine, intimate area. He rubbed and teased but it wasn't enough; she wanted more. She wanted everything he could give her.

"Digby!"

"Patience, my darling Bay. Teasing you is half the fun."

Bay sucked in her breath when his index finger pushed under the material of her thong and slid into her moist channel. Her head tipped back. "Digby, ah. Jeez, that feels good."

"Take off your bra and shirt, sweetheart."

Bay whipped her T-shirt off, flicked open the clasp to her bra and tossed the garments away. Then Digby's hot mouth was on her nipple and a bolt of heat, sensation and pure power flashed through her system, and Bay found herself teetering on the edge of a powerful wave, waiting to fly down its massive face.

Digby held her eyes as his second finger joined the first and he brushed her bundle of nerves with his thumb. "Do I make you feel good, Bay?"

"You make me feel amazing, Dig," Bay replied from a place far, far away. She was standing on that wave, waiting. Another second and she'd be flying.

"So close, Dig," she said, placing her arms behind her head and gripping hair in her fingers, trying to hold on, trying to delay her flight.

Digby rocked his fingers within her, hitting a spot deeper inside, and Bay shouted as she accelerated, skating down that warm, rolling wave with all the skill of a world champion. She felt Digby's face in her neck, his fingers digging into her hip, but she didn't care. She didn't want this intense ride, the sexual equivalent of riding one of the ocean's big waves, to end.

After sucking every last sensation out of the most intense orgasm of her life, Bay collapsed against Digby's chest, yawned and snuggled in. Like Olivia, she was exhausted, and there was nothing like fresh air, sex and the sea to lull one into sleep.

Digby stood up with her in his arms and walked into the master bedroom. He lowered her to the bed and draped a lightweight cotton blanket over her. "Sleep for a little while, Bay. I'll wake you when dinner is ready."

Bay yawned and forced her eyes open. They immediately drooped closed again. She waved in what she hoped was the direction of his groin. She had but he hadn't… "What about, you know…you?"

"I'm good." Digby dropped a kiss on her forehead. "Hopefully, we can pick that up later. But for now, sleep."

Bay yawned again and, wrapping her arms around a pillow, wishing it were Digby, dropped off to sleep.

Bay woke ninety minutes later and, after a quick shower and changing into a short sleeveless dress, checked on Olivia. She'd kicked her blankets off and spread out; Bay knew that she'd sleep through, hopefully allowing her to sleep in, as well.

Pushing her hand through her hair, Bay walked into the kitchen and inhaled the distinctive and wonderful smell of fried onions and beef burgers. Following her nose, she returned to the entertainment deck to see Digby standing by the monstrous gas grill, wearing a bright pink apron with the words Kiss the Cook on the bib.

Since that was an order she was happy to obey, Bay placed her hand on his chest and did what she was told. Digby tasted her briefly before pulling back. He sent her an easy grin. "If we start that we won't get food and I'm starving."

So was she. Bay dropped into a chair, crossed her legs and nodded when Digby offered her a beer. Eschewing a glass, she took the icy Mexican brew he offered, complete with a slice of lime, and took a long sip. "What's the time?" she idly asked.

Digby consulted his bells-and-whistles-and-the-kitchen-sink watch. "A little more than half past eight."

The sun set earlier here than it did in Cape Town and it was now fully dark. Digby had flicked on the lights to the house and entertainment area and Bay imagined that ships at sea could see straight into the house. Thank God there weren't any other houses for miles around.

"I was looking through your portfolio of drawings for the hotel while you were sleeping," Digby said, picking up his own bottle of beer and taking a sip.

Bay wrinkled her nose. "I am not happy with what I've come up with for the new honeymoon suite. It's blah..."

"I think you are being too hard on yourself—I thought it was great."

It really wasn't, but she appreciated his comment. "I'm missing something. Hopefully it'll come to me sooner rather than later."

Digby lifted the lid of the gas barbecue to check on the beef patties. "You went to Stellies, right?"

Bay nodded, smiling at his use of the nickname for her old university, the University of Stellenbosch.

"I didn't know you could do a degree in interior design there."

Bay rested her head against the back of the chair. "I didn't do a degree in interior design—I did a diploma after I graduated."

Digby looked confused. "Then what did you get a degree in?"

"Mechanical engineering."

Digby lowered his beer bottle to stare at her. "Seriously?"

Bay nodded. "As a heart attack. I hated every bloody minute of it, but yeah, I got it done. I'm even still registered with the engineering council."

Digby placed his beer down and his hands on the table, staring at her. "Wait, hold on, let me get this straight. You have a degree in mechanical engineering?"

"Yep."

"And you hated it?"

"Yep."

"So why didn't you change courses? Do something else?" Digby demanded, standing up again.

Ah, that. Bay winced, took a sip of her beer and rested her bare feet on the seat of the chair opposite her. After helping herself to a juicy black olive from the bowl next to her, she popped it into her mouth and slowly chewed. Damn, they tasted good, like the ones she had on Lesbos two years ago.

"The short answer to that is that I didn't change courses because I'm damn stubborn, especially when it comes to anything to do with my parents."

"What's the long answer?"

Bay picked the paper label from her bottle. "My dad's first choice for his three daughters was for them to leave school and marry. That's what good girls did, what my oldest sister, Jane, did. And if they did want to get a qualification, then becoming a nurse, teacher or secretary was acceptable…just."

"Does he know it's the twenty-first century?" Digby demanded.

Bay smiled. "Anyway, what my dad didn't bank on was that his two younger daughters would inherit his brains."

Bay wrinkled her nose. "Not meaning to brag but school was easy for me, as it was for Layla. I got a full academic scholarship to Foresters and so did Layla, a year later.

"I skipped a year of school and graduated early. My father wanted me to teach—I thought I'd rather put my head in an oven. In a fit of pique, I decided to show him I could do what he does, so I applied to join the Faculty of Engineering. I was admitted and I thought he'd blow a gasket. What did women know about engineering? I wasn't suited, I would drop out, I was wasting my time…"

"But you stuck it out."

"Never been so bored in my life." She didn't bother to tell him that she'd graduated third in her class and briefly considered doing her MBA. "He was ridiculously angry that the firm he worked for offered for me to join the company when I finished my postgrad degree."

"I bet."

Digby whipped the burgers off the grill onto a plate and swiftly started to assemble them from the ingredients he'd prepared earlier. Lettuce, tomato, pickles, fried onions, what looked like spicy mayonnaise.

She placed a hand on her stomach, realizing how hungry she was.

"As soon as I graduated, I immediately enrolled in a course to do a diploma in interior design. When I got that, I rewarded myself with a holiday in Thailand. Then I went to Vietnam, then to Cambodia and basically, I kept traveling for six years. I was so damn happy to be away from Cape Town, from everyone but Layla.

"At some point during my travels, I realized I was wasting my energy on my father and that my anger was destroying me, not him. It was just so damn hard to stop being angry at him." Bay stared out to sea, her thoughts a million miles away. "I saw him, you know. A day or two before I first met you."

Digby frowned. "Really? What did he want?"

"He told me that he wanted Liv, that I would be forgiven if I just handed her over. That I could be part of the family again if I agreed." Bay rubbed her fingertips across her forehead. "I was, sort of, tempted. I could give them Liv, I could go back to traveling and I'd have my family back…"

Bay darted a look in Digby's direction but there was no judgment on his face. "So, why didn't you?" he asked, his voice remaining even.

"Because I knew that he was using Liv to manipulate me, to get me to, finally, fall into line. My father doesn't like being bested, especially by a woman."

"How did you beat him, Bay?"

Bay picked a slice of gherkin and slowly chewed it as she pondered his question. "That's difficult to explain. By being as stubborn as him, I guess."

She hesitated before continuing. "I've told you that he was racist and misogynistic and I hated his views, but it went deeper than that. I mean, I loathed the fact that he had such antiquated views and we had screaming arguments about his inability to consider another point of view. But what really hurt me terribly was that he couldn't love me if I didn't have the same opinion as him."

"What do you mean?" Digby asked, pushing a plated burger over to her.

"Before I left for Foresters, I was his favorite girl. I adored him and he adored me too. We spent so much time together—I loved being with him. And when he's not being a jerk, he can be engaging and rather wonderful."

Digby picked up his burger, took a bite, his eyes and all his attention on her.

"But after I started challenging him, he withdrew. We had a dozen vicious arguments and hundreds of minor ones but instead of trying to understand, he punished me by distancing himself from me."

"I'm so sorry, baby," Digby murmured.

Bay folded her arms across her chest, her need for food gone. She stared at the dark sea, listening to the waves crashing. Thinking about her parents and the upcoming custody battle made her throat close and her lungs feel like they were being squeezed in a vise.

She couldn't lose Liv, she couldn't…

Bay heard Digby's muffled curse and then he was on his haunches in front of her, his hands on her thighs, pulling her back to the here and now. Needing to stabilize herself, she lifted her fingers to touch his cheek.

Digby moved his head to kiss her fingers. "Let's make a deal, sweetheart?"

"Mmm? What's that?"

"For the next few days, it's just us. We're not going to think about work or deals or useless parents and custody battles or my meeting with whoever my parents left their money to—"

Bay's mouth dropped open. "You're meeting them? Who is it? Do you know?"

Digby grimaced. "No idea. Radd and I will meet

with him next week. The meeting will be at the same time as your custody hearing on Tuesday."

Right. Well, Tuesday was going to be a big day for them both.

Digby ran his hands up the outside of her thighs and Bay, as she always did, wanted more. "Let's take this time, sweetheart, just for us and not let the outside world intrude. Can we do that?"

Bay slowly nodded. That sounded like heaven.

For the next few days, she was going to live for the moment, enjoy her time with Digby and face whatever came her way next week. Digby squeezed her legs and stood up.

"Excellent. So, do me a favor and eat your burger because you're going to need the energy tonight."

Now there was an incentive she could get behind. Smiling at the thought, she pulled her plate toward her and sliced her burger in two. Then she picked up one half and bit down, groaning with delight.

Digby grinned at her and wiped his mouth with a paper napkin. "Good?"

"Better than sex," Bay replied, her mouth full of food.

"Oh, it bloody well isn't and I intend to prove that to you."

Bay laughed and waved her burger in the air. "Can I finish my food first?"

Digby tapped his watch. "You have fifteen minutes, Adair."

Ten minutes later, shortly after she swallowed her last bite, Digby picked her up, tossed her over his shoulder and walked her to his bedroom.

And, as he promised, the sex was better than the burger.

* * *

Digby felt the sun on his face and adjusted his cap to keep it out of his eyes. This was turning out to be a perfect day. The sun was hot but not blistering and the sea was refreshingly cool. Earlier this morning, he'd left Bay asleep in his bed and hit the beach as dawn broke. After a long run, he'd swum out to beyond the reef and back, feeling the burn in his legs and arms. When he finally returned to the house, he rinsed off in the outdoor shower, checked whether Olivia was still asleep and climbed back into bed with Bay, waking her up with a series of X-rated kisses.

After they made love for the second time, Bay made coffee, and he'd been drifting back to sleep when a three-foot dynamo jumped on his stomach, demanding to go to the beach. She hadn't been prepared to hear the word *no*.

He'd swum with Olivia, watched as Bay made sand castles with her, and he had rubbed sun cream over Bay's skin, sneaking in a kiss whenever he was sure Olivia's attention was otherwise occupied.

Making love to Bay was wonderful, Digby decided, but spending out-of-bed time with her was as much fun. He enjoyed Olivia, loved her cheeky conversation and her piping voice and her enthusiasm for, well, *everything*.

"How are you feeling about meeting the heir to your parents' estate next week?" Bay asked him, out of the blue.

Digby lifted his cap to look at her but she was staring out to sea. After admiring her profile for a while, he closed his eyes again and readjusted his cap.

"I don't really care one way or the other."

Bay poked him in the ribs with her index finger.

"That's a cop-out, Dig—you have to feel something about the person."

She wasn't going to let this go. "Okay, I'm annoyed that some random person is going to enjoy the benefits of a century-plus of my ancestors' hard work. And they'd better not think that this tenuous connection will create a bond between him and Radd and I. I have no intention of playing happy families. Radd is all the family I need."

"Because you are a lone wolf, right?" Bay asked, her voice soft.

Yeah, exactly that. But lately, he'd started to think that he might, one day, be able to do this family thing.

Maybe.

And maybe, possibly, he might; at some point in the future, he'd even want this enough to risk having his heart mangled if it—love and a family—disappeared on him.

And maybe Bay was the one person, the only person, who could make him feel this way. She was the first woman to have him contemplating permanence and commitment. He liked her, he liked her more than any woman he'd ever met before. He adored her body, and sex was, well, a revelation. Instead of it being a nice, satisfactory, albeit a bit of a mechanical act, making love with Bay was a feast of textures and tastes and sensations and sounds. Instead of pulling back after achievement of sexual satisfaction and creating physical, and emotional, distance, Digby normally stayed where he was, wanting to hold on to the moment as long as possible. Gentle kisses were exchanged, backs were rubbed, hands caressed.

For the first time ever, he felt emotionally connected to a woman and for once, he didn't feel like running for the hills. Whatever was happening between him and Bay felt right and he was going to enjoy it for as long as it lasted. And God, although he knew that nothing lasted forever—that it *couldn't*—he hoped Bay would be in his life for the longest time.

Bay *and* Olivia. Because they were a package deal.

"You had a nightmare last night," Bay softly said, jerking him out of his rambling musings. Forcing himself not to react, Digby stayed where he was, conscious of his suddenly thundering heart. He didn't remember any dreams from last night but obviously something had happened for Bay to reach that conclusion.

Before he could ask, Bay carried on speaking. "You were horribly agitated—at some point I actually thought you might be crying."

Crap. Digby winced. *How bloody embarrassing.*

"What were you dreaming about, Dig?"

He could brush her off, tell her that it was nothing, that he didn't remember. But they were long past white lies and inanities, and to hand her either would be a monstrous insult. Another option was to tell her he didn't want to discuss the subject but then she'd be hurt and he didn't want to hurt her. She also opened to him last night; didn't he owe her the same courtesy?

He could give her part of the story; he didn't have to tell her everything.

"I dream about Radd dying, about being left alone. It's a recurring dream, something I've been experiencing most of my life." He would not, *never*, tell her that he'd dreamed about her dying too. There were some things she didn't need to know.

Her hand came to rest on his thigh, her gentle squeeze suggesting support. "Oh, Digby, that's horrible."

She had no damn idea. "I'm sorry if I woke you," Digby muttered, glad his cap was still covering his eyes.

"I don't care about that. Have you told Radd about your nightmares?"

Now why would he do that? "Uh…*no*."

"You should. It helps to verbalize fears—it makes them smaller, weaker," Bay told him, her voice empathetic.

Before he could tell her that he'd rather have his toenails pulled off with rusty pliers, Olivia sat down on his stomach and he released a pained, "Oof." Despite having a little wind knocked out of him, he was incredibly grateful for her interruption. He couldn't think of a subject he'd less like to discuss.

Olivia swung one leg over him so that her chubby knees were on either side of his ribs and her feet in the sand. She lifted his cap off his face, stared down at him and pursed her lips. "Is Mommy Bay your girlfriend?"

Digby sent her a "help me" look, but Bay seemed like she was enjoying this interrogation far too much to put a stop to it. "Bay is my friend and a girl."

Bay smiled at his triumphant dodged-a-bullet expression.

"So she isn't your girlfriend," Liv stated.

He was being put on the spot by a three-year-old. This time Bay did come to his rescue. "Stop bugging Dig, Olivia."

Olivia threw her hands up in the air. "I was just asking a question!"

Bay sighed. "Digby and I are friends, Olivia."

"Oh. I understand."

"You do?" Digby asked the little girl.

"You can't be her boyfriend 'cause Mommy Bay is too pretty for you."

Digby turned to look at Bay who was, rather unsuccessfully, trying to hide her laughter. "I might never recover from this emotional damage, Adair."

"And she's only three. Imagine how savage she is going to be when she's sixteen," Bay told him, patting his hand.

Liv took his cap off his head and put it on hers. It immediately fell over her eyes and half her face. Digby took it off her and, ignoring her squawk of annoyance, tightened the band and put it back on her head. It was still too big but didn't completely cover her suck-you-in eyes.

Digby looked at Olivia and rested his hand on her chubby thigh. She was dressed in a little rash vest and matching shorts, designed to keep her from burning. In his cap, she looked too cute for words and his heart stumbled and banged off his chest.

"Here you go, sweetie." Bay handed Olivia her cup filled with weak, unsweetened tea. Leaning to the side, she placed her lips on Olivia's, who happily accepted her affectionate gesture. "Love you, baby girl."

"Love you more," Olivia automatically replied, telling Digby it was an oft-repeated phrase.

How could Bay's parents want to split these two up? Okay, Bay wasn't her biological mother but damn, she loved her niece with everything she had. Olivia was her entire world and Digby felt a pang of jealousy deep in his heart. He was, he reluctantly admitted, jealous that he'd never had a mother who loved him like that…

He felt stupid for wanting a moment that was long gone…

But he was damned if he'd let Olivia and Bay be separated. If the judge didn't rule in her favor in the custody battle, he'd contact his lawyers and he'd find out what he could do to ensure that Bay and Olivia stayed together, that she became Olivia's mommy in all the ways that counted.

He had wealth and power and he had no problem using both to get the outcome he wanted...

Digby yawned and lifted his hand to cover his mouth. Despite making love to Bay quite a few times, he'd slept like a rock. No, he'd only thought he'd slept well because he couldn't remember the dream that woke Bay up.

Damn, would he ever be free of them? And he still hadn't managed to shake the memory of the very weird dream he had of Bay taking Radd's place in that coffin. Digby shuddered and his skin turned to gooseflesh.

"I knows what I'm going to be when I grows up," Olivia announced, her sweet voice the distraction he needed. Under the bill of her cap, her eyes radiated determination.

"Really?" Digby asked, sitting up but holding on to Olivia so that she stayed on his lap. "What are you going to be? A doctor? A scientist? An astronaut?"

Olivia looked at him like he'd grown two heads. "No, silly."

"What are you going to be when you grow up, Liv?" Bay asked her, leaning back on her elbows, her long body sporting four bright pink triangles. Digby's glance went to her stomach and he stared at her belly ring, remembering the way his tongue swirled around that small, sexy indentation. And those long, shapely, stunning legs had wrapped around his hips...

Right, couldn't think of that right now. Mustn't think of anything they did until they were alone...

"I'm going to be a penguin."

"Huh?" Digby asked, having lost track of the conversation.

Olivia sent him a "keep up" look. "When I grows up, Digby, I'm going to be a penguin."

"Good plan," Digby told her, unable to hold back his grin. Man, he loved this kid. He surged to his feet and tucked her under his arm like a rugby ball. "And do you know what penguins must do?"

"What?" Liv squealed as he headed to the surf.

"They must swim and catch fish!" Digby yelled, charging into the surf and releasing a banshee-like cry.

Olivia, being a warrior herself, did her best to outyell him.

Bay, he noticed when he looked back, just grinned before rolling onto her stomach and burying her nose in her book.

CHAPTER NINE

ON TUESDAY MORNING, back in Cape Town, Digby woke up feeling anxious and unsettled. After a long swim that failed to clear his head, he went into Green Point and the exclusive offices of Mabaso, Gumede and Klein, the lawyers dealing with his parents' estate.

It was also the day Bay would appear in court, fighting to keep Olivia. God, he wished he could be with her, giving her moral support, but his presence might harm her chances rather than help. It was a comfort to know that Mama B would be with her, as well as other members of the Samsodien family. Olivia would be in court as well and he hoped that she was too young to understand why she was there and what they were discussing.

But, because he needed Bay to know that he was thinking about her, he sent her a text message.

I'll be thinking of, and rooting for, you today. I know that the judge will make the right decision because you are what's best for Liv. You're a fantastic mom, sweetheart.

Call me as soon as it's over—I want to know how it went. Thanks for one of the best weekends of my life…

Digby turned his phone onto Silent and put it into the inner pocket of his suit jacket. Today was the day he and Radd were meeting the heir to their parents' fortune and, frankly, there were a million things he'd rather be doing today. Sure, it would be great to see Radd—he and Brin flew in late last night—but he had a million things to do and not much time to do them in.

He'd had a great weekend with Bay and Olivia but taking that time meant that he'd be working fourteen-hour days for the rest of the week to catch up. And to keep up that hectic pace, he needed to sleep, and last night, his nightmares returned with a vicious twist.

He'd dreamed, once again, of losing Radd. Then if that wasn't enough, when he finally fell asleep again, it was Bay's face in that black coffin.

He'd woken up tangled up in his sheets, his face and body wet with perspiration and his heart thundering, his arms reaching for Bay. When he realized where he was, alone in his own bed, and that he was having a nightmare, he felt nausea in the back of his throat and just—but only just—made it to the bathroom to throw up.

His nightmares, Digby decided as he entered the swish offices, were getting worse. Throughout his teens and twenties, they'd been vivid but short and he always managed to brush them from his mind. But these latest dreams were more terrors than nightmares and their negativity tended to be more long lasting, leaving him feeling unsettled and uptight for most of the day.

Digby strode up to the reception desk and handed the cool blonde a tight smile. "Tempest-Vane for Siya Mabaso, at nine o'clock."

"Nice to see you too, bro."

Digby turned around to see his brother standing behind him, casually dressed in an untucked, button-down shirt, chino shorts and loafers. Radd looked relaxed and happy, his dark blue eyes content.

Digby gripped his hand and pulled him into a hug. "Radd! Hell, I didn't even see you standing there."

"I noticed. Bit preoccupied, Dig?" Radd asked on an easy grin.

Just a bit. Mostly with a slim brunette with eyes the color of his favorite alcoholic drink. God help him.

"It's good to see you," Digby said. And it was. He and Radd had always been a team and they were stronger, and better, together. "How's Brin?"

"I left her in bed," Radd told him with a self-satisfied smile. "Though she is planning to get back to her shop today. She's feeling incredibly guilty for being away so long. She's wanting to open in six weeks."

Despite being engaged to one of the wealthiest people in the country, his future sister-in-law still wanted to pursue a career in floral design. Digby admired her for following her dream and kudos to his big brother for allowing her to fly.

Radd placed a hand on his shoulder and nodded to the sharply dressed lawyer waiting for them across the room. "You ready for this?"

Digby shrugged. "I guess. Though why this person wants to meet us, I have no damn idea."

"Let's go find out," Radd suggested.

Digby buttoned his suit jacket and followed his casually dressed brother into a conference room, wondering why his heart was thundering. There was nothing to be concerned about—his parents' heir had no connection to them, couldn't hurt them.

He was just here to satisfy his curiosity; that was all.

Then why did he feel like he did this morning when he woke after that nightmare? Shivery and sick, feeling like everything had changed.

Digby took a deep breath and greeted Siya Mabaso,

shaking his hand before looking around the small conference room. In the corner, by the window, stood a familiar figure and Digby blinked, convinced he was seeing a mirage, that she was an illusion.

"Roisin?" he asked, not caring that his voice was cracking. "What the hell are you doing here?"

"Radd, Digby, meet Roisin O'Keefe. Your sister."

Digby left the meeting feeling shell-shocked and disorientated. Siya explained that Roisin was born in the States when he was ten—that explained Gil and Zia's long absence that year—and that her adoption had been facilitated by a lawyer in the States. His parents must've realized that their fourth child was a girl and, knowing they wouldn't get a payout from the trust for not producing another boy child, decided to dump their unwanted daughter.

God, it physically hurt that he was related to them.

Thankfully, Roisin hit the jackpot with her adopted parents; the O'Keefes were a wealthy, childless couple who adored their adopted daughter.

Apparently, both Roisin and her parents had been shocked to discover that she was the biological daughter of two of the most notorious socialites in Africa and the heir to an estate worth billions.

As an only child, she'd explained, she'd always wanted siblings but she understood that, given their fame, news that there was another Tempest-Vane sibling would be explosive. Her dropping into Radd's and Digby's lives would set the tabloids on fire. And, she candidly admitted, she wanted to meet Radd and Digby first, to decide whether they were the type of people she wanted to know.

If she liked them, fine, if not, her identity could forever remain a secret.

Apparently, she liked them. Well, she liked Digby. *Hoo-bloody-rah.*

Digby, flying down Chapman's Peak on his Ducati, felt the power between his legs and gave his superbike more force, feeling his heart rate kick up a notch as adrenaline coursed through his system.

He had a sister, another sibling, God help him. He was furious that she'd lied to him, that she'd sought employment at The Vane to push herself into his life, into his world. He'd employed her to look after Olivia, had trusted her with his lover's child, with the little person he was crazy about.

Yet he hadn't known whom she was or her true agenda.

He felt like a bloody fool.

He needed to tell Bay, needed her to know that Roisin wasn't whom she said she was, that she'd been lying to him, them. But he couldn't talk to Bay, not yet.

Not until he got his head on straight.

Up until six weeks ago, he'd been happy in his single life, content to have only his brother to worry about. But now he had a sister, a sister-in-law, a lover and his lover's kid, all clamoring for a piece of his soul.

He couldn't do it. Radd was the only family Digby had, all he needed.

It was bad enough that he lived in constant fear of losing his brother but now he was also dreaming about Bay, and obviously, he was worried about losing her too. What was next, him perpetually fretting about losing her, losing Liv? Would that worry extend to Roisin, to Brin?

He couldn't do it; he didn't want the additional

emotional stress. There were suddenly too many people in his life and he couldn't, wouldn't give them the power to hijack his heart. No, he preferred to fly solo, thank you very much.

He couldn't get rid of Radd, and he didn't want to. And Brin was part of his life. But he didn't have to engage with Roisin, he didn't need a sister.

As for Bay, well, it was time to let her go. It would hurt, for a little while, but she was a risk he couldn't take. Didn't want to take. From tonight, from *now*, he was going to revert to his old life, to what he knew, to what he was good at. Casual flings, ships-in-the-night relationships, nothing that involved any risk.

Digby whipped into a turnout, kicked down his stand and switched off the engine. Taking off his helmet, he stared down to the sea kissing the rocks below and tried not to remember Bay and Olivia poking around the rock pools in Mozambique. He pushed the memory away. He'd miss them but it was better this way.

After pulling out his phone, he grimaced at the many, many missed calls—Bay, Radd and Roisin— and switched to his text-messaging app.

There were twenty, twenty-five messages, and he again ignored the ones from Radd and Roisin. But he couldn't resist opening the first of Bay's many texts.

The judge decided not to wait and made his ruling immediately! I'm officially Liv's mommy! Want to celebrate with me tonight?

Dig, I can't get a hold of you. Call me.

Digby, I really need to talk to you...

Dig, Roisin told me about today, that she's your sister. She really feels bad about lying to you, and she needs to talk to you. I need to talk to you. Call me, please.

Dig, it's been hours and hours. I'm really worried.

She didn't need to worry; he hadn't asked her to. He'd been looking after himself for a long, long time and he was fine. He didn't need her sympathy or her company, to help him work his way through this mess.

They were over...

They had to be.

Digby slapped his helmet back onto his head and revved his bike, spinning it in a tight circle to face the road. Giving the bike power, he shot away and his speed quickly climbed, then climbed some more. His heart sat in his throat as he flung the bike around the tight corners and adrenaline pumped through his body.

If he could only go fast enough to forget.

Have just heard that D used his private entrance ten minutes ago. Go kick his ass.

In the ballroom of The Vane, Bay read Roisin's message once, then again. She quickly typed her reply.

How do you know?

I made friends with one of the guys manning the security cameras. Roisin's message popped onto her screen seconds later. Let me know how it goes.

Bay looked at her computer screen and frowned at the open tabs on it.

How to Cope After a Breakup
Steps to Treating the Pain of a Breakup
How to Heal Fast After Your Heart Has Been Broken

Stupid internet and its super-stupid advice.

She needed a fall-out-of-love pill, something to erase everything she felt, to help her forget the possibilities of the amazing life they could have had together. Her vision for her future coalesced nine days ago when she'd seen the judge give his surprising verdict, shortly after he heard all the evidence around why she should keep custody of Olivia.

The judge said nice things: that anyone could see that she and Liv were a family and that they were a tight unit. It was a pity that there wasn't a father figure in Liv's life. He was concerned about the animosity between her and her parents but it wasn't a reason to deny her custody.

Maybe they could work it out, the judge suggested, before awarding her permanent custody there and then.

Instead of reacting jubilantly, Bay, her arms around Liv's little waist, buried her face in the child's hair, biting her own lip to stop herself from yelling that Liv did have a father figure in her life, a man they both adored. A man she was completely, thoroughly, impossibly in love with.

But, because he was currently running away from reality, from a situation he no longer had control over, she was alone.

She shouldn't be alone. Neither of them should. They were better, stronger, together.

Bay shut down her laptop, thinking that Digby was taking a long time to reach the same conclusion. And, she reminded herself, he might never get to that point. *You can't force people to love you the way you need to be loved, Bay, you know this.*

Love meant different things to different people: to her father, it was control, to Digby it represented fear and loss.

Either way, both the men she'd loved most in her life had taken her love, then dismissed her and left her swinging in the wind.

Damn them.

She might not be able to stop the people she loved from treating her like she was disposable but that didn't mean they could get away with it.

After walking out of the ballroom, Bay used the staff passages to avoid the guests and finally emerged at the back of the hotel. As she walked to Digby's house, the many reasons she was angry with him tumbled through her head.

In ten days, he never once called or even replied to her many, many messages. Not even to congratulate or acknowledge her winning the custody battle for Liv. He'd gone completely silent and it was no comfort to know that he wasn't talking to his brand-new sister, or apparently, as she'd heard from Roisin, to Radd either.

But while he wasn't talking to his brother, his new sister or to her, he hadn't been alone. The tabloid press had been ecstatic about his return to the clubbing and partying scene and there had been photos in the gossip columns every day this week. He'd attended many, many parties and he'd only left the clubs when they finally closed, usually accompanied by a stacked blonde. He'd run up Table Mountain, gone skydiving and free dived with sharks off Hermanus. He'd also managed to rack up a slew of speeding tickets in six days from pushing his Ducati to higher and higher speeds.

Wild Digby Tempest-Vane was back with a vengeance and the press was salivating.

Bay just wanted to bash his head in.

How dare he? How dare he act like she and Liv, Roisin and Radd, didn't matter? That they weren't important enough to let them know that he was okay? They'd had such a marvelous weekend away in Mozambique and Bay thought they were on the path to creating something special. He'd been sweet and considerate and seemed to enjoy spending time with not only her but Liv. She'd tried not to, but she'd started to think, just a little, that they had a chance of a relationship, of something permanent.

What a colossal fool she'd been. From the beginning, she'd known he was going to hurt her and she wasn't surprised by that. Although she'd never expected him to disappear, to break contact with everyone who loved him.

But someone needed to tell him his behavior was unacceptable and inexcusable. She could, just, cope with him hurting her, but she refused to condone his behavior toward Roisin.

Bay didn't bother to knock; she just stormed into his house, shouting his name. He emerged from his study, his eyes flat and his face pale. Bay put her hand on her heart and shook her head at his gaunt cheeks, his red-rimmed eyes. "Wow, looking good, Tempest-Vane."

"If you are going to be sarcastic you can just bugger off," Digby told her, walking past her to head for the kitchen. He fiddled with the coffee machine, keeping his back to her. "Actually, just go, Bay. We have nothing to say to each other."

Bay felt a red-hot surge of anger. "You might not have anything to say to me but I have a hell of a lot to say to you!"

Digby turned to face her, his hands gripping the counter behind him. "Get on with it then—I have somewhere to be."

She wasn't going to ask; she wasn't going to be *that* woman. "Who is she today? Do you even know her name?"

Really, Bay, why are you asking questions you really, really don't want to know the answer to? What is wrong with you?

Digby met her eyes and for a second, maybe less, she saw shame in his eyes. Then it disappeared and he handed her a laconic shrug. "I just call them sweetheart, they seem to like that."

Just like she had. Bay sent him a hard look and shook her head. She didn't believe him. He was bullshitting her. Yeah, she could easily believe that he'd been clubbing and doing all those other crazy things, but she knew he hadn't been with another woman.

He was being a jerk, but she knew him… He wouldn't jump from her bed to someone else's. He might've been on a tear this week, but she could see how much pain he was in; it was there in his churning eyes, in his too-tight lips, reflected in the fact that his shoulders were halfway to his ears.

She'd learned to read him and could feel the confusion and hurt rolling off him in hot waves. He didn't want to deal with the idea of having more family; he simply couldn't bear it. He'd trained himself to keep isolated, to not allow any love into his life. He already worried about losing his brother, and the idea of having a sister had, she was sure, rocked his world. Digby's biggest fear was loving and losing someone he loved, and having someone new in his life freaked him out.

And adding her and Liv to the equation was a sure way to make him panic and want to run.

"Talk to me, Dig," she said, her anger dying and sadness rising.

"Nothing to say." Digby whipped out the stinging words.

"So, you're quite fine with the fact that you have a sister?"

"We might share some genes but, as far as I'm concerned, she's just another Tempest-Vane employee. I don't intend to have anything to do with her," Digby said, his voice flat. But longing crossed his face and Bay knew he was lying through his teeth. "Radd is my family, my only family."

Every time he said that it hurt a little more. But she couldn't think of herself, she had to concentrate on trying to get Digby to move off the I'm-better-alone hill he was currently defending. Not for her but for Roisin, whom she adored and who wanted to have a relationship with her biological brother.

But mostly she wanted this for Digby. She understood that Roisin's revelation was a lot for him to come to terms with, that her coming into his life was too much for him to deal with…

But Bay understood that Digby needed more people in his life who loved him. Family was a precious gift and not something to be easily dismissed. And family wasn't confined to people with whom one shared DNA; after all, it had been Mama B who held her hand during the custody battle, Mama B who led her and Olivia from the courtroom after the verdict.

It was Mama B who held her as she watched her

parents walk away from their granddaughter without a word. Mama B remained in her life as her parents walked out of it.

Family wasn't something to be so easily dismissed, Bay thought. Especially when that family was walking toward you. When they didn't want anything from you but to be part of your life and, if you were brave enough, to love you.

"You are the reason why Roisin decided to come clean—she feels a connection to you," Bay persisted.

"I. Don't. Care," Digby said, through gritted teeth.

Bay folded her arms across her chest and looked him in the eye. "This is all pretty overwhelming, isn't it? You've fallen for me, and Liv, you have a new sister, Radd is engaged to Brin… For a guy who's always felt alone, being surrounded by people who want a piece of you must be disconcerting."

"I haven't fallen for you," Digby muttered, his tone harsh.

Oh, he so had. "You told me once that you craved attention and that you looked for it everywhere, that it fueled so many of your actions. Funny that now that you have a bunch of attention, from people who claim to love you, who want to spend their lives loving you, you are running from it. What's up with that, Dig?"

"Will you please *go*?"

Not yet. Bay decided to push him some more. "Wait, I'm trying to understand this. So, you are happy to have the attention of strangers and the press and acquaintances, but you bolt when you are faced with real love, true love?"

Digby stared at a point past her shoulder. "Bay, I am tired and pissed off and I'm done with this conversation. Will you please leave?"

He roared the last sentence and Bay forced herself not to react, to keep her expression bland. He didn't scare her; he never would.

"I'll go, in a minute. I just have a few things to say first," Bay said, her heart and stomach doing backflips.

"Get on with it," Digby growled.

Bay was desperate to get through to him but knew she would only have one shot at this. She considered and discarded a couple of sentences and when Digby threw up his hands in annoyance at having to wait, she allowed the words to flow.

"I love you, Digby."

And she always would. Sure, she'd been on the receiving end of conditional love but that didn't mean she had to give it. She knew, somewhere deep in her soul where truth resided, that if Digby was capable of giving her what she needed, he would. He wasn't doing this to hurt her, but because he'd been hurt, time and time again, by people and circumstances.

"I know that's not something you want to hear but it's something I want you to know." She saw him jerk, clocked his deep frown. He wasn't happy to hear her declaration and, knowing she had nothing more to lose, she carried on.

"Someday, I hope you realize that we could have something pretty wonderful," Bay calmly stated. "But, if you decide that you want us, you'd better be prepared to give me what *I* want, Tempest-Vane."

He lifted his chin, those blue eyes blazing. Digby didn't like ultimatums; he far preferred to give them. Too damn bad.

She refused to be intimidated by him. "I know what it's like to live with uncertainty, what it's like to live with someone who is exceptionally good at giving and then withdrawing affection. I refuse to love someone like that again. In Mozambique, you gave Liv, and me, your love and affection but, the next day, you withdrew it and dropped out of our lives. That is not acceptable behavior."

Bay pushed a weary hand through her hair. "If you come back to me, you'd better be damn sure that I, and Liv, are a priority and not an option. We'd better be the most important people in your life because I won't settle for anything less, for her or for me. If you come back, you'd better be prepared to commit to me, and to Liv, in every way that matters. Are you hearing me on this, Digby?"

Resentment flashed in his eyes. "You want me to be Olivia's dad."

She did, so she nodded. She refused to settle for anything less than everything, for even a fraction less than wonderful. "Yeah, I do. You're living in fear, Digby, and I wish you'd realize that none of us is out to hurt you.

"If you take a chance on me, I promise I will always be there for you, that I will never willingly walk away. Apart from infidelity and abuse, neither of which are in your nature, the only way you will lose me, and Olivia, is by not letting us in. I won't abandon you. Neither will your family—you just have to give them, *us*, a chance."

She'd said a lot already; she might as well get it all out. "But I also need to be able to rely on you, to know that you are not going to freak out and run when life throws us a curveball. I want to know that I can rely on you when things get tough, to celebrate with me when things go well. You have no idea how much you hurt me by not acknowledging my winning custody of Liv. I needed to share that with you but you weren't there for me. I was, *am*, gutted about that."

Desperation and guilt flared in his eyes but Bay

forced herself to ignore what she saw. "I'm also so sad that you didn't come to me when you heard about Roisin. I could've helped you make sense of it but you ran and looked for attention from people who don't matter.

"I matter, Digby. So does your family." Bay lifted her fingers to her cheeks, cursing her tears. She lifted her hands as Digby took a step toward her and she violently shook her head.

She had to end this conversation before she lost it completely and broke down in front of him.

Finding the last of her courage, she looked at Digby, his image blurry through her tears. "Make damn sure you know what you want before you come back, Tempest-Vane. And if you don't, no hard feelings. I found a way to live without my dad's love—I will do the same with you too."

Feeling a little broken, and a lot sad, Bay turned away from him and stumbled toward the door, frantically wiping her tears away.

He'd come to her or he wouldn't. There was nothing more she could do.

Because he'd slammed down a bottle of whiskey—alone—after Bay left him, and was the architect of his own massive headache, Digby decided that he didn't deserve painkillers.

He was regretting that decision as he walked down the path leading from his house to the hotel. The sun felt like a million acid-tipped needles digging into his eyeballs and he was fairly sure his head was going to drop off his shoulders at any second.

I promise I will always be there for you, that I will never willingly walk away.

You're living in fear.

I wish you'd realize that none of us is out to hurt you.

Yeah, the pain was nothing he didn't deserve.

Digby sighed and rubbed the back of his neck. After a long night and a great deal of self-examination, re-criminations and kicking his own ass, he knew he had fences to mend, explanations and decisions to make. He didn't want to do any of it…dealing with people he loved was exhausting. It was easier to pretend when he was amongst strangers. And that was why he'd run from Roisin, from Radd and yeah, from Bay.

Strangers didn't ask questions, demand more, couldn't force him to confront feelings he wasn't ready to deal with. And when he was chasing adrenaline, he had to—his life depended on it—push everything else away and focus on the task at hand. If he didn't, he could die.

He didn't want to die, but God, he wouldn't mind it if someone cut off his head to get rid of his headache.

First things first…

Standing on the edge of the white-to-pink-to-red rose garden, Digby pulled out his phone and called Radd. His brother answered on the third ring. "You alive?" Radd asked, sounding tense.

"Yeah."

Radd didn't speak again and Digby sighed. Radd wasn't going to make this easy for him; none of them, damn them, would. "So much happened very quickly."

It was a weak excuse but the only one he was pre-pared to give. "Yeah, I heard that you fell in love around the same time you heard about Roisin," Radd com-mented, his voice bland.

Digby dropped his phone to look at his screen. Shak-ing his head, he lifted it up to his ear again. "I don't know that I'm in love with her, Radd."

"Of course you are, Dig. Any idiot, apparently, can see it," Radd told him, sounding impatient. "I really like her, by the way, so does Brin. Roisin considers her to be a very good friend."

He couldn't think of Bay, not just yet. He needed to get his family situation sorted and then he'd deal with these churning, burning, crazy feelings he had for Bay.

"What does Roisin want from us, Radd?"

"Why don't you ask her yourself?" Radd asked. "And when you're done with that, pull your head out of your ass and go and talk to Bay."

Frank, older-brother advice. Not that it was needed; he was planning to do that. He didn't know if she'd accept his apology but he had to try, dammit.

But, before he ended this conversation, he needed to say one thing, just one, to Radd. Digby felt his throat tightening and pushed the words up his throat. "Radd, just don't…" his voice, to his dismay, cracked.

"Dig? Don't what?" Radd asked, immediately sounding concerned.

Digby ran his hand over his eyes, cursing the burn he felt within them. "Bay said that I should tell you that I've had nightmares about you most of my life, well, since Jack died. I dream that I'm burying you, saying goodbye…"

He shoved the words past the massive ball in his too-tight throat. "Anyway, I can't lose you so don't die on me, okay?"

Radd was silent for a long time before Digby heard his heavy sigh. "Dig, I have a life partner I love and adore—I want to have kids as soon as we can. I want my brother, and my new sister, to be an integral part of my life going forward. I have no intention of going anywhere."

He couldn't respond, too choked up to speak. But he did feel a little lighter for voicing his biggest fear.

"Dig?"

"Yeah, I'm here."

"You've got fences to mend, apologies to make, a ton-load of groveling to do if you want to win Bay back."

"Thank you, Captain Obvious," Digby told him. Then he sighed. "But hell, you're not wrong. Any advice on how to grovel? If I recall, you had to do it with Brin…"

"I did not grovel. I explained my position," Radd growled.

"Brin says you groveled and I believe her," Digby teased him, needing to distance himself from the emotion swirling between them. He started to walk again, heading toward the childcare center on the western edge of the property.

"Bloody hell, you're annoying," Radd retorted before disconnecting. Digby's smile faded as he put his hand on the door leading to the building he'd erected to entertain the guests' smaller kids. Roisin would be inside, as well as Liv.

Two of the three females causing havoc in his life…

Olivia was the first to see him and she let out a high-pitched squeal before bounding over to him, all but flying by the time she reached him. He scooped her up and closed his eyes when he felt her little face in his neck, all doubts about what he wanted fading.

He wanted to be Olivia's dad, to be Bay's husband, to spend the rest of his life loving them, and any other children they had, with everything he had.

Liv was the first to pull back and she placed her tiny hands on his cheeks, before dropping a kiss on his lips. "I's missed you."

Digby's heart skipped a beat at her shy declaration. "I missed you too, kiddo."

"I know." Liv narrowed her amazing eyes at him. "Are you going to buy me a present because you missed me?"

Digby didn't bother to hide his grin. She was smart little baggage and she'd keep him, God willing, on his toes and wrapped around her already overdeveloped finger for the rest of his life. "What do you want?"

"I still wants an elephant and a penguin."

Digby dropped a kiss on her nose. "Mmm, what if I bought you a stuffed elephant and penguin instead?"

"Like Fluffy?" Liv, her hands still on his cheeks, considered his offer. "I'll think about it. I's go play now."

She pushed against his hold and Digby lowered her to the ground, watching as she scampered off to join a little boy playing with blocks across the room. There, he thought, went part of his heart.

"She's a handful but so, so sweet."

Digby turned at the voice behind him and saw Roisin leaning against the wall, her blue eyes wary. She had his eyes, he noticed, Radd's chin, their height. With her dark hair and blue eyes, she was, absolutely, a Tempest-Vane and Digby couldn't believe he hadn't noticed it before.

"Hey," he said, wincing at the inane comment.

"Hey back," Roisin said, her arms crossing over her chest as if to protect her heart. He'd hurt her, he realized, just as he'd hurt Bay. *Enough of that now, Tempest-Vane.*

Going with his gut, Digby opened his arms and waited, with bated breath, to find out whether Roisin would accept his gesture. She sniffled, just once, before moving toward him, then hugging him tightly.

"I didn't mean to deceive you, Dig. I just wanted to go slow," she muttered against his chest.

Digby ran his hand down her long braid. "It's okay, Ro. And can I say, although it's a bit late…welcome to our dysfunctional family."

Roisin stood back and wiped her tears away with the balls of her hands. Then she covered her eyes with her hands. "I needed time to see if you were anything like your, *our*, parents. If you were, I was going to fade away, not make contact."

"Smart girl," Digby replied. Hell, in her position, he would've done exactly the same thing. After leading her outside, Digby pushed her into one of the two chairs on the veranda and sat down on the opposite one.

Roisin sniffed and pulled a tissue out of her pocket. After blowing her nose, she tried to smile. "I was only told about the inheritance when your parents died. I didn't know about them before. I was shocked at suddenly becoming an heiress."

"I bet."

"But they, according to the lawyer, kept track of me," Roisin stated. Then determination burned in the eyes that met his. "I told Radd and I'm telling you, I don't want everything they left me. I want you two to choose anything you want and I'll auction everything else."

"I don't want anything," Digby said, placing his hand on her knee. "I have everything I need."

"Radd said the same thing," Roisin replied. "But there are some boxes of jewelry, photos and knick-knacks you may want. I think it might be your grandparents' stuff—it's pretty old. Maybe you'd like to look through that, at least."

"I'd like that," Digby told her. "But sell the rest, Roisin, bank the proceeds."

"They left me enough cash for several lifetimes and I don't need that much money. I thought that I could donate the money raised at the auction to the Tempest-Vane foundation. Anonymously, of course."

They'd be grateful but it wasn't necessary, he told her. And that raised another point. "Do you want a public acknowledgment from us, Ro?"

Roisin cocked her head. "Would you give me one?"

Of that he had no doubt; he'd be proud to call her his sister. "Absolutely. It will create a firestorm in the media, but if that's what you want, then sure."

Roisin placed her hand on her chest. "You and Radd are amazing and I'm so lucky to have found you. But no, I'd prefer to avoid the press. But thank you for the offer."

Digby shrugged. "You're our sister." He heard someone calling her name and Roisin checked her watch. "It's outside playtime—I need to go," she explained as she stood up.

As if they'd been doing it forever, she stepped into his arms again for another hug. When she pulled back, he asked another question. "Why are you still working? I mean, now that we know who you are, you no longer need to pretend."

Roisin sent him a sweet smile. "I like to work and I love kids. And my friend needed me to look after her little girl."

Digby looked down at his feet, noticing a new rip in the knee of his oldest jeans. "How is she?" he quietly asked.

"Sad. But strong," Roisin replied. "Missing you. She's in the ballroom if you are looking for her."

He was. Honestly, he'd been looking for her all his life but never knew it.

CHAPTER TEN

Bay, sitting on the floor in the corner of the ballroom, lifted her head up from her sketch pad to look around the space. It was the lack of noise that first caught her attention and, yep, the room was completely empty.

She looked at her watch and frowned. It wasn't tea or lunchtime. The renovation crew should still be working; this room had to be finished in time for the Table Mountain Ball in a few weeks.

Where was everybody?

"Do you know the definition of the Greek word *philophobia*?"

Bay's head whipped in the direction of Digby's voice and eventually found him, standing next to the French doors, the sun creating a halo around his head. She almost snorted; Digby was as far from an angel as anyone could be and she far preferred naughty to nice anyway. Wearing a white linen shirt, sleeves rolled up his forearms, and ripped and battered designer jeans, flip-flops on his feet, he looked hot and sexy and hot...

She was repeating herself.

Annoyed by her instinctive, uncontrollable response to him, Bay scowled. "Did you come here to slow down work—" she looked around the ballroom, realizing he was the only person who could clear the room so fast

"—or to torment me with the meaning of obscure Greek words?"

Digby walked into the ballroom, across to where she sat, and sank to the floor in front of her before crossing his legs and placing his elbows on his knees. "It originates from two Greek words: *philos* which means loving, and *phobos* which means fear. I've been suffering from the fear of love all my life."

Bay bit her lip, wondering where he was going with this.

"I'm terrified of love, having it, dealing with it, losing it. It's easier to dismiss it, to tell yourself you didn't want it in the first place."

Bay rested the back of her head against the wall behind her and waited for him to continue.

"Then you dropped into my life and made me confront that fear," Digby told her, sounding a little cross. "I was just wrapping my head around *that* notion when I found out that Roisin is my sister, and I, sort of, lost it."

"Really? Sort of?" Bay sarcastically replied.

Digby pulled her sketch pad from her grip and looked down at what she'd been drawing. Bay started to blush as he inspected her sketch of him. She should've been working but, feeling sad and dispirited, she'd sat down in the corner, and when her thoughts went to Digby she'd started to sketch his likeness. Her sketch looked a lot like him, she thought. Complete with tired eyes and gaunt cheeks.

"Liv's right—I'm definitely not pretty enough for you."

Bay forced herself to speak. "I don't want pretty, Digby. I want real."

Digby slowly nodded. "Okay, how is this for real?" He hesitated and Bay held her breath, knowing he was about to say something momentous. "Except for Radd, I've been on my own for a long, long time. I've liked being on my own—I've loved my freedom. I've had no one to answer to.

"Over the last couple of weeks, I've met you, I've met Liv and I've met Roisin and each of you, in different ways, has taken—despite my objections—a piece of my heart. The tiny piece that's left, that's mine alone, is terrified that I will never get those pieces back." Digby looked at her, his eyes deep, dark and intense. "I'm scared, Bay. Can you understand that? You're each offering something I desperately want, but history has taught me that I don't get the things I most want."

"Like your parents' love and attention," Bay murmured.

"And the love I did have, the love I relied on more than I realized, went away when Jack died. Love, to me, is synonymous with loss, constant disappointment and unfulfillment."

Oh, God, when he put it like that, she saw the uphill climb she'd asked him to make and accepted that she'd asked for too much. He wouldn't be able to love her the way she needed him to. She'd asked for far too much.

"Let's just stop here, Digby—I can't do this," she said, her words running together. "I understand why you are hesitant to get involved but I can't be anything *but* involved. I can't be the one giving everything and not getting what I need."

She wouldn't cry; she wouldn't! She'd stand up, hold her head up high and walk out of the room. "I'll leave all my designs for the next designer and I'll get out of your hair. I'd still really appreciate a letter of recommendation if you wouldn't mind giving me one."

Bay tried to stand up but Digby's strong hand on her

leg kept her in place. "I have no intention of writing a letter of recommendation because I am not letting you go. After you finish the designs for The Vane, I need you to redesign some of the suites at the resort in Bazaruto—I've decided to purchase that place. Oh, you'd also need to decorate our new house."

"What new house?" Bay asked, utterly confused. "What are you talking about?"

"Well, the barn isn't suitable—Liv is too young to negotiate the walkway and those stairs. And, while I love your cottage, baby, it's a bit small for all three of us." His lips quirked into that sexy smile she loved so much. "And the elephants and penguins Liv is insisting I buy for her."

"What?"

"Hopefully, she's resigned to having stuffed animals but, because she's a tough negotiator and I can't seem to say no to her, who knows?"

Bay leaned forward, gripped his shirt and attempted to shake him. "Digby! What the hell are you talking about?"

Digby lifted his hand to stroke her face with his fingertips. "I'm still scared, Bay, but I'm more scared of living my life without you than I am of losing you. I love you so much, sweetheart."

"Uh…"

Was she really hearing what she was hearing? Or was she suffering from some sort of selective hearing?

"Would you mind repeating that?" she politely asked, pushing down on her chest to keep her heart from shoving through her skin.

"I love you. I love Liv," Digby told her, resting his forehead against hers. "Will you both be mine? For the rest of my life?"

Bay bit her bottom lip, blinking away her tears. Bay lifted her hand to his neck, needing to feel his warmth, his solidity. "Is this really happening?"

Digby looked around the ballroom and shrugged. "Not exactly where I thought I'd propose but…what the hell. So, what do you say, Bay?"

"To what?"

Digby smiled. "Wow, I'm really bad at this." He picked up her left hand and stroked her ring finger. "I'd like to put a ring on this finger, Bay. Because you don't seem to be grasping innuendo today, I want to put my ring on your finger, have your ring on mine. I want to marry you and I really, really hope you want to marry me."

Of course she wanted to marry him, to be his. "Are you sure, Digby?"

Digby nodded. "Very sure, sweetheart. Look, I accept that I am a bit of a mess, emotionally, and that I won't always get it right. But I promise to never run again, Bay. I promise to stick. And stay. I promise to work it out. And yeah, we'll fight but I promise that I will never punish you by withdrawing my love. I never break my promises, Bay.

"I'm not the man I was yesterday, a month ago, six months ago. You've made me better, Bay. I promise to love you with everything I am, all that I've got."

Bay stared at him, overwhelmed by his declaration, feeling like her heart was on a wild ride. She saw worry jump into his eyes, then fear. When she didn't speak, she saw him retreating, the light fading from his eyes. "I'm too late, aren't I?"

He started to rise but Bay gripped his shirt in her fist, twisting the material in her hand. "*Yes.* Yes, Dig, to everything. The new house, the job, the penguins and elephants, but only of the stuffed variety. A huge, shiny, yes, please, to becoming your wife."

She heard, and felt, his relief-tinged laughter. Burying her face in his neck, she wound her arms around it and breathed him in. "I can't wait to be yours, Dig."

Digby's broad hand stroked her back. "You have been, from the moment I first saw you. It just took my brain a while to catch up with my heart."

"I'm so very glad it did," Bay told him, pulling back to look into his lovely, love-filled eyes. "I love you so much, darling."

Digby's mouth drifted across hers. "I love you more, Bay. I always will."

And at that moment, hearing the words she and Liv often exchanged, she knew that he was, absolutely, the third point in their triangle, the compass point they'd been missing. Liv's new dad. Her best friend. Her love and her life.

In his eyes, she saw everything she'd ever need.

* * * * *

STRANDED
FOR ONE
SCANDALOUS
WEEK

NATALIE ANDERSON

For Heather—
thank you always for your support and cheer.
I hope you enjoy this one too!

CHAPTER ONE

MERLE JORDAN WAS surrounded by bubbles. White frothy ones filled the deep, wide bath, petite ones fizzed from the oversized champagne bottle she'd just opened, while the fragile glass bubbles of a sleek modern light fixture gleamed above her head. The glimmering orbs delighted her starved senses, bringing absolute bliss.

She opened the stunning glass doors which led to the balcony that stretched the length of the building and ended with a curling staircase that led down to the pool below. A massive moon hung in the sky like the biggest bubble of all, casting a rippling sweep of light across the private bay. Merle lit the candle beside the bath and switched off the pretty light overhead, indulging in the soft, muted glow of the large moon and small flame.

With a disbelieving giggle she wriggled out of her underwear. She'd barely sampled the champagne but this decadence wasn't something she'd experienced and it was heady. Merle didn't excel at self-care at the best of times and this was beyond beginner level. She'd graduated to expert in one go. Never before had she been in a bath so big, never had she seen a view so stunning, never had she stood naked and sipped champagne from a slender crystal glass. Never had she stolen time for herself.

The summer air was still warm but she couldn't resist the bubbles of the bath a moment longer. The glistening suds slipped over her like soft strokes of indulgence. Sliding deeper, Merle sipped her drink and breathed in the magnificent surroundings. She couldn't believe she was living in this 'holiday home'. She could bathe like this every night for the next six weeks if she wished.

It wasn't really a holiday home, it was a mega-mansion on Waiheke—an island less than an hour from Auckland, the largest city in New Zealand. Known as a playground for the wealthy, this property was a perfect example of the luxury homes hidden here. Incredibly private, it overlooked a beach with boat-only access and was furnished with an overflowing wine cellar, stunning swimming pool and spa. There was also a home gym, a cinema room, and even a single-lane bowling alley. The entire property was beautifully decorated with simple yet luxurious style. Richly coloured timber floors provided warmth and white paintwork offered crisp freshness, while soft-cushioned sofas and artfully placed occasional chairs invited relaxation. The gorgeous glazing of the house meant the entire building could be opened up to invite the outside in, and baskets with verdant plants accentuated that coastal, nature-loving style.

The place was ready for a magazine shoot at a moment's notice, Merle mused. Unusually for her, she liked the dearth of personal items in the decor; it made her feel it was more of a holiday venue and less as if she was encroaching on someone's private space. Besides, all those personal secrets were waiting to be discovered in the boxes currently filling the triple-car garage. She'd been contracted to sort and list their contents and prepare them either for storage or destruction.

She couldn't believe that such a property had sat unoccupied for over a year. It seemed wrong when so many people didn't have a home—including her. But she could hardly resent the obscenely wealthy owner's abandonment, given that the live-in requirement of the job gave her a roof over her head for a while. And, as it was Friday night, she'd decided it was okay to finally relax. Everyone deserved a treat after a hard week's work, right?

Sighing with pure, luxurious pleasure, she knelt up to replenish her champagne from the bottle she'd left on the ledge.

'Oh, hey, darling.'

The low, lazy murmur shocked her.

'Why are you naked in my bath?' he asked.

Half kneeling out of the bubbles, her hand stretched towards that champagne bottle, Merle froze, gaping at the man leaning against the doorjamb. For a second she only saw his eyes. They gleamed in the candlelight with an amber, almost animal warmth that didn't just dazzle, but actually stunned a woman into stillness.

Ashton Castle.

Merle breathed out, relieved because she'd instantly recognised him. He was in a photo downstairs, the one personal item on display in the place. He'd inherited this house when his father, Hugh, had died just over a year ago, but had ignored it since. Ash had been too busy to be bothered, right? He had his hands too full with every socialite or model or influencer who crossed his path. And they all said yes because not only was notorious playboy Ash Castle eye-wateringly rich, he was also appallingly good-looking.

Confronted by the reality, not a decades-old photo, Merle was stupefied. Tall, dazzling, *devastating*. She stared slack-jawed and wide-eyed at his long, muscular lines and stunningly sculpted face. She knew he also had that other irresistible-to-many facet to his nature—he was reckless. That was catnip to lots of women, wasn't it? They wanted to dance with danger, attempt to tame the untameable, bring the rich, ravishing, reckless playboy to heel…

But not Merle. She couldn't think of a worse combination.

She was sure his money, privilege and good looks meant it was too easy for him to get everything and everyone he wanted. That led to lazy arrogance and entitlement that meant the usual boundaries were ignored. She knew those sorts of men well. She'd been burned by one in her youth and she'd successfully avoided all of them since. Until now, when she was confronted with the worst of them all.

'Sweetheart?' Ash's gaze narrowed slightly.

Belatedly Merle realised she was up on her knees and, while there were masses of bubbles in the enormous bath, there weren't enough to cover her completely. Her breasts were exposed and quite possibly her...

She splashed down into the water so quickly she almost slipped right under. Desperately she threw her arms out to clutch the sides while drawing her knees up defensively at the same time. Another deep breath later, she wiped away the blob of frothy bubbles she could feel sliding down the side of her face.

Of all the people to have arrived unexpectedly. Of all the *times*. Of all the shocks.

And she couldn't stop staring. His dark grey tee hugged his broad shoulders and clung to the hard planes of his chest, while his black jeans emphasised the length and strength of his legs. They were faded in the thigh area, the paler patches drawing her eye to the core of his masculinity. She snapped her gaze from his slim hips back up past his broad shoulders, but his face only added to that impression of absolute masculinity. The shadow on his jaw highlighted its sharp, angular line. Beneath his straight nose, his sensually full lips curved into a weary but appreciative smile. And then there were those mesmerising eyes—a warm brown with an almost leonine hint in the amber. Everything about him screamed virile male. And the truly horrific thing was that her body—her weak, treacherous body—seemed to want nothing more than to melt in a purely sexual reaction. It was a primal, utterly basic response that was so new, so surprising, she couldn't pull her scattered thoughts together enough to scream at him to get out of there.

'Why are you here?' he asked negligently, still leaning against the doorjamb, apparently unfazed by her nudity and her panicked slide back into the water.

Of course he wasn't bothered. He was well used to women baring all around him.

Merle burned, mortified. That should be *her* question. But she wasn't great at speaking up, even when necessary. The truth was Leo Castle—Ash's half-brother and the man who'd confirmed her contract here—had said she'd have the place to herself, that she could take six weeks or more on the project if necessary. The prospect of having a home for that long had been incredible. She desperately needed to recover her affairs. She had no regrets about going into debt for her grandfather's health, but now that he was gone she had to claw her way out of the deep financial hole she'd been left in.

'Did someone send you, Miss...?'

Merle stiffened, perceiving slight insolence in his tone and finally found her voice. 'Leo Castle—'

'Leo hired you?' Ashton Castle's eyebrows rose, as if he was surprised. 'How did he know I was coming?' He looked perplexed as he muttered, apparently to himself, 'But he knows I don't do prostitutes.'

Merle sat stupefied all over again, suddenly unable to feel whether the water was hot or cold because everything had gone numb. Had he just said *prostitutes*?

Her heart pounded. Did he think she'd been hired to *entertain* him? That she was waiting naked in this bath with this champagne, ready to...to *please* him? A humiliation bomb exploded—bursting every one of her happy bubbles that'd been fizzing only five minutes before. And then a cloud of something else rose inside—something sinful and hot and that she couldn't bear to define.

'I think there's been a mistake,' she choked, so awash with embarrassment she was unable to continue.

'Yeah.' He strolled nearer and picked up the bottle of champagne from the edge of the bath, studying her even more closely, more *directly*—an open, unashamedly sexual appraisal. 'But worse ones have been made.'

With a twist of his full lips he cocked his head and cast that searing glance over the champagne label. '*This* was not a mistake, however. This was a nice choice.' He glanced back at her, laughter glinting in his eyes. 'At nine hundred dollars a bottle, you're not afraid to set your value high.'

What? Merle nearly choked again.

'It cost how much?' Her voice faded in a welter of shyness.

Ash smiled and Merle just about died. The transformation from serious sex god, to *smiling* sex god made every muscle inside her squeeze. She could only stare—yet again rendered stupid. He met her gaze square on. But as her brain slowly came back online she registered a tired edge in his eyes that meant that his smile didn't quite ring true. Drawing in a deep breath, she dragged her gaze back to the bottle and regretted ever thinking it was okay to accept the offer to have anything she wanted from the cellar.

'I had no idea. I'm sorry,' she mumbled, even more mortified. *Nine hundred dollars?* It was incredible to her that a bottle of anything could possibly cost that much. 'Mr Castle said I could—'

'Look, sweetheart, you fill your bath with it for all I care,' Ash interrupted her embarrassed explanation with an almost dismissive boredom. 'Bathe in every last drop if you want.'

But then his gaze skimmed across her shoulders and something else gleamed again.

She had the scandalous sensation that he was envisaging licking the droplets from her skin. And she *wanted* him to.

Merle—who'd never wanted any man near her—suddenly wanted the biggest playboy of all to do what he wanted with his tongue and her skin, and how was it possible that she was slithering beneath some wordless spell?

Instinctively sinking lower into the water, Merle felt that awful softening deep inside. It was shockingly inappropriate, and she was appalled by herself as much as she was by him. Merle didn't feel hot and bothered by *anyone*. Yet she was unable to tear her gaze away from Ash Castle. It was as if she'd met a mythological creature—something rare and impossible. People simply didn't look like this in real life. Not with glinting strength and sinfully arching dark eyebrows and casually tousled, slightly too long hair that fell just so. Not with sharply defined jawlines, even when masked by the stubble of a long day, not with full, sensual mouths that curved upwards in invitation even when in repose.

But now his expression clouded as he gazed back at her. As she watched—too flummoxed to be able to do anything else—a heated heaviness filled the atmosphere between them. Neither of them moved. Merle didn't even breathe as his expression intensified. If she weren't already going crazy, she'd think he was as captivated by her as she was him.

'Do you like the taste?' he muttered. 'Because I like the look. Very much.'

She simply couldn't reply.

'And I must be tired,' he muttered as he lifted the champagne and took a long swig straight from the overpriced bottle, his hot gaze not leaving her face. 'I'm so tempted—'

'I've been hired by Mr Castle to sort out your father's collections,' Merle blurted quickly, knowing her cheeks were blazing with a dreadful blush.

Ash stilled for a second, then slowly set the bottle back down on the side of the bath. 'Pardon?'

She didn't believe the laziness in his tone, not when she saw the lethal alertness that had sprung into his eyes.

'Mr Leo Castle hired me to sort out your father's things,' Merle mumbled miserably, barely able to inject volume into her voice and utterly unable to hold his gaze. 'I'm an archivist. I've been staying here since Wednesday. I'm working on the papers in the boxes first.'

'An archivist?'

She hesitated, taking in a breath to summon the equilibrium to explain further. She hadn't spoken this much in days. 'Aside from the rare books, there are several dozen boxes stacked in the garage. I'm also cataloguing the art and the wine collections, though expert valuers will deal with those once I've done the detailed lists. I'm only doing the storage and destruction plan for the papers.' She paused for breath and glanced up to find he wasn't really listening to her explanation anyway.

'That's why you're in my bath?'

'I didn't know it was your bath,' she said. 'I didn't want to use the main bedroom. I thought this was one of the guest rooms.'

Something flickered in his expression before he shut it back to bland. 'I guess in recent years that is what it has been. But a long time ago it was my room.' He stared at her a little longer. 'I feel surprisingly disappointed.'

Her jaw dropped. She ought to be outraged, but the awful thing was she actually felt a touch flattered. Maybe the champagne had already had more of an effect on her than she'd realised?

'How long are you here for?' His forehead wrinkled.

She had to swallow before she could answer. 'Six weeks. But it might run a little longer as there's more than was initially listed...'

He lifted one of the large, fluffy white towels from the

rack and placed it beside the champagne bottle. 'I didn't realise Leo had got that underway.'

'Mr Castle seemed to think the place would be empty for the duration of my contract.'

'Ordinarily he would've been right.' Ash's mouth tightened. 'Maybe it's best if we continue this conversation downstairs. Ten minutes, okay?'

She stared at him, shocked. Wasn't he going to apologise for thinking she'd been hired as his evening's entertainment?

He stared back at her, his head tilting as he read her expression, and that wicked smile flashed again, banishing what had barely been a hint of remorse. 'Unless you're happy to negotiate terms in here…?'

'Of course not,' she mumbled.

'Don't be embarrassed. I'm not.' He seemed amused by the colour she knew was climbing her cheeks again. 'Sex work is legal in this country.'

'I'm aware, but it's not my chosen profession.' She wanted to slide right under the bubbles, she really did.

He shrugged carelessly. 'Can you blame me for the mistake? The scene was perfectly set—candles, champagne, and you were beautifully positioned to maximise the effect of your…assets.'

His gaze didn't waver from hers—didn't drop to assess those 'assets' once more. And right now, those assets felt tight and achy and it was appalling.

'It's not unusual for you to find a woman just waiting for you in your bath or bed?' she asked huskily, shocking herself with the question. She never talked to anyone about such things.

'Not unusual in the least.' He grinned, the devilish lights in his eyes twinkling. 'It's something I enjoy. A lot.'

But he didn't pay them to be there. They arrived by choice—because of *want*.

Merle glared at him, horrified by her own reaction, her own wild thoughts. Since when did she feel anything thing like attraction to someone so…so…*smugly* sexual?

'Pleasure is something to be valued and appreciated,' he added almost piously. 'Not embarrassed about.'

And, with that pithy piece of sexual arrogance, he left.

Merle waited, almost completely submerged, until he'd vanished. The second he closed the door she scrambled out of the slippery bath. She dressed quickly in loose jeans and a tee shirt and threw on a baggy sweatshirt for good measure, despite still burning from that mortifying moment. She left her hair in its damp twist on top of her head and checked her reflection. For a millisecond she stared at her make-up-free skin and wished she was something she wasn't.

Fool. Why suddenly think of mascara and lipstick? She did *not* want his interest. Judging by the pictures she'd seen in the media, she wasn't anything like the women he usually met and that was a good thing. And, while she'd like a boyfriend one day, Ash Castle wasn't ever anyone's *boyfriend*. He was a lover, a seducer, an unrepentant playboy who doubtless left a mountain of broken hearts behind him. Merle's wasn't going to be one of them. As if he'd ever be interested anyway. It was only *context* that had made that glint flash in his face for those few seconds. She shrank in embarrassment, refusing to think about what he may or may not have seen of her in that bath. Or what he'd have thought.

'Are you usually based on Waiheke or in Auckland?' Ash called from where he stood in the centre of the atrium the second she appeared on the staircase. 'Because it's late. I'm not sure how we'll get you back to Auckland now the last ferry has already left.'

Merle descended slowly, stopping three steps from the bottom so she could keep her distance yet be able to look him directly in the eyes. She couldn't leave here. Not tonight or any other night for the next six weeks.

'I came here to do some work. I need space and peace,' he added when she didn't reply, and his gaze grew pointed.

'You'll have that,' she muttered, hoping to assure him despite the sudden racing of her pulse. 'You won't even know I'm here.'

His mouth tightened, then curved into a slow, deliberate smile that yet again didn't quite reach his eyes. 'Won't I? When you're naked in my bath and sleeping in my bed?'

She stared, sure he'd worded that deliberately to put those inappropriate images in her mind and unsettle her all over again. 'I'll switch to another room, of course.'

She tried to breathe away the blush she felt beating across her face and trained her own gaze a little lower. It wasn't the wisest move. He had the most perfect cheekbones; they were like blades, angling towards the arrogant set of his chin and his full mouth. And she really shouldn't look at his mouth. The full sensuality of it made her think of hunger and kisses. She forced her focus back up to his eyes. They were intent upon her, but within their heated gaze there was more than unhappiness growing. There was misery. *Why?*

'Delay your work for a week,' he said abruptly. 'Head home for a holiday. Full pay, of course.'

She instantly forgot her curiosity. Head home? To *where* exactly? She stared, unable to think of a reply as her anger built. Why did he need this enormous house all to himself? Why this one, when he had all those others? Aside from being a whizzy finance billionaire in his own right, she knew he was the heir to the Castle Holdings luxury apartment empire in Australia. His father had amassed a huge amount of property over there—where Ash Castle was supposed to be living right now.

But the man standing before her was obviously used to getting everything his way. To 'full paying' away any annoying inconveniences. And, not so deep beneath her surface, she smarted from the sting of his rejection. It was stupid, especially given the fact that she was well used to rejection.

For once in his life Ash Castle wasn't getting everything he wanted. At least, not tonight. He'd arrived on a whim and it was too bad for him that she was already here—under contract and with nowhere else to go.

'I don't need a holiday,' she said stiffly. 'I need to do my job. Which means I need to stay here.'

'Until tomorrow.' He nodded. 'Then you can go home for a week.'

She gritted her teeth. 'Unfortunately, I'm between residences at present.' She hated having to inform him of the deeply personal fact.

'Between residences?' he echoed bluntly, his gaze sharpening. 'You mean you're homeless?'

She tensed even more. 'As I spend my time going from contract to contract, I've no need to set up a permanent residence.'

It was a lie. Very few jobs were live-in and the only reason she'd got this contract was because she'd been able to leap on a plane at short notice. Sonja, the manager of the archival company she worked for, had been going to do it but her early pregnancy had been reassessed as high risk and she'd asked Merle to step in at the last minute.

Unsurprisingly, Ash Castle stared disbelievingly, making her feel as if yet more mortifying explanation was necessary. She'd spoken more in the last five minutes than she had all week and her voice was still rusty.

'Archivists don't get paid incredibly well,' she muttered.

'You amaze me.' That untamed gleam glinted in his eyes and his lips twitched.

An odd little fire in her ignited. There was no need for him to be facetious.

'Plenty of incredibly important jobs are low-paid.' Her heart thudded at her daring. Merle didn't stand up to anyone. Certainly not a man like this. Her grandmother would've torn strips off her if she'd seen her even look at him.

'Is archival work incredibly important? I wasn't aware.'

She had the feeling there were a lot of important things he was unaware of.

He was watching her closely and his sudden smile was both irreverent and tantalising. 'Do you think there are things you can teach me?'

With that soft-spoken drawl he revealed himself completely. Jaded. Experienced. Cynical. Incorrigible. Everything she wasn't. But yes, she could teach him some things. Manners, for a start.

'It's not my job to teach you anything,' she said with a bravery she was far from feeling. 'You're a grown man and I'm sure you'll be able to figure things out for yourself. Eventually.'

For the merest moment Merle basked while he stared at her, his mouth slightly ajar. She ought to be cautious, as if she'd just prodded a sleeping dragon, yet she was strangely exhilarated.

'If you're prepared to delay the completion of the archival process and pay for me to stay in a nearby hotel and holiday for the week, while on full pay,' she said warily, feeling a wholly foreign confidence trickle in her veins, 'then of course I'll do as you wish and leave first thing in the morning. However, it's a weekend in the height of summer and this is a small, popular island with not that many accommodation options. Do you think you'll find me a place?'

He stared at her for a long second. His mouth compressed. 'You want *me* to find you a place?'

'*You* want me to leave.' She couldn't hold his gaze and found she needed to study the floor intently as that damned fire beat across her face. 'Alternatively, you could be the one to stay elsewhere.'

'What?' He sounded flummoxed.

A hitherto dormant imp of mischievousness took over her mouth. 'Would that put you out?' She darted a glance up at him and the rest spilled out softly. 'Are you not used to working for what you want?'

There was another moment in which he just stared at her. That unhappy emotion had vanished from his eyes, and there was only gleamingly sharp speculation now.

'Oh, I work hard to get what I want,' he said pointedly. 'And I always get it.'

How nice to be him. But as he held her gaze with a fierce intensity, Merle's bubble of bravado popped. Breaking into a sweat at her temerity, she dropped her gaze and surreptitiously watched him pull a phone from his pocket. It was a latest release, squillion-dollar tech toy. Of course.

'It's late to be making calls.' She worried her lower lip, already regretting her runaway, rogue tongue moment. She should have stayed quiet. She couldn't afford to lose this job. 'I—'

'But not too late to check an online bookings app,' he interrupted before she could apologise.

Merle watched, partly glad because he didn't deserve her apology. As he tapped and swiped the screen over the course of the next six minutes, his frown deepened and his jawline hardened. Merle's heart raced as his expression turned positively rigid.

'You're going to have to stay,' he finally gritted.

Was it bad to relish the fact that the man couldn't get his way? Doubtless it was a rare occurrence for him. And a *very* rare victory for her. A thrill shivered through her. She'd stood up to him and she'd won.

'You stay in my old room. I'll take the master suite.' He squared his shoulders and his smile was bitter-edged. 'Might as well exorcise all the demons while I'm here.' He lifted his gaze to ensnare hers once more, his lips twisting in a mocking smile. 'You'll have to work extra hard now you know I'll be here watching you.'

Her sliver of success melted in the face of what could only be described as a...*promise*. A veiled, heated, *inappropriate* promise.

Her pulse thickened and she regretted his change of mind. Wouldn't it be better for her to be as *far* away from him as possible while he was here? What had she been *thinking*? She'd wanted to win one over on him—the kind of guy who got everything his way all of the time. 'I thought you wanted space.'

She hadn't meant to say anything more but somehow it slipped out.

He regarded her beneath half-lowered lids. Merle found she was unable to move beneath the intensity of his gaze. Was this how he did it? Seduction by a simple stare?

'I thought I did,' he murmured. 'But I also enjoy watching interesting things, Miss...'

He didn't know her name. He'd made all kinds of assumptions and he didn't even know her name.

'Merle Jordan,' she said stiffly. And she wasn't 'interesting'.

'I'm Ash Castle.' He mock-bowed. 'But you already knew that.'

She nodded. It had been his arrogant, own-it-all air that had given him away but she awkwardly offered a more polite explanation. 'Your photo's in the study.'

A young Ash with his parents, captured on the beach just outside. His eyes widened, exposing a flash of that other emotion before his expression shuttered again.

Inside, she was feverishly panicked about getting

through this. She'd avoid him entirely for the next week. Fortunately, she was well used to staying out of sight and silent. All those years of hiding like a mouse in the wings of her mother's performances would finally come in handy. Not to mention hiding from her grandmother's shouting. It wouldn't be hard at all to avoid him in a house this size, plus she had all those boxes to bury herself in.

Yet, intriguingly, as he hesitated his expression turned more than serious, more than sombre, more akin to misery. It didn't suit him. A tinge within Merle tugged her down the stairs towards him.

'No one knows I'm here,' he said. 'Not even Leo. I'd like to keep it that way.'

'Of course,' she mumbled.

He didn't realise she had no one to tell and she was far removed from anyone in his world. But she did need to stay here. Not only did she have nowhere else to go, but this was also an important job for her professionally. She had debt to clear and a future to forge.

'You won't even know I'm here.' But as she earnestly attempted to reassure him, she saw the look in his eyes morph once more.

CHAPTER TWO

You won't even know I'm here.

Well, *that* was impossible. Ash scowled. How was he going to forget the sight of her gleaming in the moonlight like a welcome beacon? She'd been rising out of that bath like a dryad at a magical spring, complete with champagne fountain and a flushing allure that had transfixed him. Only he'd been so jaded he'd mistaken her for a woman of the night and said so. Even for him it had been inappropriate, an unthinking utterance of the first possibility his tired brain had come up with. *Wishful* thinking, if he was being completely honest. The fantasy of her waiting nymph-like to give him pleasure had made perfect, albeit impossible, sense. He should've held his outrageous, rebellious tongue, but he never yet had.

And now?

He *needed* to be alone, but he'd never been going to stay a full week. It was going to be a couple of days max. He'd just wanted her well out of the way so he could be clear of any human contact while he absorbed the shock of what had been done to the place. But now he was stuck with her. Yet he wasn't feeling as irritated about that as he had been only a second ago.

Yesterday's headline should've been easy to ignore. The newspaper article comparing 'playboy rebel Ash' to his il-legitimate half-brother, Leo, the 'responsible leader', had been rubbish. Yet it had forced him into the action he'd been deferring for months. Almost a year ago, Ash had in-herited everything. His father, Hugh Castle, had refused to recognise Leo right to the end. He'd also refused to believe Ash's own refusal to be involved in the family business. No matter that they'd been estranged for a full decade and that Ash hadn't once set foot inside the company headquarters or any of the family properties in all that time. Or that he'd deliberately set out to make his own fortune—taking risks purely to have the satisfaction of being more successful to spite his father.

None of that had mattered. His father, as always, didn't listen, didn't care and only did what *he* wanted. As Ash was Hugh's first-born, legitimate male heir, it was onto his un-willing shoulders that the company had been foisted. But Ash had immediately moved to ensure *all* Hugh Castle's heirs got their fair share. He'd intended to liquidate all as-sets and split the wealth. But Leo had asked for a different solution. It wasn't that Ash had 'abandoned responsibility', *forcing* Leo to take over Hugh's company, Leo had insisted. He'd been determined to take over. Ash had simply stood aside and let him. How could he say no when Leo had been denied so much by the Castle family already?

Ash had half expected his half-brother to raze Castle Holdings to the ground. He wouldn't have blamed him, in fact he would've enjoyed watching. But Leo hadn't done that. Leo had obviously inherited integrity from his mother. Maybe growing up away from the malignant force that had been their father had benefited him.

Whereas Ash was utterly his father's son. Careless. Ruthless. Selfish.

But there was one particular problem Ash *had* been avoiding. This last personal property—the former family holiday home on Waiheke Island. The press would never think to look for him here. No one would, which was why he should've realised the idea of Leo arranging a woman for him was ridiculous. It wasn't in his ultra-responsible half-brother's playbook. Truthfully, it wasn't in his either. And

this woman was no courtesan. She couldn't underline that
fact more boldly than with the monstrously oversized clothes
she'd hurriedly thrown on. But the swamping swallow-her-
whole trousers and sweatshirt were too late. Ash had seen
her naked and one part of him had already made meticu-
lously detailed plans for her very luscious body.

'The place is large enough for us to avoid each other
completely,' Merle Jordan reiterated in that shy, low, sexy-
as-sin voice.

Ash stared as the colour in her luminous skin increased
and her beautiful brown eyes darkened. His gloom evaporated as his intuition purred. He had to suppress a satisfied smile.

She was *bothered*. It wasn't just because of what he'd
said or done. The underlying cause was as obvious as it was
reciprocated by him. Instant interest—the immediate recognition of physical, pleasurable, possibilities. Admittedly,
they were possibilities she seemed determined to reject.
Yet *she* was the one who'd insisted on staying here. Who'd
insisted he discover for himself how impossible it was to
find other accommodation on the island. Who'd wanted
to teach him a lesson. It had actually pleased him to learn
that he'd be able to sell even this ultra-expensive property
quickly and easily, given the popularity of all pricing levels of accommodation. So her plan hadn't only backfired,
it'd also had a beneficial consequence.

'Don't you think?' she added.

Maybe there could be more than one benefit. But then he
saw the anxiety lurking in the backs of those beautiful eyes.

*She's bothered because she's worried about being home-
less, you idiot.*

At his silence that blush swamped her face again. She'd
almost stammered as she'd pushed past her shyness to
fight for her place here. It had cost her to admit to him the
truth of her circumstances. The confession hadn't been an

attempt at manipulation, but rather dragged out of her in raw embarrassment. It drew a response from deep within him too. The feeling shimmered again now and reminded him of another woman who'd also been alone and vulnerable and awkwardly shy. One who he'd stepped forward to help. But back then the flare of protectiveness within Ash had ended in a destructive mess.

Back. Away.

He should leave. Yet the temptation to do the absolute opposite almost overwhelmed him. He wanted to reach out and slide his fingertips down her neck, to push aside that baggy sweatshirt and explore her skin, to draw her close and kiss her past comfortable and right on to pleasured. The concentration required to stop himself made him ache. This chemistry at first sight was explosive. For all of his success with women, it *wasn't* something he was used to. He played around but never foolishly. Now it was as if a fever had taken hold. He forced his gaze beyond her, focusing on the house to pull himself together.

It was exactly the shock he needed.

The beach house had always stolen his breath—one moonlit glimpse of the inky water was enough to invoke that old sense of freedom. But the house itself had been altered beyond recognition—entire walls were gone, replaced with larger, newer elements. He'd yet to see all the renovations, but what he could see was so changed. That first feeling of freedom was strangled in seconds by anger. Regret. Self-recrimination. The last time he'd been here was the last time he'd seen his mother alive. And he'd disappointed her so badly.

He refused to remember. But he'd been refusing to remember for a long time now. And after yesterday's article?

The piece had celebrated his 'sainted' father before speculating and comparing his disparate sons' lives yet again. Ash still couldn't fathom how his father had been held in such high esteem for so long. Even after Ash had exposed Hugh Castle's cheating soul to the world by providing Leo with a DNA sample to prove he was Hugh's illegitimate son, his old man's other successes had overridden any punishment he should have faced. Hugh had been miraculously forgiven not just by his beloved 'society circles', but by the media and court of public opinion too. Even though the lying old jerk had spent years denying Leo's birthright, years destroying Leo's mother's reputation.

Who could blame Hugh for a few transgressions when he'd suffered the heartbreak of a dying wife for so long?

As though his father were the victim. Empathetic explanations were offered and forgiveness assured. But not by Ash. Never by him. The falsity of it all was something he couldn't forget. Indeed, the abbreviation of his name was apt. Because all Ash could offer were the acrid, smoking remnants of what had once been. And all he wanted to do was destroy what was left of his father's legacy. For him this place on Waiheke Island was the core—the most obvious construct of his father's deceit. It was the ultimate symbol of his father's ability to build over the truth with nothing but a fabrication of perfection.

That article had forced all those feelings up and he'd finally come to face the poisonous betrayal of his father's last actions. To say his final, bitter goodbye so he could forget it all for ever. To finish it, so Leo didn't need to trouble. But his capable half-brother had already stepped in. He'd hired Merle Jordan to sort out the vast personal collections that had been dumped here in the aftermath of their father's death. Was there any need for Ash to stay here at all?

Bitterness and an acrid sense of futility swamped him— scouring off the old scab and exposing the raw wound he'd been hiding for years. He'd been helpless the last time he was here, too—watching his desperately unwell mother. Disappointing her beyond redemption. But there *was* one last thing he needed to do for her—despite his inability to ever secure her forgiveness. And that task wasn't right for a stranger's hands—not even the soft, light, careful hands of the archivist standing before him. It was a job only for Ash. He couldn't avoid it any longer. He had enough regrets regarding his mum already. So he had to stay for a day or so at least to accomplish this last for her—he'd go through her things and dispose of them himself.

Like most people, Ash infinitely preferred pleasure to pain. And the memories he couldn't restrain now were the worst of his life. So what else could he do but glance again at the welcome radiance of his initially unwanted house-mate?

The luscious Merle Jordan's hair was still mostly tied up in that messy pile while a few wispy curls lingered from the damp heat of the bath. She wore not an ounce of make-up but her pouty lips were a tantalising pink and her eyes were like dark pools in secret caves—their depth indeterminable, possibly dangerous, but still so damn inviting. His senses begged him to step closer, to stare deeper, to touch and discover if she was as soft and yielding as she looked. Sex had always been an escape and he needed escape more than anything in this bitterest of returns.

'I'm hungry, Merle.' He couldn't resist voicing his thoughts.

Her eyes widened and he could've sworn the pulse at the base of her neck fluttered faster.

'Is there anything delicious to eat?' he added lazily, unable to resist the pleasure of watching her react to such a very little tease.

She swallowed. 'Um…'

'Or do I have to find that out for myself as well?'

He suppressed the smirk at her visible flare of irritation.

'There's…' Her voice faded away.

'Not much?' he gathered drily, wondering how much

more it would take to provoke the real response he just knew she was thinking.

Her expression turned mutinous. Her lashes fluttering her eyes a direct stare into his pitiful soul.

'Didn't you bring anything with you?'

He smiled. It was the slightest of stands with a hint of scorn. She thought he was spoiled and, yes, that was exactly what he was. He'd make no apologies for it or for any of his other faults. But he liked that tiny glimpse of her spirit. He wanted to see more of it. More of her—all over.

Frankly, he didn't expect to have *all kinds* of appetites roused here and now.

But as he gazed at her, suffering her wide-eyed scrutiny, something else tugged inside him. A very small desire to do a little better. He abruptly turned and stalked to the kitchen. But he was keenly aware of her following him with that intriguingly subversive look barely hidden in her expression.

Once there, he scoped the shelves, but there were limited signs of her presence. In the fridge there was a single block of cheese. On one shelf in the pantry there were a few small tins of fish, a couple of packets of instant noodles and a box of crackers. Just looking at her pathetic supplies made his stomach rumble.

'What do you exist on?' he grumbled, glancing over to where she stood on the other side of the large kitchen counter, primly holding her hands together and pursing her very kissable lips.

'I have sufficient supplies.'

'Sufficient?' he echoed drily. 'How sad. Why have merely sufficient when you can have *satisfying*?'

Colour tinged her cheeks again. He couldn't resist acting up the outrageousness he knew she expected from him. She thought he was an irresponsible playboy? He was quite happy to perform if it meant he kept seeing her blush.

'Instant noodles.' He groaned. They weren't even decent flavours.

'They're delicious.'

'I prefer my noodles hand-pulled and fresh.' He knew he
sounded awful, but it was too much to keep from pulling
another eye-roll from her. He poked through the tins and
came across a small stack of individual steamed puddings—
complete with caramel sauce. They were little single-serve
tubs to go in the microwave.

'Oh, here we go.' He glanced at her slyly. 'So you're not
afraid to spoil yourself in secret?'

Of course she wasn't. Hadn't he just caught her indulging in a luxurious candle-lit bubble bath while sipping overpriced champagne? She had a decadent, sensual streak.

She stared at him, those eyes widened in shock. Then
he saw her chin tilt.

'You want to eat my little dessert?' Her voice was impossibly breathy.

No. He wanted to eat her. And they both knew it. He
stared at her, stilled by the glimpse of steel in her eyes.
And of heat.

'You think you can just swoop in and take what you
want?' she added, despite the blush mottling not just her
face but her neck too. 'No matter who it belongs to?'

Wasn't she a deliciously pointy creature when she let
herself out?

'I'll always take what I want from someone who's willing to offer it to me,' he assured her.

He watched her warring with whether to speak again or
not. He couldn't move, desperate for her to say it.

'I'm not offering anything,' she finally claimed.

'Not even one little bite of pudding?' he drawled.
'Damned if I'm going to spend the week living like I've
been shipwrecked.'

She shouldn't settle for that either.

'You can't cope with a constraint on your appetite even for a little while?' she asked.

The little punch pleased him an inordinate amount.

'I don't like to be denied decent sustenance,' he answered lazily. 'I like delicious. It doesn't have to be a lot, but it does have to be quality.'

'A man like you will always want more than a morsel of perfection,' she said quietly. 'You wouldn't stop at one of those puddings, you'd want *all* of them.'

A morsel of perfection? He leaned against the bench and laughed. 'You think I have a voracious appetite?'

She slowly nodded, her baleful, brilliant gaze locked on him. 'Absolutely.'

'That's where you're wrong, my sweet,' he said lightly and then shot straight to the crux of the matter. 'I only ever have one bite. One night with a woman.'

She blinked. 'Only one night? Wow,' she muttered in that husky voice. 'That's too mean of you. Are you afraid she'll get bored if you let her stick around for longer?'

Ash regarded her steadily, masking the adrenalin and anticipation burgeoning inside. Merle Jordan had gone from a mortified, tongue-tied bundle of embarrassment, to a worthy opponent displaying claws and wit and he wanted to see so much more of it from her. 'I'm not afraid,' he countered softly. 'I'm merely protecting her from the inevitable heartbreak.'

'Oh, so it's *chivalry*,' she mock-marvelled, even as she dropped her gaze from his. 'How heroic of you to save her from yourself.'

'Quite,' he purred. She was an absolute, intriguing challenge. 'Now, Ms Jordan.' He held up one of the single-serve puddings. 'Are we going to label and lock away what's mine and label and lock away what's yours, or are we going to pool resources and share?'

At that, she gazed back up at him, despite her blushing

breathiness. He could see the tremble in her fingers she was trying to hide and he respected the effort it took for her to hold his gaze. He willed her to say whatever pithy thing she was thinking. Because she was *definitely* thinking and he ached to know what about.

'Exactly what resources are *you* planning to bring to this party?' she finally asked.

Suddenly he had plans. Lots of very good, very pleasurable plans.

He'd thought he wanted to be alone to face this final goodbye and dispose of his mother's things. But perhaps, while he was here, alone was the one thing he *shouldn't* be. This disapproving woman might be the perfect antidote to take his mind off the mess of emotion this place conjured within. He *badly* needed distraction from the task he'd been dreading for almost a decade and here she was in bountiful, curvaceous perfection. Maybe he could tempt her out of her prickly shell? He could disarm her stand-offishness, break down her reserve…

If he got her to deign to talk to him? If he got her to laugh, that would be a bonus point for sure. And if she dined with him that would be a total win. He relished each possible challenge in a game he suddenly ached to play.

'Haven't you figured it out yet, Merle?' he teased, assuming full arrogance and amusement. 'I'll bring everything you could ever want.'

CHAPTER THREE

FIRST THING IN the morning, Merle had shut herself in the study with one of the many boxes from the stacks in the multi-car garage. While she wasn't contracted to work weekends, given the circumstances it seemed a good way of staying out of sight and out of trouble. The enormous wooden table in the cavernous room was perfect for sorting the mountain of papers and the work would occupy her completely for weeks.

Unfortunately, the floor-to-ceiling windows spanning the length of the study overlooked not just the gorgeous sea, but also the stunning infinity pool. And Ash Castle had been making the most of that pool for *hours*.

Last night he'd said he was here to work, but to Merle it didn't look as if he was doing anything other than hardcore exercising. He swam length after length. Every so often he emerged to perform push-ups and burpees on the beautifully landscaped deck. Given he was clad in nothing but black swim shorts, it was hard not to notice his lean, muscled strength. But it was his single-minded focus that fascinated her more. Intensely driven, he pushed himself like a man possessed.

Merle couldn't stop herself watching, equally impressed and aghast as he brought weights out from the gym and lined up the kettle bells into some sort of terrifying poolside circuit. He seemed determined to exhaust himself—which took a lot of effort because apparently the man was ultra-marathon-fit. Maybe the work he meant was some kind of one-week extreme make-over? Was he was going to be modelling or something? Or did he have some super-hot date next weekend that he wanted to be in peak shape for?

Merle couldn't think of anything worse.

Worse than that, she couldn't think of anything *else*. Ash Castle infuriatingly appeared in every thought—her sly mind kept replaying that mortifying moment when he'd walked in on her in his bath. And she kept seeing the wicked laughter in his eyes, the outrageousness in his tone…but the glimpse of tiredness and the fleeting depth of discomfort intrigued her even more. She suspected the man was more complicated than his superficial perfection presented. To make matters even worse she'd actually dreamt about him.

I'm hungry, Merle.

His frank admission had meant something else and her suddenly unreliable body had responded so inappropriately.

Everything you'd ever want.

She knew he meant sexually. And, as inexperienced as she was, she knew he *wasn't*. He'd deliver.

Annoyed with her basic instinct fixation, Merle pulled more papers from the box, determined to regain her customary indifference to men and the thought of sex in general. Men and Merle didn't mix. Ever. Actually, *people* and Merle rarely mixed. It wasn't surprising; she'd had an unusual childhood—hiding in the wings of her mother's shows, then suppressed by her strict disciplinarian grandmother who'd never really wanted her, then isolated at school, where her only escape had been hours at second-hand stalls with her quiet grandfather. She'd become even more isolated while caring for him. But now things were going to change and as soon as she'd got herself on a firm financial footing she'd feel braver about moving forward. Getting this job done would help immeasurably. Squaring her shoulders, she focused on the boxes. Ash Castle was a distraction she couldn't afford.

It turned out Hugh Castle had been old-school—keeping an extensive collection of everything from business files to correspondence, to orders of service from state functions, to menus from society weddings, to feature articles—mostly about himself. It wasn't surprising. The man had been massively successful. She labelled each item and inputted the details into the database she'd set up. But she still couldn't help thinking about his eldest son just outside. Reportedly, the cause of the division between Hugh and Ash had been Ash's wild lifestyle—all reckless partying and playboy rebellion. But Ash had forged his own success through high finance and venture capital—risky deals that had paid off. He had the gift.

Of course he did.

When Hugh died a year ago there'd been speculation regarding who'd inherit the vast estate—the wayward acknowledged son or the illegitimate son Hugh had refused to recognise. Ash had notoriously declined anything and everything to do with his father for years, yet even so it had stunned people to see Leo, the son Hugh had always denied, taking over the management of the flagship property company Castle Holdings.

Merle's own curiosity burgeoned, exacerbated by the physicality of the man outside the window. Why had Leo, not Ash, taken over? In a flash of weakness she typed his name into an online search engine—but it was the images that caught her attention. As she scrolled down the never-ending expanse of photos her stomach knotted. There were brunettes, blondes, redheads, women with long hair, bobs or elfin crops, thin and curvy and everything in between... The only thing they had in common was their smug, 'look at me' smiles. Merle sharply inhaled, staving off the acidic emotion. Surely she wasn't jealous?

Apparently Ash Castle had dated a huge, eclectic number of women over the last decade. Of course he had—wasn't it 'one night' only for him? Indeed, rarely did one woman feature in more than a few shots. Yet, while they all wore that satisfied smile, the look in *his* eyes didn't reflect the same. The gleam wasn't desire, more like resentment, and in many he'd raised his hand to block the blinding flash or push away the paparazzi blocking his path. The photos went back years, documenting a familiarity with a party lifestyle Merle hadn't experienced. She didn't want to. She liked her life as it was—*safe*.

She shut down the web browser. The pointless search hadn't assuaged her fascination. If anything, she was more curious. Ash didn't just operate in a different world, but a whole other stratosphere. She glanced again at the family photo on the mantlepiece in the study. He stood between his parents in front of the beach. He looked about ten in the picture, but his eyes were unmistakable. Merle thought it interesting that, despite their estrangement, Hugh Castle had put this one personal picture pride of place in his holiday home.

She glanced out of the window and saw Ash swimming yet more lengths. Envy rippled over her. The afternoon heat had seeped into the study but she couldn't open the doors the way she had earlier in the week. Not with Ash only yards away and her determined to remain invisible. But it would have been nice to take a dip. Instead, she adjusted the air conditioning so it basically blasted ice at her.

Once she was finished here she'd sneak up to her suite for the evening. The room upstairs was opulent with a comfortable study area and balcony overlooking the pool and the bay, so she could hardly complain about being stuck in there. But she felt a pang of disappointment at the thought of the luxurious home cinema she'd spotted on her first day with its vast digital library. Tonight had been going to be her movie night—after Friday night's champagne bath pamper treat. She'd been looking forward to working out that fancy popcorn machine… Yet suddenly the fantasy scrolling through her head like some romance movie was of her curling up on that amazing lounge suite and watching a movie *with* Ash Castle…

Fool. That wouldn't be a romance, but a tragedy. Or, worse, a mockumentary. A prank plot line where the out-of-her-league girl thinks the perfect guy has become genuinely interested in her. It would end with her as the punchline. Again. She'd been humiliated by a perfect-looking popular guy once before and she wasn't up for a repeat. Those guys knew they were attractive, and they got it too easy, so they got bored and played games. Cruel ones. She knew, she'd been the target. So that fantasy bubble could just pop and disappear for good.

Besides, Ash Castle wasn't perfect. He was a playboy. The type she'd been warned about all of her life by her super-strict grandmother—though truthfully, her grandmother had warned her about *all* men, and to be wary of her *own* desires. It was from her mother's experience that Merle knew the heat-of-the-moment temptation a man like Ash could inspire was nothing short of life-changing. That mistake wasn't one Merle was about to make. So, instead of the movie and the popcorn, she'd curl into that cosy armchair in her room with cheese and crackers. She'd celebrate surviving one whole day, and in a week he'd be gone.

Ash floated on his back and gazed up at the house through narrowed eyes, wondering if he'd actually imagined the whole woman-in-his-bath moment last night. Had she been some wishful mirage from his overtired brain? A wistful fantasy of female perfection?

No. Not even *his* fertile mind could have conjured up such a stunning, ethereal yet earthy sample of femininity, nor the horrors of her outfit afterwards. Now, the studied silence and stillness of the house irritated the hell out of him.

Merle Jordan was the avoidance champion of the world. He ought to *appreciate* that she was being quiet and staying out of sight, given he'd told her he'd come here for space when he'd tried to banish her from the premises.

Of course, peace was the last thing he could find. It was the first time he'd been back in years and memories tortured him. Echoes of old arguments rang in his head like faint wails of distant sirens, keeping him eternally on edge. That aim to sort his mother's things was impossible when he couldn't even bear to look around him. His father's redesign of the property was massive and so bitterly pointed. Every element of his mother's input had been erased. There wasn't just a new pool, but also a whole new guest wing with the private cinema and bowling alley, and the wine cellar had doubled in size. But it was the changes in his mother's beloved garden that had angered Ash to the point where he couldn't bear to walk beyond the pool area to see the full devastation. He'd tried to burn the fury out with a brutal workout, hoping to exhaust himself and finally silence his overthinking brain. It hadn't worked. He kept on thinking—though increasingly he kept thinking about *Merle*. She was an infinitely preferable subject.

Merle Jordan, mouse-like woman of mystery. What was she doing in there? How was she managing to stay so quiet? So out of sight? So deliberately invisible?

A fling wasn't what he was here for. And, despite the undeniable awareness flickering between them, she clearly didn't want it either. But of course, to Ash Castle and the contrary, spoiled mood he was in, that made her even more enticing. He liked a game and he liked to win. Isolation wasn't what he wanted any more. Not here, where the house that had once held such happiness had been so destroyed. Of course, it wasn't the renovations that had wrecked everything. That had been Ash himself. His own weakness was the culprit—the one he'd inherited from his cheating jerk of a father. He breathed in sharply and determinedly—blessedly—thought of Merle Jordan instead. She'd been mortified when he'd caught her naked in the candlelight but later she'd revealed a little sass. He wanted to see more of that—he was sure it was there. When she wasn't biting her tongue.

His skin tightened as he thought of her mouth. It was that fever again—he wished his extreme emotions would ease. Except, regarding Merle Jordan, they weren't really emotions. They were hormones. Sheer, mere, lust. But part of him welcomed the warmth of it. For all the partying, he'd been feeling cold these last few months. He'd attributed it to too much of the same game as always—long work hours, jaded social scene, easily won escapades. Boredom, in other words.

Merle Jordan wasn't boring. Merle Jordan wasn't like anyone he'd ever met. A very serious, homeless archivist.

By the late afternoon he was out of patience to wait any longer for when and how she might appear. He strode to the study, where he knew she'd set up her archival operation. He blinked as his eyes adjusted from the bright sunlight outside. He avoided looking at the cardboard box open on the floor, nor did he glance at the papers spread on the large table. He still wasn't ready.

Merle was standing by the table, a page in hand, staring at him, and he stared right back because *what* was she wearing? The white inspection gloves on her hands he could understand, but those coveralls? Akin to a hazmat suit, they enveloped her completely, only instead of white or blue or high-vis neon, they were all black. They were, without doubt, the most shapeless sack he'd ever seen.

'Is something wrong?' she asked nervously.

He could still only stare. Beyond the suit her skin was as luminous as he'd remembered and he lost himself in her dark brown eyes. They reminded him of rich chocolate, that sort he'd like to play with—to melt, then lick. As he watched, her eyes widened and grew darker. Velvet delicious. Her long brunette hair was held back in a loose braid that hung down her back. Utilitarian, yes. Also, stunning. He still couldn't stop staring.

'Mr Castle?'

That snapped him back to reality. 'Mr Castle' was his father, Hugh. He was Ash.

'How are you getting on?' he asked.

'Well, thank you.' Her polite response wasn't enough to sugar-coat her wish to dismiss him and only worsened his irritation. His own contrariness was killing him.

'Did you find a body in the bunker?' he muttered.

Her brown eyes widened fractionally before a flinch compressed her features. 'A...what?'

'A body. In the bunker,' he repeated unrepentantly and grinned as he gestured towards her. 'Hence the forensics fashion.'

He knew he'd been out of line, but he wanted her to unleash the spirit flaring in her eyes.

Her chin lifted. 'Very funny.'

Vitality flowed through his veins. It might be a frosty reaction, but he'd got her to speak.

'A lot of the boxes are dusty.' She iced her explanation with the coolest of tones. 'My "forensics fashion" protects my clothes.'

Even as fiery embarrassment stained her skin, the determined dignity in her restrained response made him squirm. To his amazement, Ash experienced a rare moment when he regretted his teen-acquired tendency to say whatever outrageous thing popped into his head. And what kind of sub-human was he for being annoyed that she was so well-covered by her clothing?

But as he watched, her smooth forehead wrinkled and

her coolly assessing gaze narrowed. 'You were joking about a bunker, right?'

'You mean you don't know?' he drawled, as he realised an opportunity had suddenly opened up. She'd fallen for bait he'd not intended to set.

'If only you had a moustache, you could twirl the ends,' she muttered. 'Obviously I don't know, or I wouldn't have asked.'

He paused to savour the surprising sass of her answer. She was crisply to the point and her quietly crackling energy stoked his.

'There's a secret bunker,' he said, determined to snare her interest now.

'A relic from the war?' She frowned. 'Here on the property?'

'Sadly no, not a historic one. That would've been fascinating. This one is more…' *Bonkers.* He cleared his throat. 'It's new. My father had it installed.'

Her eyebrows lifted. 'You mean a panic room?'

'I think it's a little more over the top than that.' He'd not checked it out yet. He'd missed its construction entirely and had only become aware of its existence when he'd read through the list of current contractors the estate was paying for. Because he'd been so out of sorts at his glimpse of the garden, he'd avoided investigating in full the other changes to the grounds. Having Merle with him while he did might be a good diversion.

'Why would your father want a bunker?' She looked confused. 'Why *here*?'

'Why indeed?' He had no idea, he just wanted to avoid his history by focusing on her and he didn't want her to disappear on him again yet. 'Want to see it?' he purred.

Her eyes darkened even more, melting into delicious pools of an unreadable emotion.

'I'm partway through this box,' she muttered.

It was a weak show of reluctance. An absurd level of anticipation swept through him. Surely this was like catnip to a woman who liked historical records and old things?

'It'll still be here when we're done,' he replied easily, trying not to let his eagerness for her company show too obviously. 'Apparently, it's only in the garden. It shouldn't take long.'

He watched, conscious of the increasing awareness between them—the rising colour in her cheeks, the thrum of heat in his blood.

'There might be all kinds of things stored in there that should be considered for the archives,' he tempted.

'You don't know for certain?'

'I've not been in there yet.'

Surprise flashed. 'You've not yet ventured into a secret bunker that's been built here?'

He shook his head, suppressing the instinctive rejection of anything his father had built and focusing on her. 'Could be exciting, right?' he said blandly. 'Like discovering Tutankhamun's tomb?'

He watched as her mouth quivered, but she couldn't suppress her smile for long. A hard lump in his chest eased. One point on the board—he'd made her smile. And it had been worth the effort.

'Let me just finish up with this letter.' She put the document she held onto the table, drawing his attention to his father's things. Things that made his skin crawl. Things he wanted to burn.

'You don't wear glasses?' he asked, distraction a necessity as she marked up something with her pencil.

'Stereotype, much?' she muttered coolly. 'Bookish girl must need glasses?'

He laughed. *This* was what he'd needed, a little sparring with someone determined to remain uninterested. Except she already was. He *knew* she was. And that wasn't all arrogance. Sparks like this were never one-sided.

'Actually, I asked because of the lamp you're using. It casts an unusual light.'

'It's to avoid damaging the documents,' she explained as she added something else to the paper. 'It's not for my eyes. I have perfect eyesight.'

'Perfect?' he echoed with amusement. 'You can see right through me, huh?'

She glanced over and shot him an instant kill look. That heaviness in his chest thawed fractionally more. 'You already know I can.'

'Yet you've been avoiding me,' he said when she finally stepped away from the table.

'You came here to be alone,' she said, her expression devoid of the coy flirtatiousness that he was used to from women. 'I've been giving you the space you asked for.'

He'd been regretting that request since the moment he'd made it. Though, contrarily, he equally regretted not insisting that she leave. Truthfully *he* was the one who ought to leave. He shouldn't have come back. It had only dredged up memories he'd fought hard to forget. A reminder of who he was and the family failings he couldn't ever escape. A frank reminder of his own damned, futile existence. Maybe he should leave his mother's things in her hands. But he was curious about Merle now too.

'Besides, I have work to do,' she added.

That 'work' didn't include entertaining him. But she was watching him and he realised the thoughtfulness on her face had slid to concern—and compassion. He stiffened. Did she think he was distressed about his father's death? He didn't want her pity.

'You're paid to work the weekends as well?' he asked shortly.

That colour rolled back into her cheeks. 'I thought I may as well get on with it, seeing as I'm to remain hidden.'

'Well, take a moment—let's go and see if there's anything worth saving down there.' He didn't think for a second there was, but if he was wrong he wanted rid of all of it immediately. It was only for Leo and for his cousin Grace that he'd agreed to assess everything before selling. For transparency and honesty. They'd missed out on so much, he'd ensure they weren't short-changed in anything else ever again. The other property sales were already completed and all personal effects had been shipped here for a final sort.

'Apparently the entrance is via a hidden trap door in the back of the pool house,' he added, desperately needing to think about anything other than Leo and Grace and his father's awful shame.

'Seriously?'

'Yes.'

Merle knew this was a Bad Idea, but she couldn't resist. Like the home cinema, she'd only briefly glanced at the pool house earlier in the week, opting to explore the leisure activities as a weekend reward for work done. She'd been keen to assess how much work there was ahead of her because Leo Castle's brief had been sketchy. He hadn't known how many boxes were onsite or even the state of the property. But since Ash's unexpected arrival she'd been confined to the study.

Apparently there was no lazing about with a long weekend lie-in for Ash. Which had meant not for her either. It had been impossible to lie in bed listening to him splash about this morning. It had put all sorts of inappropriate images in her mind—and that was already distracted enough by that shockingly hot dream. She was mortified that she was thinking about him in such an inevitable way. Even right now she was trying not to stare at him and not get bothered by the fact he was still wearing only swim shorts. It was perfectly appropriate attire. This was a holiday home and he'd been swimming all morning, but she was too aware of all that *skin*, and her fingertips tingled with the appalling temptation to touch.

As she followed him she desperately fixated on the stunning grounds. There were a couple of alfresco dining areas—an enormous table overlooked the pool, a sweet setting for two was in the corner, while sun loungers and comfortable chairs were placed in sheltered spots where the views over the bay to the sea beyond were sublime.

'The bunker was put in when the pool and tennis court were done. As far as I can tell from the plans, they dug up the entire area and basically buried a prefabricated structure.' Oblivious to her feverish thoughts, Ash moved aside a rug on the pool house floor. 'According to the notes I have…' He trailed off and pushed on one of the inlaid tiles.

To Merle's astonishment, four of the tiles slid back to reveal a dark cavity. 'Oh, wow. There really is a trap door.' She chuckled. 'It's like something out of a spy movie.'

'I know,' he muttered. 'Ridiculous.'

As she stared down, lights flickered on to reveal a steep flight of stairs.

'Shall we?' He glanced at her with a wicked smile.

Her heart pounded. It was crazy to feel this frisson. 'We leave this open, right?' Merle double-checked.

'Of course,' he answered.

The staircase was so steep she could almost slide down it. At the bottom, Ash pulled open a heavy-looking steel door. Yet more lights flickered on as he walked through. Her heart still thudding, Merle followed.

'Oh, wow.' She gazed about the gleaming space in absolute astonishment. 'Wow. This is…'

'Insane?' He circled around on the spot, shaking his head as he took in the set-up.

This was no weird, prison-like cell or futuristic survival bunker. This was pure luxury—like a plush hotel penthouse.

'You'd *never* know it was here.' She wouldn't have believed it possible. Not when above them was that perfect, smooth, manicured tennis lawn beside the pool. There were no tell-tale lumps or hollows giving away the secret beneath the ground.

'Which is the point, right?' He crossed the room.

'It's big.' Merle slowly followed him across the smooth wooden floors that echoed the warm, coastal luxury of the mansion above ground. Cosy leather sofas furnished the room.

'My father wouldn't have anything less than opulent.'

'How does it smell this fresh when we're this far underground?'

'Good maintenance,' he muttered. 'There's a ventilation system. The control panel is in here…'

Merle tuned out as she took in additional details herself. The wall carefully concealed a series of cupboards providing impressive storage space. Digital frames had lit up, creating 'windows' to a virtual garden. The kitchen was compact yet still luxurious. While every space was utilised, it wasn't crammed. It was, she had to admit, absolutely stunning.

'What was the man thinking, having this installed here?' Ash's growl impinged.

'It is pretty unusual.' She released a helpless laugh. 'Did he think he was in danger or the end of the world was nigh?'

'No.' Ash shook his head. 'I think it was the accessory *du jour* and he wanted to feel superior to his friends in his club. He'd hint and whisper but confirm nothing. My father did like keeping secrets.'

Hearing underlying rancour in his tone, Merle stilled. That edge of emotion flickered in his eyes. It made him even more beautiful. Merle stiffened. *Never* had she thought a man beautiful before… The bunker no longer felt spacious. Or safe. It was scarily exciting.

He rubbed his arm absently as he looked about the luxury lounge.

'Are you cold?' she unthinkingly observed aloud. 'Maybe you should wear more clothes.'

He snapped his head back and turned a wicked smile on her. 'Don't you like to swim?' he teased and stepped towards her. 'It's very warm this afternoon.'

It was *extremely* warm this afternoon. Truthfully, she was melting this second, but she wasn't about to tell him that. She'd lost her ability to speak again and she just knew another scalding blush was mottling her skin.

'You're not a pool person? What about the beach?' He cocked his head and chuckled at her. 'Or is it just bubble baths for you?'

'I didn't want to disturb you,' she muttered.

'Too late, Merle.' A heated glint flickered in his eyes. 'But I've been hogging the pool, haven't I?'

'This is your home. I'm just working here.'

'You're also *living* here. You're not supposed to work all day, you're supposed to have breaks. If you like, I'll vacate the pool area at a time that's convenient to you.'

She met his gaze, stilling when she saw seriousness stealing that glint away. Stupidly another wave of heat overwhelmed her—how could she find him even more attractive just because he was being almost human?

She walked down the narrow corridor, more to escape him than to explore. But fascination and curiosity took hold as she ventured further into the pod. There was a bunk room gorgeously decorated in light colours, a sleek bathroom and beyond that a luxurious bedroom for two. The whole place was pristine and perfect and surprisingly cosy. It would be easy to forget you were deep underground. But then Ash followed her into the room and she remembered just how alone and isolated they were.

'It's better finished than most homes,' she commented, purely to pierce the thickening atmosphere. Certainly it was nicer than the house she'd grown up in. 'For a space likely never to be used, it's extravagant, isn't it?'

He merely nodded. Embarrassed, she realised that for him this wasn't extravagant. He probably thought it sparse, given the luxury he was probably used to.

'Anything archive-worthy?' Ash asked.

'I'm not sure.' She glanced again at the concealed drawers and cupboards. If she were bolder, she'd check them out to see if anything was inside. But being down here was confusing her thinking. With Ash in the luxurious bedroom beside her, it felt as if the space was smaller. Intimate. Inescapable.

Her gaze was unerringly drawn back to him. He was watching her. Too close. The temperature soared. Her lungs squeezed and she swivelled to nervously step past him. She needed to get upstairs so she could breathe again. It wasn't that she was claustrophobic, she was just too close to him. All of her usual reticence and caution had evaporated and she was tempted to act...*wantonly*.

It was imperative to put distance between them. Not because he was dangerous in a threatening way, more that he was too wicked and her own mind was turning towards temptation. She'd avoided temptation all of her life—but then, she'd never been confronted by anything or anyone who ignited it within her like this. But the current of awareness that sparked to life whenever Ash Castle so much as stepped into her line of sight wasn't just unsettling, it was also unstoppable.

'I'll just…' She breathed out, unable to regulate her racing heart. 'I'll just head back up.'

She glanced over again and was instantly snared in the crucible of his attention. She lost time—she didn't know how much—as she strived not to crumble beneath the intensity of his killer eye-contact. Her temperature climbed and her pulse skipped and worst of all she was so sure he *knew*. Yet seconds stopped in the heat of that stare.

'I'll be back up in a moment,' he muttered eventually.

Scalding humiliation flooded her as she scurried towards those steep stairs. That mortifying moment made her even more aware of her internal reaction to him. That raw physical response that was so strong, so primal. She had to get away and get herself under control. She climbed carefully, keeping her eyes fixed on each steep stair. But ten steps from the top she stopped, finally realising that there was no glow of sunlight shining down on her. No space where the hatch had been left open.

'A-Ash?' Sound struggled to emerge from her suddenly tight throat. '*Ash?*'

'Yes?' A second later he appeared on the bottom step. 'What?'

But he could already see. He took the stairs two at a time and in a blink was too close behind her. Her heart galloped as she heard his sharply inhaled breath.

'Merle?'

She could feel him only a step from her now but she couldn't bear to face him as she admitted the awful truth. 'I don't think we can get out.'

CHAPTER FOUR

'MERLE...' A LOW hum of laughter emanated from him. 'What did you *do*?'

'I left it open. I know I left it open.' Merle retreated down a few of the stairs to let Ash try the hatch, even though she was fatalistically certain he wasn't going to be able to open it.

'It must've closed automatically,' he drawled.

'Which means it must open automatically again, right?' she rationalised, striving for calm. 'With some other secret mechanism?'

'Sure,' he agreed, too equably.

But there were no levers or buttons or anything near. 'If this place is that high-tech...isn't there some retinal scan that would unlock the door in seconds?'

He glanced at her then, droll amusement oozing from him. 'And if I had my dad's eyeball in my pocket we could use that. Sadly, I don't.'

Why wasn't he bothered by this the same way she was?

Because he's not bothered by you. Her subconscious whispered the biting truth. Or maybe it was because he knew exactly how to get them out and was merely teasing her?

She narrowed her gaze on him. 'So are we stuck in here for the next sixty years until the nuclear winter has passed?'

'Would that be so terrible?' His eyebrows lifted.

Unable to maintain eye contact, Merle turned and went back downstairs, pretending she was calm but in reality far too aware of him a step behind. Dear heaven, she was stuck

deep underground in a luxury doomsday bunker with billionaire Ashton Castle. Some might consider that a dream
come true. But for Merle? In her current mode of *uncon-
trolled inappropriate lust*…it was a nightmare. She paced
across the space that was growing smaller again with every
second—where was it he'd said the control panel was?

'I refuse to believe we're stuck. Isn't a bunker all about
safety?' Her tongue rattled ahead of her brain. 'There must
be a second way out—an emergency exit. What if there
was a fire?'

'Bigger than the one currently burning you up, you
mean?' He watched her walk back and forth with undis-
guised amusement.

She gritted her teeth. She wasn't panicking and becoming hysterical. Okay, yes, she was panicking. Not because
she thought they were going to be stuck in here for ever
and *die*. It was a more intense issue terrifying her. It was
the intimacy of being in here with *him*. And that amused
look on his face? A sudden suspicion struck. 'You did this
deliberately, didn't you?'

He oh-so-slowly, oh-too-innocently widened his gorgeous amber eyes. 'I wasn't the one who shut the door.'

A wave of indignation swamped her. 'I *didn't*.'

He laughed.

She glared back at him. 'It's not funny.'

'The look on your face is. Honestly, what do you think
I'm going to do?'

'Nothing,' she snapped.

It wasn't what *he* was going to do. She didn't think for
a second he'd actually make a move on her—not without
her explicit acquiescence or invitation. No, the problem
was the appalling desire that kept bubbling up from where
she'd tried to shove it.

'If it's not me, then what is it? Are you claustrophobic?'

'No,' she muttered, trying to haul her wits together. 'It's nothing major. I'm just…'

'You don't trust yourself to be alone with me any more?'

She stilled and glared at him. Of all the arrogant— unfortunately *accurate*—things to suggest.

'You said yourself you've been avoiding me.' His smile broadened. 'And…' He waved a hand at her boiler suit.

She sighed dramatically. 'My clothing choice has nothing to do with you or anyone else. I find it comfortable to work in.'

'No shorts on a hot day?'

'I'm usually in a dusty warehouse.' She was suddenly determined to somehow flip this so he was the one feeling as if *he* was the bug beneath the magnifying glass in the sun and about to frizzle to death. Make *him* feel desperate to escape the bunker. 'Do you ever wear anything *other* than black swim shorts?'

He laughed. 'I do, as it happens. When I'm at work I wear a suit.'

'It's very considerate of you to cover up all your muscles so your poor workers aren't distracted.'

He glanced at the spark in her eye. 'Why, Merle, stop it, you'll make me blush.'

'Is that possible?'

'Probably not.' He grinned.

What was she thinking, talking to him like this? It didn't help that she was starving. She'd not had lunch for fear of running into him and somehow the afternoon had slid away from her. Eager for distraction, she opened the first of the many sleek cupboards in the kitchen area. To her amazement—and relief—there were packets and packets of food. 'Oh, wow, these supplies are amazing.'

'Amazing?' He sounded appalled. 'It's all tins and bottles.'

'It could be worse.' She shot him a sideways look. 'There could be instant noodles.'

'True. That would be terrible.'

'You've obviously never cooked them properly.' She pulled out a tin of peanuts and opened it. The sooner she stabilised her blood sugar, the sooner she got a grip on her crazy hot thinking, right? And if she stuffed her mouth full she'd stop saying things she really shouldn't. And usually wouldn't, but for Ash Castle's influence.

'Are you hungry?' He was still watching her with unconcealed amusement. 'I guess that's not surprising, given you've not been eating anything decent.'

She paused chewing long enough to shoot him another death look.

'Instant noodles are for starving students,' he opined. 'This is not the place for them. I won't allow it.'

'You won't *allow* it?'

'It's unnecessary. Didn't you notice the delivery arrive earlier?' he asked. 'Or are you only interested in the contents of the wine cellar?'

Heat flooded her. 'Mr Castle said—'

'I know what Leo said.' Ash rolled his eyes. 'I also know that if you'd had any idea of the cost you would never have opened it.' He cocked his head. 'Have dinner with me tonight.'

She nearly choked on the next nut. 'Dinner?'

'Yes. Dinner,' he repeated calmly. 'I refuse to work round the clock and definitely not on the weekend. And it's silly for us to avoid each other completely and waste resources cooking two separate meals.'

'You don't seem the type who has to worry about wasting resources.'

'I'm doing my bit for the planet, Merle,' he countered limpidly. 'It's always better to share.'

His echo of last night's words made her skin sizzle. But

last night she'd turned and walked out on him without replying. His soft, mocking laughter had trailed her all the way up the stairs to her room. Now she had no choice but to stay and face him. To better him with her own wits. Somehow.

'Say you'll have dinner with me and I'll be inspired to remember the code to open that door,' he said.

So he did know the code. She ground the nuts between her teeth, hard. 'There's a century's worth of food in here,' she said after swallowing. 'I don't need your dinner. I can just stay put.'

His eyes glinted. 'You'd choose to be stuck with me for ever? Isn't that a hellish proposition?'

It was an appallingly appealing proposition. Since when had she become a masochist—to want to remain stuck inside a spacious yet small-feeling safe room that was so *not* safe—at least not for her peace of mind. Or her libido. Or her self-control.

'Besides,' he added, 'there's no *fresh* food. I do like it fresh, sweetheart.'

Merle summoned the little self-control she had left. 'Are you really going to keep me locked in here until I agree to have dinner with you? Doesn't that seem a little coercive? I wouldn't have thought you'd have to resort to abduction tactics.'

'Abduction?' That wicked glint flared in his gaze. 'Asking for a dinner date is nothing,' he said softly. 'It could be far worse. I could demand a kiss for the key code.'

She stilled. 'You wouldn't dare.'

'*I'm* not the one afraid to be daring, sweetheart.'

He was the most aggravating man alive. *This* was what he wanted—for her to rise to his provocation. Well, perhaps she would—just not in the way he wanted. Couldn't she teach him a lesson? Admittedly, she had little likelihood of success. She was a lamb against a lion. But there was something beyond irresistible about the prospect of putting him in his place.

'Merle?' He leaned against the counter as he watched her staring at him. 'What are you thinking?'

His hands were loose, his expression neutral, but his awareness had flared. She felt it too. It locked them both into position—on edge. *Ready.*

'I'm thinking...' she mused softly, 'that who dares, wins.'

'Do you dare?' he drawled. 'Is that what I can see in your eyes?'

He was so bold. And somehow *she* was emboldened. Because she'd pull back at the last moment. She'd tease him and win.

'What you can see,' she said softly, 'is frustration with your insistence on strutting around in nothing but...' She gestured at his swim shorts.

His eyebrows skyrocketed and she felt a ridiculous pleasure that she'd surprised him. She'd surprised herself too. And quite liked it.

'Then look the other way,' Ash taunted. 'I'm not going to change the way I dress for you, sweetheart. Just as I don't expect you to change the way you dress for me.'

A molten sensation stormed through her. She was never dressing *for* him, or anyone. She refused to think about what he thought of her appearance. She already knew he loathed her coverall.

'It's not appropriate,' she argued anyway.

'I'm on holiday at a beach house, Merle,' he said blandly. 'I've been in the pool most of the day.'

Yes, she was *acutely* aware of that fact.

'This whole thing isn't appropriate,' she continued, on a roll now. 'You're my employer.'

'I most definitely am *not*,' he answered instantly. '*Leo* is paying you. I have nothing to do with that.'

She met his fierce gaze and his lips curved in an inviting smile.

'Come closer, Merle. I dare you.'

'Do you really think I'll respond to such little provocation?'

His shoulders lifted and, despite that lazily wicked smile, intensity burned in his eyes. 'Beats me, but I really hope so.'

That absolute honesty stole the wind from her sails.

'You *would* have to be the most outrageous man I've ever met,' she said, breathing out in annoyance.

'Yeah? I bet I'm also the most honest. And here's my truth, Merle. I've been thinking about kissing you every bit as much as you've been thinking about kissing me.'

'I have *not*...' But she blushed at the complete lie.

'No?' He grinned triumphantly. 'It's only chemistry. Nothing more meaningful than a few compounds that spark when struck together. I know you don't actually *like* me.'

'*Like* you?' She rolled her eyes. 'You just want me to disagree and say you're actually not that arrogant, not that inappropriate, not that *appalling*. I'm not falling for it.'

He merely laughed. 'That still doesn't mean you don't want me.'

The cockiness of the man was astounding. 'You're swaggering round, practically naked, like you're some sort of sex gift to the nearest woman—'

'I think you're awfully judgmental about people's clothing.' He flipped to pious with a blink of his unfairly long eyelashes. 'It's personal expression, Merle.'

'Oh, please, you were the one trashing my "forensics fashion".'

'I know, and I was wrong.' He nodded. 'And I've decided, upon reflection, that it's appealing. There's an allure of discovery in what lies beneath.' His lips quirked. 'Of course, I already know the visual delights to be seen under yours...'

She burned with embarrassment. She should have turned down his invitation to explore the bunker. Avoidance wasn't just the best solution for dealing with this man, it was the *only* solution. Except, much to her annoyance, Ash Castle was easy to like. He was sharp and funny and she knew he took pleasure in deliberately provoking her. He didn't mean most of this talk—there was that spark in his eye, a devilish gleam knowing he was taking it too far. Frankly, she was enjoying trying to better him. It was a game she'd never played. A game she wanted to win.

And now? Now there was a part of her that wanted nothing more than to wipe that smug challenge off his face and topple his assurance the way he'd obliterated hers.

The way he watched her was unashamedly interested, underlined with curiosity. She was different, that was all. Not like the other women who slid into his bed with ease. Surely she couldn't be the only woman ever to have said no to him?

He outstretched his arms and took hold of the counter's edge. 'I promise I won't let go, so you can be assured there'll be no wandering hands. Then you can get it out of your system.'

She was sure he was joking. Yet he was still and serious and she had to dig her heels in to stop the temptation slithering through her. Somehow time blipped, somehow she stepped nearer. A hard blaze lit his eyes and she couldn't tear her gaze from him.

'A kiss for the key code? Is that the deal?' she asked.

'If that's the deal you want to make.'

'And dinner?'

'Is happening regardless and it will be a much more leisurely, sumptuous affair than instant noodles followed by a bite of pudding.' His eyes gleamed as he waited, alert, for her response.

His confidence was extreme. He was certain in his arrogant assumption that she wouldn't dream of turning him down. Truth was, she didn't want to refuse him. In any of these things. But she would.

'Just a little closer, Merle,' he whispered with full arrogance on display. 'What's the worst that could happen?'

There were so many worsts that she could think of. He could laugh. Humiliate her. Tell her he hadn't meant it. Hadn't she had that experience before—to be led along a path by a handsome man, only to have him humiliate her publicly? Proving her grandmother's ridiculously dire warnings that men were to be avoided.

Only, there was an intensity in Ash's expression that she couldn't turn away from, and he was so very still that she couldn't resist stepping that breath closer.

She would whisper 'never' to him. She would refuse to give him any kind of satisfaction. 'I ought to…'

'To what?' He breathed heavily.

She couldn't remember what she'd been going to do any more. Her brain had shut down.

'Run,' he finished for her in a raw, low growl of bitter honesty. 'That's what you should do, Merle. You should turn around and run, right now.'

Maybe she should. But a flare of need had unfurled. Because she knew he'd meant it, but she also knew it was the last thing he wanted. It was the last thing she wanted too.

He wasn't smiling any more. All that laughing arrogance, all the careless flirting, had vanished and all that remained was that almost angry look in his eyes as he fiercely stared, as if trying to compel her with his thoughts. Even with his arms stretched wide, his biceps were flexed as he gripped the bench tightly. But that stance made him vulnerable. She could get close to his body.

'Why did you dare me, then?' Her own anger bloomed. 'To *make* me run? To prove my cowardice? To put this all on me so you don't have to answer for it?'

Was he trying to prove that her inexperience was something to be embarrassed about? And that it was her own fault? That there was something wrong with her?

'Merle.' His mutter was almost an apology.

It changed everything again. The intensity between them shifted to something more than sensual. Something devastatingly intimate. And emotional. Anger—and another emotion too powerful to ignore—overwhelmed her into action. She rose on tiptoe and held his gaze. Feeling fire scurrying along her veins, she was about to tell him exactly what she thought of him. Except she was frozen. Less than an inch away from him, she suddenly couldn't move.

Yet his heat emanated, burning her, inexorably pulling her closer. And then he tucked in his chin, lowering his head just enough for their lips to brush. It was little more than a swift press but a shock of pleasure struck her insides. She felt taut as a bowstring, ready to fire. But she didn't. She pulled away, immediately hoping he'd take it as a mockery of the real thing—that she'd offered only a pretence, given his request was so outrageous.

'No,' he muttered hoarsely. 'Come back.'

Not a line. Not an arrogant command. A raw plea that escaped gritted teeth.

She hadn't exactly gone anywhere. Only a breath away, she could see the warmth of his eyes, more mesmerising than ever. Whoever wanted to step into a crucible? To willingly fling themselves into flames? But these were searing licks of pleasure. These were irresistible.

'My turn.' He bent his head closer.

Still, she didn't step away. Even when she'd told herself that was exactly what she was going to do—veer close, only to swerve at the last minute. Like some game of chicken. Only she'd discovered that a collision was the far more preferable option.

'Just stay there,' he growled. 'Just for a minute.'

They were close enough for their mouths to brush as he spoke. For her to feel his warmth, his breath on her skin. She could feel him watching her, feel the light nuzzle of his nose against hers. Gentle, careful. Searingly sensual. It only took the tiniest lift of her chin to catch his lips again and hers clung to his without conscious intent. But then—without releasing that counter—he somehow moved, somehow took control.

His mouth roved over hers, gentle, then with a subtly increasing strength. She closed her eyes, lost in the kiss instantly. She leaned closer and inadvertently grazed her fists against his bare skin. The sizzle was intoxicating and she unfurled her fingers, shivering at his scorching heat. And then she simply melted. Her belly pressed against his, her palms spread on his solid chest and her head fell back as she let him kiss her to life. It was pure electric vitality now crackling through her veins. She heard the low groan from the back of his throat and an answering echo, a moan from deep within, escaped her.

Both sounds impinged on her mind, dragging her back to reality. Stunned at the intensity and speed with which she'd lost herself, she tore away, snapping the contact.

This time he didn't try to stop her. He just watched, his beautiful eyes lit by his potent, wild spirit. A cloud of sensuality wafted from him, tempting her to get close again. Not a cloud—*chains*. If she wasn't careful she might be locked in his thrall for good.

There wasn't satisfaction on his face. Nor the smug arrogance she'd expected because he'd got what he wanted. Got it so easily. If anything, he seemed as breathless, as speechless as she. But that was impossible.

Breathing hard, she broke free of those invisible bonds and stepped back. She didn't want him to know how deeply that had affected her. She'd spent so many years hiding by staying silent. For once, she was going to have to speak up to cover up. She was going to have to pretend.

'I've changed my mind.' She expelled a shaky breath. 'I don't need your key code. I've come to consider the bunker a safe haven. I'll happily stay down here.'

A smile spread across his face and that arrogance gleamed. 'You were that moved, huh?' He nodded. 'So now you're too scared to have dinner with me.' He lifted his hands from the bench and shook them. 'Has that one kiss made you too frightened of what else you might find yourself wanting to do?'

That was so accurate she wanted to hit him.

He stepped forward. 'Do you really think you'd be safer now, stuck in here with me? In this teeny, tiny space?'

'It's not that tiny,' she said, desperately defending her position, and decided to appeal to his humanity. 'And I really think you're not the animal you make yourself out to be. You're not that desperate for anything.'

'No?' He half laughed. 'I'm glad you're so certain. Because I'm not. And now I can't escape the sight or scent of you? Now I've had a taste?'

He stalked towards her, but at the final moment, when she was bracing for impact, he swerved and stepped past her—pulling off the move she'd planned but failed to perform.

And the sudden sense of loss? Of disappointment? In that second she hated her own body—the chemicals and hormones that had been so thoroughly turned *on*. She watched him viciously prod a discreet panel in the study area of the living space. Only a second later she heard a hissing sound and the clang of some mechanism.

'The door's open, Merle.' Ash glanced at her. 'I suggest you return to the real world.'

CHAPTER FIVE

THE PROBLEM WAS that the 'real world' was no different. Above ground, breathing fresh air, forcing physical distance, Ash still wanted her more than he'd wanted any woman ever. He rolled his shoulders, unable to release the tension that had been building since the second he'd first seen her. Tension that was now unbearable after he'd touched her. What had begun as the most chaste kiss of his life had ended as the most unforgettable. How was it possible that he'd been left aching with such desperation? It wasn't like anything he'd experienced before. It was no lie that he'd needed to get them out of there as fast as possible.

When she'd professed her desire to stay locked down there? He'd had to move before he took her up on it.

Ordinarily, most kisses didn't end like that. Not so suddenly. Not with his lover walking away. Ordinarily, most kisses ended with all clothes off and multiple orgasms on. Not with Merle Jordan though. Of course it couldn't be ordinary with her.

She was so tantalising. He'd never been as careful, absurdly terrified that he'd scare her off somehow. But then he'd lost track of any planned seduction. His mind had hazed. All that had remained was sensation in that sweet, scorching moment when he'd had his mouth on hers. Then she'd put her hands on him.

There'd always been a clinical element to Ash's conquests. A decision to accept the offer of some mindless, emotionless physical relief and pleasure. This was different. This was a visceral ache in his core. Desire he couldn't deny. Every other time it had been easy enough to walk away. Now he couldn't. It wasn't because he was trapped here. For all his hedonism, all his copious enjoyment of easy pleasure, he'd never been so fixated. Now he feared he was on the edge. That he'd do almost anything to have Merle Jordan in his bed was a frankly alarming feeling.

And there'd been inexperience in her kiss. Ash didn't fool around with women who didn't know the score. Not since he'd broken a young woman's heart a decade ago. He didn't like to think of Rose but her visage flickered in his mind. Of course it did—his treatment of Rose had been the reason for his mother's anger here, that afternoon when his whole world had been turned upside down.

He slammed the door on those recollections. Things were very different now. While Merle's initial shyness had reminded him of Rose, she'd shown herself to be very different just beneath the surface. Merle wasn't some sweet-sixteen, never-been-kissed, awkward girl. She was an adult—fully capable of handling this attraction and of standing up to him more devastatingly than most people he'd met. He knew she wanted nothing more than to put him properly in his place. And when she let her tongue off the leash? When she was provoked enough not to hold back?

He wanted that too. Because he wanted her. But, given the inexperience that he intuitively sensed, he needed her to come to him. He *needed* her to be more than sure. He needed her to be in charge. Instead, she'd vanished back into that study.

He paced through to the kitchen, grumpily fixing on the perfect displacement activity. He was no great cook but he also wasn't afraid to source expert help when necessary. Seeing those little puddings of hers last night had made his mouth water, so he'd been deliberate in the groceries he'd ordered for delivery from one of the local delis this morning. He'd tempt every one of her tastebuds until she could do nothing but ask for more.

Ninety minutes later, he appeared at the door to the study where she was still hiding.

'Hey, darling.' He leaned against the doorjamb. 'Dinner's ready.'

Merle had spent the afternoon locked back in the study, buried in the boring business papers from his father's box, keeping calm and carrying on as if nothing drastically life-changing had happened. But Ash hadn't gone back to his usual routine. He hadn't appeared at the pool to swim for endless hours. She wished he had. The truth was, she'd realised, she wanted to swim *with* him.

But now he led her to a beautifully set small table overlooking the pool. It offered spaciousness, room to escape, a stunning view across the bay and an even better view across the table—to him.

Merle gazed down at the vibrantly coloured curry instead. 'This looks amazing. Thank you.'

She perched, keenly aware of the awkward silence that immediately descended, but she was unable to think of anything to break it. *Don't be pathetic.* She chewed, furious at overthinking everything. Why couldn't she relax? Why couldn't she shut down that searing, shockingly sexual response?

Merle didn't have sexual responses to anyone. Why now, with such a known playboy who took nothing and no one seriously? Perhaps that was the problem. Had his reputation sparked a primal response within her subconscious? Had she inherited some genetic predisposition to bounders? She'd always rejected the way her grandmother had labelled her mother—as a foolish woman who'd 'fallen' and brought shame on the family by getting pregnant, unmarried and young—yet that lingering burn curled through her as she heard the strident echo of her grandmother's displeasure.

Stay away from men. You don't want to make the same mistake as your mother.

Everyone made mistakes. Having sex wasn't necessarily one of them. Merle knew her mother was brave and loyal and loving. And frankly, it would be nice to have a sexual response to someone *some time*. Temptation whispered, telling her that an experience with Ash Castle might be perfect, might teach her much, *without* costing her heart. She desperately needed to stop thinking about any of this. She'd initiate a safe conversation instead. The one topic she had in common with him was her work.

'Is there anything in particular you would like me to do with the diaries?' she asked, pleased to have thought of something innocuous to discuss.

'Diaries?' He glanced up.

'Your father's diaries. I found a few in one of the boxes today.'

His mouth compressed and emotion flared in his eyes. 'Direct any questions on his things to Leo. He's the one paying you.'

'But—'

'I don't want to know about it,' he clipped. 'As far as I'm concerned you can burn it all.'

Merle focused on her plate, taking a moment to digest his snap.

He sighed heavily. 'Don't look at me like that.'

'I'm not looking at you,' she answered equably.

'Exactly.' He half-laughed, half-groaned and then sighed. 'Do you really enjoy cataloguing the detritus of people's meaningless lives?'

Oh, wow, there was some bitterness to unravel there.

'Yes, I do,' she said calmly. 'Archives of all sorts, records of people's thoughts and experiences, are valuable.'

'In what possible way?' he asked as if any valid reason was impossible.

'It's the connection to the past, isn't it? Things tether us, help us learn things about our heritage.' She hesitated. 'Sometimes I deal with the records or things other people can't bear to face yet,' she said softly. 'I put them in an order so they're there when people are ready.'

'And if they're not?'

'I put a date on each box for when the contents will be reassessed. If it's deemed no longer valuable it goes to a secure facility to be destroyed.'

His lips twisted. 'That sounds perfect. Make the date tomorrow.'

She shook her head. 'Not in the protocol, sorry.'

'There's a protocol?'

'Sure,' she said softly, but firmly. 'Because these things matter.'

'They really don't.'

She held his gaze.

He cocked his head and blinked. 'You think I'm protesting too much.'

She hesitated. 'I think strong feelings provoke strong reactions.'

'Oh, indeed.' He stared at her for another pregnant moment. 'You're assuming that what's written in those diaries is even true.'

'Actually, I'm not assuming anything. Of course, a historian would study other sources to confirm if one person's account of things is true. But I don't have to worry about that, and discovering dead people's secrets is something I enjoy.' She mirrored his cock of the head and blinked back at him. 'Those of the living too, actually.'

'Allow me to disappoint you early, darling. I don't have any secrets. Secrets are never any fun, despite what others will try to tell you. Take that bunker—it's an unnecessary, expensive monstrosity. And it wasn't my father's only secret. Nor was it the biggest in his life, unfortunately.' Ash coolly reeled off a list. 'Illegitimate offspring. Hidden bank accounts. Shady dealings.' His blandness was too studied. 'And for years I had no idea. It's amazing how little you can know someone even when you live under the same roof.' His direct gaze seared through her. 'Maybe you'll know him better than I did once you're done. Or maybe, as I said, you should just burn it all.'

She was curious about *him* right now, not his father. 'Everyone has *some* secrets.'

'My family life was a family lie,' he said. 'Which I hated. So if I'm going to do something, I'm going to do it with full transparency. No secrecy. No shame. No regrets,' he said with proud finality. 'That's why it's a good thing my half-brother is now in charge of my father's company, not me. Leo's the responsible one. He'll keep an eye out for those employees. Ironic, isn't it? That the child my father denied for so long is the one willing and able to preserve all he built.' He glanced down at his steaming curry and then looked back up at her, his expression even more alert than usual. 'Do you have family treasures of your own?' he asked. 'A mountain of old letters and recipe books and chipped china?'

Merle didn't answer. She'd had to sell everything to afford the care bills for her grandfather, and now she was homeless she had no space to store anything big anyway. But she'd always found solace in *other* old things that she had no direct connection to. Not that she was about to tell deeply cynical Ash Castle that; he'd only scoff.

'Things can be destroyed, Merle,' Ash drawled, proving her point immediately. 'What's the point in holding on to things so tightly when, with a strike of a match, they can be lost for ever?'

'Says a man who accumulates more things than most people.'

'Only money,' he corrected.

'People can be lost too,' she muttered.

'So *things* are sometimes safer than people?' he asked astutely. 'Is that why you surround yourself with them?'

'What makes you think I do?' Her defensiveness rose.

'You spend your days prioritising and protecting material things from other people's pasts,' he asserted. 'But not around actual, real live people.'

She tilted her chin at him, feeling that frisson—that kick from his light teasing. 'And here *you* are,' she said pointedly, 'avoiding actual, real live people.'

'It's a momentary hiatus, not a *habit*, for me.'

'Well.' She breathed softly, absorbing the hit. 'We *all* have bad habits, Ash.'

She took a mouthful of the curry, feeling her tastebuds zing. But her nerves were zinging all the more from the appreciative grin he flicked her. Suddenly, he pushed back from the table.

'I've forgotten something vital.'

Before she could question what, he went inside. She took the chance to release a breath she'd not realised she'd been holding. Instinctively, she knew they were dancing around something more serious than either of them wanted to recognise. Maybe she ought not to open the lid on those hurts, yet she couldn't resist her curiosity.

He returned brandishing a bottle of champagne. She eyed it warily. 'Is it as expensive as that other one?'

'More.' He laughed negligently and popped the cork. 'Will you help me drink it?'

'I imagine you could manage it on your own.'

'Are you referring to my insatiable appetite?'

That awareness fizzed inside her, the bubbling sensation mirroring the miniature ones in the glass. She lifted the glass he filled for her and took a haughty sip because he'd set a challenge she didn't have the strength—or will—to ignore.

Ash had tried to distract himself by mucking about in the kitchen, but now she was sitting across the table and it felt like the most intimate date he'd had in years. Which was crazy, because it wasn't really a date. They were just two people staying in the same house sharing dinner. His body begged to differ. His brain? That needed respite from the edginess in their conversation. They'd veered close to topics he didn't discuss. He needed to raise shields, and to do so he fell back on customary form—to be outrageous and turn this to a totally superficial skin-to-skin tease. He'd make the most of their chemistry. It was the perfect distraction.

'Are we going to talk about it?' he asked bluntly. The colour in her cheeks deepened in that gorgeous way. 'The kiss, I mean.'

She sipped her champagne to avoid answering.

'Don't worry, darling,' he purred. 'You're not the first woman I've rendered speechless.'

'Well, *you* are the most arrogant man I've met,' she said calmly—no flirtation couched in mock-outrage.

'Am I?' He grinned and went in search of some truth. 'Or maybe it's just that you've not met many men.'

'Actually I've met several arrogant jerks over the years.' She lifted her chin. 'You're by far the worst.'

Again, no hyperbole. Just a calm, direct comment. Ash stifled his surprise. Somehow he'd imagined her to be a complete innocent—permanently hidden away from the eyes and attentions of other men, like some Rapunzel trapped in a tower of archival boxes. But she'd met several guys? When? Who?

'The thing is, you don't have to be,' she said, derailing his curiosity. 'You attract women easily.' She angled her head and a gleam shone in her deep eyes. 'Of course, mostly it's your bank account,' she said flatteningly. 'But your looks help. And your confidence to a degree. You just take it too far.'

His looks? His confidence *to a degree*? He was used to women being attracted to him and to all kinds of attempts at flirtation or to capture his interest. But sweet, shy Merle's serene stocktake of his eligible bachelor qualities didn't feel like a flirtation attempt. The realisation was both refreshing and disappointing.

'But the "one night" thing that you admitted to last night,' she added. 'That's purely for *self*-preservation.'

'You're incorrect,' he drawled. 'That's for *their* benefit. I'm not a marrying man, Merle. I never will be.'

'Oh, really?' She pouted and looked downcast. 'Perhaps I'll learn to live with the disappointment, eventually.'

He chuckled. 'Miaow.'

Her lashes lifted and those deep brown eyes stared soulfully into his. 'As if that's not the reaction you wanted.'

What he *wanted* was becoming untenable. Not to mention impossible.

It was his turn to take another sip of champagne to buy time. Easy banter usually stood him in good stead. He enjoyed setting the mark and establishing the very basic rules he lived by. He generally glided towards the inevitable conclusion that chemistry such as this inspired. It was all anticipation—in the parry and thrust of prospective pleasure. But Merle seemed determined to stamp out the sparks showering between them with absurdly prim, pragmatic denial. Didn't she know desire like this could only be destroyed by as explosive means as possible? The frankly animal urge to reach out and rouse her spirit disturbed him. For the first time he was truly trapped by lust. And it was *crazy*.

'You're blushing.' He was so tense he sounded husky.

'It's the champagne,' she muttered.

'It's not the champagne,' he muttered back.

She lifted her chin with a defiance that undermined itself with its own fierceness. 'It's not you either.'

'Then there's only one thing remaining.'

'And that is…?'

'You.' He smiled as triumph roared at the realisation. '*You're* bothering yourself.'

Her flush receded, leaving her a little pale, but her gaze didn't shy from his. 'Is that something you're familiar with?'

Clever woman, wasn't she? Reflecting his barb back at him and forcing a fragment of honesty to escape from beneath his veneer. 'Sure. I get very sick of myself.' He stiffened. 'But I know how to escape my own thoughts.'

'Via rakish escapades?' Her gaze was relentless.

'Rakish?' He chuckled at her old-fashioned terminology. 'Why not? There are worse ways, I think.' He cocked his head and challenged her. 'What are you going to do to escape your thoughts, Ms Prim?'

'Just because I won't slither beneath your spell, you say I'm prim. *Really?*'

She was opting for diversion—setting up another superficial spar to escape answering with actualities. He knew the gambit well, as he'd played it many times himself.

'Don't worry, I'm not taking it personally.' He smiled. 'Because I don't think it's just me—I don't think you'd slither beneath *anyone* in any great hurry.'

She tossed her head to the side. 'Because no one would want me to?'

Actually no, that wasn't at all what he'd meant. The flash of vulnerability on her face let him know that wasn't a play for compliments. In fact, he'd scored an unintended foul. The vein of rejection that everyone had apparently ran particularly deep within her. *Why?* Protectiveness—that rare sensation for him—surged.

'We both know one guy who definitely wants you to,' he muttered almost angrily. 'And there's no way I'd *ever* be the only one.'

'This is what you do, is it?' she asked. 'Flatter any female in the vicinity. Is it a compulsion to seduce everyone into liking or wanting you?'

Was that the effect he was having on her? He hoped so. But he realised she didn't believe he actually meant what he'd said about her. 'So judgmental, Merle. Why?'

He waited as she looked down at the empty plate before her, hiding her mesmerising eyes from him. Then she glanced back up and he saw a new bitterness in the heat of her rich gaze.

'I'm jealous of you.'

Surprise silenced him.

'You swing through life, apparently not giving a damn about anything, yet getting *everything* you want.'

'I've already told you I work for what I get,' he pointed out.

'In business, sure. But in your love life?'

'Love life?' He scoffed. 'I don't have a *love* life.'

'Sex life, then. It comes so easily to you. You have no idea how hard it is for normal people.' She paused. 'Shy people.'

That hot wave of protectiveness washed over him again, only this time it was merged with an equally powerful surge of possessiveness. *Both* feelings were foreign. Both were undeniable. 'All you have to do is ask, Merle. All you have to do is say yes. Have you ever done either?'

Colour swept over her skin and clued him in to her true status.

'Never *ever*?' His eyes widened. 'Not to anyone for anything?'

'I went on a date once.'

'*Once?*' Prim wasn't the word for her. But something compressed his chest, a premonition of her pain. 'You were hurt?'

Her attention flashed back to him. 'Only my pride.'

He was relieved, but that underlying irritative effect she had on him flared up again. 'So because that happened *once*, you've not said yes again?'

She shrugged dismissively. 'No one's ever asked again.'

She'd been ignored? No. His gaze narrowed and he slowly shook his head. 'Maybe that's because you work locked away in isolated rooms with only old, dusty things for company. How do you expect to meet anyone if you don't go where the living are? I bet you've never downloaded any dating apps.'

She bet *he* never had either. Merle shuddered at the thought of trying to make herself sound attractive on an app in twenty words. 'What would you have me do? Wear a tiny bikini and pout in a profile pic?'

Annoyed by him and by her own wayward thoughts, she stood and carried the plates inside to the kitchen with ruthless efficiency, as if she could wipe this heated awkwardness away like harmless crumbs.

'Merle—'

'I've something to show you,' she interrupted. Distraction all the way.

She'd prove to him things from the past were worth preserving. That slightly wicked gleam lit in his eyes again and she had to catch her laugh. She went back down the corridor to the study. It only took a minute to grab the boxes she'd found and bring them back to the kitchen. 'Look at these—it's an amazing collection. I think they're all vintage.'

She put them on the bench in front of him. There were a number of traditional games—chess, snakes and ladders, dice games and puzzles. Glancing up, she saw he'd paled slightly.

'Where'd you find those?' he asked gruffly.

'In a cupboard in the study.'

'Curious thing, aren't you?' His gaze was locked on the games in front of him. Tension bracketed his sensual mouth, stealing away his customary smile.

'It's my job to notice interesting things tucked away in dark corners,' she answered lightly. 'Someone did a good job of collecting these. They would have been hard to find. Especially in such good condition as this—they'll be worth a lot. This compendium alone is worth thousands.' She placed the last antique wooden box down carefully.

'They weren't collected for their value,' Ash said softly. 'They were my mother's.'

'Your mother's?'

He now reached for the nearest. 'I thought they were long lost.' He frowned. 'Everything else of hers seems to…'

Merle paused, unsure how to respond.

'All those things in the boxes you're sorting,' he added softly. 'All the art, the books, the collections. They're all his, right?'

Her heart sank at the hurt in his voice. She'd not meant to upset him, merely distract him. 'I'm sorry—'

'Don't be. I'm glad the games are still here.' A half-smile tugged his lips. 'She loved a challenge.'

Merle was intrigued. 'Was she a risk-taker, too?'

'Oh, she was a player and she liked to win.'

'So that's where you get it from.' Merle glanced up when she heard his choking laugh. She was stupidly pleased to see his smile return.

'She made a couple of bad bets in her life,' he said. 'Her husband being one of them. She had a chronic health condition, so she wasn't on the sports sidelines when I was a kid. She had a lap table she'd set up on her bed and we'd play. Board games, puzzles, cards.' He lifted the lid off one box and ran a finger across the wooden counters. 'I haven't seen these in for ever.'

It took a moment for everything he'd just said to really sink in. How sad for his mother and for him. Yet they'd had good times.

'So which was your favourite?' she asked. 'Which are you best at?'

She saw that dangerous, playful light in the amber.

'You want to play with me, Merle?'

'A *board* game,' she stressed. 'Why not?'

'It's not too much of a risk for you?'

'I think you have your own code of conduct.'

'High praise,' he mocked. 'You think I play around, but I play by the rules.'

'*Your* rules, yes. One night, right?'

He drew back and shot her a serious look. 'No cheating. No children. No commitment. Fun and done.'

'In that one night? Truly? You don't ever want more with someone?'

'What is more, Merle?' he asked sardonically. 'It's only messy.'

'What's so wrong with mess?'

'People are greedy. And selfish. Everyone is, at heart. Especially me.'

'I think that's just an excuse,' she said cheerfully. 'To make it easier for you. You don't even have to *try* to be better.'

He laughed then drew in a steadying breath. 'You want to see if you can beat me, Merle?'

'I'm not afraid to *try*.' She lifted her chin. 'A *board* game.'

Satisfaction flared between them both.

'You pick the game,' he ordered. 'I want you to have some kind of chance.'

'Snakes and ladders,' she said promptly. It was the only one she actually knew the rules to. 'A roll of the dice and you can win or lose.'

'You're relying purely on chance? You're not willing to back yourself and pick a strategy game?'

'Who says you can't have strategy in snakes and ladders?' She scooped up the dice and shook them in her hand.

'You're not going to kiss them?' he teased.

'I don't think that will bring me any extra luck.' She rolled and made the first move on the board.

'Kiss mine for me,' he jeered.

She puckered and made a loud popping sound with a fake kiss. He promptly rolled double sixes.

'Thanks, darling.'

She didn't reply. She was too busy fuming at the man's luck. That wicked grin spread over his face as he counted out the spaces he got to move—landing on a ladder, naturally enough. Three rolls along she rolled the dice and found herself on the head of a snake and slid back to the beginning again, while he was already onto his next move.

'You play a fast game,' she noted. 'Barely taking the time to consider your options.'

'Because I know what I need to do.' He slid his counter on the board and lifted his intense gaze to hers. 'Look at that,' he said softly. 'I won.'

'Wasn't it inevitable, given you're so much more experienced?' She gazed across the game to meet his intense stare.

'If you're not used to playing games, why are you so willing to try?' he asked.

'Because there's always hope, right? There's always a chance there might be an *exception*.'

'You want to risk everything on chance? On the possibility of being an exception?' He shook his head and laughed. 'Maybe you're more of a risk-taker than most.'

He was wrong. Yet once again she was tempted to take all the risks with him. Once again she was a hot mess of confusion and conflict. Of desire and denial. And of silence.

He cocked his head and smiled slowly as he studied her with that relentless intensity. 'I bet I know what the troubling thoughts are.'

'Do not, I beg, reveal your appalling arrogance yet again.'

For him it was merely an entertaining escape, but for her it was pure, tantalising mystery.

He leaned back. 'You can't stop thinking about that kiss any more than I can.'

Was he really thinking about it? Or was that one of his many practised lines? *Did it really matter?* Because for her it was the truth. He was magnetic.

'Why not a repeat?' he asked.

'There are so many reasons,' she muttered. 'But I think you just want what you can't have,' she said. 'You want the woman who doesn't want you.'

'Is that what you think you are?' He chuckled. 'I've met many women who didn't want me and I've never felt the need to persuade them otherwise. You're only saying no because you can't stand to say yes to me. You don't like it when I win, because you think that means you lose,' he muttered. 'But I promise you won't lose. And, if you like, you don't have to say anything at all. You can choose to stand there, or you can move to that other room and have your own space. Your choice. But I know what I want.'

'And you always get it?' She shook her head. 'I don't believe anyone gets what they want all of the time.'

'Then why not get what you want when you *can*,' he suggested with a smile, 'when it's right here, waiting for you to simply admit it?'

He made it sound logical and easy and as if it meant nothing. Which, of course, it did for him.

'You're so annoying,' she muttered feebly.

He stepped closer. 'Why shouldn't you get what *you* want, Merle? Why shouldn't you get to have some fun?'

'A one-time limited offer?' She paused.

'Games end, Merle.'

True. And no matter how he tried to spin it, there was always a winner and a loser. She knew she was nothing but another challenge to him. Once conquered, the challenge of her would be destroyed and his interest would wane. He was mercurial, a creature easily bored. Never truly satisfied.

But *she* could be satisfied. She could finally experience the one thing everyone else in the world seemed to go crazy for. And if the hint she'd had earlier was any indication? It would be so worth it. Couldn't *she* be the winner? But a streak of insecurity undermined the warmth flowing through her. 'Is this because I'm the only woman around for miles? Because we're stuck here together and you need a release? Because you're bored? Because—'

'You're magnificent and fascinating. Because you've snared my interest and I want to work out why. Because I desperately want to make you feel good enough to stop questioning everything and just enjoy our explosiveness.'

His fierce interruption silenced her. Was this explosive for him too, then? Was this something a little less ordinary for him? The prospect tempted that weak part of her.

'There's nothing wrong with sex,' he breathed. 'Did someone tell you there was?'

Merle froze. He'd veered so close to the truth there. She'd tried to mute her grandmother's endless lectures about being 'good', about not bringing shame home. She'd linked shame so explicitly, so wrongly with sex. Her mother's fears for her still echoed too. She'd never seen an example of women allowed to simply have fun, let alone anything loving.

'So there has to be something wrong with me because I'm saying no to you?' She turned defensive.

'But you haven't said no to me yet.' He held up his hands. 'Be *honest*.'

That was an altogether different dare from him.

'I've told you the rules I play by,' he said. 'You know I don't cheat. I don't lie.'

'And I do?'

'To yourself, maybe. Isn't that what you're doing right now?'

Emotions were heightened. Desire was heightened. But so was doubt. She'd been burned before.

'I'll admit we have some chemistry. That doesn't mean I'm going to say yes. I like pudding a lot, but I'm not going to over-indulge because it wouldn't be good for me. There's such a thing as balance.'

'But you're not indulging at all. There's no balance there either.' A smile curved his lips. 'Why don't you just sample a little? You can say "enough" any time you like.' He gestured towards the oven. 'You know there's pudding on offer here tonight.'

She glanced at the oven and laughed. 'I couldn't possibly. I've had sufficient.'

'Oh, Merle,' he chastised softly. 'Since when was *sufficient* ever enough?'

CHAPTER SIX

ARE WE GOING to talk about it?

Not only had Merle never had such kisses to discuss before, but she'd never had anyone to discuss them with either. She'd stayed in the shadows, silent almost all of her life. She'd been taught—by her mother, her grandmother, and her own small experience—that invisible equalled safe and that men meant trouble. But Ash hadn't let her hide. And, while they'd danced with banter and tease, at the core was a challenge for honesty. For her to embrace her own desires. Now seductive possibilities fired her blood, pushing her pulse faster. He was leaving at the end of the week, their paths would never intersect again, no one would ever even know they'd met, no one would ever care—certainly not him. He was a hedonist who lived in the moment and who took advantage of all good opportunities when they arose—in business and in pleasure, right?

Maybe she could learn more than a few things from him.

She paced the length of her suite, unable to unwind. She'd run away after dinner—wary that her feelings were going to topple her into making a rash decision that couldn't be reversed. But wouldn't she be crazy not to claim such a chance? To experience something most other people enjoyed? It wasn't as if she was at risk from him when she knew exactly what she'd be getting. And not getting. She'd not been saving her virginity. It was more that she'd not met any possible takers until now.

Hot and bothered, she ran a cold bath, hoping to relax and settle her runaway thoughts. But she couldn't stop thinking about him. Ash offered brevity, but intensity. A night at his island hideaway. Wouldn't it be a chance for her to freely explore and accumulate one great memory? She didn't need to take everything so seriously, did she?

Because she couldn't ignore this ache. This burning temptation that not even icy water could soothe.

When she finally got out of the bath she heard a splash coming from outside. She glanced out of the window and stilled. Ash was back in the pool, taking a swim at nearly midnight. Occasionally, the light that spilled from the house caught him—making the droplets of water on his body glint like diamonds. Beautiful, powerful, impossible to tame and so tempting. But even as her heart thundered and her blood raced, she stepped back and turned away, too schooled in self-denial.

In silence.

But the tension in her body didn't lessen through the sleepless night. That temptation no longer whispered, it clamoured. She worked in the study all morning, thoughts circling incessantly until a low anger throbbed in time with the building pain in her temples. She was annoyed not by the ideas he'd planted in her head, but by her own cowardice. Her own docility. She was sick of doing as she'd been told half her life. She was sick of staying quiet. She was sick of missing out on what she really wanted. And she was so tired of him swimming in that damned pool, flaunting his perfect body.

She stalked out of the study onto the patio. His magnetism was too strong for her to resist any longer. She wanted to have what she wanted—*who* she wanted. He looked up. The immediate expression in his eyes scorched away the last of her shyness so that certainty flooded her.

He hoisted himself out of the pool in one powerful action, picked up a towel from a lounger and wrapped it round his waist. 'Going to roll the dice, Merle?'

He knew already. But now *he* waited. Yet, by just being near such a source of outrageous vitality, she finally felt emboldened and empowered enough to step from the shadows and speak up.

'I've decided I want…' She broke off, battling the furious blush she felt swamping her skin.

He stood more still than she did. 'Want?'

She breathed out. This still wasn't easy. 'What you dared. You. Here. Now.'

Ash's customary wicked smile didn't light up his face. Instead, he continued to look alarmingly serious. 'You said you never over-indulge and ran away the second I offered dessert.'

She had. She'd turned tail and fled, overwhelmed by the thoughts in her own damned mind. 'You said I don't indulge at all. You were right.'

His gaze locked on her more intently.

'I want to finish what we started in the bunker.' Merle's wish slipped out. 'In fact, I want more.'

He didn't move. He didn't answer. He just stared at her, expressionless.

Merle counted down the achingly slow seconds until doubt exploded in a ball of fire in her stomach. She'd just thrown herself at him and he wasn't reacting at all how she'd anticipated.

'Merle…'

The strained whisper was so unlike him. His tone holding nothing short of…regret?

Merle flinched, mortified. Hadn't she seen the flicker of interest in his eyes just then? Hadn't he spent all of dinner last night tempting and teasing her into saying yes? Cold horror struck as her doubts mushroomed. Had it all been a ploy to see if he could get her to *yes*? Had *that* been his real game? Had it been a prank—with him taking cruel pleasure in seducing her, only to say no?

Had history just repeated itself—only way, way worse? *Why* had she thought he'd be any different? He was the worst of them all. Taking a trip on an ego ride, pulling a woman he didn't actually *want*. Well, he'd won, hadn't he?

Only now she was humiliated. Now she had to get away. She hated her foolish naivety. She shouldn't have done it, shouldn't have trusted him. Shouldn't have thought she could ever have something easy and light in her life. Something just for herself. Shouldn't have thought, even for a second, that someone like him would…

On a gulp of horror she turned to rush away. But he caught her from behind, stopping her headlong retreat, his arms like steel.

'Merle.'

A harsh, raw growl.

His heat, his thundering heart, pressed against her back briefly. Then he turned her around in his arms so it was her chest pressed to his. She bowed her head and closed her eyes for good measure. Not resisting his hold, not wanting to look in his eyes and see smugness, or rejection. Or, worse, anything like an apology. She would survive his mortifying explanation and then slink to her suite to wallow.

Ash stared down at her, furious with himself as confusion threw him into unaccustomed silence. Having her come to him like this was everything he'd wanted. He should've been kissing her already—glorying in the gorgeous silk of her body and celebrating the electricity that arced every time he got within ten feet of her.

Yet the second she'd said it, something felt wrong. Damned if he knew what or why. There was just a knot in his gut that had tightened to the point where he'd been unable to move. Until she'd started to run. Then he'd gone purely on instinct.

Now he couldn't let her go because her running away would be worse than anything. And, now he had his hands on her, he was unable to resist touching her more. But the tension in her body made him wary. His muscles felt prepped, ready to fight an internal war he didn't fully understand the reason for.

'You don't do this, Merle,' he said.

Was that it? Was that what was bothering him? Her innocence? He growled beneath his breath as that spectre from his past flickered in his mind. The shy, innocent girl he'd humiliated and the horrific repercussions that had followed for him. 'I'm not going to be responsible for your broken heart.'

Merle stiffened and drew an audible breath. 'Of all the arrogant things to say,' she muttered. But she didn't pull free of his arms and she easily, easily could have. 'You're not going to break my heart. That's not what I want.'

'What do you want, then?' Ash glared at her as that strange fury within rose.

Her request had been so spartan, so dispassionate. She wanted him as if he were some kind of take-away option in a food court. It niggled. Even though it was exactly all he ever did.

'Don't panic,' she snapped. 'I'm not about to request your hand in marriage. I have that message loud and clear.'

He couldn't even pull together a grin. 'You—'

'Don't need rose petals or candles, or anything sappy like that.'

Her cynicism punctured his lungs. Her rejection of anything romantic made him feel worse. 'Nothing sappy?' He cupped her chin, making her look up so he could see into her eyes. 'So what, shall we just make a time to meet in your bed? A half-hour appointment or something?'

A wall of red scaled her face—a swirl of embarrassment and hurt. Finally she tried to twist away from him. 'Forget it—'

'No,' he said flatly. He refused to do that. Refused to release her. But the second she stilled he softened his hold, treating her like the wild bird she was—fragile and flighty, a creature who needed freedom to feel safe. He couldn't resist caressing her gently, smoothing his hands down her back, tracing her beautiful shape. He wanted her in his bed—more than anything he'd wanted in a long time. But he didn't want it quite like this. Not so clinical and cold. Not when she made him feel anything *but* cold. Anything but himself. Hell, she made him feel as if he had to do the honourable thing.

And what's that? he mocked himself. To be protective? Chivalrous? Assume he knew better than she? What was he *thinking*? More importantly, what was *she* thinking?

'Don't you want more than this?' he growled. More than a night that meant nothing and would go nowhere?

'Are you asking that because I'm a virgin?' Her eyes sparked with that dangerous edge.

The word winded him, even when he'd known.

'Probably,' he admitted, helpless to be anything but honest in the intensity of her gaze. 'You don't strike me as reckless and you've held on to your virginity for a long time.'

He'd have had her yesterday if they'd stayed in that bunker, which was why he'd unlocked it. That one kiss had been incendiary. When she was in the vicinity his reasoning escaped him completely, but Merle Jordan wasn't a player on an equal footing to him. He had to remember that.

'What makes you think this is reckless?' she said. 'Perhaps I've taken the time to think it through.'

'It's barely more than twenty-four hours since we met.' He huffed out a tense breath.

'I bet you've slept with women you've barely known half an hour.'

He couldn't actually deny that. But *she* couldn't say the same. She was a thinker. Measured. Cautious and deliberate. So what had changed? He needed to know her *why*. 'Have you formulated a list of pros and cons?' he asked.

'Actually, yes, I have.'

He almost laughed. 'Tell me.'

Her shoulders tensed. She might be reliant on reticence, but she had courage when it counted. Even though he knew she was mortified, she summoned the strength to speak.

'On the negatives, it might be a little...uncomfortable.' She shot him an awkward look and her blush burned again. 'But your experience will be a good thing. One of us will know how to...what to...'

'Right,' he muttered, saving her from further stammering. 'Any other possible negatives?'

She bit on her lower lip. 'I have the feeling I might like it a lot.'

He nearly choked. 'That's a negative?'

'That kiss was...a revelation,' she said. 'Obviously. That's why I'm here now.'

An inordinate amount of pride flooded him because he knew her descriptor was an understatement. He was always considerate with a lover but never had it mattered as much. Never had he really *cared*. He wanted her to experience the absolute best.

'So the problem is I might want more than what you're able to offer,' she murmured.

More than what he was able to offer? In what way? He didn't want to know.

He had to move on. 'And the pros?'

'I'll finally get to experience what most other women my age have been enjoying for years.'

Desire held him in thrall, yet there was that irritation on

the underside of his ribs. That resistance within him still. He didn't know why. It was a hitherto unawakened instinct, rapidly being overridden by another one—that usual hunt for hedonism. Why was he worried this might end in a mess? It'd only be a night like any other. But that whisper rose again, telling him that walking away now would be the right thing to do.

Right for whom?

A different, far louder whisper mocked. Because damned if Ash ever did the right thing. He was Hugh Castle's son, after all. He wasn't supposed to have a conscience.

'What if there's a worst-case scenario?' he growled. 'What if the contraception fails and you end up pregnant?'

'It's unlikely,' she said. 'You've managed not to get anyone pregnant before, right?'

'You've thought of everything.' Whereas he'd been consumed by pure lust. Barely able to think of anything else all day.

'But here's the biggest problem.' She put her hands on his chest as if to steady herself. 'I want more, remember?' She gulped. 'I don't want one night, I want *every* night that you're here.'

Every night? For the first time the prospect of more than one was undeniably arousing. Because this was Merle—shy, wary Merle, saying exactly what she wanted. And it was him.

A shocking possessiveness surged, shooting satisfaction through every muscle, but he couldn't move. Couldn't answer. It was the strangest sensation to be so transfixed. To be so tempted. To be so touched.

She gazed up at him—reading something in his face—and began to backpedal. 'You don't have to...you can just forget it. I'm sorry. You were probably just bored and—'

He kissed her. It was the only way to smash away her defensive barrier. It was the only thing he wanted. He could no longer resist the need howling inside him. Never had he been as conflicted about, as fascinated by someone.

But suddenly all that indecision inside was burned off by the far more important need to coax her sweet, sultry response. To his pleasure, it took the merest moment. With the softest of moans her soft, yielding body pressed against his. Satisfaction sluiced through him. He had no doubts now. He'd give her what she wanted. *All* that mattered was *her* satisfaction.

Merle couldn't catch her breath. She could feel his energy coil and passion build in his kisses. Her heart thundered as her doubts remained. He'd looked so surprised, so conflicted…she didn't want him doing this from pity. But as the dominance deepened in his kiss he held her with more assurance, more purpose. As if sensing her final concerns, he pressed her against the hard evidence of his arousal so she could make no mistake. He wanted her. His barely contained energy washed away the sting of rejection she'd felt only moments earlier.

'I have to go back on Sunday. So I will give you a week,' he promised slowly, his eyes glittering. 'But you have to give me time too.'

She frowned, still dizzy, not understanding.

'The *days*,' he clarified, possessively running his hand down her spine and pressing her more firmly against the steel wall of his body. 'You'll take the rest of the week off work and spend every moment with me.'

His request shocked her. While she wanted all the nights, somehow the days seemed more intimate. More intense. More terrifying.

'I have work to do.' She licked her dried lips.

'You worked all weekend.' He watched her intently from beneath lowered lids, his usual easy amusement veiled. 'I bet you're already ahead of your contractual obligations.'

'But—'

'Leo will be sued for flouting health and safety rules if you don't take days off like you're supposed to. He'll get done for providing an unsafe work environment. And Leo, I know, is a stickler for the rules.'

A flash of fear gripped her. He wanted *everything*.

Relax, fool. It'll just be a holiday fling.

Wasn't that exactly what she wanted? All Ash was doing now was tweaking this new game. Raising the stakes, out to win what *he* wanted. The gleam in his eyes intensified, the curve of his sensual mouth deepened and he bent his head to brush his lips across her cheekbone. And that was the point at which she surrendered.

She could barely think for the way his fingers slid over her, for the heat in his gaze as he studied her mouth, for the way temptation was unfurling fronds of anticipation from deep in her belly. She didn't know why he'd hesitated before. Maybe she'd misread that—her own doubt demons amplifying what had merely been a moment of surprise. Honestly? It didn't matter any more. Not when he was touching her like this.

She breathed out slowly. 'You want…'

'Your company.' His lips roved. 'All week. If this is what you want, then we're going all in.'

All or nothing.

It was up to her whether to take it or leave it. That was when she realised Ash Castle would always win, whatever the game he was playing. He had that intense, focused determination to make the play as perfect for himself as he could. But Merle couldn't walk away from what he could make her feel. She didn't want to. So she finally uttered the one little word she'd been biting back since the moment she had first set eyes on him.

'Yes.'

His lips met hers again—luscious kisses that were intoxicating and everything she'd wanted. Yet the need burning through her body wasn't soothed. Until with infinite, terrible, wonderful slowness he unzipped her coveralls.

'Merle…' He muttered so low, his words almost slurred together '…do you have any idea how beautiful you are?'

'Don't—'

'Speak the truth?'

'Flatter me.' She closed her eyes as he caressed the skin he'd exposed.

'Is it so hard to believe I might be being honest?'

'Can't you just kiss me? We don't need to complicate—'

'Not complicate,' he corrected with a smile. 'Communicate. I want to know what you like, sweetheart. What you want. What you need. Be honest with me.'

She stared into his eyes—dazed, confused, aching. Hadn't she just been honest? Hadn't she just asked? She didn't know what else to say…

His hand swept across her shoulder and up her neck. His fingers splayed and he cupped the back of her head, holding her so he could see into her eyes, so he could lean so close she could feel his breath, so he could tease… But that burn within her was too strong. She glared at him.

'Okay.' He chuckled and, drawing her close, pressed his mouth to hers again.

Such a contrasting, delicious mix of hot and soft and hard and irresistible. She leaned into him as with sure, bold strokes he fanned the flames igniting inside her. Her yearning built as he created sensations she'd never experienced but wanted so much more of. Her toes curled as he nibbled her earlobes and then gently sucked them into soothing submission. It was the most shockingly erotic, intimate thing.

'Sweetheart.' His sigh was tense as she shuddered. 'You're making a mess of all my good intentions.'

'What intentions?' she breathed shakily.

'To do what I've been dreaming about for ever.' He toyed with the silky slip of a bra she wore.

She shook her head, unable to speak. But he'd not been dreaming about her for ever.

'Pleasing you,' he muttered. 'I ache to please you.'

His mouth was on hers again, so she couldn't answer, while his fingers had slid south and were wreaking havoc on her most secret places. Teasing, exploring and so infuriatingly, magically wicked, he brushed against the soft fabric of her panties and she was so glad she'd been too hot to bother with anything but her underwear beneath her coveralls today. The slide of his tongue in her mouth matched the slide of his fingers against her aching, hungry core. She moaned at the insistent, playful pleasure. Oh, he was big and strong and wicked. She clutched at his shoulders, barely able to stay upright, gasping as it suddenly sneaked up on her.

'Like *that*, Merle.' His rough growl of approval sent her over the edge.

'Ohhhhh.' An orgasm. *The* orgasm. So easy—from so little. But it was hard and quick and almost unbearable in its sudden impact and delight.

She closed her eyes, resting her head on his chest while she caught her breath. With her coveralls slipping from her shoulders and her legs trembling like those of a newborn deer, walking was impossible. Ash laughed delightedly and picked her up as if she were little more than a feather. Truthfully, she was a lot more.

'Seriously?' she half spluttered as he carried her inside and up the stairs to the second floor. She needed to provoke a little tease, to hear his voice so she could be reminded that this was just for fun. Just for now. 'You want to flex your superior strength?'

'Oh, I plan to flex everything, darling.'

Her little laugh faded as he placed her on the centre of

his bed. She paid scant attention to the room or its stunning view across the bay. The view she couldn't ignore was right in front of her. The focus in his eyes ignited her senses even more.

He stood back and studied her supine on the bed before him, trying to suppress the desire to squirm her hips. His lips twitched. But then he glanced about, his energy almost crackling as he moved. She rose up onto her elbows to watch as he pressed a button and blinds closed out the rest of the world. He went into the en suite and returned a moment later with one of the gorgeously lush candles that were artfully placed everywhere.

'What are you doing?' she asked.

'Making it perfect.' He lit the candle and placed it on the table by the bed.

He didn't need candles to make it perfect. He just needed to touch her.

Amusement flickered in his eyes, dancing like the flame of the candle he'd just lit. 'You don't think you're worth going to any trouble for? Taking time for?' he teased very gently as he slowly removed her shoes. 'Because you couldn't be more wrong about that.'

She didn't know how to answer him. And then she simply couldn't, as with care and heat and wicked intent he slowly pulled the zip of her coveralls the rest of the way down to reveal her body to him.

He leaned over her and cupped the side of her face, regarding her with impossible seriousness. 'If you don't value yourself, sweetheart, no one else will.'

'You sound like an inspirational social media meme,' she said in a small voice.

At that he laughed. 'You're so defensive. Don't be shy, Merle.'

Easy for him to say. But she was more than pliant, she was willing and helpful as he peeled her coveralls from her.

'Accept nothing less than you deserve,' he muttered. 'You should be satisfied every time you allow a man near you, that's the bottom line—the minimum of what you should get from your lover.'

She didn't want to think about being with someone else in the future.

He, too, suddenly looked serious. 'Your body is for savouring, for worshipping,' he muttered, and the lowest of growls escaped him. 'It's for me.'

The determination in his gaze, that glittering assurance of so much more, melted her.

'I'm going to kiss every inch of you, Merle.' It was half seeking permission, half savage promise.

She could barely nod, she could only enjoy as that tension swirling inside built. More than curiosity, more than yearning, it became hunger. Fierce, impatient hunger. Unclipping her bra, he tossed it to the side to leave her clad only in her plain black briefs. He returned to kissing her—teasing one tight nipple with his tongue while torturing the other with the tips of his too-clever fingers. Then he slowly pushed the panties down her legs, until she was completely bared. Despite that overwhelming heat, now there was vulnerability and her shyness returned. She'd never been naked in front of a man before. She wanted to pull up the sheet to cover her. But the only covering she received was Ash himself. He lay beside her, one leg across hers, his hand splayed across her stomach. His fingers loosely skittered over her skin, helping to ground her. Yet still rousing her. She looked into his eyes and knew what he wanted to do. And she wanted to let him.

With infinite patience he kissed her. Starting again. Melting away every one of those last inhibitions and shreds of self-consciousness. Slowly he kissed every speck of her skin, gently, hungrily working his way to her most private places. Until she was no longer shy, until she was aching for him to reach the destination that was now slick with anticipation for his touch. For his tongue. For the gorgeously wanton way she knew he'd make her feel. Where before she'd thought she wanted a sheet to cover her, now she didn't care. She was so hot, writhing in pursuit of more of the ecstasy he'd given her before. She was suffering such wicked delight beneath the ministrations of his hands and lips and teasing hot breath. But she trusted him with her body. With every intimacy.

He kissed her until she moaned, breathless and hot and aching in all those secret parts he'd stirred to life. Her hips lifted and his hands swept over them—heavy and sure, and kisses followed. Merle closed her eyes. Even the flickering candlelight was now too much to handle. All she could do was focus on the sensations as he licked and nibbled her with the most torturous slow rhythm that was utterly relentless, utterly rapacious. She gasped as the tension within— the tension he'd roused—finally snapped, tossing her once more into shuddering, fantastic ecstasy. Longer this time. Sharper. She had to scream through it.

He gently kissed her back to calmness. And then he pulled her past it to a place where she was restless again, where there was an ache, an unfinished sensation. This wasn't enough. Not yet.

He looked into her eyes and obviously saw the silent wish. He moved off the bed and shoved his swim shorts down. *Finally.* Even all those hours she'd seen him in little else had not prepared her for the impressive, erotic vision of him before her now. His skin was smooth and glittered slightly as the sheen of sweat caught the candlelight. That time beneath the sun had tanned him and it emphasised the fabulous bulges and dips of every hewn muscle. She began to tremble as her whole body ached with recognition and longing. He caught her gaze, held it—and her—transfixed.

A half-smile curved and he returned to brace himself beside her on the bed.

'You're sure about this?' His fingers teased up her thigh.

If she hadn't been before she certainly was now. 'Yes. Please. So sure.'

He was as breathless as she and he held her with such reverence. As if there was nothing in the world he wanted more than this. Thoughtful, teasing deliberation preceded every touch. He was so damned careful, so responsive to her reactions. She shifted beneath him restlessly as he took his sweet, savage time to stir her all over again. She didn't want him to be *restrained*, determined to make it special for her because of her inexperience. He probably wasn't, of course. He'd be this considerate with any lover. Because it was the way he was. His innate courtesy lay beneath the teasing playboy persona. He was multi-faceted—with depths he didn't usually like to display. That realisation peeled away something else within her. He'd bared more than just her body. He had her heart in his hands too. Suddenly she was so vulnerable, so exposed, so much more than physically.

He paused. 'You okay?' Somehow he'd sensed the shift within her. 'We can stop any time. If you change your mind…' He puffed out a difficult breath. 'Just say.' His whisper of reassurance was more of a groan.

His awareness, his concern, undid her even more.

'I don't want to stop. I don't want *you* to stop.' She wanted this more than she'd ever wanted anything. More than an ache. More than desperation. She shivered as that trust surged and the truth escaped. 'I just want you. As amazingly out of control as I feel.'

Something flared in his eyes. A satisfaction. A hunger. But then restraint swept in and his jaw clenched. 'Later.'

'*Now.*' A whispered, heartfelt command.

He stared into her eyes and she saw then his internal,

then physical shift. Instinctively, she slid her legs further apart as he pressed close. She was so focused on him she forgot everything but what was happening in this moment. Ash with her. Ash holding her. Ash sliding inside her, finding his way into her tight-held confidence. He moved slowly, but with a heated strength and a powerful surety that made her shiver even as she welcomed his penetration. It was shockingly real, shockingly good as he gently rocked into her.

'Oh,' she groaned. She could hardly breathe. Hardly believe.

'Okay?' he muttered through clenched teeth. 'You need me to go slower?'

She shook her head and drew in a shuddering breath at the pleasure-pain, the overwhelming sensation, of his first possession. 'Don't stop.'

She wanted this. She liked this—she had the dawning feeling she was about to *love* this.

She sighed as he pushed deeper still, then ebbed, allowing her a chance to breathe. To adjust. And then he slowly pressed again—pushing closer to her. He smiled as she gasped again at the pure sensation. All she could do was curl around him, her hands sliding across his muscular back to find purchase and hold him closer still.

'Ash…' It was so sensational, she was so enraptured, she'd lost her speech.

His gorgeous smile quirked. 'Too gentle?'

It was a blissful, sweet torture. She wanted it exactly the same, yet he was right. She wanted a touch more. So gentle, so fierce, she felt so *full*. Somehow he worked his hand between them, teasing her to slipperiness to ease his occupation. Patience and confidence in his touch, in his relentless, claiming rhythm. It overpowered her again— sudden and hard. She convulsed in spasms of pleasure as the orgasm smashed through her. He growled as she came apart. She clutched him passionately, the fierce power and strength of her own body a surprise as she clamped about him, locking him inside her.

'Merle…' he breathed rawly, almost a warning.

Pressed deep into the mattress by his strong body, she was breathless, almost broken, floating on a current of bliss even as aftershocks made her tremble. Yet he still hadn't had his release. The breathlessness she'd sensed in him before was under control now. Why was he so in control? Didn't he want to finish? Doubts rivered through her even as she felt the hard hunger of him still inside.

'Isn't this good for you?' she asked. She had to ask now. 'Ash—'

'Don't worry about me.' He rested his forehead on hers briefly, his eyes looming close but still so alert. Then a smile tore through his tense expression. 'Demanding woman, aren't you?'

'I just want you,' she said.

He was powerful and strong and she wanted him to be entirely *hers*. The way she'd just been *his*. He was so controlled—too controlled. But at her words that glint lit in his eyes. He lifted his head and pulled his hips back, only to surge close again—anchoring himself deep within her. Impossibly, excitement flowed again, firing her lax muscles into anticipation. Into movement. She rocked beneath him, provoking another fierce thrust from him. She held his gaze—proud, uninhibited. He was in her, with her, and he would give her what she wanted. Himself. That delicious sensation arrowed from her core out to every extremity, curling her muscles in the tight torture of bliss.

'Ash.' She could barely think of her words. 'I want you…'

She didn't know what to do with herself. She was so unprepared for the emotions tumbling through her. And he knew. In the triumph that flashed just before his self-control crumbled she saw his satisfaction. But then he moved—faster, harder, finally out of control, and his grip was tight and his intensity ferocious. His breath came short and quick to match hers as he thrust deeper and harder. And she loved it. She absolutely, hungrily, desperately loved it. She moaned, unrestrained, her response flying full and free, and she revelled as he groaned in reply. He talked, then, in a low growl, expressing the desire, the pleasure, the want, the sheer celebration of finally being right here. Like this. With her. In her. Again and again and again.

The words, the action, the kiss, the carnal completion pushed her to a place she'd never imagined. To a place where time stilled and sensation soared. She arched in a moment of sensual agony. And then devastatingly fierce fireworks exploded from the centre of her body, cascading in blinding brilliance. She screamed as she shook and then tears tumbled as the sensations overtook everything. She was torn to pieces by pure pleasure.

He cried out too. Growling her name with a desperate moan as he lost control in her arms.

But he didn't let her go. He held her. He stroked her hair back from her face, brushed away the few tears that she couldn't stop. They were of pleasure and wonder, gratitude and, okay, yes, with a whisper of sadness. Of not having known for so long that life could and should include *this*.

He kissed her gently as she slowly calmed. He caressed her carefully until the oversensitivity of her skin was soothed and she accepted the extent to which she'd just been irrevocably altered. Not just by having sex, but also by the joy of having someone treat her with passion and tenderness and with utter focus on her needs. Of being gifted an experience so profoundly intimate and pleasurable. One she would never regret, never forget.

And then he did it to her all over again.

CHAPTER SEVEN

'DO YOU NEVER sleep in?'

Ash chuckled at Merle's drowsy question as he set a coffee beside her. He'd always had more energy than he knew what to do with.

'No lie-in *ever*?' She stifled another yawn.

'Drink this and get dressed—'

'Dressed?' She half pouted. 'Is that necessary?'

He paused to appreciate the glimpse of unguarded, luscious laziness. Quiet, primly hard-working Merle had melted into a warm, messy woman who'd whispered what she wanted and destroyed him.

'You're not tempting me back to bed with you,' he said firmly.

Actually, she totally was, but after last night he wanted to see if he could resist—even for a few minutes. He needed fresh air to clear his head and the warmth of the sun on his skin to bring back his energy. And he wanted to share that with her.

'I have plans.' He tempted her with a little mystery. 'Good ones, I promise.'

'You *promise*?' She eyed him with teasing amusement. 'That's big.'

'Not the only thing that's big.' He winked and walked out, chuckling at the groan that followed him.

Fifteen minutes later he smiled again at the sight of her. Back in the black coveralls, she had a hint of heat in her cheeks despite her teasing banter just before. She looked at him and their gazes meshed. Neither of them spoke, yet everything from the night before flickered in his mind. Her gaze suddenly slipped and she intently studied the basket on the kitchen counter as the colour in her cheeks rose. His heart missed a beat and for a moment that feeling returned—the hesitation, the confusion of whether this was the right thing.

Too late now.

He'd taken her—had his way with every inch of her body. Yet he'd not had his fill. Thank heaven he had the week to satisfy her. He'd thought it pure novelty, but now fierce determination flooded him, drowning that uncommon tendril of doubt that had sprouted again. He'd give her an affair she'd never forget.

She reached for the basket. 'We're going...'

'On an adventure.' He batted her hand away, not letting her see what he'd packed. 'You might want to bring a swimsuit.'

Her smile flashed back. 'You just want me out of my coveralls.'

'You just think I'm shallow.' He scooped up the basket and led her to the shed down by the water. 'Are you okay with boating?'

'Do we have to paddle?' She shot him a sideways look.

'No.' He laughed as he unlocked the door. 'We have a motor.'

'Oh, wow.' She stared at the classic motorboat that was stored pride of place in the shed. She fluttered her fingertips along the smooth, highly varnished wood as he opened the rear doors out onto the ramp. 'It's fabulous—we should be on the Italian riviera.' She looked at the other equipment stored in the big shed. 'You really do have all the toys.'

He glanced around the walls briefly before focusing back on the boat he'd not been out in for a decade. 'Most of it's new, but we've had this beauty for as long as I can remember. My mother bought it but I guess it was too valuable for my father to part with,' Ash muttered. 'Even when she was too unwell to walk, I'd carry her down for a spin on the water.'

'That must've been hard.'

'It was kind of normal.' He tried to pull together some perspective. 'There were good moments here.'

But there'd been bad moments too. And the last tainted all other memories of this house. Disappointing someone who really mattered, hurting them irreparably, was the worst. And he had to live with it for the rest of his life. He couldn't change it. Forgiveness could never be attained.

'Ash?'

At that soft query he reluctantly glanced over. The compassion in Merle's gaze had deepened. He didn't deserve it. 'Shall we see if it starts?' He turned away.

The engine coughed, then roared to life.

'First try.' She picked up the basket and came down to the end of the ramp. 'Does it go fast or is it just for show?' She shot him a look as she shrugged on the life jacket he handed to her.

That look was like a spark, bringing him back to the present. He smiled. 'It goes fast.'

Merle beamed. 'I expected nothing less.'

Onboard he let the engine go, whizzing them out along the coastline and past the next couple of bays. Then he headed inland. Merle curled cross-legged on the navy cushions, her face tilted towards the morning sun, her eyes closed. Ash realised almost too late he wasn't watching where he was steering. He cut the engine so he didn't crash them into the dock by accident. Merle blinked at their destination, directing a questioning look at him a second later.

'You must be hungry—you haven't had breakfast.' He stepped from the boat onto the dock.

'Isn't there food in the basket?'

'No. That has other essentials.' He tethered the boat securely.

'Surely it's too early for it to be open?'

Five stars and famous, the restaurant had a waiting list a mile long, so he couldn't quite understand Merle's audible reluctance. 'We're just picking up a package. It won't take a moment. Come on.'

Ash knew the owner and had phoned ahead to ensure they had what he needed. Up at the building, the door was open.

'Hey, Josie.' He gave the waiting woman a quick hug.

'It's been for ever, Ash.'

'It has,' he acknowledged briefly. 'Thank you for doing this.'

'Of course.' Josie smiled, not even trying to hide her curiosity. 'Are you staying long? What are your plans for the house?'

'I'm not sure yet.'

A total lie. He'd have an assistant finalise the sale as soon as he returned to Sydney. Interested buyers had been trying to contact him for months but he'd avoided their calls. Having seen the house now, understanding the changes, there was no question what he'd do. His heart seized and he instinctively turned, seeking his favourite distraction. Besides, he didn't want Merle thinking he didn't want to introduce her to Josie. But she'd vanished. Frowning, he looked more keenly for her and spotted a flash through the window. She'd disappeared into the shadows just outside to intently study some sign.

He thanked Josie again and hurried to catch Merle before she disappeared altogether.

'Why didn't you come in?' he asked as he walked her back to the boat.

'You didn't want anyone to know you were here. I imagined you wouldn't want to be seen with anyone else either.'

She didn't realise that he was pretty much always seen with someone—that it was more unusual for him to be alone in social spaces. Maybe her decision had nothing to do with him. Maybe she'd been playing safe, the way she always did around other people. And she said nothing more now. Did she not talk to people unless they spoke to her first? Did she always hide? Always only work? His curiosity escalated. Why was that? And why the hell was she *homeless*? She was intelligent and did a good job. What had gone wrong in her life for her to be as alone as she seemed to be?

As they chugged back out into the bay, he watched her relax. He wanted to see her step out into the sunlight again. Her knew she liked the warmth of it. He thought she needed it. But he said nothing, knowing when to hold and when to play his hand. Fifteen minutes later, he slowed the boat and guided it to the small private bay that the outgoing tide had exposed.

She glanced back at him. 'Ash. This place is magical.'

Yes. It was the perfect place for the Merle he'd first met that night—the Merle who'd been in her element in her bath full of bubbles and beauty.

'It's actually still our property, but it's only accessible by boat and only at the right time with the tide.' He jumped into the water and held up his hand to help her down.

'So you timed this 'specially?'

He had.

'And this is your idea of breakfast?' Merle giggled as he unpacked the container Josie had handed to him. 'Champagne and oysters?'

He grinned. He'd known she'd appreciate it—and sharing this with her? This was fun. 'Aren't you going to have any?'

He'd poured the champagne and shucked four oysters already, and apparently all Merle could do was stare.

'I've never eaten them,' she confessed.

'Ever?'

She shook her head.

'Here's to another first, then.' Suddenly he had so many firsts in his head for her. He couldn't help teasing. 'You've heard they're an aphrodisiac?'

'Ash.' She glanced at him with those gorgeous eyes. 'I don't think I need an aphrodisiac. Right now I need something to calm me down and make me rational again.'

Her slightly husky, sassy honesty stopped his heart.

'But I like irrational Merle the best,' he countered.

'Is it hard to shuck them?' She watched him pull another shell from the container, chips of ice scattering onto the sand.

'No. I holidayed here every summer all my youth.' He laughed and passed her a half-shell. The plump oyster gleamed.

'You first,' she muttered, looking very doubtfully at the succulent blob.

He obliged, then raised his brows at her. She took the next one he held out and drew a breath. He watched as the salty treat disappeared between her sweet lips.

'Thoughts?' he asked when she'd swallowed.

'I'm…not sure.' Her nose wrinkled.

He laughed, again enjoying her honesty. 'Try another.'

She sipped her champagne to wash it down and Ash broke into the fresh-made fluffy bread and the twist of paper with home-churned butter that had also been in the parcel from the restaurant. She was *very* appreciative of that combination. He smiled, hiding the aching urge to kiss her, but he knew where that would lead and he still had that odd yearning to prove self-restraint to himself.

Merle finished her bread, licked her lips and suddenly stood.

'Are you going in the water?' he asked as she stepped across the sand.

She glanced back at him. 'I thought I would.'

'Not in those coveralls—you'll drown.'

'Then I'd better take it off.' A flicker of colour built in her cheeks. 'I need to clear my head.'

She had a simple black tee beneath and she slipped that over her head to reveal scarlet underwear. *Scarlet.* He sat back on his hands, tickled. She hadn't had the opportunity to go shopping in the last twenty-four hours, so those scarlet strips of silk weren't new, weren't bought specially for his benefit nor any other lover's. These were hers, bought for her *own* pleasure. The heat in his belly exploded. He liked that she indulged herself—those little individual puddings, the bubble bath, the scarlet silk. Her combination of inexperience and earthiness, of sensuality and hesitation with that occasional unpredictability fascinated him.

The urge to chase her was growing. His muscles tensed with the need to wrap her legs around his waist and hold her close. But this was more than his usual desire for release—more than a merely physical ache. This was more fun and more precious. He made himself remain still and watch—appreciating her full, gorgeous curves and inner effervescence as she giggled at the temperature of the water. He only lasted ten seconds before he threw aside any stupid thoughts of self-restraint. He only had a week and it suddenly felt like nothing. He quickly pulled what he needed from the basket and stripped off.

Moments later, he dived after her like the shark he was. He wound his arm around her waist, and to his infinite satisfaction she curled her arms around his neck. Kissing her was pure pleasure. He couldn't deny her. Couldn't deny himself. Even after last night, he wanted her more. She'd unlocked a vault of hunger in him. He carried her out of the water and set her down.

'This is a gorgeous rug,' she practically purred.

'Essential,' he breathed.

He'd tossed it down in those frantic seconds before joining her in the water. Because he didn't want her sand-burned, didn't want her soft skin marked in any way. He rolled onto his back so she was above him. Time stretched. A treasure trove of possibility spread over him. He peeled away the scarlet to bare her breasts. She was stunning and he could hardly stand it as she swept her hands, her mouth, her body over his. This was a woman lost in the throes of desire, exploring her sensuality with him. And he'd never felt as lucky. It felt like a first time for him too—this discovery.

'Like that?' she asked, a breathless sweet echo of his own check-in with her last night. Ensuring understanding, acceptance, pleasure.

The blue sky was a background to her beauty. Brilliant, almost blinding, the whole world seemed hot and vital. She writhed above him—with a moan, with a choked laugh. His heart beat painfully. She killed him. Never had he experienced such sweet, heady enjoyment. She was fresh and intoxicating and wicked. She didn't offer the slick moves of a lover aiming to please another. This was too innocent, the expression in her eyes too dazed. Joining her in this was a privilege that he could only strive to deserve—vowing to make it better for her still. She groaned as he worked his hand between them, feeling her flaring response—and his own complete unravelling.

'You're stunning.' And he was helpless. Unable to think of anything more intelligent to say as she made him arch and shout, 'Merle!'

'I didn't think it could get better than last night.' Merle drowsily studied Ash but couldn't get a read on what he was thinking. He sipped his drink, gazing across the water, his breathing taking time to slow. And as she too slowly recovered, she began to imagine the full extent of the week's possibilities.

He glanced down and met her gaze, his mouth quirking. 'You look like a satisfied kitten.'

'Kitten?' she echoed with mock outrage. She did not want to be a *kitten*. 'Can't I be a panther?'

He answered with another bitingly gentle kiss and suddenly she was all out of shy patience. She didn't want more games. She just wanted *him*. She broke free from his gorgeously decadent lips and breathlessly asked him to take total advantage of her again.

'You've gone to so much trouble,' she muttered as she pulled the soft blanket higher up her shoulders another half-hour later.

'I really haven't,' he laughed lazily.

Perhaps for him it wasn't a bother. Perhaps all these things that were luxuries for her, were simply normal to him.

'Well…' she smiled a little sadly '… I appreciate it, so thank you anyway.'

He turned that intense gaze of his back on her and she saw questions in his eyes.

'Talk to me,' he muttered. 'Tell me everything.'

She shook her head. 'I'm pretty boring, Ash.'

'No. You're an enigma.'

'As flattering as that is…' She shuffled lower in the rug he'd cocooned about them. 'You're in for disappointment.'

'You're not used to talking about yourself?'

'Not used to someone being interested.' She laughed to let him know she was joking. Except they both knew it wasn't a joke. It was a sad, self-piteous truth that she instantly regretted uttering.

'Let me in, just a little.' An Ash Castle dare.

She met his gaze. 'Will you do the same in return?'

'Sure.'

She laughed for real then. 'Are we really going to play emotional strip poker?'

'I'm asking for history, not emotion.'

'You don't think they go together?'

'No. There are just facts. Points along the way.'

'Points that move and shape you.'

He rolled his eyes. 'Why not show me just *one* of the cards you hold so close, Merle?'

She'd let him in—literally—so this shouldn't be difficult. And she wanted him to reciprocate because she wanted to understand what drove him to be as determined—as resolute—as he was. And as recklessly, relentlessly unattached. That he was obviously as curious about her? That tilted the balance. Was fascination as mutual as the desire between them?

'Come on,' he tempted. 'Where did you grow up? When did you get your first coveralls? Why did you go into archival work? I want the whole—'

'Biography? Really?' She tugged the rug higher. She didn't want to tell him about her past. She didn't want him to pity her. Although she had the horrible suspicion he already did.

'Absolutely.' He leaned back and surveyed her, humour dancing with curiosity in his eyes. 'Why not start with the coveralls?'

'You can't cope with them, can you?'

'I've already told you I changed my mind about them.' Ash laughed.

And every time Ash laughed, Merle found herself slipping further under his spell.

'How and why did they become your go-to style?' He was like a terrier.

She sighed and relented. 'When I went to live with my

grandfather I picked up a pair from his workshop and they were comfortable. I felt like I could do anything I liked in them.'

Ash leaned closer. 'There are so many things to unpick in that, I don't know which question to start with.'

She rolled her eyes but tightened her hold on the rug at the same time.

'Your grandfather,' he decided swiftly. 'When and why did you go to live with him?'

Merle gave in. There was no reason to hide this from him and telling him about it suddenly seemed easy. 'My mother was a back-up singer for a series of bands. She spent most of her time on the road, gigging here and there. It was hand-to-mouth and hard but she loved the lifestyle.'

He toyed with the edge of the rug near her fist. 'But how did you fit in with that lifestyle?'

'For the first decade I waited backstage. When I was very small others in the band would watch me and as I got older I quickly learned to be quiet and stay out of the way. Half the time the headline artists didn't even know I was there. That's how I liked it and how she kept me safe.'

'Safe?'

'She worked late nights at downmarket venues. It was good to be invisible when I was a young girl.'

His frown set her on the defensive.

'Don't disapprove,' she said. 'Mum was amazing. She took great care of me. She taught me how to take care of myself.' Merle had known their situation was precarious and that she had to stay silent and good. 'She wasn't supposed to have me there, but she didn't want to leave me with strangers. I sat on a stool in the wings and read. She could see me from the stage. We were okay.'

'Then what happened?'

'When I was about twelve, she sent me to live with my grandparents. She said I needed to go to school, that I was too bright to be held back by her lifestyle. She wanted more for me.'

Ash's expression remained serious. 'Did you know your grandparents before you went to live with them?'

'My mother was young when she had me.' Heat built in her cheeks. 'Very young. They didn't want her to keep me. In the end she left home before I was born. They didn't approve of her choices but she was hardworking and she did everything she could to give me the best.'

'Did they approve of you? Of your choices?'

'Well…' She half smiled. 'My grandmother was determined I wouldn't make the same choices my mother had.' She'd lectured Merle about her mother's 'downfall' so many times. She'd been so controlling, so strict. But Merle had swallowed back the rebellion and resentment and she'd stayed silent. Knowing again that she had to, to survive.

'How did that determination play out?'

Merle's smiled twisted sadly. Ash was too astute—honing in on the most vulnerable angles in her answers.

'She could yell. A lot. It was best to be quiet. Fortunately I was good at that.'

Be silent, be good, be as unseen as possible. Even though she'd hated having to do so. Hated not being able to stand up for her mother. The one time she'd spoken up, she'd suffered a horrible slap-down. Literally. A punishment that had gone on far in excess of what her 'crime' had deserved. But now she shrugged the worst memories off.

'She lectured for hours. She wanted to control my every minute. So I tried to stay out of her way, out of sight really. I tried not to cause any trouble and not give her anything to be disappointed about.'

Her grandmother hadn't realised how hellish school was for Merle—there was no danger of her falling in with a 'bad crowd', because no crowd was interested in Merle.

Ash's frown didn't lessen at all. 'Where was your grandfather?'

'Out in the garage. He was a second-hand goods trader and he had a garage and shed full of everything you could possibly imagine. The safest, easiest way to avoid my grandmother was to be with him. I went with him to all the markets.' He'd given her safe haven from her grandmother. And from school.

'But he didn't stop your grandmother from shouting at you?'

'He did by taking me with him,' Merle countered. 'And when I was home I studied in my room. I did chores without question.' She looked at him and saw he still didn't understand. 'She wasn't well,' she whispered.

'So you had to be quiet and out of sight your entire childhood,' he said grimly.

It hurt, even though it was true. 'You're awfully good at judging.'

'Maybe.' He leaned over and looked into her eyes. 'You're awfully good at making excuses for all three of them.'

Her heart stuttered. 'They were the only family I had,' she answered simply.

'That I do understand.' His lips twisted in a gentle smile. 'So they *were*? What happened?'

She'd known he was going to ask but it was still hard to articulate. Her voice would hardly work. 'When Mum was on tour in Australia there was a fire at the lodge. They didn't have batteries in the fire alarms and they didn't have an up-to-date guest list. She died of smoke inhalation before they realised she was still in the building.'

She knew Ash was looking at her but she couldn't meet his eyes. She never spoke about this. Most of the time she tried not to even remember it.

'I'm sorry, Merle.'

She nodded mutely, her throat too tight for sound to emerge.

'You could've been there too,' he said softly.

She coughed. 'I know.' She'd stayed at that same lodge several times before the move to her grandparents'. 'I was a light sleeper as a kid,' she whispered. 'Maybe if I'd been there I would've heard something, maybe I'd have woken. Maybe I could have saved her.' She dreamed she had sometimes. Then she'd wake and remember the worst was real.

For a moment there was silence. But it wasn't strained, it was oddly connecting.

'I was devastated when my mother died,' Ash said gruffly, looking out across the water. 'Even though I knew it was coming, it wrecked me.'

His quiet admission devastated something within Merle.

'She had a heart condition all of her life,' he said. 'I always wished I could've done something about it even when I knew I couldn't.'

Merle's heart ached at the guilt echoing in his voice.

So he was human. He wasn't always supremely confident, floating through life with bulletproof, brilliant ease. He had hurts too. She'd known that. And whatever had happened with his father had cemented his slide into rebellion. It wasn't that he didn't care. Maybe it was because he cared an awful lot? And he didn't want to.

'How old were you?' she asked.

'Eighteen, at the end of my final year of school.' He frowned and looked back at her, that alert curiosity lighting his eyes once more. 'How was school for you—when you finally went?'

'Horrendous. I was never going to be popular like you.' She laughed a little sadly. 'And don't even try to tell me you weren't. People can't cope with someone being a bit different and I was *very* different. I'd never been to school, I had no clue how to play the social clique game...' She broke off.

'So how did you survive?'

'The same way as always. Stay quiet. Stay unseen. Sometimes it's better not to be noticed.'

'Merle—'

'Most of the time I succeeded,' she interrupted before he could contradict her.

It was easy to be invisible. Easy to avoid eye contact. Easy to avoid answering calls and replying to emails. Easy to be forgotten about.

'Most of the time?'

He'd heard the wistful edge of regret that she'd been unable to mask. But she didn't want to go there. Too embarrassing. There was a long moment of silence that she refused to break.

'Where are your grandparents now?' He didn't relent.

She sighed. 'Three years after I went to live with them, my grandmother had a stroke. She became more difficult. It was a hard couple of years before she had another stroke that left my grandfather on his own with me. He was worn out from caring for her and it took me a while to realise his cognitive abilities were declining. In the end, I couldn't manage him on my own, not with needing to work as well to support us both. So he went into a facility. I sold the house, and everything else, to ensure he got good care. He passed away eight months ago.'

'That's why you're between residences? You sold the house to cover his care costs?'

She nodded. 'I only got this job because my boss at the records management company is pregnant and needed someone who could take a live-in job. I did an interview online with Leo. I was lucky and I need to do a good job here.'

A flash of guilt curdled her blood. What was she doing taking the week off work? Worse—spending it with Ash like this? Fraternising with her client's half-brother was surely a huge mistake—the most unprofessional thing she'd done in her life.

'Don't panic.' He read her mind. 'I'm gone at the end of the week, remember? There won't be any repercussions. You'll get the job done. What's happened between us won't have any impact on the future.'

Wouldn't it? That seemed impossible. She wasn't the same person she was yesterday, was she? Or perhaps this wanton lover had been inside her all along, just waiting for Merle to allow that part of herself to be unleashed. There was no locking her away again now.

'That's why I'm not going to "burn the lot" like you keep telling me to,' she said softly.

'The only reason *I* haven't is out of respect for the volunteer firefighters.' He grimaced.

'You don't want to keep any of it?' She didn't quite understand why. 'You have good memories here.'

'I have bad ones too.'

She hesitated but had to ask. 'Did she die here?'

He nodded slowly. 'But I wasn't here at the time.'

He didn't want to talk about it. She recognised the reluctance because it mirrored her own. Digging too deep hurt. This week with him was only an interlude, an experience. One she had to handle *lightly*.

She threw the blanket off and stood up on the sand, shaking free of the melancholy that had briefly descended. 'I think it's time for another swim.'

CHAPTER EIGHT

ASH SAT ON the deck absorbing the morning sun and reading while waiting for her to wake. He'd swum, then prepped a simple breakfast that was on the table beside him. Letting her rest was hard. The selfish part of him wanted to go in there and wake her. But she needed her sleep; they'd shared yet another very late night.

He couldn't concentrate on his book. Memories stirred and impatience tightened his muscles. He hadn't holidayed in years. For all the nights out or weekends partying on a yacht, there'd always been a laptop on the desk, a call to be made, business to be done. But he hadn't checked his emails in four days—the longest stretch ever. Time had slipped easily and deliciously like those plump oysters had slid down his throat two days ago. Hours could be lost in the simple pleasure of kissing Merle Jordan and long, sunny days had bled into long, hot nights. It was easy to forget why he'd come here in the first place and that he'd never intended to linger like this. He focused only on Merle. Together, they'd discovered she had a penchant for skinny dipping and she'd laughingly embraced her sensual, hedonistic side. She also had a hidden decadence that was dangerous to his peace of mind. They laughed, ate and drank and duelled over anything and everything light and simple. Drawing her out, engaging her, was rewarding. She was a quick learner and fiercely competitive and now she held nothing back. Her teasing smile alone sent anticipation rippling down his spine.

She'd blossomed before his eyes. But even though she'd

let him in, he was more curious than ever. She'd been lonely, her early life lacking in laughter. He'd had to teach her the rules to the most common of board games. *That* was why she'd been so quick to choose snakes and ladders the other night. It was the only game she'd known how to play. He wanted her to experience more of the things she'd missed out on. And he wanted her to experience them with *him*.

Half an hour later she joined him, her eyebrows lifting. 'You wear glasses.'

'I do.'

'So there's *something* less than perfect about your body,' she teased.

'You think the rest of my body is perfect?' He smirked.

'It's not like you don't already know that.'

'Still, I'm touched, given it's *you* who thinks so.'

'My opinion matters?' Half disbelieving, half flirt. Wholly gorgeous.

'Very much.'

She rolled her eyes and angled her head to read the spine of the book he was holding. 'It's an amazing library in there. Someone took time and effort to amass a good collection.'

'My father bought someone else's lifetime effort. He didn't carefully select each item himself. It was an investment,' he said drily. 'Like the art and the wine. It was for money, not love.'

'He loved the actual *collecting*.'

'He was avaricious. *Not* for love but for show. There's a difference.' Merle, Ash suspected, would always collect things for love. Things that held meaning to her. 'I still can't believe you don't have piles of dusty old things perfectly arranged in boxes with ridiculously detailed labels, keeping everything for ever and ever.'

She giggled and picked up the small bowl of fresh fruit he'd sliced for her. 'You think I'm a future hoarder?'

'Yes.'

She shook her head. 'Most of my mother's things were lost in the fire and her parents didn't keep any of her childhood things, so…' She shrugged. 'I guess that's why I went into archive work. Because I know what it's like to lose everything. I know that some things are irreplaceable.'

Her smile twisted when he failed to hide his sceptical expression.

'I watched my grandfather lose his memory,' she said. 'Maybe that's why it's important to me to help people hold memories for another. I think sometimes that's all we can do.'

'You don't think sometimes people hold on to things for too long? Everything eventually wears out as things rot or break—either way, they're rendered useless. Don't they just become a burden?'

'You don't have to keep hold of everything, Ash. You get to choose. Keep what matters and let go of the rest.'

He rested his head back against the chair. 'You make it sound easy.'

'You treasure these games now you've found them again,' she pointed out. 'You wouldn't part with them now.'

She was right, of course. Aside from Merle herself, they were the best thing about coming back. His mother was the reason he'd stayed away so long, but she was also the reason he'd returned now. He'd needed to see the place one last time. To say goodbye. For all of his teasing, Merle's words had an effect on him and he found himself seeing things from her point of view. There ought to be more here than those games of his mum's. There should be her personal papers and effects. The things he should have taken care of so much sooner.

'You really don't have anything of your own you treasure?' he asked. Surely someone who put sentimental value on things had *something* she prized?

'I once had a gorgeous copy of *Jane Eyre*. I got it at one of the car boot sales I went to with my grandfather.' Reminiscence softened and warmed her brown eyes. 'It wasn't exactly a first edition but it was old and lovely and had the nicest inscription.'

Ash frowned, confused. 'The inscription was from your grandfather?'

'No, *I* bought the book. The inscription was to someone else—the previous owner, I guess.'

She'd treasured a book that had been gifted to someone *else*?

'I know it sounds weird.' She laughed sheepishly at the look on his face. 'But it had obviously been treasured; it was in such perfect condition and it had been gifted with love. I didn't think it should just be thrown away.'

'You think the book itself was imbued with importance?'

'For me, yes. It deserved to be treasured—for itself, for the care between the two people. It shouldn't have been forgotten.'

'You don't think it stayed perfect because no one picked it up? Maybe it was put on a shelf and ignored for decades?'

'Why do you need to destroy my dreams?' She shot him a baleful look. 'Why can't I believe?'

He felt bad for suggesting it—but he doubted that the pristine condition of her book meant it must have been treasured. He'd long ago discovered that perfect facades, perfect stories, often hid horrible lies. But Merle still believed in generosity and sincerity, in humanity and kindness. *She* was genuine. And she believed in the gift of love from one person to another, even though she'd been neither a giver nor a recipient of much herself. For all of her self-protective measures, she was a romantic. And that tendril of doubt, of hesitation, turned to a touch of remorse.

'Did you like the actual story?' he teased. 'Did you even read it?'

'Of course I read it and I loved it.' She tilted her chin defiantly. 'Jane had a tough time, but she was strong and true to herself.'

'So you still have it?'

She nibbled her lip and put the bowl down on the table. 'I took it everywhere with me. I was sixteen and okay, yes, I was idealistic. It was just Grandad and me and I guess I was lonely and it became like a talisman of something...'

Of hope? Ash couldn't speak for the sudden ache in his chest. Concern for her grew, because he knew too well that things rotted and relationships were ripped away. *That* was reality. So something bad had happened to her lovely book. 'What happened?'

'I got a little lonely and made a fool of myself with a guy in my class. He started paying attention, acting as if...'

Ash tensed as she shrugged sheepishly. He had the horrible feeling he knew where this was going.

'I was gullible.' She confirmed the basis for his anxiety. 'I was easy pickings for a guy like him.'

'Like him?'

'Good-looking, popular...he had everything.' She frowned. 'Though I know he probably didn't, no one has everything all of the time.'

'Not even us privileged rich boys?'

Her smile quirked. 'He was curious about my book. I didn't realise people had noticed that I always had it. That they wondered about it. I was just oblivious to all that. He asked to borrow it. I'd inspired him to read it, apparently. I was flattered and I didn't want to deny him. Maybe he didn't realise how precious it was to me.'

'Don't let him off lightly, Merle,' Ash muttered. 'He knew.'

And Ash knew how it was to be young and thoughtless.

'Yeah. They all did.' She looked at him sadly. 'There was a clique, you know? I asked for it back days later. He laughed even as he said sorry. He said he'd lost it. He'd put it in his sports bag and it must have fallen out or something.'

'You don't believe him?'

She shook her head. 'I think they just wanted to know what it was and why I always had it. Maybe they thought it might've been a secret diary and they wanted to mock my innermost thoughts. Maybe they were just mean.'

It hadn't been a precious diary, but it had mattered as much. She'd cared about it.

She'd given the idiot something that was precious to her and he'd trampled it—crushing her fledgling trust in the process. And she'd scuttled back into her corner, hiding in the shadows and attempting that damned invisibility.

'It was the deceit that got to me.'

Ash's chest tightened. *He'd* been deceitful. He'd cheated. And he'd hated how bad he felt for it. 'I won't lie to you, Merle.'

'I know. You value honesty.' She glanced at him somberly. 'Someone lied to you.'

'Yes.' That was true. Yet he felt as if he was letting her down by not being completely honest now. 'But I've lied too,' he added. 'I was just like that jerk. When I was that age I was awful.'

'What did you do?'

'I cheated.'

Her eyebrows lifted. 'You were in a relationship at that age?'

It had hardly been a relationship. 'She wanted more than what I could give her and I was a coward.'

Merle paled. 'But you've learned your lesson?'

'Oh, yes, I've never done it again. Never will.'

She nodded slowly.

Amazed, Ash stared at her. She'd just accepted his word? She was too forgiving of shabby treatment. Too generous. But his mistake couldn't be forgiven by the one person who mattered most. It wasn't Rose—his 'girlfriend'—who'd suffered the most, though her humiliation had been total. It was his mother who he'd destroyed with his selfish carelessness. The truth he'd discovered then was that he was *less.* He didn't have Merle's depth of compassion. He didn't have her ability to hold someone's precious feelings—not their heart. He never had, never would. Because he was his father's son.

Normally he didn't think about it. He lived in the moment, lived by the rules he'd designed to keep everyone else safe. Because he'd learned who and what he truly was and he wasn't hurting anyone else again. Merle would be okay. She knew this was only for these few days. He'd made sure she understood. But he couldn't resist his own curiosity about her—couldn't help wishing he could make things better for her.

'So was that the guy you meant when you mentioned you'd said yes once?' he asked. 'That was secondary school, Merle. There must've been something since.'

'No one's asked again.'

'Maybe because you hide and avoid any situation in which that might become possible,' he suggested softly.

'Maybe because I've been busy,' she said defensively. 'I was looking after my grandfather, I was studying…and struggling financially, so I worked as well. There hasn't been the time for fun.'

She was right and he was an idiot for assuming she'd have had the time to be as frivolous as him.

'There's time now,' he said.

'Yes.' She lifted her head. 'There is now. With you.'

And she was embracing it. Except being here with him was still within her safe boundaries. This was her with him, but still hidden. He wanted her to have more. And yes, *he* wanted to have more too.

'Let's go out,' he said suddenly. 'Dinner and dancing.'

She looked startled. 'You mean like a date?'

'Yeah, why not?' He smothered his smile as he saw her hesitation. He bet there was a pro and con list leaping into her mind.

'You really struggle to do nothing and relax,' she said.

He laughed. 'You really struggle to be seen. And to have fun. You ought to go out.'

'So I know what to do for next time?' she asked.

A cold ball clenched in his stomach. 'So I get the pleasure of doing it with you first,' he said huskily. 'I want more of your firsts.'

Her eyes widened. For a moment he'd rendered her speechless.

Then she swallowed. 'What kind of dancing?'

'Any kind you want.'

She sank a little lower in her seat. 'I don't understand the appeal, to be honest.'

'Of going out dancing?'

'I saw the patrons at the clubs mum performed at and they were just... I don't know. Were they having a good time?'

'Have you never gone dancing yourself?'

'I haven't been in a club since I was a kid.'

'Your mother warned you off?'

'Sometimes the guy lingering around the stage door thought the back-up singers might be available for other services if their offer was enticing enough. Then my grandmother was all, *don't make a mistake like your mother. Sex is bad and shameful and men are dangerous. You're too young...*' She laughed bitterly. 'What chance did I have, really?' She tossed her head. 'But I'm not too young now. I know they both had baggage. I don't have to carry it for them. Sex can be fun and feel good and doesn't need to be over-complicated or over-emotional, right?'

The problem was this didn't feel all that *uncomplicated*

to him. This was the most complex relationship he'd had with anyone—in years. And yet in some ways it was the easiest.

'We're definitely going on a date,' he said.

'We definitely don't need to do that,' she said, but then an alarmed look crossed her face. 'Are you bored?'

'Of course not.'

She didn't relax. If anything, she looked more concerned. 'I don't want you doing this because—'

'There's a difference between pity and simply sharing an experience with someone,' he interrupted her.

She narrowed her eyes. 'You wanted quiet and solitude.'

'I'm talking one night, Merle.'

'Always it's "one night" with you.' She pulled a face. 'But we've been on a date—when we went boating the other day.'

'Not the same thing. We'll fly to Auckland. Have dinner and stay the night. We'll return early the next morning.'

She still didn't say yes.

'Have you ever dined at an award-winning restaurant?' he cajoled. 'One with a live band?'

'As opposed to a dead one?'

'Ha-ha.'

'If it's so amazing, how are you going to get a booking at such short notice?'

He just smiled at her.

'Really?' She folded her arms across her chest and raised her brows. 'Money talks?'

'Generally speaking, yes.'

'Yet you couldn't find alternative accommodation for me so easily the other night, for all your money.'

'True,' he acknowledged. 'But you have to admit that's ended up working in my favour.'

He was ridiculously pleased to see she still blushed.

But she tilted her chin. 'Not even you can wear swimming shorts to dinner.'

'I'll have a suit delivered to the hotel.'

He suppressed his amusement at the stunned expression that flitted across her face. Then her expression fell. Her next worry was already evident.

'You want me to wear coveralls to a fancy restaurant?'

'You can wear whatever you want,' he answered easily. 'I'll find you as delectable as ever.'

She gazed at him and sighed, almost sadly. 'You do it so easily, you're not even aware of it.'

'Do what?'

'Seduce me into saying yes.'

CHAPTER NINE

ASH LEANED BACK against the table, drumming his fingertips on the wood behind him and debating whether he ought to knock on the door and ask if she was okay. She'd been locked in the bedroom of their hotel suite for over an hour. Was she worrying? Was she literally hiding again? *He* felt uneasy and he *never* felt uneasy. But she'd been taking too long. He straightened up, deciding to go, and then the door opened. Adrenaline blasted, stopping him dead. He was only able to stare.

'What are you wearing?' he croaked.

He'd not meant to say that. Not meant to question her choices or sound judgmental and make her self-conscious. But her smile flashed. Not just any smile—brilliant, unguarded, a tiny bit self-satisfied—so he knew she'd not taken his moronic question any of those wrong ways. She'd heard the underlying truth—he was stunned and too caught up in staring at her to care.

'I like how it feels,' she said.

Anticipation tightened every muscle. His beautiful secret sensualist was wearing a jumpsuit unlike anything he'd ever seen. A week ago he'd never have thought he'd find any kind of coveralls sexy, yet here it was happening again. But these weren't for protective purpose. They were scarlet and silk and sleeveless, and skimmed her body, clinging to the fullest points of her curves. The deep vee drew his eye and the fabric flowed as she walked towards him—in scarlet high heels to match. She'd left her hair loose so it hung down her back in a rich brunette swathe. Impossibly, her skin was even more radiant. She'd look less visible in a little black dress that revealed far more skin. This was so much better than that. This was Merle doing her thing, her way. The smile in her eyes felled him all over again.

'Are you okay?' she asked.

'I don't think so.' He groaned, literally backing away from her. 'We'd better go.'

He barely noticed the restaurant, barely tasted the food, was barely aware of the service or of anyone else present. He could only see her. He didn't know how he kept up with her banter. It was as if his brain had been stupefied.

'Will you dance with me?' he asked, unable to sit still a second longer.

For the first time all evening doubt shadowed her eyes. 'It might be more stand and sway than spin, okay?'

Stand and sway sounded perfect. He ached to get his hands on her—to anchor himself, to ensure she was real. As they walked towards that darkened area, he was aware of heads turning. Of course people looked—she was stunning. But it hauled up other concerns. While he wanted the world to appreciate her, he also wanted to keep her to himself. Suddenly he felt possessive.

Even here in Auckland he was recognisable. The media in Australia had followed him for years. When he'd first turned his back on his father he'd welcomed the stupid society gossip blogs, annual most-eligible lists, relentless speculation and stories, all fuel to which he was the flame, to shame his father. But he didn't want Merle exposed to any negativity. If people found out what he'd been up to this week? It could totally be construed as a scandal. He'd seduced an innocent. Kept her in his holiday home to be his lover. It sounded as bad and mad as if he'd locked her in that damn bunker.

Wasn't it worse than humiliating Rose? Never had he

been as selfish. But Merle was an adult—she'd *asked*. She'd wanted and she'd taken. This was a scandal they'd *both* desired and they were both determined to make the most of. But he couldn't help pointing out the problem to her.

'People are watching,' he muttered. 'Are you okay with that?'

'Oh, I'm fine.' She grinned. 'They're watching *you*.'

They were not.

'Okay—' she shot him a sideways look, together with an impish grin '—they're looking at me too. But I don't mind.'

He'd wanted to spoil her. He'd wanted her to have a night where the spotlight was on and she could see she could do more than survive in its light. He'd wanted to see and feel the world through her perspective some more because that hope, that optimism she had, was tantalising when he'd lost his so long ago.

'If you'd had cameras in your face all the time, trust me, you'd start to mind,' he muttered.

'Maybe.' Merle nodded.

Right now she didn't really care about anything—she was too busy basking in the glow of Ash's attention. How he'd worked out that people were watching them she didn't know because he'd not taken his eyes off her and it was thrilling. But it was more than his attention: it was his influence and his outrageousness that encouraged her own sense of liberation. He'd bluntly pointed out her right to speak up. That he lived and moved with such confidence inspired her to answer back, to be as blunt and as honest.

It wasn't that she didn't care about consequences, of course she did, but she wasn't afraid of them in the way she had been for half her life. She felt alive, as if she had vitality and fight within her to stand not just beside him but also in front of him and be bold. It was invigorating. Enriching. Addictive. She spread her hand across his chest, feeling his tension, the powerful thump of his heart against her palm. Ash did not stay still. He was full of vigour and vitality and humour. He had more energy than anyone she'd ever met—a freewheeling force of nature. But he'd been so careful with her. Tender. He'd channelled all that energy, focused it on her pleasure. There was nothing as seductive as all of his attention.

She'd not realised how stuck she'd become. How constrained. Why had she let things hold her back for so long? She'd not wanted to see the problematic issues from her upbringing but perhaps he'd been right about that too— that she'd made too many excuses for too long, ignoring the impact on herself. She loved her family and she knew they'd done their best but it hadn't been easy for her—she'd not been the priority. But now she had absolute freedom and she could live her own life on her own terms. And she wanted to.

'What are you thinking?' Ash suddenly asked.

She glanced up at him and smiled.

His hold on her tightened. 'You're more luminous than ever.'

She laughed. 'It's the lighting in here.'

'No.' The question in his beautiful amber eyes was unrelenting. 'Tell me what you're thinking.'

How could she resist him anything when he looked at her like that?

'That I'm happy.' She blinked back a sudden burn behind her eyes. 'I'm enjoying the freedom to do what I want. How I want. When and where and with whom I choose.'

And that was with Ash.

She felt the response ripple down his body. He wasn't perfect, but he didn't claim to be. He'd been honest— letting her know he had flaws and had made mistakes. And he'd made her appreciate that other people in her life hadn't been perfect either. Despite her tendency to try to see the best, sometimes it was good to accept an honest assessment.

And honestly? She adored her new jumpsuit. She'd searched online and had it delivered direct to the hotel—living like Ash Castle himself. It had arrived on time and hadn't even needed alterations. It was comfortable yet sexy and she didn't regret blowing some of her pay on it. It had been so long since she'd done something for herself.

Aren't you doing this for him?

Maybe partly—and his reaction? So worth it.

'Merle?' he asked again. 'Why are you chuckling to yourself?'

'I'm thinking that I don't care what anyone thinks.' She smiled, aware of her blossoming sensuality and confidence. 'Except you. But I know you like my outfit.'

'Not just your outfit.'

A ripple of sensual awareness skimmed down her spine. The pleasure, the sensations, of this evening? Stepping out with him, teasing him, enjoying every mouthful of that stunning food, the restaurant's stylish decor and the sexy beats from the live band by the dance floor... *Everything* had been perfect. It wasn't an experience she wanted to just remember, but an experience that she wanted *again*.

Ash Castle had opened up her world. He'd pulled her free of the shroud beneath which she'd hidden for so long—*not* her coverall, but her tendency to stay safe back in the shadows. He'd given her more than he'd promised. More than the sexuality she felt safe exploring with him, more than the light jokes and games between them. More than the serious conversation too.

But there was another, rarer element curling around all these things, threading them together, forming an unbreakable, undeniable core within her. Something invisible, something strong, had melded to her central framework and become inseparable from her very soul. She gazed up at him, lost in the world of memory and sensation, laughter, spark and sensuality. The world that was totally, utterly Ash.

Ash's clothes felt too tight. His collar especially. It made breathing difficult. Thinking was simply impossible. That weird protectiveness rearing within tensed all of his muscles. But Merle held him close. She had rhythm. But then, he knew that, didn't he? She moved so well in his arms. In sync and breathing together, they sensed and anticipated each other's movements.

He was desperate to be alone with her. Yet he didn't want to short-change her on the night out he'd promised. But she cupped his jaw. And she tempted him.

'Shall we continue this dance upstairs?' she murmured.

She saved him.

As the lift rose, taking them to their hotel suite, his tension scorched. 'Merle...'

'Yes?'

Something broke apart within him then. Her simple, sweet response. Affirmative. Listening. Willing.

It was everything he wanted from her. And it terrified him at the same time. He had no idea how he unlocked the hotel room or what he did with the damn key card, just that somehow they were inside the door and alone. Thank heavens.

This wasn't just superficial desire, but also physical need underpinned by bone-deep longing. A fast release wasn't going to work. But he was unable to stop himself from trying. The sexiest outfit ever had just become the source of the most insane frustration. Somehow he worked it out and the scarlet shimmered down her body in a slither of sexy colour and then she stood so close to naked, clad only in a tiny bra and thong, in matching scarlet. Ash had never felt as honoured in his life. Not even their first night together compared to this. He was utterly lost for words.

She smiled at him again. 'Thank you for tonight. It was a lot of fun.'

Fun? He couldn't stand the compressed sensation inside his chest. It was as if his heart had been clamped by some medieval instrument of torture. He couldn't bear to look into her beautiful eyes but he couldn't look away and something once held fast slipped loose inside. In another breath, every last semblance of his control was lost.

He tore the condom wrapper between his teeth. Her eyes widened with humour and arousal. A gorgeous, intoxicating, provocative mix that made him even more desperate to take her. Now. To his eternal gratitude she stepped forward and reached for his belt, intuitively understanding the level of pain he was in right now. Two strokes of her gentle hand up his turgid length was two too many for him to handle. He growled. Her gaze lifted to his. A smoky, sensual pride gleamed in those brown eyes.

He buried his thoughts by kissing her, rejoicing because it wasn't a response that she gave him, it was an action of her own—the dance of her tongue against his, the slide she'd learned so quickly, tore at the last of his self-restraint. The way she wanted him destroyed him. This was a pure celebration of their physical selves—of desire and pleasure to be found with each other. But it wasn't just that. The sudden tightness in his chest hurt.

He spun her to face the wall so he couldn't see her expressive face, because he was so close to something else. He hooked his thumbs into the waistband of that tiny scarlet thong and tugged it down. Seconds later he'd unhooked her bra and taken a moment to skim his palms across her tight-budded breasts before sliding his hands to settle heavy and hard on her hips, holding her where he needed her to be. This was sex. This was just another night. This meant *nothing* more. But then she braced her hands on the wall in front of her and pushed back, sliding her curvy derriere into him. Claiming her space. No longer hiding, no longer content to be invisible—not around him.

He could only take pleasure in her stance. Pressing her against the wall. And she was hot and wet, the silken pull of her muscles sending his into overdrive. He tensed at the base of his spine. His release so close. Too close. Too soon.

He fought to regain himself and slow it down. But her hair was loose and fragrant and her moans of delight, of demand, rang in his ears. He couldn't resist pressing a kiss at the side of her neck and once there he was lost, tempted again by those sweet, small earlobes just made for him to nibble. She shuddered and cried out, her lithe body shaking. Passion and pleasure rushed over him at her response. His skin rippled as goose pimples lifted everywhere. He swiftly slipped his hand down to delve and delight her and heard her harsh, high-pitched cry of pleasure. He closed his eyes but the shock waves of her detonation went through him anyway and sucked the last of his control with it. He gripped her tightly and pumped hard, all control gone.

His heart slammed against his ribs. He didn't want it to be over. He didn't want this just to be…that. A night. A good time. A meaningless moment. Because that was the last thing this was for him. This felt like so much more and, even though he'd tried to deny it, he couldn't any more. He tried again—slammed on the mental brakes, trying to stem the unfettered feelings flooding his body.

He wasn't even undressed. His trousers were around his ankles as though he were some out-of-control teen. His shirt was stuck to his back, slick with sweat from the searing heat she'd roused in him. He'd ravished her. He could feel her legs trembling as she rested her forehead against her arms, taking support from the wall in front of her.

'I'm sorry,' he groaned. 'Too fast.'

But she tilted her head back, resting against his shoulder and exposing the long, vulnerable column of her throat, and laughed. A brief, sexy chuckle that rang with pleasure and unvarnished, unashamed *pride*.

The jumble of concern in his head faded away. 'You liked that?'

She chuckled again. 'You seemed as if...'

'As if?' he said quietly. 'As if I couldn't stop myself? As if I couldn't wait? As if I wanted nothing more than to be locked in here with you? Because that's exactly what happened.'

At the dewy, deliciously dirty satisfaction in her eyes he was hard again. And, given the way she pressed her lithe, lissom body back against his, she knew exactly what she'd just done. She was the sweetest vixen. He'd forgotten that this was supposed to only be sex. He'd forgotten that it was ending. He'd forgotten that he couldn't give her what she most needed.

All he wanted now was to make love to her for hours and hours.

CHAPTER TEN

MERLE SIPPED HER fresh-squeezed orange juice and wondered whether she should wake him. For the third time in the hour she opted not to. He needed the rest. And she needed more time to *process*. Last night had been…*indescribable*. No words could explain the sensations she was still floating upon. The intensity followed by such tenderness. He'd kissed her, kissed her, kissed her. Now she tried to stay in the present, tried not to panic about the fact the week was almost over and he'd be returning to Australia soon. She had to be grateful for the experience, right?

But she wanted more.

She wanted the man who'd come apart before her very eyes last night. She wanted more of that kick to the heart she'd felt when she'd seen his reaction to her scarlet jumpsuit. That thrill of pleasure. She wanted more of his attention, his wit, his warmth.

'Merle? Why didn't you wake me?' He walked through the door already dressed in those dark denim jeans and tee that skimmed his muscular frame.

He looked as if he'd had a hard night—his hair rumpled, stubble on his jaw, the sight of which sent a tingle to her fingertips. She wanted to touch him all over again. She didn't want the night to be over. Ever.

'You were in a really deep sleep,' she said huskily.

For a moment their gazes meshed. But his lips twisted and his lashes lowered. 'Come on. We'd better get back. I've missed a bunch of messages from the pilot.'

'Oh—'

'It doesn't matter,' he said negligently. 'He'll be ready the minute we get there.'

She nodded. Things moved that way for Ash. Instantly and at his summons. Because he didn't want to stay.

Her heart sank as she realised. He *never* stayed.

Ash strode across the tarmac, gritting his teeth to suppress another yawn. Strange, he'd never felt this exhausted. Maybe he was coming down with the flu? Maybe that would explain his behaviour last night. He'd never lost control like that. Never been so overcome by lust he'd barely paused long enough to ensure his partner was there with him. But Merle had been. In fact, she'd been a step ahead. He'd heard it in her breathing, seen it in her glazed eyes, felt it in every inch of her body. She'd stayed a step ahead of him the rest of the night too. She was still a step ahead of him now. He followed her into the helicopter. He didn't speak. The bright sunlight made his eyes ache.

Last Friday he'd arrived on Waiheke at night and the house had been cloaked in dusky darkness. For the first day he'd focused on the pool. Then he'd been so focused on Merle he'd not noticed the property—he'd avoided it. But this time, the midday sun was bright and he was so focused on *not* looking at Merle that he couldn't help but see it. *All* of it. A wall of hurt and regret slammed into him. The helicopter lifted up as soon as they were clear and walking towards that wretched lawn court. In only a few minutes silence returned. He glanced to see Merle watching him. Beyond her, the house loomed. He couldn't decide which caused him the most discomfort.

'This is the last time I'll be here,' he muttered unthinkingly. He had to be done with it.

'This week.' She nodded.

'At all,' he corrected flatly.

She paused on the path. 'You're not coming back?' Her

soft lips parted on an audible breath. 'Are you planning to sell it?'

Her shock lifted his heart for a second—before it smashed back down like a stone hitting concrete.

'Why does that surprise you?' he asked. Surely she understood this place held little happiness for him?

'You love it here.'

'No.' His blood ran cold here. 'I wasn't going to come back at all. But in the end I couldn't let it go without...'

He growled, because he'd never expressed it aloud—never wanted to. But he was tired and somehow he couldn't resist the compulsion to tell *her*. As if she were justice herself—a scale with which he could weigh the decision—even though he already knew it tipped him towards guilty.

'I had to see what he'd done to wreck the place,' he muttered in frustration.

'You think this is *wrecked*?' Merle's gaze shot back to the house briefly before returning to shine that steadfast belief into his. 'Ash, this place is beautiful—'

'You're wrong. It *was* beautiful.'

She didn't understand the level—or the layers—of destruction. She didn't know that the last time he'd visited was branded in his brain and had left a wound that would never heal. He'd regret the pain he'd caused for the rest of his life. There could be no redemption. His mistakes were unforgivable.

'The heart of it got ripped out, and a new facade put in place,' he said gruffly. 'It looks like perfection but there's nothing real.'

His skin tightened but the misery swelling within couldn't be contained. He stood even more rigidly, resisting the threatening emotional explosion. He didn't want this. He couldn't even walk inside. Instead he gazed around the garden.

'Ash?'

'There used to be an orchard where the tennis court is,' he muttered. 'Apples, peaches, plums… I used to climb up and pick something and take it to where Mum was watching from the balcony. She always knew where the best ones were but she let me find them.'

He was too lost in memory to register the long pause.

'That would've been awesome,' Merle eventually responded with her softness.

'They ripped it out when they put in the bunker and the tennis court.' He stared at the green expanse that had shocked him so completely. 'The garden was everything to her. She couldn't do the physical work but she designed it. She was good friends with the groundsman and they kept a record of the produce each year.' He surveyed it, remembering how much there'd once been. 'I guess nothing of any real depth can grow when there's a lump of cold metal just beneath the surface.'

Which was him too, right? Fine superficially, but beneath—what was there really? For the first time he felt how lacking in depth, how empty inside he was. A sense of futility stunned him—for all of his success, his years proving to his father that he didn't need him, that he could do better than him. What, exactly, had it all been for? His father had foisted the inheritance on him anyway. Ignoring Ash's years of anger and absence. He'd still assumed that Ash was his true son—*just like him*, the worthy recipient of what he'd created.

'I haven't been back here in almost a decade,' he admitted quietly.

Friday night had been the first time he'd seen that the trees had been replaced with perfect lawn, that the comfortable old house had been renovated into soullessness with stripped-back decor and nothing intimate or personal about the place. He knew it was maintained by a team of strangers who swooped in and set everything 'just so'. Even now, a year after his father's death, they maintained its flawless facade. It irritated him intensely. Even after his death his father was all about false appearances. About destroying what should have been wonderful—purely because of *greed*. Everything had been an investment, but Hugh didn't value true treasure. Like those damned trees.

'Why haven't you been in so long?'

He'd simply been unable to. But it had come to a point when he couldn't avoid it any longer.

'After Mum died, I fell out with my father. I refused to have anything to do with him or the company, I avoided all our properties and built my own,' he said. 'Now I've finally come back and discovered my worst nightmare was reality. He's scrubbed everything of her from the place. He's destroyed everything she'd created to fulfil some stupid desire for some gadget he thought was essential.'

'You came here a lot before she died?'

'When Mum's health declined, she moved here permanently.'

Merle stood very still beside him. 'But your dad was still in Sydney?'

He nodded. He could hear the confusion in her voice. He'd already told her his family life had been more of a family lie. But she still didn't realise just how messed up it had been. And he couldn't seem to stop himself from remembering.

'Did you divide your time between them?' Merle asked when he didn't immediately answer.

'I went to a very *prestigious* boarding school a few hours north of Sydney,' he explained with full sarcasm. 'It offered every advantage for a young person, you know. Then I'd come here for the holidays.'

He had rarely seen his father—so he didn't impact on the secret lifestyle his father had enjoyed. Glancing over, he saw her deepening frown, and Ash shook his head. 'Yeah, no denying my teenage years were dysfunctional.'

'But why do you want to sell it now?' she asked. 'I don't think you hate this place, Ash. I think you still love it. It's just that you were hurt here. Maybe being here makes you remember what you lost.'

Being here made him angry. And powerless. Because there was no fixing any of it.

'Mum's passing was awful,' he admitted. In an almost naive way he hadn't realised how ill she was. He'd thought she would go on as she was for years—in a kind of weak but strong stasis. He'd thought he'd have a chance to make things right again once she'd got over her anger. But there'd been no chance. 'I'd already lost everything before that. Because *I'm* the one who inflicted the pain here.'

Her steady, unflinching gaze stabilised his careering emotions.

'What happened?'

He'd known she'd ask. Who wouldn't when given a statement like that? He'd wanted her to. He wanted her to know. Because then? Then she'd know the truth. She'd know him for who he was. And that light in her eyes when she looked at him? That would dim.

'It was my fault my mother died when she did,' he said harshly.

'What?' Merle's soft voice lifted. 'How?'

'I broke her heart.' And it had already been so damaged, the harm was irreparable. His own heart tore every time he so much as thought of it.

But Merle stayed still, her gaze true and calm. 'How did you do that?'

'I proved to her that I was just like him.'

Didn't I teach you to play fair? Not to cheat? Never cheat, Ashton.

His mother's recriminations echoed. Even after all this

time they scalded his vital organs, making it feel impossible to breathe. If he told Merle the whole truth she'd recoil. She'd step back. She was too much of a believer in good things not to shrink away from something awful. And maybe after last night that would be best. Because last night had changed this.

'I cheated,' he added bluntly. 'Just like him.'

And the fallout had sent him on a spiralling path of excess and oblivion—pointedly different to his dad's secrecy. Ash had been boldly, openly provocative. He'd developed his own code.

But Merle didn't flinch. She merely nodded, almost matter-of-factly. 'That girl—when you were young.'

It hadn't been a matter-of-fact mistake. 'Her name was Rose Gold.'

At a muffled sound from Merle he grinned ruefully. 'Yeah. Trust me, no one hates that more than she does.'

'But you were at school.'

'She came to my boarding school, yes.'

'So this was a youthful, schoolboy mistake. Secondary school,' she reiterated.

But it had been no minor indiscretion and the awful repercussions had been permanent. Merle still gazed up at him, clearly waiting, and, as much as he regretted starting this, the anger within made him continue. She needed to know what he'd done.

'It wasn't teenage foolishness, it was massive. Rose was in the year below mine but she was even younger. One of those super-smart kids, she'd been accelerated up. Apparently we'd already met because she was the daughter of one of my mother's friends, but honestly I didn't remember her. Mum asked me to be kind, ensure she was included. She was shy. I think she'd been unwell or something.' He sighed. 'She was pretty nerdy. A society princess but shy at that point.' He paused and frowned as he realised Merle's skin had pinkened.

'Come on,' he muttered. 'We should get out of the sun. It's burning at this time of day.'

But Merle resisted. 'Tell me what happened.'

'I will, when you're in the shade.'

Merle walked ahead of him again but once she'd passed the pool she turned and blocked his way into the house.

'Okay, I'm in the shade. Tell me the rest.'

Ash grimaced. 'I became her champion, I guess. I didn't think anything of it. People assumed we were dating because I'd sought her out and she hadn't said anything to the contrary. It amused me to see her popularity rise. I didn't take it too seriously. I didn't think she had either. We weren't exactly physical—I thought we were more friends. But she was flattered, I guess.'

'I bet she…' Merle mumbled. 'I bet she had a massive crush on you.'

'I only asked her to go to that damn dance because Mum asked me to. To make sure she had a good time. But I…'

'What happened at the dance?'

He shifted on his feet, obviously uncomfortable. 'I got filmed with another girl.'

'Filmed? Oh…' Merle's gaze slid from his.

'Two girls, actually,' he confessed angrily. 'I got stood down from school for misconduct. Never went back. Got summoned here. Mum was more furious than I'd ever seen her. *How could I have done that to Rose?* She tore strips off me. *"You're just like him."* Direct quote.'

'Ash—'

'The thing was, I'd not known. About Dad, I mean. I didn't know *any* of it until that afternoon. I'd never seen Mum so agitated. She cried about things that didn't make sense. Later, I asked her what she'd meant but she'd calmed down and shut me out and wouldn't say. She sent me away. Back to Sydney. To Dad. And I found out the truth.'

The lies. The cheating. The absolute betrayal.

'Do you know what he did?' He looked at Merle.

Merle tried to stay calm, but every muscle had tensed. She was still reconciling what he'd told her about that girl, Rose. A shy, quiet girl whom he'd humiliated so *publicly*. But this about his father was going to be bad too. No son had such a visceral reaction to the mere mention of his father without serious reason.

'Leo Castle isn't my only half-sibling,' Ash said harshly. 'It wasn't just that Dad was a serial cheater and lazy when it came to contraception. He was a risk-taker who didn't think he'd ever get caught.' He flinched at his inward recollections. 'It turned out he'd also seduced my aunt. Mum's younger sister. So my cousin Grace is actually my half-sister. That's why she was so angry with me for turning out just like him, *despite* her efforts.'

'But you're not like him.'

'No? Not selfish? Not arrogant? Not a cheater?' He shook his head. 'I never saw Mum again,' he muttered. 'She died less than a week after she'd sent me back in disgrace.'

The deeply etched pain in his voice scraped Merle's nerves.

'I literally broke her heart.'

Merle ached for the horror and guilt he felt. 'I think your father might've already done that, Ash.'

His eyes widened and for a moment he froze. 'But I ripped it right through,' he said hoarsely. 'I was the one thing she believed in. I let her down. And she died.'

'Ash—'

'I'd had no idea he was unfaithful at all, let alone so completely,' he said hurriedly. 'It's embarrassing when with adult hindsight it's so bloody obvious. I had to find out what she'd meant. I confronted him when I got there. He didn't even try to deny it. He was more interested in the details of what had happened with those girls in the bathroom at the dance. He actually *congratulated* me. He said I needed to work on my discretion, but he was proud. That's when I realised what he was like. I searched online and found a reference to Leo in an old newspaper. I tracked him down and offered to do the DNA test for him to prove our dad's paternity.' Ash's smile was both satisfied and sad. 'My father never forgave me for *that*. He was so angry, he admitted the truth about Grace with vindictive pleasure. He said I couldn't escape who I was—his son. With his flaws. His predilections. And he was right. I'd already proved that. So I acted out, with no discretion at all.'

'It was *one* mistake, Ash.'

He shook his head. 'I was careless and selfish and went for what I wanted then and there.'

'But you learned from it. You said you've never cheated since.'

'I've never had a relationship since.'

'To be honest, it doesn't sound like it was much of a relationship with Rose.'

He paused. 'No. We never even slept together but it meant more to her. I think I knew that and I didn't want it and I took the coward's way out to end it. I broke her trust and I humiliated her.'

Merle felt a horrible affinity for the girl. She could understand how easy it would be to fall—to imagine there might be more—when Ash Castle had his full attention on you. 'Where's Rose now?'

'Still at university, I think. An academic. Very good at...her subject.'

Merle smiled a little sadly, feeling for Rose. 'You don't know what it is, do you?'

'She's not spoken to me since and I don't blame her.'

He winced. 'People had phones everywhere... I just didn't want...'

'To say it to her face?' she guessed.

'It was like I'd kicked a kitten.' He rubbed his face.

Merle could imagine all too well how mortified poor Rose must have been. Then Ash had been sent away from the school. It would've been horrendous to have been left there with everyone in her class knowing. And she would have had such a crush. It was impossible not to crush on Ash Castle.

But, while he'd made a mistake, Ash's *world* had been obliterated. He'd disappointed the one person who mattered to him most. He'd discovered appalling, devastating truths. He'd have felt such shame for his father. And in turn himself.

'You didn't get to see your mother again?' she asked softly.

He stood very still, not looking at her, not seeming to see anything but the bitter memories lodged inside. 'We didn't even speak on the phone. I was angry because I felt guilty. Angry because I was shocked. *Everything* had been a lie. Her husband had an affair with her own sister. Can you imagine the betrayal?' He closed his eyes briefly. 'And it happened when they both knew she was unwell. That was why I'm the only child. The only one she could have and I...' He pushed out a heavy sigh. 'Hell, no wonder Grace never holidayed with us here.' He glared at the pool and then turned that tortured gaze back on Merle. 'Why didn't she leave him? Why did she stay and put up with that for so long?'

She understood why he asked. Ash hadn't stayed. He'd been so hurt, felt such guilt, he'd rejected his father totally. But his anguish and the questioning of his mother's hard choices were ultimately unanswerable. Merle could only guess, only imagine.

'Maybe she didn't have the strength,' she suggested gently. 'Maybe the battle for her health was the only one she had the energy to fight.'

He didn't reply for a long time.

'What was she like?' Merle asked.

'When she had the energy, she was so much fun.' His expression fell again. 'And I devastated her. I broke her heart.'

'But you *didn't* kill her, Ash,' Merle said softly. 'She'd been unwell a long time, right?'

His nod was jerky.

'And you weren't much more than a kid yourself. Packed off to boarding school. Isolated from your parents through a very sad time. Burdened with a ton of external expectation and no real support to help you cope. I'm not surprised you sought a way out—however you could—especially at that age, when everything's overwhelming. You were so alone.'

'Don't feel sorry for me, Merle. I don't deserve it.'

She disagreed. He was beating himself up over something that had happened a long time ago. A series of events had morphed together into a tangle from which he'd drawn conclusions that weren't necessarily true. She could understand how he had when such deep, devastated emotions were at play. That was because of the person Ash was. And *that* was the point.

'You're different from your father,' she said urgently, aching for him to believe her. But she saw his instant negation. 'You are—'

'Some things can't be changed,' he interrupted bitterly. 'I am who I am.'

'Workaholic, fiery, full of energy and independence,' she said. 'And you try to hide it, but you're a man who *cares*.'

He turned a burning gaze on her but she held it defiantly, daring him to deny it.

'I don't believe you want to give this place up, Ash.'

'I can't keep it like this.' He glanced across at the lawn again. 'He destroyed everything she built.'

'Then rebuild it. No one says you can't do what you want with it. Things can change, Ash. People can too.'

'Eternally optimistic, aren't you?' But his small smile didn't reach his eyes.

'I don't see that as a negative.' She put her hand on his arm, hoping to somehow get him to believe her. 'Everyone makes mistakes. Everyone screws up. Everyone hurts someone—intentionally or not. That's part of being human,' she said. 'Maybe the trick isn't to try to erase it, or even to ease it, but just to accept that it happened. That it's there. So there's a little weight you carry and maybe you'll always have it, but that's okay.' Beneath her hand, she felt his tension. 'Because you'd do things differently now, right?' she said softly. 'Facing the same situation now, you wouldn't do that again.'

'Of course not.'

'So—' she smiled '—you've learned something. It's just very sad you didn't get to see your mother again so she could see that too. And it's sad your father took everything of hers away. I'm so sorry he did that.'

Ash looked directly at her again. She saw pain in his amber eyes. And tiredness.

'Thanks, Merle.' A gruff whisper of appreciation.

Yet Merle felt as if he was slipping away from her. That her words hadn't comforted him at all—they'd been futile. Like seeds scattered on hardened, dry land.

He stepped away. 'I think I need a swim.'

She watched him walk away, feeling oddly bereft. This morning she'd dressed in the scarlet jumpsuit she'd worn last night. Partly because the silk felt heavenly against her sensitive skin but mostly because she hadn't wanted her fairy-tale night to be over yet. But the heat of the day had built and now the sunlight was harsh. He'd been right. It had been seconds away from burning her skin. And what he'd told her lingered. The parallels she felt with Rose made her wince. How easy it would've been to wish there might be more meaning in Ash's actions. He'd have been spellbinding, a force of nature even then, with that ferocity of intent. But she also knew how easy it was to misinterpret someone's intentions. And *he'd* certainly learned from the resultant horror. He didn't let any woman get the wrong impression now. Not relationships. Only sex. And in business he'd been driven to succeed on a scale impossible to most people, desperate to build something bigger and better than his father.

Her heart ached for him as she showered and dressed. He was still swimming length after length, so she didn't interrupt him. She sensed he needed time to clear his head. So she went in search of a displacement activity of her own.

It was another two hours till he came in. He was back in his shorts, a white tee skimming his broad chest. Her heart bumped against her ribcage.

'What have you been up to?' He didn't quite meet her gaze.

She didn't want things to be awkward, so she tried to keep it light as she surveyed the mess she'd made in the kitchen. 'I cooked dinner. Elevated instant noodles.'

He shot her a glance. To her relief the old smile flickered in his eyes. 'Elevated? They're still instant noodles.'

'Are you not prepared to give them a chance?' she asked primly.

'I'll try them. For you.'

The merest hint of his old flirt lifted a bubble of hope in her. She set dinner out on the table of one of the smaller dining nooks, still with a stunning view across the bay, and opened another bottle of champagne.

'Champagne with noodles?' he queried.

'The perfect accompaniment.'

'And is that lobster tail I see in there?' He stirred the contents of his steaming bowl with a fork and began to laugh.

'Elevated, as I said.' She grinned impishly at him. 'Isn't it amazing how satisfying something can be, even when it's pulled together from sparse ingredients?'

He shot her a look across the table. 'I don't think we can consider lobster sparse.'

'Still full of flavour and delicious. Still satisfying.' She wilfully ignored his interruption. 'And yet it can still leave you wanting more.'

His lips twitched and she finally saw him fully relax with a long sigh. 'Oh, Merle. I definitely want more.'

CHAPTER ELEVEN

MERLE WALKED THROUGH the eerily quiet house. It was stupid but she was almost afraid to call out to him—afraid there would be no reply. So she crept quietly, slowly searching each space, hoping to find him. Fearing she wouldn't. While 'playful' Ash had reappeared last night at dinner, by the time they'd gone to bed he'd fallen silent. But he hadn't slept. He'd turned to her—touched her, taken her with a wordless, gentle intimacy that had been different yet again. The tender intensity had devastated her, yet she'd held him too—feeling the emotions humming within him. It hadn't been a fiercely passionate escape into the physical. It had been deeper than that—there'd been no escape from the emotion, there'd been a silent exposition of it. Of need. Of wonder. Of connectedness. And she'd loved it. Loved *him*. Until she'd finally fallen asleep, still holding him close.

But when she'd woken only five minutes ago, he was already gone. She'd touched his pillow, and there was no residual warmth. No sleeping in for a second time for Ash.

She glanced out from the balcony but the water in the pool was still. The bay in the distance was a pure landscape, no human or other animal giving movement to the picture-perfect landscape. She walked through to the kitchen but it was empty. It felt like the whole place was oddly untouched. A horrible premonition ate away her security. Had he left already? Without even saying goodbye?

Anxiety shot nausea to the back of her throat. Because she knew now—this wasn't some light affair for her. Not some fun 'experience' that she might go on to have again with some other guy. There'd never be another guy. Not like Ash. What she felt for him? It was immense and over-whelming and so wonderful that it terrified her.

But he didn't want it, did he? She fervently, desperately wished he did or would. She needed more time with him. They needed so much more time. So where was he now?

She checked the pool again. The study. For a moment she wondered about the bunker, but then she heard a sound in the distance. Walking around the side of the house, she saw one of the garage doors open.

'Ash?' She blinked, her eyes adjusting to the change from the bright morning sunlight to the dim interior. There were towers of boxes she'd yet to open and categorise. But Ash had ripped open several and was standing in the cen-tre of a pile of stuff.

'What are you doing?' she asked.

He glanced up at her grimly. The emotion that he usu-ally kept so deeply buried was now glinting sharply in his eyes. This place dredged it up. Increasingly over this last week memories had risen until he'd been so bothered, he'd been devastatingly honest with her. He'd revealed that well-spring of pain—the mistake he'd made that had unleashed the truth of his parents' marriage and what he feared had hastened his mother's death. Merle had hoped that, just by listening, she might've helped. But now? She didn't think she had. A trouble shared wasn't always a trouble halved. It was still just a trouble.

'I'm sorry for making a mess and making your job worse than it already was,' he said gruffly.

She didn't care about the mess. She cared about him. But he was avoiding looking at her again.

'Were you searching for something in particular?' she asked.

He stood stiffly in the centre of that heap. Merle saw

some of the paperwork was damaged. Water must've somehow gotten into those boxes.

'I thought, maybe, in all the boxes, there might've been something worth keeping. You know, didn't he want to keep my old swimming trophies?' The bitterest smile barely curved his lips as he shrugged sarcastically. 'I guess not. It's all just his stuff. He expunged every *last* thing of us both. There's nothing of her. None of her diaries. The garden journals.'

He'd wanted something of his mother's to treasure. And he'd not found it. His desolation swept over her.

'I guess he only kept her games because they were in good condition and valuable,' he said. 'Not because he wanted any real reminder of her. They're an investment. Like everything he held on to.'

Had he once considered Ash an investment too? The heir groomed to take over the company? The one he was proud to have follow in his footsteps? Whom he'd wanted to corrupt? And the man had shipped his wife to a whole other country. Out of sight and out of mind for her final years. Merle hated him.

'Why do you think he kept that one photo?' she asked.

'For show. He probably put it face down when he was here. Or,' he added acidly, 'maybe he used it as a reminder to his new lovers that he'd already had a wife and child and didn't plan on making that same mistake again.'

'Ash—'

'It's true. Apparently he vowed he'd never marry again after Mum died. But it wasn't because he was heartbroken. He just didn't want the expense of a divorce. He collected girlfriends—a new model every couple of years in the decade before he died. There would've been more, of course, those ones on the side he had in secret. So he could still look like the loyal, grieving widower.' Still not meeting her gaze, he kicked at the pile at his feet. 'I can't believe you have to go through all of this.'

'It's my job to go through everything. It's not personal for me the way it is for you. It's not painful.'

His jaw clamped.

'Why don't you come inside and have breakfast?' she suggested.

'Food isn't going to make this better, Merle. I'm not a hangry two-year-old.'

Ash couldn't stand to see the disbelief he knew ought to instantly flash on Merle's face. He couldn't even manage a joke. The irritation scratching down his spinal cord like nails on a chalkboard was impossible to ignore. And his irascibility, his impatience, was all amplified *because* he was so irritated and he knew he shouldn't be. He shouldn't care at all. He'd thought he hadn't for so long.

He was supposed to have come here briefly to see what had been done to it and to sever all ties. An acidic, isolated homage to all that had been and all that he couldn't change. He should've been able to handle that. Then he'd discovered *she* was staying here. Merle. His own house nymph—all temptation and temporary effervescence. He should've been able to handle her too. Except she'd put *possibilities* into his head. And he'd stayed. He'd taken what he shouldn't. He'd done so many things that he never allowed himself to do.

Now he couldn't even hold eye contact with her.

He stared down at the piles he'd rummaged through in a furious frenzy this morning. They were now scattered in a haphazard mess at his feet. Any remnant 'piles' had tumbled into a shambolic heap. He didn't know why he'd thought he'd actually find anything that mattered.

'No wonder you like to wear the gloves and the hazmat suit,' he growled.

'The boxes shouldn't have been put straight onto the

floor,' she said. 'I'll fix that. Dry out these items and prevent more damage.'

Her tone was soft and gentle. As if *he* was the object being treated with kid gloves. That irritated him even more. He didn't deserve gentleness. He didn't want her or anyone touching this rubbish. It really all ought to be put on a bonfire. But he didn't mention it. He couldn't seem to manage a joke. 'I'll put it back in the boxes for now.'

'Do you want some help?'

He certainly couldn't look into her eyes now. He knew he'd see sympathy and concern. And other things.

'No.' He didn't want anything from her.

'Ash—'

'You should go and have breakfast,' he dismissed her abruptly. 'I'll be along in a bit.'

There was the barest hesitation before she left.

Ash drew in a sharp breath because now he knew. Last night something ordinarily impossible had briefly become imaginable—like a wisp of a magical fog that promised growth. But that wisp had evaporated in this morning's light. All that remained here now was a musty, mildewy pile of meaningless *stuff.* There was nothing worth keeping. Especially not now the rot had set in.

He needed to leave.

He'd thought this trip would be simple enough. That he wouldn't care. Instead, he'd discovered he still loved the place. Even with the changes there was something that would always move him here. And, in showing it to Merle, he'd remembered moments beyond those last painful ones when he'd faced his mother's disappointment. Ironically, the hurt that came with those other memories was almost worse.

He'd tried to bury himself in Merle to avoid it all again. Only he'd woken this morning with the realisation that *she* was the problem too. Not just part of it but as much of a *cause* as any old memory. She'd shown him the world through her eyes, with an appreciation that was somehow contagious. She'd shown him *more* than this place: she'd shown him herself. And what had he done? He'd told her everything. Because she was real and right here. And she'd been gentle and accepting and she'd wrapped him in that wispy mirage of something impossible. He'd believed in it. In what she'd said. The importance of small things. So he'd come to check this morning. But it hadn't taken long for reality to return. There was no point in unsealing old boxes. Not when the contents were half-rotten and couldn't be fixed. Not when there was so little of any value left.

And when the wisps of promise were blown away, the truth remained. That hesitation he'd felt when she'd first come to him? He should have rejected her offer that night. Because the gorgeous Merle was asking for something in her bottomless eyes that he could never, ever give her. She deserved so much more. Even if he tried, he knew that in the end he couldn't deliver. It wasn't in his DNA to be there for someone, or to promise not to let them down. He could never guarantee that he wouldn't disappoint her. He couldn't bear to do that.

So he needed to leave here. He needed to leave *her*. And he needed to leave *now*.

Merle didn't know what had changed in Ash's thinking, or why. All she knew was that he was restless and angry. The usual amusement—even sarcastic joking—had been snuffed from his eyes. Her tension built the longer he stayed away.

Anxiety made her want to hide. To slip back to the shadows and stay safe. But she fought it. She wouldn't retreat into those old habits.

He didn't join her for breakfast, so she ate alone. She went for a quick swim, splashing a little extra-loudly, but he didn't appear. He didn't invite her for a ride on the boat or challenge her to a game. Two hours passed excruciatingly slowly. In the end, she decided to catalogue some effects in the study because she didn't know what else to do. The loss of time pressed like a sharp blade against the sensitive, thin skin of her neck—the sense of danger, of desperation tightened. Tomorrow would be Sunday—a full week since their bargain. Which meant he was due to leave. So this was their last day together. Shouldn't it be good—couldn't they forget that ticking clock for just a little longer?

Despite the warmth of the sun beating onto the deck, she felt chilled to the bone. Seconds staggered by slower than a sloth crossing a stretch of forest floor. Something was wrong. He'd gone from being open—being vulnerable—to being both physically and emotionally remote. It devastated her. Because last night they'd made love. She'd known the difference. There'd been an unspoken but deep empathy—that caring, that tenderness in their touch. She'd embraced him, showing her understanding, wanting him to know she understood, that she was here for him. Accepted him as he was. It hadn't just been fun, hadn't just been pleasurable. He'd *held* her and she'd held him back. Hadn't that meant something?

Was it his departure that was bothering him now? Was he too wondering whether this situation—this time between them—could be extended? Maybe he might even consider coming back for another visit while she was still working here?

No. It wasn't important enough for him to even think about. He was working through the agony of his history here.

'Merle?'

That bubble of hope rose from her belly into the tightness in her chest—pushing for breathing space.

'I'm in the study,' she called.

But she followed the direction of his voice and stepped out through one of the glass doors, onto the deck by the pool. The second she saw him that bubble got stuck—instant ice stopping its upward float. Ash was dressed, actually *dressed,* in dark denim jeans and a creaseless grey tee that hugged his hewn body. But it was the shoes that gripped her attention. They were not casual trainers or poolside sandals, but boots. Shoes for a journey.

'Are you going somewhere?' She hoped he'd deny what was so obvious.

'I need to get back to Sydney.'

That bubble inside her burst. 'To do what?'

He didn't reply. He was regarding her so seriously, but she could read the thoughts in his eyes. There was nothing urgent for him to go back to.

'I have meetings to prepare for,' he muttered.

'You can't do that here?'

She didn't know why she maintained the fiction with him. Why she didn't just challenge him outright to speak the truth.

In answer he simply shook his head.

'Why not?' she asked.

'The environment is too distracting.' A wisp of a smile.

But Merle couldn't smile. That he was leaving was bad enough. That this was over was devastating. But that he was ending it *earlier* than she'd expected? Right when the balance had tipped and it had become raw, but so good? Right when they were on the brink of something so much more? He was stealing away all possibility. Denying them any kind of chance—this was like someone tipping over the board and scattering the pieces before the game was won.

It *hurt.*

Because it meant he didn't care. His time with her had been good, but not good enough. *Distracting* but not anything important enough or meaningful enough to stick around or change plans for. Except he *had* changed plans. Hadn't he shortened it? Her gaze narrowed as she tried to understand *why* he was ending this *sooner*. If she was just a distraction, if this wasn't that meaningful, why, then, did he have to escape here—and her—earlier? That bubble re-formed and floated up again.

'You've had enough time here?' she asked.

He didn't move.

'Enough of me?' she asked. 'You don't want one more night?'

He swallowed but still didn't answer.

'Are you running away, Ash?'

His jaw clenched. 'It was always coming to an end, Merle. That was the agreement.'

'Agreement?' As if this really was some sort of blood-less business arrangement? As if emotions hadn't tangled between them? 'Why now, though? You've ended the game early. Reneged. Why?'

'You're that determined to have your last night with me?'

She paused, then stepped forward, which took all her courage. 'Why does it have to be the last night at all?' she asked bravely. 'You could come back here while I'm still working.'

He didn't give an inch. 'I told you I'm never coming back.'

'Aren't you allowed to change your mind?' she asked. 'You told me I could change my mind any time. Why are the rules different for you?'

His expression hardened. 'You know I don't go past one night. Our fling was only longer because of…circumstance. I thought you understood that.'

It wasn't because of circumstance. He'd *chosen*. And so had she. 'You don't think things have changed?'

He didn't waver. 'No.'

'You don't think this matters more than some brief fling?' Her voice wobbled. '*I* don't matter more?'

'Merle—'

'Don't lie,' she interrupted. 'Don't offer a platitude. Be honest. Why are you leaving early?'

'Because I can't stand to stay here a second longer.'

The buzzing sound in her ears was getting louder. It wasn't an internal hum of frustration, it was a real noise. Her blindsided brain finally recognised it was a helicopter. Noisily, brutally drowning out the beautiful birdsong and the once calm environment. He wasn't just leaving. This was an *extraction*. There was no other word for it. A precision operation to retrieve him from this hell zone as quickly as possible and return him to the soulless world in which he lived. Saving him from having to face things he'd once loved. Things that hurt.

But she was the one hurt. So very hurt. 'You're leaving right *now*?'

'It's the right thing to do.'

'Right thing for who?'

Because he didn't want to face her reaction for too long? Suddenly she was angry. Too bad for him. She'd never complained before—never stopped her mum and asked her to stay. Never stood up to her grandmother. Never asked her grandfather for help. She'd never fought for something that she'd really wanted. She'd never told them how their actions had really made her feel.

Not. This. Time.

Not when it was Ash himself who'd pulled this strength from her. Who'd shown her. She couldn't stop the hurt and anger from bubbling out of her now.

'You thought you could get away that easily?' She stepped towards him. 'You thought I'd say nothing—just smile and wave because I'm meek and useless at standing up for what I want?'

She had been. She wasn't doing that any more.

He didn't flinch. Didn't smile. He looked as angry as she felt. 'What do you want?'

'*More,*' she said bluntly. 'And I think you do too. But you're afraid. You got spooked yesterday. Because you talked to me and now you're worried…'

He stilled. The helicopter had landed, the pilot cutting the engine so there was a fading whine.

'What am I worried about?' he asked harshly.

'You want to stay like this for ever, don't you?'

'Like what?'

'Angry. Denying yourself or anyone else in your life anything more.'

'I'm not—'

'You're *so* angry. Because you're hurt. And scared. You think you're running away because you don't want to deal with *my* emotions, but it's your own emotions you're really running away from.'

She'd gone too far. But it felt good—exhilarating even. She couldn't silently let him leave.

'What emotions do you think they are?'

'That you love it here. That you've had a better time with me than you expected. That maybe…' It seemed brazen to even think it and she couldn't *quite* voice it. 'You swim endless lengths to nowhere to avoid what's right here in front of you.'

'*You're* right in front of me, Merle.'

Her heart pounded in her throat. 'Exactly.'

He stared at her. 'You've been the perfect distraction.'

And that was all she'd been? *No.*

'I told you right from the start that I could never be anything to anyone,' he argued. 'Certainly not to someone like you, Merle.'

'Someone like me?'

'Someone who deserves *more*—'

'We *all* deserve more,' she snapped. 'Everyone deserves to love and be loved. People only seem to become less deserving when they've had that love lacking in their life too long. When they *think* they don't deserve it. Then they start to act in ways that ensure they don't get it.'

That was him. Cutting things short.

'We want different things, Merle. You know there's no point drawing this out.'

'Different things?' She took another step nearer to him. 'You never want to find love? Never have a family?'

She didn't know why she asked. He'd already said he'd never marry and, given his scrupulous attention to avoiding an accidental pregnancy, she knew he didn't want to be his father with secret children everywhere. But worst case for Ash wasn't just an accidental pregnancy but *any* pregnancy at all. He'd never want children. But Merle did. To build her own family and ensure they had everything she'd missed out on.

'If I stay now, you'll only be more hurt,' he said brutally. 'You don't have to stay to finish the job.'

The breath was sucked from her. 'Of course I do,' she said heatedly. 'I need this job.'

'I'll pay—'

'I don't want your money!' she yelled at him, furious that he'd reduced this to a transactional debate.

He didn't look repentant. In fact, anger mottled his skin. 'You know I didn't mean it like that.'

'There's no other meaning to it. What exactly would you be paying me for?'

He clenched his teeth. 'Merle—'

'Ask *me* for more, Ash.' She'd lost it and now her most desperate wish poured out. 'Ask me for *all* my firsts.'

An endless second of silence followed. He looked shell-shocked. And as he shook his head, he barely breathed. 'I never should have—'

'Don't even start with that. Don't pretend it meant more to me than it did to you.' She sizzled with sudden certainty. 'You want more too but it terrifies you,' she said. 'That's why you're running away. But too bad, Ash. Because here it is and you have to listen anyway. I want more. I want you. I want everything from you. With you.' She clutched the back of the nearest deckchair to stop herself from shaking. 'I want your first *I love you.*' Her deepest wish broke free. Because she was damned certain he'd never said that to anyone. '*That* should be *mine.*' She drew a fierce breath. 'And you want to know why? Because I love you, Ash. I've totally fallen for you.'

'Merle…'

The sorrowful but bitter rejection in his eyes stilled her. In an awful moment she realised just what she'd blurted out. There was no hiding. A horrible heat of humiliation swept up and smothered her. She was that naive fool all over again, believing that someone like him could ever be interested in her. Her anger seeped out because she'd taken a risk and lost. Because she'd humiliated herself. Because, despite that fact, she couldn't believe that he didn't feel this the way she did.

'Don't let him win, Ash,' she muttered. 'If you stay isolated? Never finding someone the way you should? Never having happiness and security? Never being loved and loving? That's letting your father win.'

'Merle…'

In the way he said her name she heard it all. The regret. The refusal. The *rejection*.

'*You* told me to be honest,' she chastised him bitterly.

Yet even though she hated this, *she* couldn't regret the difference within her. She didn't want to return to reticent, invisible Merle. She wanted to stay bold, stay ready to get stuck into life and love. Stay strong enough to make these stupid mistakes. Because maybe one day it wouldn't be a mistake. She'd just wanted that day to be *today*. She wanted Ash.

'You're a romantic,' he dismissed her. 'And I'm an idiot for ever thinking you could handle this. I'm sorry.'

No. She rejected his assessment. She was *not* Rose. She wasn't hoping—imagining—there was more to this than there really was. She'd seen it in his eyes. She'd felt it in his body as he'd moved in hers. And she was *not* letting him tell her otherwise.

'You might deny your own feelings, but you don't get to tell me *my* feelings aren't real,' she said. 'This is special. What we have could be amazing. It is amazing.' They were more than lovers. They were a match.

'I have to leave.'

There was a pilot in that helicopter who could probably see her desperation in this pathetic scene in front of him, but Merle didn't care.

'You can't. We're still talking—'

'There's nothing more to say. There's nothing here for me any more.'

Even though she didn't believe him, she could see how badly *he* wanted to believe it. How badly he was fighting against listening to her. Fighting the tension within himself. It wasn't easy. Which was why he'd arranged such an immediate escape. A quick goodbye because he was a coward. Because he wasn't sure he could complete it?

Now he wouldn't even look her in the eyes.

'You told me I was too focused on seeing the good in people, that I didn't want to consider how they'd treated me. That I avoided seeing that truth. But no one is as good at avoiding things as you are,' she said angrily. 'Why not face the problems, Ash? Why not try to fix them? Instead of hiding for ever and letting them grow so big they consume you? If you always run away, you'll never find peace.'

Or love.

The waves of hurt kept coming as he didn't acknowledge her words. He just moved, picking up the small leather carry-all from the deck and stepping away. It was shockingly, unnecessarily sudden.

'You're the one who can't handle this,' she said. 'You're the one eternally isolated by fear.'

His shoulders stiffened. 'I have to go.'

'Kiss me goodbye, then, Ash.' She hurled the challenge at him. 'I *dare* you.'

His face paled, his jaw clamped—highlighting even more his spectacular angular cheekbones. Sharp, and angry, and barely controlled.

Silence screamed between them. She held his gaze as he stepped nearer. But the flare in his eyes gave him away. Or at least she hoped it did. Angry as she was with him, she needed him to know *her* truth. This wasn't a plea for him to stay any more. It was a pure expression of her own emotion.

I love you.

The press of his mouth on hers was hard, his lips compressed. Merle arched her neck, taking the almost bruising weight and then pushed back—with a softening of her own lips, with the slide of her tongue. She heard a choked sound in the back of his throat as he relented and released his hold on himself. And she stole in—all loving, passionate strokes. Warmth flowed, relief flooded in. Touching him like this? Feeling his rising response? Her heart soared. Love in a kiss. Love in a wordless, honest gift—

That he suddenly tore free from. He stared down at her, his breathing heavy. But he said nothing.

Reality slammed into her. She was never going to see him again. And she was angry with him for making her think even for a moment that she could have had more. That she could even dare *ask* for more. She went back to gripping the back of the damned deckchair. For support. To stop herself from following him and crying. From throwing herself in front of that damned helicopter in lovelorn desperation. To squeeze tightly to ride through the wave of pain as he turned and strode across that perfect tennis court that he despised.

They could've been more. They could have had more. They could have had everything that mattered. He couldn't see that. He completely disagreed.

Which had to mean that she'd been wrong.

CHAPTER TWELVE

ASH STRIVED TO stay busy, setting himself a hellfire week of work. He read reports, organised face-to-face meetings, inspected new prospects. But whenever he thought he'd found the sweet relief of pure focus, an image flashed into his mind—a shot of her in the pool, the gleam in her eye at a mid-play move of a board game, a portrait of her smile. Stills that switched the rest of the world off, meaning he could see only that moment, feel again the ripple of pleasure…only to suffer a tearing ache the milli-second he realised it was a mere mirage. His sadistic mind spasmodically tortured him with emotion-drenched memories that were too deep and good to be real. And he couldn't shut it off.

By midweek, he'd decided he'd reflect. Maybe if he remembered it all, if he methodically thought over every interaction, of every day, he could then compartmentalise it into his mental history box and move forward. But remembering made his skin burn hot and then goosebump. It made that tearing ache in his chest rip even wider. It made his breathing uneven and restlessness surge. He closed his eyes and willed for some perspective.

He wasn't missing *her*.

Maybe he could class it as a warped holiday romance? That—particularly given the location—he'd succumbed to a complicated set of sensations. He'd sought physical escape from the horrible recollections and unhappiness of discovering how fundamentally the property had been changed… and the switch from misery to delight had been so intense he'd attributed more meaning to the pleasure he'd felt with her. The problem with that classification was the disservice to Merle. *She* was much more than a distraction. She was much more than someone he'd had good sex with. She was more than a moment in time.

By the end of the week he'd realised that yes, he missed *her*. With every breath, every beat of his heart, he ached with loss. Beneath that, a feral anger prowled deep, growing exponentially bigger. She didn't contact him. He didn't contact her. It had to be finished. It was for her benefit. And this misery he felt now, he deserved. Because she deserved more than him—in every way.

He hated who he was. Not good enough. Not committed enough. He would inevitably let her down. Better now than in the future though, when it would only be worse.

But her words—that declaration—tormented him.

Ask me for all my firsts...

On the Saturday following his return to Sydney, Ash arranged a brief meeting with his half-brother. There were issues that had been outstanding for too long, and somehow catching up with him felt more important than it ever had.

Leo was impeccably on time, of course. His starched white shirt hurt Ash's jaded, sleep-deprived eyes. His half-brother was a half-inch shorter, neater and more legitimate-looking with his short hair and sharply fitted suit. So incredibly serious. There was only a glimmer of a smile in his eyes as he joined Ash at the waterfront cafe for a coffee. It had been a few weeks since they'd last caught up. Their interactions were mostly via messages, and mostly they only discussed heavy decisions regarding the business.

'You've been keeping well?' Leo's eyes narrowed as he glanced at Ash and took the seat alongside him.

The fact Leo had asked meant Ash knew he must look like death.

'Yeah. Fine.' Ash coughed the rasp from his throat and

moved straight to business. 'Thanks for arranging the archival work on Waiheke.'

Leo studied him impassively. 'Have you considered the options for the property?'

Yes. Decisions needed to be made. It wasn't fair on either of his half-siblings to drag out the process any longer. They'd already divided the proceeds from the other personal properties three ways. 'I can't sell that one. If you and Grace agree, I'd like to buy you out.'

He didn't actually need their consent—the house was his. But he wanted to do right by them.

'You want to keep the beach house in New Zealand?' Leo didn't look surprised. 'Fine by me.'

Ash breathed out. He already knew Grace wouldn't object. She'd been so appalled to discover her true lineage last year that she'd said she didn't want anything from the estate at all. Ash didn't blame her for that anger. But he refused to let her give up all of her claim. He'd transfer her share to her—what she then did with it was her choice.

As for the beach house? Selling it no longer seemed right. Merle's assessment had hit a nerve. It shouldn't be the preserve of one wealthy family—a paradise that only a few privileged people got to enjoy. Somehow he'd work out some way to restore some soul to it.

'Are you sure you want to stay on at the company?' he asked Leo.

He'd been astounded that Leo had stepped in to take over as CEO after their father's death. When he considered that Hugh had refused to acknowledge Leo even after the DNA test had proven his paternity, the fact Leo had wanted to turn around the sliding fortunes of the company was impressive. Ash wouldn't have been bothered to see the business fail. But the business supported so many *other* people…there was the rub. Leo had an intense sense of responsibility and honour that Ash respected. Though the fact that Leo had defiantly taken the Castle name while Hugh was alive enough to be apoplectic about it still made Ash smile.

Now Leo nodded. 'I'm enjoying the challenge.'

Leo generally looked so serious; Ash wondered if he ever really enjoyed anything.

'You have my full support, you know that, right?' Ash grimaced. 'If you ever need me to do something.'

'I know.' Leo sipped his coffee. Drinking strong coffee was a habit they shared. 'You're busy with your own empire though.'

'That hasn't stopped you managing two.'

Leo shot him some serious side-eye. 'But I don't have a social life or any other…distractions.'

Ash smiled and shook his head. Leo was a workaholic machine with no balance at all.

'They're not distractions.' Ash tried to assume a semblance of his usual attitude. 'They're like mini-breaks. For medicinal purposes. All work and no play…'

But Ash didn't believe his own words. He didn't feel like having a social life ever again. Apparently he'd been cured of the penchant for frivolous one-night bursts of fun.

A frown furrowed Leo's brow as he contemplated the depths of his coffee. 'Actually…' Leo suddenly glanced at Ash. 'There's a charity event at Kingston Towers tonight. Half of Sydney society is going to be there.'

'Your ideal market,' Ash noted.

'But not my ideal night.' Leo took a mouthful of coffee before releasing a sharp breath. 'You don't want to show up and help take the heat off me?'

Ash mirrored his half-brother and sipped the scalding black coffee to avoid speaking immediately. It was the first time Leo had asked him for anything, and it would be the first time in years that Ash showed up at a Castle Holdings event. It would be—in society and business pages—a notable occurrence.

His first impulse was to decline. Not because it was his father's company—he saw it as Leo's now. But because he'd felt a physical rejection inside at the thought of socialising. But he *should* accept. Maybe if he returned to his usual lifestyle, he'd feel better sooner. Maybe he'd made a mistake this week by staying isolated in his penthouse and at work. Maybe he needed to get back on the party horse...

That tearing ache in his chest widened. He finally recognised it as emptiness. And he knew speaking sassy nothings with a series of society babes on the never-ending party circuit wasn't going to fill the void. But there was another reason, a far more important reason, to say *yes*.

He'd lived most of his life without knowledge of either of his half-siblings. Now he knew about them and, while Grace preferred not to engage, Leo was here. Maybe the two of them could make something more from the little they had between them? Ash could show up for Leo.

'Sure,' he said firmly. 'What time should I arrive?'

Ash had regrets the moment he walked into the gorgeously decorated ballroom. The usual were present—the old money, the newly famous, the current influencers, the prettiest, the most 'interesting'... Phones and cameras were everywhere—capturing the stunning set-up, glamorous make-up, fantastic food. Ash wasn't hungry for any of it. But he could fake it with the best of them.

He had, he realised, been faking it for a long time now. Finally he realised everything he'd pushed so deep down for so long had floated back to the surface. And he had to face it. More than anything, he had to face what Merle had said to him. What she'd opened up in him. What she'd made him *feel*.

A sense of urgency swept over him.

He needed to go. He needed to—
Be there for Leo.

He slammed on his own brakes. He could build at least *one* better relationship in his life, couldn't he?

He chatted to a few people before deciding he needed a glass of water to clear his head. On his way to the bar he passed by a redhead. He glanced again because there was something familiar in her slightly oddly angled stance. That was when he recognised her. She looked vastly different to the awkward girl who'd come to school all those years ago. With her black skirt and silk shirt and her hair tied back from her face, now she looked capable and confident.

'Rose? What are you doing here?' he asked before thinking better of it.

But she didn't flinch or look embarrassed as he'd have expected from her. Rather her eyes widened and she actually smiled. 'Ash Castle!' she exclaimed. 'It's been ages.'

'Yeah.' He felt a little winded at her easy friendliness. Of all the people to bump into—why here and now after all this time? What *was* she doing here? 'I'm sorry about what happened back at school,' he suddenly blurted because it was right at the front of his mind. He instantly regretted it. What an idiot to bring that up in public.

Rose frowned in confusion, then he saw the penny drop. To his astonishment she actually giggled. 'Oh, you mean *that*.' She laughed again but then sobered and suddenly looked apologetic. 'You poor thing, that must've been hell for you. Your mother was so unwell and none of us knew how bad it was.'

Um. Was she feeling sympathy for *him*?

'Yeah, but I acted…' He didn't even want to say it.

'Ash, that was *years* ago.' There was no distress in her eyes, no embarrassment, no concern. She certainly wasn't blushing. Because she really wasn't bothered. If anything, her smile had grown bigger and more carefree. 'Have you been feeling bad all this time?'

He hesitated.

'Forget it,' she said. 'Truly.'

He'd thought he'd devastated her. That he'd blighted her life. He clearly hadn't. She barely batted an eyelash about it now. She didn't look at him with any adulation, any interest even. Just courtesy. He mocked himself bitterly—it had been so arrogant of him to assume he'd truly hurt her. But he'd thought he'd really damaged her. The way his mother had been damaged. Had he confused the impact on Rose with the devastation his mother had felt? And his mother had so many *other* reasons to react so angrily, so devastatingly, to that foolish, selfish act. Everything had got jumbled up inside him, and he'd been so upset he'd thought of everything in extremes.

Now he'd never been so relieved to be wrong about something.

'You seem really well,' he said feebly.

'I am, thanks.' She glanced past him. 'But I'm afraid I need to get going—there's someone I really have to see.'

'Yes. Of course.'

Yeah, she wasn't interested in lingering to talk to him. She wasn't interested in him at all any more. She'd grown up and moved on. Whereas he? He'd got stuck back there—in that hot mess of guilt and betrayal and hurt. But maybe he didn't need to be there any more. Maybe he'd been an idiot.

He kept a grip on himself long enough to chat to a few more guests. From a distance he saw his half-brother shoot him an appreciative nod of the head. A few women smiled, 'available and interested' signals lighting their eyes. He smiled but kept his distance and talked up Leo's new development plans some more as, inside, feelings crystallised into hard rocks of unavoidable truth.

Suddenly he couldn't stay a second longer. He couldn't find Leo to say goodbye. He'd send him a text tomorrow. He asked his driver to just drive. He didn't want to go to his empty penthouse, didn't want to stay at the party, didn't want to take up any of the offers he'd had.

Instead, he took the back seat and closed his eyes, partially soothed by the low hum of the powerful engine and the constant movement. That sensation of escape was essential. But what he was struggling with was stuck inside him. There was no escape from that.

He'd been wrong. Seeing Rose had made him reassess the fallout of those actions of so long ago. Leo was bold and in control. Grace happily doing her thing in Melbourne. Rose was clearly confident and in control of her life. Apparently the only person still bogged down in all that horror was him—stuck in resentment and isolation and self-loathing. Stuck so he couldn't get out to where he wanted—and needed—to be.

Merle Jordan didn't like good-looking or popular guys. She didn't trust *anyone's* motivations. Ash didn't blame her. She'd judged him, and that long-burning rebelliousness in Ash had meant he'd encouraged her to. He'd made it so easy for her—playing up to that image. He'd been everything she'd been wary of. But then, with that perfect eyesight of hers, she'd seen through him. She'd seen more in him than *he'd* wanted to believe was there. She'd seen right from the start that he was hiding.

Of course he was hiding—he'd been hiding, faking, for years. Just as his father had. No matter that the lies were *different*, he was still living a lie. Still using a facade to hide behind. He'd hated who he was beneath it. And now he hated that he couldn't be the guy she needed. The last thing he'd wanted to do was hurt her, but he had. Badly. He'd hurt himself too. The cavernous hopelessness had become a physical pain. She deserved so much better than what he'd offered. Than what he *was*. Or what he'd *thought* he was. Because maybe he'd taken it all too far?

For so long he'd thought he was just like his father. For so long he'd tried not to be but felt that hopelessness deep inside. That there was something within him that he couldn't escape. That he was someone who'd hurt the people he loved the most. But that wasn't entirely true, was it? Because he hadn't hurt Rose the way he'd thought. Or maybe he had, but she'd long forgiven and forgotten and moved on to better things. Because people failed and people made mistakes but they tried again. Ash wasn't used to failure in a business sense. He didn't have much experience of trying again. But couldn't he? Couldn't *he* be better?

Because the person he'd hurt recently? She was the one who mattered most. Her words—the ones he'd tried not to listen to—rang in his ears like town hall bells pealing through the county.

Don't let him win.

Was that what he was doing? Wasn't she right? Wouldn't having a committed, happy, *honest* relationship be the ultimate act of rebellion against his father's memory? Even when facing the worst, Merle had hope and strength. She wanted more for him. But also for herself. Because she could admit how she felt. She had courage. He wanted to be better for her—brave like her. And he didn't give a damn about his bloody father any more.

He didn't want Merle to be alone, and the last thing he wanted was for her to find someone else. In time, she would. She was too beautiful, too loveable not to. Suddenly his old arrogance soared inside. No one else—*no one*—could give her what he could give her. He wanted her to have everything she'd missed out on. Not material wealth or luxury. It was simpler than that. Scarier. But how did he create a bond that would only strengthen them? How did he reach out to her? How did he do *any* of this? For all of his supposed intelligence, he was absolutely clueless.

It felt as if that empty ache inside was filling with his own blood.

I want your first I love you.

That plea had devastated him. But she didn't realise she'd already had some of his firsts. Things he'd never told anyone. Things he'd never done before. Spending that time with her. Laughing like that with her. *Playing* in a way that was more than superficial, in a way that formed serious foundations.

But she didn't know, because he'd not told her. Because he'd been a coward. It turned out he was better than Merle Jordan—the hide-away queen herself—at avoidance. He finally accepted that he'd run away not to 'protect her' from him. He'd been protecting himself. Because he didn't want that pain of loss. Because he didn't want to be rejected. Because he didn't want to be a disappointment. So he'd got in first. Everything that terrified him, he'd done to her. He was a jerk.

And now he felt terrible for it. The biggest mistake of his life had left him balancing on the narrowest ledge of a cliff. He didn't have long to stop himself falling. Merle Jordan was like a sprite. She'd lit his life for only a short time, but he'd not appreciated her true value. So he'd left her. He'd lost her. He couldn't lose her for ever. He couldn't let her disappear, never to be found again. So how did he reach out? How did he try to make this better? How did he fix what he'd broken?

With the truth.

CHAPTER THIRTEEN

MERLE WAS SICK of being stuck in a mega-mansion all by herself riding the roller coaster of heartbreak and hope. She'd spent the week storming through the boxes in silence, determined to still do a good job. But determined to do a *fast* job. The sooner she was done, the sooner she could escape, and the sooner she could recover. Because the hope side of the equation was slipping.

A couple of days after Ash's abrupt departure a load of groceries had been delivered. A mass of fresh fruit and vegetables, meat and fish and, yes, even more instant noodles. She hated that he'd been that thoughtful when he'd refused to care. Was it only pity? With a sprinkle of guilt perhaps. Either way, it was a scattering of emotional crumbs she really didn't want from him. Because she wanted *everything*. Instead, Ash Castle had left her with only ash—the remnants of her pride, of her memories of that last week, with her burned heart.

She'd worked through the whole week, then the weekend. She had that week off with Ash to make up for anyway. She'd focused on cataloguing one item after another, not letting her gaze wander to the pool outside, not letting her mind wander to wisps of conversation, to the echo of laugher and sweet sighs. And she was never, *ever*, thinking of that last kiss—where she'd tried to pour her soul into him. To show him what she felt in the hope he wouldn't have been able to hold back. But he had.

She'd half-hoped to find something of his mother's, knowing it would mean so much to him. But there was nothing. There wouldn't be even that littlest of happy endings.

She needed a break now. She needed to restore some balance to herself. She'd avoided the places they'd been together. Most especially the pool. But it was a stunningly hot day and she refused to deny herself the simple pleasure of a dip. She refused to let the heartache stop her. She was brave. She could handle it, couldn't she?

Ash couldn't remember feeling anxiety like this. His hands felt damp, his pulse raced, skipping unpredictably. The helicopter couldn't fly fast enough. Yet, as it descended towards the grassy helipad at the far end of the tennis court, he suddenly wanted time to slow. He wanted a chance to think through his plan once more. But there wasn't time. Nor was there any real plan.

There was no way she could've failed to hear his arrival. Unless, of course, she'd already left the property. His heart pounded even more irregularly. He walked towards the house and the helicopter lifted away behind him. As its noise faded he heard another—a splash. He moved more quickly to be sure, but there she was. In the pool. His nymph, swimming as if she hadn't a care in the world. But as he walked nearer he saw her eyes, and the expression in them smote his heart. She was pale and her fine features drawn, but she'd never looked more beautiful. She held her head high as she climbed the ladder and reached for a towel, hiding from him.

'You're still here.' His voice sounded croaky. The paper bag he carried felt both too small and too heavy.

'I told you I'd stay.'

'I wouldn't have blamed you if you'd left,' he said. 'Most people would've already.'

'I had a job to do.'

Was the only reason she'd stayed because she was contractually obligated? Because she needed the money? Or was it because she'd made the commitment and Merle saw her commitments through—even to people who'd hurt her? That was what she'd done for her family, wasn't it? She'd done what was right.

'Why are you here?' she suddenly asked. 'You were never coming back.'

'I needed to see you. I have something I wanted to give to you.'

She stiffened. 'You don't need to give me anything just because you feel guilty about…whatever.'

'Merle—'

'You didn't need to come back here and try to make… I don't need this from you.'

'Please, Merle.' He held it out to her.

It wasn't even wrapped properly. She pulled the small volume out of the brown paper bag and when she read the cover her eyes widened and her colour leeched, leaving her looking ghostly.

It wasn't some pretty edition like she ought to have. It was a mass-produced paperback that cost only a few dollars. He'd wanted to gift her something meaningful. That she would treasure not because of its financial value, but for the thought behind it. He wanted—hoped—she would understand. 'I found it at the airport on the way,' he muttered apologetically. 'I thought about a rare edition, hoped for a hardback even, but there wasn't time.'

He'd been desperate to get to her once he'd realised what a damned fool he'd been.

A touch of pink stole into her cheeks, combatting her pallor. 'This is better,' she said. 'Ordinary things can be loved too.'

'But I bent the spine when I wrote in it,' he added, even more apologetically.

'You wrote in it?' Her gaze flashed back to him.

A tiny bubble of hope formed in that cavernous ache in his chest when he saw the intensity in her expression. He hid his tense fists in his trouser pockets and resisted the burning urge to drag her against him. He'd never felt such uncertainty. But if he knew Merle at all, he knew she would appreciate this.

Now there was a rosy depth to her cheeks. Now her beautiful brown eyes were gazing right into his and he couldn't look away from them. He couldn't help but hope that he was really seeing what he so badly wanted in those eyes.

'The ink is archival quality, apparently,' he mumbled helplessly. 'So it'll last. It won't fade. Even if you put it in the sun.'

But she didn't open the cover to read what he'd written. She didn't even look down at it. Her gaze was fixed on him and suddenly he felt too exposed. Too raw.

'Ash Castle,' she murmured softly and stepped closer, 'are you blushing?'

More than that—his hands were shaking and he felt hot and cold all over. He really didn't like the vulnerability. 'Just read it,' he said. 'Tell me you love it.'

Tell me you love me.

He wanted to hear that again. He was desperate to record it and keep it so he could replay it over and over. His pulse hammered. But she still didn't look at the book. She held it out to him.

'You read it to me,' she said quietly.

He stared at her. He saw wariness still in those beautiful eyes, but he saw hope too. The shy desire for so much more. His throat was unbearably tight. He didn't need to take the book that she held in visibly trembling fingers. And it was her trembling that tore him apart. Her trembling that showed how much this mattered to her. It mattered to him too. So impossibly much.

'"For my beautiful Merle."' He paused to cough away

the huskiness, but it didn't work. He didn't think he could get to the end of it. But he had to try. '"Because precious things matter. Because you're my treasure. Because I want you to have all my firsts that truly matter and everything else I have to give. Because I love you and I will for ever and for always. Ash."'

Merle couldn't move, couldn't breathe past the massive lump of emotion weighing her down. 'That's why you came back?' she whispered.

'For you. Yes.' A storm of emotion swirled in his eyes. A world of promise. 'Because it's awful without you. Because I've been such an idiot. But mostly because I'm in love with you and I can't stand to be apart from you any longer.'

He'd just said it again. The words she'd wanted so much. The ones that meant the world.

She clutched the book to her chest. It was so simple, so perfect, and what it symbolised was so precious. He'd listened. He'd understood. And he cared.

'Merle...' His voice dropped.

Goose pimples feathered across her skin at the ache evident in his voice. Her eyes stung. He meant it. He stood so rigidly, as if he couldn't trust himself even to breathe.

He was waiting. For her.

She began to shake so badly she had to wrap her arms around her waist and tightly grip the towel and the book all together in a damp mess. All the emotion was leaking out as if her body were a sieve. And as it did, it exposed a hard knot of agony deep in her chest. The knot that had formed when he'd rejected her, when he'd walked out and left her alone. And now it was impossible to move.

'Merle?' That old smile bubbled up into his eyes—a hint of his tease. 'One last chance?'

Taking a step seemed impossible, but that knot loosened and she moved. He met her halfway and his arms were around her and his heat and strength warmed where she'd been so cold.

'I'm sorry,' he mumbled against her hair. 'I've been such a fool. I thought I was broken. I thought I wasn't worthy. But I want to try. I want to be better for you.'

That tight, hard knot unravelled. Tears spilled as he pressed her so close that she felt his racing heart as it pounded against her breast. The tremors in his muscles matched hers and that disbelieving desperation made her cling to him.

And he held her. 'You were right. So right. I've been hiding. I went to see Leo. And I saw Rose.'

She stilled, listening intently, her heart clogging her throat.

'She was fine, Merle. So's Leo. Seeing them both made me realise that I might've been wrong about the fallout from what had happened back then. And if I'd been wrong about that, then I was likely wrong about other things too. Most importantly, I've never felt this way about anyone other than you. And I can love and I can commit and I want everything. *With you*,' he added, his hands roving, pressing her closer. 'I missed you.'

Her eyes closed and she melted, tucking her face into the warmth of his neck, breathing in his scent, his nearness. Finally believing this was real.

'I don't want anything else. Not anyone, anything,' he growled. 'I just want you. With me. All the time. Okay?'

Someone wanted her. Not just someone. *Ash*.

She wasn't some distraction from this house, not some project to assuage old guilt. She wasn't some mere affair either. She was his *treasure*. As he was hers.

'Sweetheart?' He slid his hands in her hair and tilted her head.

Merle lifted her chin and he met her halfway. The kiss

was more than scorching, it was acute—almost agonising—perfection and it melted the remnants of that knot inside and allowed the most precious of all of her feelings to flow freely towards him.

'I love you, Ash.'

His breath shuddered. This time he didn't ignore her. This time he answered with touch, with heat and infinite care. It was as if his sole purpose was to give her pleasure, to show her how passionately he felt about her. How much he'd missed her. How much he needed her. How much he loved her.

He loved her and loved her and loved her.

She felt it in every kiss, every touch. She responded—unable to restrain anything, and she didn't want to. She caressed him and the ache and emptiness that had been a constant these last few days dissolved. She needed to share and show her feelings for him. She shuddered as he peeled away her swimsuit. He stroked her tenderly, his hands shaking as badly as hers were. They stumbled together until he took some semblance of control and tumbled her down onto one of the sun-loungers.

'It's too sunny out here,' he said.

She smiled tremulously. 'Then we'll be quick.'

He half laughed and, to her eternal relief, obliged. She just needed him *with* her.

His groan of pure joy when he pushed home was magical to her ears but she could only moan in return and lift her mouth to kiss him once more. They moved together, slick and desperate, and it was so joyous she cried again.

'I love you,' he whispered, kissed, vowed as he held her closer, pushing faster and fiercer.

Her head arched back as the sensations overwhelmed her—he was really here, loving her hot and hard, making her world shatter. And holding her still. Holding her through it all.

* * *

Eventually, she snuggled against his chest, loving the firm weight of his arm around her, holding her to him. She rested her chin on his ribs to steal a glance at his face. He looked back at her, so much more relaxed, so handsome. That old arrogance tinged his smile but there was an unguarded openness that was new.

'You were right,' he said softly. 'I've been avoiding real intimacy for years. But you got to me, Merle, and I couldn't handle it. I still…' He gazed at her so intently. 'I don't want to let you down.'

'Ash, I love *you*.'

The kiss was the sweetest, the hottest of her life and she didn't want it ever to end. He seemed to sense it, his arms tightening around her.

'It's okay, sweetheart,' he promised. 'I'm not going anywhere. I'm going to work here while you're finishing the archiving,' he murmured. 'I'll have to go to Sydney occasionally for meetings. Will you come with me?'

'You want me to?'

'I don't want to be away from you. Not for long, anyway.'

He wanted her front and centre in his life. Not hidden in the wings. Not with him under sufferance. Not unseen.

'Would you like that?' he asked after a moment. 'Your choice, Merle. I want you to have and do what you want.'

She smiled at him even as tears sprang forth all over again. 'I'd like that very much.'

They were cuddled close on the deck and Merle followed the direction of his gaze, up to the house. 'I'm sorry I didn't find anything of your mother's.'

'But you did.' He kissed her gently. 'You found the games. They brought us together.'

Her heart lifted as she saw the warmth and acceptance in his eyes. So they had.

'Are you still going to sell the house?' she asked.

Beneath her cheek his chest rose as he drew in a difficult breath. 'Actually, I was thinking you were right about it being a shame that more people don't get to come here and enjoy it. I thought we could offer it as a holiday home for cardiac patients and their families. For during their recovery or as an escape or something...' He cleared his throat. 'There might be a charity that could help us arrange that. If there isn't, we can establish one.' He paused. 'What do you think?'

She sat up to lean over him and look directly into his beautiful eyes, seeing the flash of vulnerability there. 'I think that sounds amazing. I think *you're* amazing.'

That smile broke across his face. 'Shall we go for a swim, sweetheart? And then maybe play another round of snakes and ladders?'

A bubble of pure happiness fizzed from deep within her, culminating in a satisfied giggle. That simple invitation was the most special of her life. She was with him now—included—and together they made laughter and love.

Ash Castle had opened up in the most gorgeous way and given her everything she ever could have dreamed of.

'That'll be just perfect.'

CHAPTER FOURTEEN

One year later

MERLE DECIDED THIS summer on Waiheke Island was particularly stunning. Every day had been highlighted by a brilliant sun, cloudless bright skies and views of that calm, endless sea. Today her floaty fabric jumpsuit was vibrant and cool. She loved the silky feel of it as Ash firmly gripped her hand and led her down the balcony stairs.

'What are you doing?' She giggled at his determined pace. 'Where are you taking me in such a rush?'

'To my secret underground lair.' He glanced back with a suggestive waggle of his eyebrows. 'Where else?'

'The bunker?' She'd not been down there in ages. Most of the time she forgot it even existed. 'Why?'

He didn't answer. There was just another playfully suggestive smile.

They were almost a week into their month-long holiday here. They'd made Ash's old bedroom their suite, mostly so they could indulge in a decadent bubble bath most nights. During the days they pitted wits over the selection of board games. They'd taken their favourite, most precious ones back to their home in Sydney, but they'd bolstered the collection here so that the families who stayed could enjoy them. His idea of a respite holiday home had been embraced and now the house was used every weekend, even through the heart of winter.

They swiftly descended the steep stairs down into the bunker. Merle looked around, taking in the changes that had occurred since the first time she'd been in here. Ash had obviously been down here earlier because on the counter there was a bottle of champagne on ice and a selection of fresh cut fruit on a platter, together with her favourite crackers.

'What have you planned?' She shot him a laughing glance.

He paused, his head cocked at a distinct rumbling sound. 'I think the hatch just closed. I'm afraid we're locked in. Oh! No!'

Amused at his theatrical 'distress', she rose on her toes and leaned towards him. 'Are we, now?'

'Mmm. Maybe we can find a way out. I think... Is that a clue?' He peered in exaggerated fashion at the fruit platter.

She looked and saw there was something scratched on the edge of the plate. Numbers.

'Oh, yes!' She turned back to face him in mock-amazement. 'I think it might be.'

Merle knew the bunker was often used by the children who came to stay. Ash had contracted a games designer to work out an 'escape room' challenge for the guests to enjoy as part of their holiday. It was a thoughtful touch that had melted Merle's heart when he'd run it past her, but she'd not given the challenge a go herself yet. But according to the messages left in the guest book in the main house, it was one of the most popular activities.

'But this isn't fair if you know the answers to the challenges.' She laughed as he handed her a glass of champagne.

'But I *don't* know them.' He winked. 'We'll have to work it out together.'

A series of challenges took them through the bunker—one puzzle led to another, from the living area, to the kitchen, to the corridor... Working out an anagram gave them a code to unlock the bedroom at the end, and once they had made it in there they found a tiny key. Merle was entranced and fascinated, and realised that, indeed, Ash had no clue about most of the answers. It fired up the competitive nature that he'd brought out in her. She was delighted to be the one to discover a small projector that made a hologram appear. It gave them another clue to search one of the storage cupboards. When that finally unlocked, it revealed a miniature treasure chest inside.

'Do you think the key will fit?' Ash waggled his brows.

'I wonder,' she joked.

'I guess the code from the hatch will be inside,' he muttered.

Merle unlocked the little chest and lifted the lid. Then stilled.

There was no code. No next clue. There was a midnight-blue velvet cushion and carefully placed on it was a stunning solitaire.

'Merle?'

There was no denying what kind of ring that was. Her eyes were instantly watering but she glanced up at him anyway. She couldn't not. He compelled everything from her. *'Ash.'*

He was wickedly gorgeous and that smile—the one that melted her—now spread across his face. He knew her answer already, just as she knew the question. She loved his playfulness. She loved his effort. She loved *him.*

But he spoke so seriously. 'I love you. Please will you marry me, Merle?'

Even though he knew her answer already, she heard the rough edge of vulnerability. Emotion, *truth*, throbbed. She knew that for him, too, nothing else mattered.

'Yes,' she answered swiftly and simply as tears warred with her smiles. 'There's nothing I'd like more.'

He lifted the ring from the treasure chest.

'It's beautiful,' she whispered.

Relief lit his eyes. 'There's a code in the engraving.'

'Meaning?'

'You'll have to work it out.' Holding it carefully, he angled it so she saw the stunning, intricate pattern engraved along the band and a small black stone set right inside it.

'It has a secret stone in there?' She was amazed.

'An ash-coloured diamond.' He glanced at her a little sheepishly. 'My heart.'

It was both traditional and modern, serious and playful with a hidden heart—his. Of course there was. Because Ash knew her love for symbolism, for tying memory and emotion to little treasures. So he'd made sure this ring had it all for her.

'Do you like it?'

'It's such a precious thing,' she breathed. 'You've put so much thought into it. It's *perfect,* Ash.'

So unique, so *intentional.* She adored it, but most of all she adored him. She held out her hand urgently, half-laughing as she saw how her fingers trembled. He slid the ring home.

'I'm never taking it off,' she vowed.

His smile flashed and he tugged on her hand to pull her against his body. 'What if we take everything else off?'

'Yes, please.' She could say nothing but yes to Ash Castle.

He helped her out of her pink jumpsuit, chuckling at the emerald bikini beneath it. Colour was now Merle's friend. She loved exploring all kinds of combinations, all kinds of everything, with Ash alongside her for the ride. And now, as she gazed into his eyes, her heart burst, overflowing at the hope and love she saw. In his delight at their future together. They'd both finally found love. For ever.

* * * * *

MILLS & BOON

Coming next month

HIS BILLION-DOLLAR TAKEOVER TEMPTATION
Emmy Grayson

"Mr. Cabrera?"

The husky feminine voice slid over his senses and sent a flash of heat over his skin. He took another deliberate sip of his wine before turning his attention to the second woman who had invaded his space this evening.

Her.

The blonde woman he'd locked eyes with before Alejandro's arrival now stood before him. The neckline of her dark blue gown plunged down in a V to the silver ribbon wrapped around her slender waist. From there the dress flowed into a long, billowing skirt that reminded Adrian of the waters of the Mediterranean before a storm.

His eyes drifted back up to her face in a slow, deliberate perusal. Lush silver-blonde curls enhanced her delicate features. Violet eyes stared back at him, and her caramel-colored lips were set in a firm line.

"Yes," he finally responded, his voice cool, showing that, despite the unusually intense effect she was having on him, he was still in control.

She stepped forward and held out her hand, bare except for a simple silver band on her wrist. Adrian grasped her fingers, pleasantly surprised by her firm grip.

"My name is Everleigh Bradford. Congratulations on your Merlot. It's exquisite."

"Thank you." He arched a brow. "While your compliments are appreciated, was it necessary for you to ignore the 'Balcony Closed' sign and invade my privacy?"

Everleigh's chin came up and her eyes flashed with stubborn fire. "Yes."

Intriguing... There were plenty of men who would have cringed at the slightest hint of his disapproval. But not this woman. She stood her ground, shoulders thrown back, lips now set in a determined line.

"You're a busy man, Mr. Cabrera. I need to speak with you on an urgent matter. I'm sorry for breaking the rules, but it was necessary for me to have a moment alone with you."

Her honesty was refreshing. A night with someone as bold and beautiful as Everleigh would more than make up for his past few months of celibacy.

He infused his smile with sensuality as he raked his gaze up and down her slim form once more, this time letting his appreciation for her body show. "I would greatly enjoy a moment alone with you."

Everleigh's cheeks flushed pink. The blush caught Adrian unawares. Was she an innocent or just playing a role? Much as it would disappoint him, she wouldn't be the first to go to such lengths to catch his attention.

"This has nothing to do with sex, Mr. Cabrera."

"Adrian."

Her lips parted. "I... Excuse me?"

"Please call me Adrian."

Those beautifully shaded violet eyes narrowed. "This is a business discussion, Mr. Cabrera. First names are for friends and family."

"We could become friends, Everleigh."

What was wrong with him? He never teased a woman like this. He complimented, touched, seduced... But with this woman he just couldn't help himself.

Perhaps it was the blush. Yes, that had to be it. The delicate coloring that even now crept down her throat toward the rising slopes of her breasts...

"We will never be friends, Mr. Cabrera," Everleigh snapped. "I'm here to discuss your proposed purchase of Fox Vineyards."

"Then let's talk."

Continue reading
HIS BILLION-DOLLAR TAKEOVER TEMPTATION
Emmy Grayson

Available next month
www.millsandboon.co.uk

COMING SOON!

We really hope you enjoyed reading this book.
If you're looking for more romance, be sure to
head to the shops when new books are
available on

Thursday 27th May

MILLS & BOON

THE HEART OF ROMANCE

A ROMANCE FOR EVERY READER

MODERN

Prepare to be swept off your feet by sophisticated, sexy and seductive heroes, in some of the world's most glamourous and romantic locations, where power and passion collide.

HISTORICAL

Escape with historical heroes from time gone by. Whether your passion is for wicked Regency Rakes, muscled Vikings or rugged Highlanders, awake the romance of the past.

MEDICAL

Set your pulse racing with dedicated, delectable doctors in the high-pressure world of medicine, where emotions run high and passion, comfort and love are the best medicine.

True Love

Celebrate true love with tender stories of heartfelt romance, from the rush of falling in love to the joy a new baby can bring, and a focus on the emotional heart of a relationship.

Desire

Indulge in secrets and scandal, intense drama and plenty of sizzling hot action with powerful and passionate heroes who have it all: wealth, status, good looks…everything but the right woman.

HEROES

Experience all the excitement of a gripping thriller, with an intense romance at its heart. Resourceful, true-to-life women and strong, fearless men face danger and desire - a killer combination!

To see which titles are coming soon, please visit

millsandboon.co.uk/nextmonth

JOIN US ON SOCIAL MEDIA!

Stay up to date with our latest releases, author news and gossip, special offers and discounts, and all the behind-the-scenes action from Mills & Boon...

 millsandboon

 millsandboonuk

millsandboon

It might just be true love...